Presented to

_____

From

_____

on

_____

CHILDREN'S ILLUSTRATED BIBLE

Published in 2006 in the U.S.A. by Spirit Press,
an imprint of Dalmatian Press, LLC
Copyright © 2006 Dalmatian Press, LLC

Adapted from *The Story Bible Series*
by Eve B. MacMaster,
published by Herald Press

Editorial Direction *Kathryn Knight*
Editorial Assistance *April Rhodes, Bill Greendyk*

Art Direction and Layout *Kathryn Knight, David Meyer, Gina Rhodes-Haynes*
Production Management *Renee Morton*

Cover illustration *Tom Newsom*
Interior Illustrations *Utopia, Inc., Jerry Dillingham,
and the entire* Children's Illustrated Bible *team*

The SPIRIT PRESS and DALMATIAN PRESS names are trademarks
of Dalmatian Press, LLC, Franklin, Tennessee 37067.
No part of this book may be reproduced or copied in any form
without the written permission of Dalmatian Press.

ISBN: 1-40371-610-2
13859

Printed in the United States of America

06 07 08 09 VHM 10 9 8 7 6 5 4 3 2 1

Children's Illustrated
BIBLE

Children's Illustrated
BIBLE

Adapted from *The Story Bible Series*
by Eve B. MacMaster

SPIRIT PRESS

TESTAMENT

THE NEW

*"...we have seen his star in the east,
and are come to worship him."*
—Matthew 2:2

TESTAMENT

HITTITE EMPIRE

Haran

SYRIA

GREAT SEA
(MEDITERRANEAN SEA)

Sidon

Tyre

Cana

Damascus

Samaria

Jordan River

Bethel

Shechem

Jerusalem

Jericho

CANAAN/JUDEA

Sodom

Gaza

MOAB

Hebron

Beersheba

EDOM

SINAI

Goshen

Mount Sinai

MIDIAN

Memphis

EGYPT

Nile River

RED
SEA

★ = *Possible Locations*

THE CREATION OF THE HEAVENS AND THE EARTH

THE FIRST DAY

In the beginning, GOD created the heavens and the earth. The earth was bare and without form, and darkness covered the face of the deep. GOD's breath moved like a wind over the face of the waters.

And GOD said, "Let there be light." And there was light.

GOD saw that the light was good, and GOD separated the light from the darkness. GOD called the light Day, and the darkness HE called Night.

There was evening, and there was morning: the first day.

THE SECOND DAY

GOD said, "Let there be a dome in the middle of the waters, and let it divide water from water."

GOD made a dome, and it divided the water beneath the dome from the water above the dome. And so it was. GOD called the dome the Heavens.

And there was evening, and there was morning: the second day.

THE THIRD DAY

GOD said, "Let the waters under the heavens be gathered in one place, so the dry land will appear." And so it was. GOD called the dry land Earth, and the gathering of waters HE called Seas. GOD saw that it was good.

GOD said, "Let the earth grow grass and plants—green plants and flowers, bushes and trees, fruits and vegetables and grains." And so it was. The earth put forth mosses and ferns, grasses and flowers, bushes and trees. GOD saw that it was good.

There was evening, and there was morning: the third day.

THE FOURTH DAY

God said, "Let there be lights in the dome of the heavens to divide the day from the night. They will be signs for the seasons and days and years, and they will be lights in the dome of the heavens to light up the earth." And so it was.

God made the sun to rule day, and the moon to rule night. He also made the stars. God set them in the dome of the heavens to light up the earth, to rule over day and night, and to divide the light from the darkness. God saw that it was good.

There was evening, and there was morning: the fourth day.

THE FIFTH DAY

God said, "Let the waters swarm with living creatures. Let birds fly over the earth across the dome of the heavens."

God created the great sea creatures and fish to fill the waters, and He created every kind of bird. God saw that it was good.

God blessed them, saying, "Be fruitful and multiply, and fill the waters in the seas, and let the birds multiply on the earth."

There was evening, and there was morning: the fifth day.

THE SIXTH DAY

GOD said, "Let the earth bring forth living creatures of all kinds—cattle and crawling things and wild animals." And so it was. And GOD saw that it was good.

Then GOD said, "Let US make a human in OUR image, in OUR likeness, to rule over the fish of the sea and the birds of the heavens and the cattle and the animals and all the crawling things that move upon the earth."

GOD created humans in HIS image, male and female. GOD blessed them and said to them, "Be fruitful and multiply. Fill the earth and manage it. Rule over the fish of the sea and the birds of the heavens and all the animals that move upon the earth."

GOD said, "Behold! I have given you every seed-bearing plant and every fruit-bearing tree that grows on the face of the earth, to be food for you. The grasses and plants will be food for all the animals of the earth and all the birds of the heavens." GOD saw all that HE had made, and it was very good.

There was evening and there was morning: the sixth day.

THE SEVENTH DAY

Thus the heavens and the earth were finished, and all that was in them. On the seventh day, GOD ended HIS work, and HE rested. God blessed the seventh day and set it apart as a holy day, because on that day HE had rested from all the work HE had done.

This is the story of the Creation of the heavens and the earth.

THE STORY OF
ADAM AND EVE

The LORD GOD had not yet caused rain to fall on the earth, but a mist went up from the earth and watered the soil and the plants.

And the LORD GOD molded and shaped the wet dust of the earth and formed a human. GOD breathed into his nostrils the breath of life, and the human became a living soul.

The LORD GOD planted a garden in the east of Eden. There HE put the human whom HE had formed. The LORD GOD caused beautiful trees and trees with delicious fruit to grow out of the soil. In the middle of the garden also grew the Tree of Life and the Tree of Knowledge of Good and Evil.

The LORD GOD took the human and set him down in the Garden of Eden to take care of it. HE commanded the human, "You may eat fruit from every tree in the garden, except one. You must not eat from the Tree of Knowledge of Good and Evil; for on the day that you eat from it, you will be doomed to die."

Then the LORD GOD said, "It is not good for the human to be alone. I will make a partner and helpmate for him." So HE took dust from the ground and molded and shaped it into animals and birds. HE brought each one to the human to see what he would call it. Whatever the human called each living creature, that was its name.

"Chicken. Cow. Lion. Tiger. Cat. Kangaroo. Alligator. Dog," called the human, until all the animals and birds were named. And the human was named Adam, meaning Man and of Red Earth." But among all the animals, Adam could not find a helpmate.

The LORD GOD caused a deep sleep to fall on Adam. While he was sleeping, the LORD GOD took one of Adam's rib bones and closed over the flesh where it was. HE formed the rib into a woman and brought her to Adam.

"At last!" said the man. "This one is bone of my bones and flesh of my flesh. This one will be called Woman, because she was taken from Man."

The man and the woman became husband and wife. The two of them were naked and were not ashamed.

The man and the woman were happy in the Garden of Eden. They took care of the plants and animals and enjoyed being together. Life on earth was good, and everything was in order as GOD had made it, until that order began to fall apart.

THE TEMPTATION AND THE FALL FROM GRACE

Now, the serpent was the slyest animal that the LORD GOD had made. It said to the woman, "Has GOD said that you must not eat from any of the trees in the garden?"

The woman told the serpent, "We may eat any fruit, except the fruit of the tree in the middle of the garden. God said, 'You may not eat from it, nor even touch it, lest you die.' "

"Die?" said the serpent. "You're not doomed to die. GOD knows that on the day you eat from it, your eyes will be opened, and you'll see things in a different way. You'll become like gods, knowing good and evil."

The woman looked at the ripe fruit on the tree. How delicious it looked! How lovely and desirable it was—to make a person wise like a god!

She picked some fruit from the tree and ate. Then she gave some to her husband, and he ate.

And the eyes of the two of them were opened, and they saw that they were naked. For the first time they felt shame. They sewed fig leaves together to cover themselves.

In early evening they heard the voice of the LORD GOD as HE was walking in the garden. The man and his wife hid themselves from the LORD GOD among the trees of the garden.

"Where are you?" the LORD GOD called to Adam.

The man said, "I heard YOUR voice in the garden. I was afraid because I was naked; and I hid myself."

"Who told you that you were naked?" said the LORD GOD. "Have you eaten from the tree from which I commanded you not to eat?"

The man said, "The woman whom you created to be with me—she gave me fruit from the tree, and I ate."

And the LORD GOD said to the woman, "What is this you have done?"

"The serpent tempted me, and I ate," she said.

The LORD GOD said to the serpent, "Because you have done this, you are cursed above all cattle and above every beast of the field. You will crawl on your belly and eat dust all the days of your life. You and the woman will be enemies, and your children and her children will hate each other. They will bruise your head, and you will bruise their heel."

To the woman God said, "I will greatly multiply your sorrows. You will suffer pain when you bear children. You will depend on your husband for happiness, and he will rule over you."

And to the man HE said, "Because you listened to the voice of your wife and ate from the forbidden tree, the soil will be cursed for you. In sorrow you will till the soil all the days of your life to earn your bread. Thorns and thistles will grow in your fields. Your face will be covered with sweat from your labor until you return to the soil, for out of the soil were you taken. Dust you are, and to dust you will return."

And so it was. The LORD GOD made suits of animal skins and HE clothed them. And Adam named his wife Eve, meaning Life, because she was the mother of all that lives.

Then GOD said, "Now that humans have become like gods, knowing good and evil, they might also take fruit from the Tree of Life and live forever."

So the LORD GOD drove Adam and Eve out of the Garden of Eden. At the east of the garden, the LORD GOD placed winged Cherubim. Then HE placed a great flaming sword that whirled in every direction to guard the way to the Tree of Life.

THE STORY OF CAIN AND ABEL

When Adam and Eve left the garden, their life of pleasure became a life of pain. Adam worked in fields filled with thorns and thistles. He dug out rocks and pulled up weeds until his hands were rough and sore, and his face was covered with sweat.

Adam and Eve knew that the LORD still cared about them, and they made an altar where they could pray to HIM. Adam gathered big stones from the field and piled them up with a wide, flat stone on top. They placed gifts of plants and animals on the top stone and burned them. The smoke from the burnt offerings rose to heaven with their prayers.

Adam and Eve had two sons named Cain and Abel. When they grew up, they joined their parents in the fields and at the altar. Abel became a shepherd, and Cain a farmer.

One day Cain brought some plants from the field and offered them to the LORD. At the same time, Abel brought as his offering the best parts of the best lambs from his flock. The LORD was pleased with Abel and his gift, but HE was not pleased with Cain and his gift. Cain was so angry, his face fell into a deep frown.

"Why are you angry?" the LORD asked Cain. "Why is your face downcast? If you plan to do good, let your face show it; but if you don't, beware! Sin crouches at your door like a wild beast, ready to devour you! But you can rule over it."

Cain didn't listen to the LORD. Instead, he said to his brother Abel, "Let's go out to the field."

When they were in the field, Cain attacked his brother Abel and killed him.

The LORD said to Cain, "Where is Abel your brother?"

"I don't know," said Cain. "Is it my job to watch over my brother? Am I my brother's keeper?"

"What have you done?" said the LORD. "Listen! Your brother's blood is crying out to ME from the soil. You will be cursed by the soil that opened its mouth to take your brother's blood from your hand. If you try to work the soil, it will produce nothing. You must leave your home and your fields and be a restless wanderer on the earth."

"My punishment is too great!" said Cain. "You're driving me away from the face of the earth, and I must hide from YOUR face. I'll be a restless wanderer on the earth, and whoever finds me will kill me!"

"Don't worry," the LORD said to him. "I will watch over you. Whoever kills Cain will be punished seven times."

Then the LORD put a mark on Cain so that whoever found him wouldn't kill him.

Cain went away from the LORD, and away from his home and his fields. He settled east of Eden, in the land of Nod. Cain and his wife had a son, and Cain built a city and named it Enoch, after his son.

Adam and Eve had another son, and Eve said, "GOD has granted me another child in place of Abel because Cain killed him." She named him Seth, meaning Granted.

NOAH AND THE GREAT FLOOD

But one of Seth's descendants found favor in the eyes of the LORD. His name was Noah.

Noah was a righteous man who followed the ways of GOD. He was the father of three sons: Shem, Ham, and Japheth.

When GOD saw that the earth was corrupt and filled with cruelty, GOD said to Noah, "I have decided to put an end to all living creatures. The earth is filled with cruelty because of them. I will destroy them, for I will destroy the earth.

"This is what I want you to do: Make an ark of cypress wood. Make it with many rooms, and put tar on the wood, inside and out, to waterproof it. Build it four hundred and fifty feet long, seventy-five feet wide, and forty-five feet high. Make three levels and put an opening for light and air at the top. Put an entrance on one side.

Seth had many children and grandchildren, and the earth began to be filled with people. But when humans began to multiply on the earth, they did evil things and thought evil thoughts.

The LORD saw that the evil of humans was great on the earth. HE was sorry HE had made humans, and it grieved HIM to HIS heart.

"I'll wipe humans off the face of the earth," HE said. "I'll wipe out everything I've created—humans and animals and crawling things and birds of the sky. I'm sorry I made them."

"And, behold, I—even I," said GOD, "will send a flood upon the earth to destroy all living creatures that have the breath of life. Everything on the earth will perish.

"Go into the ark with your sons, Shem, Ham, and Japheth, and your wife and the wives of your sons. Bring to the ark seven pairs of the animals used for offerings and pairs of all the other kinds of birds and animals. Bring them in, two by two, male and female, so they can multiply and fill the earth after the flood. I want you to take plenty of food and store it in the ark for yourself, your family, and the animals.

"After you finish building the ark, I will send rain onto the earth for forty days and forty nights. I will wipe out all the living creatures I have made from the face of the earth."

Noah built an enormous wooden box, an ark, just as GOD commanded. When the ark was finished, Noah, his sons, and Noah's wife and the three wives of his sons went inside. Behind them came the animals and the birds, male and female of every kind, just as GOD had commanded. When everyone was safely inside, the LORD shut them in.

And it came to pass after seven days that the order of Creation began to come apart. The fountains of the great ocean and the windows of heaven opened up. Hard rain fell on the earth for forty days and forty nights.

The water surged mightily over the earth and lifted the ark from the earth, and the ark floated on the face of the water. The water rose until all the mountains were covered, and the dry land disappeared.

All living creatures of the earth died—all the birds and cattle and wild animals and all that creep upon the earth and all human beings. Everything that breathed the breath of life in its nostrils died in the flood. Only Noah remained, and those who were with him in the ark.

And the waters prevailed upon the earth for a hundred and fifty days.

But GOD remembered Noah and all the animals with him in the ark. HE sent a wind over the earth and quieted the waters. The fountains of the great ocean and the windows of heaven were closed up. The hard rain was held back.

Month after month, little by little, day by day, the waters went down, and the ark came to rest on the mountains of Ararat.

After forty days on the mountain, Noah opened the skylight of the ark and looked out to see whether the waters were drying up. He let out a big black raven, and it flew back and forth. Then he let out a little white dove. The dove found no place to rest its foot, and it returned to him. Noah reached out his hand and brought it back into the ark.

Noah waited another seven days, and then he let the dove out again. It came back in the evening, and in its beak was a green olive leaf. The waters were drying up.

Noah waited another seven days and let the dove out again. This time the dove did not return.

Noah took off the covering of the ark and looked out, and, behold, the earth was dry!

GOD said to Noah, "Go forth from the ark, you and your wife and your sons and your sons' wives. Bring all the animals and all the birds, so that they can be fruitful and multiply on the earth."

Noah went forth, along with his sons and his wife and his sons' wives. All the animals and birds went with them, two by two. Then Noah built an altar to the LORD. He took some of the animals and birds used for offerings and burned them on the altar as a gift for the LORD.

The LORD smelled the sweet smell of the offering, and HE said in HIS heart, "I will never again curse the soil because of human beings, no matter what evil they have in their hearts. As long as the earth remains, seedtime and harvest, cold and heat, summer and winter, and day and night will never cease."

GOD blessed Noah and his sons and said to them, "Be fruitful and multiply and fill the earth. All the animals on the earth and all the birds in the sky and all the fish of the sea will fear you. They are in your hands. Every moving thing that lives will be food for you. But anyone who sheds human blood must have their blood shed, for in the image of GOD I made human beings. As for you, be fruitful and multiply. Fill the earth and rule over it."

GOD said, "I will make a covenant with you and your children and all the people who will ever be born, and all the animals and birds that came out of the ark. This covenant is a promise that will last forever. I promise: Never again will all living things be destroyed by the waters of a flood. Never again will a flood destroy the earth.

"This is the sign of the promise: I am setting my bow in the clouds. When I send clouds over the earth, the rainbow will appear, and I will re-member the everlasting covenant between me and you and all the creatures who live on the earth."

THE TOWER OF BABEL

After the flood, Noah's sons and their wives had many children and grandchildren. Everyone on earth lived in one place and spoke one language.

As they moved from the east, they found a fertile plain between the Tigris and Euphrates rivers and settled there. The clay soil was good for brickmaking, and there was tar for mortar to hold the bricks together. "Come!" they said to each other. "Let's make bricks and bake them hard and build houses."

They made bricks, and then they said, "Come! Let's build a city for ourselves, and a tower with its top in the heavens. It will make our name known and keep us from being scattered all over the earth."

The LORD came down to see the city and the tower that the mortals were building. "Behold," HE said. "They are one people with one language. If this is how they are going to act, there will be no limit to their schemes. Come! Let US go down and confuse their language, so they won't be able to understand each other."

And so the people became confused because they were all suddenly speaking different languages. Since they couldn't talk to each other, they stopped building the tower. They left the city in groups of families who spoke the same language. Each group became a separate nation, and thus were the people scattered over the earth.

The city and the tower were called Babel, meaning Confusion, because that was where the LORD confused the language of all the earth.

GOD CALLS ABRAM

In the beginning, GOD had created life and abundance out of nothingness. And now GOD was going to create a family, and from that family HE would create a great nation.

One of Shem's descendants was a man named Terah. He lived in the land of Ur, east of the great river Euphrates. He was the father of three sons: Abram, Nahor, and Haran.

Haran was the father of Lot, and Haran died in Ur. Abram's wife was Sarai, and Nahor's wife was Milcah. Sarai was barren: she had no children.

Terah took his son, Abram, and Haran's son, Lot, and his daughter-in-law Sarai, and they left Ur and went toward the land of Canaan. They settled in the city of Haran, in Syria, and there Terah died.

Now the LORD said to Abram, "Go from your father's house and from your homeland to a land I will show you. I will make a great nation of you. I will bless you and make your name great, and you will be a blessing. I will bless those who bless you, and I will curse those who curse you. All the families of the earth will be blessed through you."

Abram went, as the LORD had said. He took his wife, Sarai, and his nephew, Lot, and all the possessions they had gained in Haran and set out for the land of Canaan.

When Abram came to the land of Canaan, the LORD appeared to him and said, "I will give this land to your descendants."

There was a famine in the land, and so they went down to Egypt. Egypt was a dangerous place, but the LORD protected them. Abram came out of Egypt a rich man, with much silver and gold and many sheep and oxen and donkeys and camels and servants.

Abram's nephew, Lot, was now a rich man, too, with large flocks of sheep and goats and herds of cattle and many tents. The rocky hill country was good for sheep and goats, but the cattle didn't have enough pasture. The men who were herding Abram's cattle quarreled with Lot's herdsmen. There were too many animals and not enough grazing land for all of them to stay in the same place.

"Please!" Abram said to Lot. "Let's stop quarreling! It's not good for us or our herdsmen to argue. We are family. There's enough land here for both of us if we divide it fairly. Let's separate. You choose the direction you want to go, and I'll go the other."

Lot looked out and saw the whole plain of the Jordan River. At that time, it was as beautiful as the Garden of Eden. It was as rich in water and good soil as the land of Egypt. Lot chose the plain of the Jordan.

Lot went east, and Abram stayed in the west. Lot pitched his tent near the city of Sodom—a prosperous but wicked city.

After Lot left, the LORD said to Abram, "Look around. I will give all the land you see, in every direction, to you and to your children forever. I will make your descendants as many as the dust of the earth—if you can count the dust. Get up and walk through the land, from one end to the other, and all across it. I am giving it to you."

God's Promise to Abram

Some time after this, the LORD came to Abram in a vision. "Don't be afraid, Abram," HE said. "I am your shield. Your reward will be very great."

"My LORD," said Abram, "what good are YOUR gifts to me? YOU still haven't given me a son to inherit my possessions. When I die, my chief servant will inherit everything I own."

"That one won't be your heir," said the LORD. "The one who comes from your body will be your heir."

HE took Abram outside and said, "Look up at the heavens and count the stars—if you can. So will be the number of your descendants."

Abram trusted the LORD, and the LORD counted his faith as righteousness.

A few days later, GOD said to Abram, "I am the LORD WHO brought you out of Ur, to give you this land as an inheritance."

"How can I know for sure?" said Abram.

The LORD said, "Bring ME a calf, a she-goat, a ram, a dove, and a pigeon."

Abram brought the animals and birds, cut them, and placed one line of pieces opposite the others. Vultures swooped down on the carcasses, and Abram chased them away. As the sun was about to set, a deep sleep fell on Abram, and a great dark dread came over him.

The LORD said to Abram, "Know for sure that your descendants will be strangers in a foreign land. They will suffer as slaves for four hundred years. But I will bring judgment on the nation that enslaves them. Afterward they will escape with great possessions and return to this land. You will die in peace and be buried at a ripe old age."

The sun went down, and it was very dark. A smoking fire pot and a flaming torch appeared out of the darkness and passed between the pieces of animals and birds.

This ceremony was called "cutting a covenant." The LORD was making a solemn promise to Abram, and HE said, "I give this land to your descendants, from the river of Egypt to the great river Euphrates."

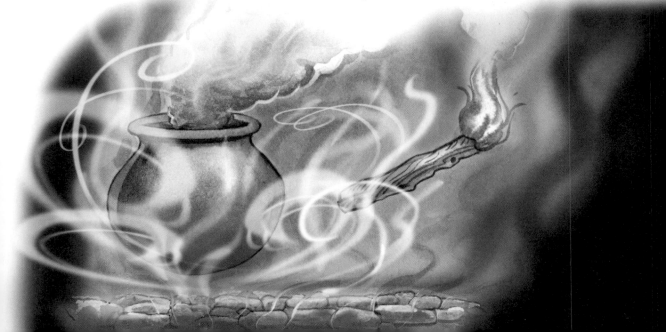

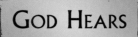

GOD HEARS

"She is in your hands," said Abram. "Deal with her as you please."

Sarai was so angry that she was cruel to Hagar, and Hagar ran away. She went out into the wilderness, along the road to Egypt. When she came to a well, she stopped to rest.

The angel of the LORD found her and said, "Hagar, servant of Sarai! Where have you come from? Where are you going?"

"I flee from the face of my mistress Sarai," she said.

"Return to your mistress and submit to her," said the angel. "I will multiply your children. You will have so many descendants, no one will be able to count them.

"Behold, you are with child. You shall bear a son, and you shall call him Ishmael, meaning GOD HEARS, for the LORD has heard your troubles. Your son will live in the wilderness, as wild and free as an untamed colt."

Hagar went back to Sarai, as the LORD had told her. A few months later, her baby boy was born, and Abram named him Ishmael. Hagar continued to work as Sarai's servant-woman, but Ishmael grew up in the tents of his father.

Sarai and Abram had lived in the land of Canaan for ten years, and they still had no children.

One day Sarai said to Abram, "I want a baby, but I'm an old woman, past the age for giving birth. Here is Hagar, my Egyptian servant-woman. Take her as a wife, so I can have a son through her."

Abram listened to Sarai and took Hagar as his wife. When Hagar became with child, she was no longer respectful to Sarai.

"Must I suffer such insult?" Sarai said to Abram. "I gave Hagar to you, but now that she is with child, she looks down on me. This is your fault!"

Thirteen years later, the LORD appeared to Abram and said:

"I am GOD Almighty. I will make MY covenant with you and multiply you greatly."

Abram bowed down, and GOD said, "You will be the father of a multitude of nations. From now on, your name will be Abraham—Father of a Multitude.

"I will give you and your descendants all the land of Canaan, where you are now a stranger. I will give this land to them as an everlasting possession, and I will be their GOD.

"From now on, Sarai's name will be Sarah. I will bless her and give you a son by her. She will be the mother of nations."

Abraham laughed and said to himself, "An old man like me a father? I'm ninety-nine years old, and Sarah is ninety! We're too old to have a baby." Then he said out loud to the LORD, "Bless my son Ishmael."

"I speak not of Ishmael," GOD said. "I'm talking about the baby Sarah is going to have. Call him Isaac. I will establish MY covenant with him and his children after him. As for Ishmael, I hear you. I will bless him and multiply him and make him a great nation. But I will establish MY covenant with Isaac, Sarah's son, who will be born this time next year."

GOD finished speaking with Abraham and ascended from him.

The LORD appeared to Abraham in the middle of the day as he was sitting in the shade at the entrance of his tent. Abraham looked up and saw THREE men standing nearby. He knew that THEY were the LORD, and he ran to meet the visitors and bowed low.

"My LORD," he said, "I'm honored that YOU've come here. Please stay and let me serve YOU. Let me send for a little water so YOU can wash the dust off YOUR feet. Rest in the shade and let me bring YOU a little food so YOU can refresh YOURSELVES before YOU continue on YOUR way."

"This would be good," said the visitors. "Do as you said."

Abraham hurried into the tent and said to Sarah, "Quick! Three measures of the best flour! Knead it and make fresh hot loaves."

Then he ran to the herd and picked out a good calf and told a servant to prepare it. He brought some yogurt and milk and set them in front of his guests with the roast meat. While THEY ate, he stood near THEM, under the tree.

"Where is your wife Sarah?" THEY said.

"Over there in the tent."

"I'll return this time next year," said ONE of the visitors, "and your wife Sarah will have a son."

Sarah was listening at the entrance of the tent, and she laughed to herself. "I'm old, and my husband's old—too old to have a baby."

The visitor said to Abraham, "Why did Sarah laugh and say she's too old to have a baby? Is anything too hard for the LORD? I will return this time next year, and the baby will be born. Sarah is going to have a son."

Suddenly Sarah felt afraid. "I didn't laugh," she lied.

"Yes, you did," the man said. "You laughed."

If they do, I will keep the promises I made to him."

Then the LORD said, "Great is the outcry against the cities of Sodom and Gomorrah. Their sin is grievous. Let ME go down and see if this report be true."

Two of the men went on toward Sodom as messengers, and the LORD was still standing in front of Abraham. Abraham stepped forward and spoke.

"Are YOU really going to destroy the innocent with the guilty?" he said. "What if there are fifty innocent people in the city? Will YOU really wipe it out? Won't YOU spare the place for the sake of the fifty? YOU wouldn't put the innocent to death with the guilty! Won't the JUDGE of all the earth do justice?"

"If I find fifty innocent people in Sodom, I will forgive the whole place for their sake," said the LORD.

Abraham spoke again. "Please, let me presume to speak, although I am mere dust and ashes. What if the fifty innocent lack five? Will YOU destroy the whole city because of the five?"

"No," the LORD said. "I won't destroy it if I find forty-five."

"What if YOU find forty?"

"I won't for the sake of the forty."

"Oh, please don't be angry if I speak again. But what if YOU find thirty?"

"I won't do it if I find thirty."

"What if YOU find twenty?"

"I won't destroy it for the sake of the twenty."

"Please don't be angry if I speak just one more time. What if YOU find ten?"

"I won't destroy it for the sake of the ten."

When the LORD finished speaking with Abraham, HE went on HIS way, and Abraham returned to his place.

The visitors got up to leave, and Abraham walked along to see THEM on their way. THEY looked down at the city of Sodom and talked among THEMselves.

"Shall I hide from Abraham what I'm about to do?" the LORD said. "I've called Abraham so I can bless all nations. My plan is for him to teach his family to be righteous and do justice.

Lot's Narrow Escape

Abraham's nephew Lot was sitting in the city square when the two messengers arrived at Sodom. As soon as he saw them, he got up and greeted them with a bow.

"Please, my lords," he said, "let me serve you. Come to my house to spend the night and wash your feet. In the morning you can get up and be on your way."

"No," they said, "we'll spend the night in the city square."

But Lot insisted, and they went with him to his house. He prepared a meal and baked some bread, and they ate.

But before they went to bed, all the men of Sodom, young and old, came and surrounded the house. "Where are the men who came here tonight?" they called out to Lot. "Bring them out to us! We want to harass them!"

Lot went out to them and shut the door behind him. "Please, friends!" he said. "Don't be so wicked! Don't do anything to these men, for they have come under the shelter of my roof."

"Step aside!" they said to Lot. "Who do you think you are? Foreigner! Alien! How dare you judge us! Now we'll treat you worse than we'll treat them!"

They pushed and shoved against Lot. The messengers inside the house reached out their hands and pulled Lot back into the house and shut the door. Then these messengers struck the men who were standing outside the house with dazzling light, so they couldn't see to find the door.

The messengers said to Lot, "Do you have any relatives in the city besides your wife and daughters? If you do, get them out of here. We're going to destroy this place and its people. The enormous outcry against them has reached the LORD. HE has sent us to destroy the city."

Lot went out and spoke to his sons-in-law. "Get out of here!" he said to them. "The LORD is going to destroy the city!"

But his sons-in-law thought he was joking.

The sun was rising, and the messengers urged Lot to hurry. "Go!" they said. "Take your wife and your two daughters and move fast, or you'll be swept away in the punishment of the city."

When Lot delayed, they seized his hand and his wife's hand and the hands of his two daughters, because the LORD had pity on him. They took him and his wife and daughters and led them out of the city.

"Run for your lives!" they said. "Don't look back! Don't stop anywhere on the plain. Escape to the hills, or you'll be swept away."

"Oh, no, my LORD!" said Lot. "You've shown me great kindness. YOU saved my life; but I can't escape to the hills. I'm afraid to go that far! See that little town over there? It's close enough for us to get to before the sun comes up. Let me run there. See how little it is? We'll be safe there."

The LORD said to Lot, "I'll let you have your wish. I won't destroy that little town. Now hurry! Run fast. I can't do anything until you get there. And remember—don't look back!"

The sun was rising over the earth as Lot reached the little town. Then the LORD rained fire and brimstone on Sodom and Gomorrah. The earth shook and flames shot into the air and fell back down upon the earth. The LORD overthrew those cities and all the people who lived in them and everything that grew in the soil.

But Lot's wife could not resist: she looked back—and she turned into a pillar of salt.

Lot was so frightened, he left the little town. He took his daughters and escaped to the hills and hid in a cave.

Abraham got up early in the morning and returned to the place where he had stood in the presence of the LORD. He looked out over Sodom and Gomorrah and all the land of the plain. He saw thick smoke rising like the smoke of a giant furnace.

When GOD destroyed the cities of the plain, HE remembered Abraham and sent Lot out of the upheaval to safety.

Sarah's Laughter and Hagar's Tears

A year passed. The LORD took notice of Sarah, and did for her as HE had promised. Sarah gave birth to a baby boy, and Abraham named his son Isaac, which means Laughter.

"GOD has made laughter for me," said Sarah. "Everyone who hears of this blessing will laugh with me. Who would imagine that Abraham and Sarah could have a baby?"

Abraham held a great feast on the day Isaac was weaned. During the feast Sarah saw Hagar's son Ishmael laughing, and she said to Abraham, "Get rid of that servant-woman and her son! I won't have that servant's son sharing the inheritance with my son Isaac."

This saddened Abraham, because Ishmael was his son. But GOD said to him, "Don't be concerned about the boy or your servant-woman. Listen to what Sarah says. Your descendants will be counted through Isaac. But I'll make the servant-woman's son a nation, because he is your child."

Abraham got up early in the morning and took some bread and a jug of water and gave them to Hagar and sent her away with Ishmael, who was but fourteen.

Hagar got lost in the wilderness. When all the water was gone, she left the child crying under a bush and went away from him. She sat down and wept, saying, "I can't stand to see the child die."

GOD heard the boy's voice, and the angel of GOD called out from heaven, "What's the matter, Hagar? Fear not. GOD has heard the boy. Pick him up and hold his hand. I'm going to make a great nation of him."

GOD showed her a well of water in the wilderness. She went and filled the jug and let the boy drink.

GOD was with Ishmael. When Ishmael grew up, he became an expert with the bow and arrow. He settled in the wilderness, and his mother found a wife for him from the land of Egypt.

GOD TESTS ABRAHAM

And GOD was with Abraham. Abraham lived near Beersheba with Sarah and Isaac, the beloved child of his old age.

It came to pass that GOD decided to test Abraham's faith and obedience.

"Abraham!" GOD said.

"Here I am," Abraham answered.

"Take your son, your only one, your beloved son Isaac, and go to the land of Moriah. Give him to ME as an offering on a mountain that I will show you."

Abraham got up early in the morning and saddled his donkey. He took two young servants and his son Isaac.

He split wood for the offering and went toward the place GOD had told him about.

On the third day, Abraham looked up and saw the place in the distance. He said to the young men, "Stay here with the donkey, and let me and the boy walk ahead. We'll worship and then return to you."

Abraham took the wood for the offering and laid it upon his son Isaac to carry. He took in his hand the flintstone for making fire, and a knife. And the two of them went together.

Isaac said to Abraham, "Father?"

"Here I am, my son."

"I see the flintstone and the wood, but where is the lamb for the offering?"

Abraham said, "GOD will provide the lamb for the offering, my son."

So the two of them went together, and they came to the place GOD had told Abraham of.

29

Abraham built an altar and laid out the wood. Then he took and tied his son Isaac and put him on the altar on top of the wood.

Abraham reached out his hand and took the knife to sacrifice his son.

The angel of the LORD called to him from the heavens:

"Abraham! Abraham!"

"Here I am," he said.

"Don't lay a hand on the boy," said the angel of the Lord. "Don't do a thing to him. Now I know that you are in awe of GOD. You haven't held back your son, your only one, from ME."

Abraham looked around. There was a ram caught in the thicket by its horns. He took the ram and offered it up instead of his son.

The angel of the LORD called to Abraham again, "The LORD says, 'Because you have done this and haven't held back your son, your only son, I will greatly bless you. I will greatly multiply your children. They will be as many as the stars of heaven and the sand on the shore of the sea. Your descendants will defeat their enemies. All the nations of the earth will be blessed through your descendants, because you listened to MY voice.'"

Abraham returned to his servants, and they got up and went back together to Beersheba.

FINDING REBEKAH

Isaac grew up, and Abraham and Sarah grew very old.

Sarah died at Hebron in the land of Canaan, and Abraham mourned and cried for her. Then he went to the leaders of the people of the land and paid four hundred pieces of silver for a burial plot. He buried Sarah in a cave in a corner of the field of Machpelah near Hebron.

The LORD had blessed Abraham, but there was one more thing Abraham needed to do before he died. He had a son, but his son had no wife.

He called his chief servant and said, "Swear to me that you won't let my son marry a Canaanite woman. Go to my homeland, to my brother Nahor and his wife Milcah. I've heard that they are living in Haran, and they have twelve sons. Go to them and find a wife for my son Isaac."

"But what if I find a woman and she isn't willing to come here?" said the servant. "Should I take your son back to the land you left?"

"No," said Abraham. "Never take my son there. The LORD took me from my father's house and promised to give this land to my descendants. He will send HIS angel ahead of you, to lead you to a wife for my son. Whatever you do, don't take my son there."

The servant took ten of his master's camels and many gifts and went to the city of Haran in Syria, where Abraham's brother Nahor lived. He stopped at a well outside the city and made the camels kneel down. It was evening, the time when women came to draw water.

"O LORD, GOD of my master Abraham," the servant said, "please give my journey success. The young women are coming to the well. I'll ask one of them to let down her water jar so I can drink. If she says, 'Drink, and I'll water your camels also,' let her be the one YOU have chosen for Isaac."

Before he finished speaking, he saw a beautiful girl with a water jar on her shoulder. She went down the steps of the well and filled her jar. When she came back up, the servant ran to meet her.

"Please," he said, "let me have a sip of water from your jar."

"Drink," she said, and she quickly lowered her jar and poured him a drink. When he was finished, she said, "I'll water your camels also." She hurried and emptied her jar into the trough and ran back to the well and drew water for all his camels.

The man stood staring at her. When all the camels had finished drinking, he took out a gold nose-ring and two gold bracelets and gave them to her.

"Whose daughter are you?" he asked. "Tell me, please, is there room in your father's house for us to spend the night?"

"I'm Rebekah, daughter of Bethuel, the son of Milcah and Nahor," she said. "We have plenty of straw and animal feed and room to spend the night."

"Blessed be the LORD, GOD of my master Abraham!" he said. "HE has shown loving kindness. HE has led me to the house of my master's family."

The girl ran and reported these things to the people in her mother's house. Her brother Laban was excited when he saw the expensive nose-ring and the bracelets on Rebekah's arms. When he heard what the man had said, he ran out to the well. He found Abraham's servant standing by the camels.

"Come in, O blessed of the LORD!" Laban said. "I've prepared the house and a place for the camels."

The man went to the house and unharnessed the camels. Laban gave him straw and feed for the animals, and water to wash his feet and the feet of the men with him.

When they put some food in front of him, he said, "I won't eat until I've told my story."

"Tell it," they said.

"I am Abraham's servant," he began, and he told them the whole story. "Now," he said, "if you're going to be faithful and kind to my master, tell me. If not, I'll go somewhere else."

"How can we argue?" said Laban. "This is from the LORD. Here is Rebekah. Take her to be the wife of your master's son."

Abraham's servant bowed to the LORD. He took out silver and gold jewelry and clothing and gave them to Rebekah. He also gave expensive presents to her brother and her mother. Then he and the men with him ate and drank and spent the night.

The next morning he said, "Let me go, so I can return to my master."

Rebekah's brother and mother said, "Let the girl stay with us a week or ten days. Then she can go."

"Don't make me wait," he said. "The LORD has given my journey success. Now I must return to my master."

"Let us call the girl and ask her," they said, and they called Rebekah.

"Will you go with this man?" they asked.

"Yes," she said, "I will go."

They kissed Rebekah good-bye and gave her a farewell blessing. Then she and her maids got up on the camels and went away with Abraham's servant.

They came to the southern region of the Negev in the evening. Isaac was taking a walk in the fields, and he looked up and saw the camels.

Rebekah was riding on one of the camels. When she saw Isaac, she got down and said to the servant, "Who is that man walking through the field toward us?"

"That's my master," he said.

She took her veil and covered her face.

The servant told Isaac everything he had done. Then Isaac took Rebekah into the tent of his mother Sarah, and Rebekah became his wife. He loved her, and she comforted him, for he mourned his mother's death.

Abraham breathed his last and died, an old man full of years. His sons Isaac and Ishmael buried him in the cave in the field of Machpelah, next to his wife Sarah.

Before he died, Abraham gave all that he had to Isaac. GOD blessed Abraham's son Isaac, and Isaac settled near Beersheba.

Abraham's son Ishmael had twelve sons. They became chieftains of twelve tribes, and they lived in the wilderness between Egypt and Syria.

JACOB AND ESAU, THE FIGHTING TWINS

Isaac was forty years old when he married Rebekah. They were married for twenty years and had no children. Isaac pleaded with the LORD for his wife, because she was barren.

The LORD answered him, and Rebekah became pregnant with twins. But inside her womb, the babies were wrestling with each other. She was in so much pain, she cried, "Why is this happening to me?"

She went to inquire of the LORD, and the LORD said to her, "Two nations are in your womb. Two tribes will come from your belly. One will be greater than the other, and the older will serve the younger."

When the twins were born, the first to come out was covered with thick red hair. They named him Esau, meaning Hairy. Then his brother came out with his hand grabbing Esau's heel. He was named Jacob, meaning Heel Grabber.

The boys grew up. Esau became an expert hunter, and Jacob was a quiet man who preferred to stay home. Isaac loved Esau for the game that he brought him from the hunt, but Rebekah loved Jacob.

One day Jacob was making a stew when Esau came in tired from the field. Esau said to Jacob, "Feed me some of that red stuff, I beg you. I'm fainting from hunger!"

"First sell me your birthright," said Jacob.

By law, the firstborn had the right to inherit most of the possessions and property and become head of the family when the father died.

"Here I am, starving to death," said Esau, "and you want to talk about the birthright! What good is that to me?" He reached out for the food.

"Swear to me," said Jacob. "Swear to me this day that the birthright is mine."

And Esau did. He sold his birthright to Jacob for some bread and lentil stew. He ate and drank and rose up, and went his way.

Thus Esau lost his birthright.

JACOB CHEATS ESAU

Isaac grew old, and his eyes became so dim that he couldn't see. But he could hear the sheep and cattle in the field. He could feel the heat on the top of his head. He could smell the warm soil under his feet. He was content. Soon he would die, and his older son would take his place.

But Isaac had one disappointment. Esau had married two Canaanite women. Yet the big hairy hunter was still his favorite son. It was time they had a talk.

"Son!" he called to Esau.

"Here I am!"

"See; I am old and I may soon die. Please do one last thing for me. Take your bow and arrows and go hunt for wild game. Cook the meat the way I like, and bring it to me. I'll eat it and give you my blessing before I die."

Rebekah was listening. When Esau went out to hunt, she said to Jacob, "I heard your father speaking to your brother Esau. He asked him to hunt some wild game and cook it for him to eat. He wants to give Esau his blessing before he dies.

"Now listen to me, son. Do as I say. Go out to the flock and get me two fat young goats. I'll cook the meat the way your father likes. Then you take it to him to eat, and he will bless you before he dies."

"But my brother Esau is a hairy man, and I'm smooth-skinned," said Jacob. "What if my father feels my skin? He'll know I'm cheating him. I'll get a curse instead of a blessing."

"Let me worry about that, son," said his mother. "Just do what I say. Now go get those goats."

Jacob went out to the field and got the goats and brought them to his mother. She cooked the meat in the special way his father liked. Then she took some of her older son's clothes and put them on her younger son. She put pieces of hairy goatskin on his hands and the back of his neck. He didn't look like Esau, but he smelled like him.

Then she gave Jacob the meat and some bread, and he went to his father.

"Father!" Jacob said.

"Here I am." Isaac turned his head toward the entrance of his tent. "Who are you, my son?"

Jacob said, "I'm Esau, your firstborn. I've done what you asked. Now, please sit up and eat the meat I hunted, so you may bless me."

"How did you find it so fast, my son?"

"The LORD your GOD gave me success," said Jacob.

"Come closer, my son, so I can feel whether you are my son Esau or not."

Jacob came closer to Isaac.

Isaac felt him and said, "The voice is Jacob's, but the hands are Esau's." Isaac didn't recognize Jacob, because the hands were hairy like his brother's.

But just as he was about to bless him, Isaac said, "Are you really my son Esau?"

"I am," said Jacob.

"Bring the meat close and I'll eat the game my son hunted. Then I'll give you my blessing."

Jacob brought it close, and Isaac ate. Jacob brought him wine, and he drank.

Then Isaac said, "Come close and kiss me, my son."

Jacob came close and kissed him.

Isaac smelled the damp, earthy smell of his clothes. "Ah," he said. "The smell of my son is like the smell of a field that the LORD has blessed!"

He put his hands on Jacob's head and blessed him. "May GOD give you rain from heaven and much grain and wine from the earth. Nations and tribes will bow down to you, and you will rule over your brothers. Curses to those who curse you, and blessings to those who bless you."

As soon as Isaac finished blessing Jacob, and just as Jacob was leaving, Esau came back from the hunt. He also cooked meat and brought it to his father.

"Please, Father," he said, "get up and eat this meat I hunted, so you can give me your blessing."

"Who are you?" Isaac asked.

"I am your son, your firstborn, Esau."

Isaac began to tremble.

"Who is it that hunted game and brought it to me?" he said. "I ate of it before you came. I gave him my blessing, and now the blessing is his forever."

When Esau heard his father's words, he cried out with a great, bitter cry. He said:

"Bless me—me too, Father!"

"I can't," said Isaac. "Your brother came with deceit and took away your blessing."

"That is why he is named Jacob," said Esau. "Heel grabber! Cheat! He has tripped me up two times. First he took my birthright, and now he has taken my blessing! Father, didn't you save a blessing for me?"

Isaac said, "I've already said he will rule over you. I blessed him with grain and wine. What's left, my son?"

"Don't you have more than one blessing, Father? Bless me—me too, Father!" Esau began to sob.

Isaac put his trembling hands on Esau's head and said, "Your home will be far from the crops of the earth and the rain of heaven. You will live by the sword and serve your brother. But in time you will tear his yoke from your neck."

Esau hated Jacob because of the blessing. He said, "When my father dies, I will kill my brother Jacob."

When Rebekah heard what Esau said, she sent for Jacob.

"Your brother Esau wants to kill you," she said. "Now, listen to me. You must get away from this place. Go to my brother Laban and stay with him until your brother cools down. When he forgets what you did to him, I'll send for you. You can't stay here and let me lose both my sons in one day."

Rebekah went to Isaac and said, "Esau's Canaanite wives make my life miserable. What will I do if Jacob marries a woman from this land?"

Isaac sent for Jacob and said, "You must not marry a Canaanite woman. Go to Syria, to your mother's family, and marry one of Laban's daughters. Now may GOD Almighty bless you and multiply you."

When Esau saw how his father was offended by his Canaanite wives, he went to Ishmael, his father's brother, and married one of Ishmael's daughters.

And Jacob went to Laban, his mother's brother.

JACOB'S LADDER

Jacob came to a certain place and stopped there for the night. He took some stones of the place and put them for his pillows and lay down.

He dreamed, and in his dream he saw a giant stairway set up against the ground like a ladder with its top reaching the heavens. He saw angels of GOD going up and down the ladder. Then he saw the LORD standing above it.

The LORD said, "I am the LORD, the GOD of Abraham and Isaac. I am with you. I will watch over you wherever you go and bring you back to this land. I give it to you and your descendants."

Jacob woke up from his sleep.

"Surely the LORD is in this place, and I didn't know it," he said fearfully.

"What an awesome place this is! This must be the house of GOD. This is the gate of heaven!"

He got up early in the morning and took the stone he had put at his head and set it up as a pillar. He poured oil over the top to dedicate it to GOD. He called the place Bethel, meaning House of GOD.

Jacob said, "If GOD is really with me, if HE watches over me on my journey and gives me food to eat and clothes to wear—and if I return in peace to my homeland—then the LORD will be my GOD."

Then he promised GOD, "This stone which I have set for a pillar will be GOD's house. And of all that YOU give me, I will give a tenth back to YOU."

LABAN CHEATS JACOB

Jacob came to the land of the Easterners and saw a well in a field with three flocks of sheep lying beside it. A huge stone lay across the mouth of the well.

Jacob greeted the shepherds who were standing in the field. "Friends, where are you from?"

"We're from Haran."

"Do you know Laban, son of Nahor?"

"We know him."

"Is he well?"

"He's well. Look! Here comes his daughter Rachel now, with the sheep."

"But it's the middle of the day," said Jacob. "It's not time to gather in the animals. Let them have some water and grass."

"We can't water them until the stone is rolled away," they said. "We're waiting for all the shepherds to gather so we can roll the stone away."

While they were speaking, Rachel arrived with her father's sheep. And it came to pass, when Jacob saw Rachel, the daughter of his mother's brother Laban, that he stepped forward and rolled the stone from the mouth of the well and watered Laban's sheep. Then he kissed Rachel, and lifted up his voice, and wept.

He told Rachel that he was her father's relative, Rebekah's son, and Rachel ran and told her father.

As soon as Laban heard about Jacob, he came to meet him. He hugged and kissed him and took him to his house.

Jacob told him everything that had happened, and Laban said, "You are my bone and my flesh."

Jacob stayed with Laban for a month, helping with the sheep and goats. Then Laban said, "Just because you're my relative, why should you serve me for nothing? Tell me what I should pay you."

Laban had two daughters. The older one was named Leah, and Rachel was the younger one. Leah had tender eyes, but Rachel was very beautiful to Jacob, and Jacob fell in love with her.

"I'll serve seven years for your younger daughter, Rachel," Jacob said.

"It's better to give her to you than another man," said Laban. "Stay with me."

Jacob served seven years for Rachel. To him, the years seemed like days because of his love for her. Then Jacob said, "Give me my wife. My time is done. Let me marry her."

Laban gathered all the people of the place and held a wedding feast. When evening came, he took his daughter to Jacob, and Jacob married her. When morning came, Jacob saw his bride in the light. It was Leah!

"What have you done?" he said to Laban. "Didn't I serve you for Rachel? Why have you cheated me?"

Laban said, "It's not the custom in our place to give the younger daughter before the firstborn. Wait one more week while we finish the feast. Then I'll give you the other daughter—for seven more years of service."

Jacob waited. When the wedding week was finished, Laban gave Jacob his daughter Rachel. Jacob married her, and he loved Rachel more than Leah; and he served Laban seven more years.

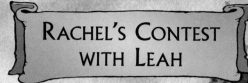

When the LORD saw that Leah was unloved by her husband, HE let her become with child. But Rachel was barren.

Leah gave birth to a son. "See! A son!" she said. "The LORD has seen my affliction. Now my husband will love me." She named her son Reuben, meaning See, a Son.

She gave birth to another son and said, "When the LORD heard that I was unloved, HE gave me another son." She named him Simeon, meaning Hearing.

She gave birth to another son and said, "Now my husband will join me." She named him Levi, meaning Joining.

She gave birth to another son and said, "This time I'll sing praises to the LORD." She named him Judah, meaning Sing to the LORD. Then she ceased bearing children.

When Rachel saw that she couldn't have children, she was jealous of her sister. She said to Jacob, "Give me children, or I will die."

Jacob's anger flared up against Rachel, and he said, "Am I GOD, to prevent you from giving birth?"

Rachel said, "Here's my servant-woman Bilhah. Take her as a wife so I can have a son through her."

She gave Bilhah to Jacob, and Bilhah gave birth to a son. Rachel said, "GOD heard my plea and did justice." She named the boy Dan, meaning Justice.

43

Bilhah gave birth to a second son, and Rachel said, "I am wrestling with my sister, and I'm winning." Rachel named the boy Naphtali, meaning Wrestle.

When Leah ceased bearing children, she took her servant Zilpah and gave her to Jacob as a wife.

Zilpah gave birth to a son, and Leah said, "What good luck!" She called him Gad, meaning Luck.

Zilpah gave birth to a second son, and Leah said, "What happiness!" She named him Asher, meaning Happy.

Leah was even happier when she gave birth to a fifth son herself. She said, "GOD has paid me for giving my servant-woman to my husband." She named him Issachar, meaning Pay.

Leah gave birth to a sixth son and said, "GOD has given me a precious gift. At last my husband will appreciate me, for I have had six sons." She named him Zebulun, meaning Precious Gift.

Finally Leah gave birth to a daughter and named her Dinah.

GOD remembered Rachel and she became with child. She gave birth to a son and said, "GOD has taken away my misery." She named her son Joseph, meaning Add. "May the LORD add another son to me," she said.

JACOB ESCAPES FROM LABAN

After Joseph was born, Jacob said to Laban, "Let me go home. Give me the wives I served you for, and my children. Let me go."

"Don't leave," said Laban. "GOD has blessed me because of you. Tell me how much I must pay you to get you to stay."

Jacob said, "I've taken such good care of your animals, they've become a multitude. But I need to provide for my own family."

"What do you want?" asked Laban.

Jacob answered, "I'll stay and take care of your flocks if you let me have some animals for myself. Let me have the striped and spotted goats and the dark-colored sheep. Most of the animals are white, so I'm not asking for much. It will be easy for you to check my honesty. If you find any white ones in my flocks, they are yours."

"Agreed," said Laban. But that same day he took all the striped and spotted goats and the dark-colored sheep and hid them among his sons' flocks.

Jacob noted any newly born dark lambs, and then bred the sheep so that all the strong ones had dark-colored lambs. He bred the goats so that all the strong ones had striped and spotted kids. Then he separated them from the white animals. Jacob's flocks grew larger and stronger while Laban's grew smaller and weaker.

Jacob heard Laban's sons saying, "Jacob grew rich by stealing from our father," and he saw that Laban's face wasn't friendly toward him anymore. He called Rachel and Leah out to the field, where no one could hear them, and said, "I see that your father isn't friendly. But the GOD of my father is with me. I've served your father with all my strength, but he has cheated me and changed my pay ten times. GOD has told me in a dream to return to my homeland."

Rachel and Leah answered, "Our father treats us like foreigners. He sold us to you, and you made him rich. Do whatever GOD says."

When Laban went to shear his sheep, Rachel stole the little clay gods he kept for luck in his house. Then Jacob took his children and his wives and all the possessions he had gained in Syria and set out to go to his father Isaac in the land of Canaan.

Three days later, Laban learned that Jacob had fled. He took his men and chased after him into the high country of Gilead. But GOD said to Laban in a dream, "Watch what you say to Jacob."

The next day, Laban caught up with Jacob. "Why have you deceived me?" he said. "You carried my daughters off like prisoners of war! Why did you sneak away? I didn't even kiss my grandchildren good-bye. I could harm you, but last night the GOD of your father told me to watch out."

"I was afraid," said Jacob. "I thought you would rob me of your daughters."

"I understand," replied Laban. "You are homesick. So go back to your father's house. But why did you steal my gods?"

Jacob did not know that Rachel had stolen the gods. "If you find your gods with anyone here," he said, "that person

won't live. If you recognize anything of yours, take it."

Laban went into Jacob's tent and Leah's tent and the tents of the two servant-women. He found nothing. He went out of Leah's tent into Rachel's tent. Rachel had put the gods inside a camel saddle. She sat on them while Laban searched the whole tent.

"I don't feel well," she said to her father. "Please don't be offended if I don't get up."

Laban searched the tent, but he didn't find the clay gods.

When Laban didn't find anything, Jacob was angry. "What's my crime?" he said. "Why did you race after me? You searched all my possessions, and what have you found? Show me."

Laban said nothing, and Jacob began to scold him. "For twenty years I took care of your sheep and goats!" he said. "I served you for twenty years—fourteen for your daughters and six for your animals. You changed my pay ten times. The GOD of my father was with me, or you would have sent me away empty-handed."

Laban answered, "These are my daughters! These are my children! These are my animals! Everything you see is mine. But what can I do? Come, let's make a treaty."

Jacob took a stone and set it up as a pillar. He told his men to gather stones and pile them into a mound.

They shared a meal, and then Laban said, "This mound is a witness between us. May the LORD watch between us when we are out of each other's sight. I won't cross over the mound to harm you, and you won't cross over to harm me."

The next morning Laban kissed his daughters and grandchildren and retuned to his place.

JACOB'S MIDNIGHT WRESTLING MATCH

Jacob went on his way, and the angels of GOD came out to meet him. When he saw them, Jacob declared, "This is GOD's host."

As Jacob came near the land of his father, he sent messengers to his brother, commanding them, "Tell Esau I am coming. Say to him, 'Your servant Jacob has lived with Laban until now, and comes with oxen and sheep and cattle and donkeys and servants.' Tell him I want to find favor in his sight."

The messengers returned to Jacob saying, "We went to your brother Esau, but he is already coming to meet you with four hundred men."

This news frightened and distressed Jacob. He divided his people, and the sheep and cattle and camels, into two camps. He said to himself, "If Esau attacks one camp and destroys it, then the other camp will escape."

Then he prayed, "O GOD of my father Abraham! GOD of my father Isaac! YOU said to 'Return to your homeland, and I will deal well with you.' I don't deserve YOUR loving kindness. I crossed the Jordan River with one staff in my hand. Now I return with two camps. Please save me from the hand of my brother Esau. I'm afraid he'll attack me and the mothers and the children."

He spent the night preparing a gift for Esau: two hundred she-goats and twenty he-goats, two hundred ewes and twenty rams, thirty milk camels with their young, forty cows and ten bulls, twenty she-donkeys and ten he-donkeys.

Jacob handed them over to his servants, herd by herd, and said, "Cross the river ahead of me, and put distance between the herds. When my brother Esau meets you, tell him these are a gift from his servant Jacob. Tell him I'm right behind you."

He said to himself, "I'll wipe the anger from his face with the gift. Perhaps he'll show me a kind face."

During the night, Jacob rose and took his two wives and his two servant-women and his children and sent them across the river with all his possessions.

Then Jacob was left alone. That night, a man appeared who wrestled with Jacob until the sun came up. When the man saw that he couldn't defeat Jacob, he struck the socket of Jacob's hip and put it out of joint. But Jacob continued to struggle with the man.

"Let me go!" the man said. "The sun is coming up."

"I won't let you go unless you bless me," said Jacob.

"What is your name?" asked the man.

"Jacob."

"You will no longer be called Jacob, the Heel Grabber," replied the man. "You will be called Israel, GOD Fighter, for you have fought with GOD and men and have won."

Jacob said, "Please tell me your name."

He said, "Why do you ask my name?" and he gave Jacob a blessing.

Jacob said, "I've seen GOD face to face, and I'm still alive!"

The sun was rising as he left that place, limping because his hip was out of joint.

Then he looked up and saw Esau coming, and with him, four hundred men.

Jacob and Esau Reunite

Jacob divided the children among Leah and Rachel and the two servant-women. He put the servant-women and their children first, Leah and her children in the middle, and Rachel and Joseph last. Jacob himself went in front, bowing low as he came closer and closer to his brother.

Esau ran to meet Jacob and threw his arms around him and kissed him. They both cried.

Esau looked at the women and the children and asked, "Who are these people?"

Jacob answered, "The children God has given to me, your servant."

Esau pointed to the herds. "What's the meaning of all the animals?"

"I hope you'll look at me with favor," said Jacob humbly.

"Keep what you have," said Esau. "I have plenty, brother."

"Please," said Jacob, "if I've found favor in your sight, take the gift. Seeing your face is like seeing the face of God. God has shown me favor, and I have all I need."

He insisted, and Esau took the gifts, saying, "Let us travel on together."

Jacob said, "My Lord knows the children are weary, and the baby sheep and cattle are in my care. If we drive them too hard, they'll die. Please go on ahead. I'll travel slowly behind you."

"Well, then," said Esau, "let me leave some of my men with you."

"No, thank you," said Jacob. "It's enough that you have looked at me with favor."

Esau started back that day on his journey to the land of Edom. Jacob traveled in the opposite direction, to Succoth. He stayed there a short time and then moved on.

Jacob came in peace to the city of Shechem in Canaan and made his camp facing the city. He bought a piece of property for a hundred pieces of money. There he spread out his tent and built an altar. He would have stayed at Shechem, but his sons fought with the men of the city, and they had to leave.

At GOD's bidding, Jacob said to his family, "Change your garments and make yourselves clean before the LORD. Let us go to Bethel. I will build there an altar to the GOD WHO answered me when I was in trouble. HE has watched over me wherever I have gone."

GOD appeared to Jacob at Bethel and said, "Israel! I am GOD Almighty. I will give you many descendants. Your children's children will become nations. Kings will come from your lineage. And I'll give your descendants the land that I gave to Abraham and Isaac." And GOD went up from him in that place where HE talked with him.

Jacob set up a pillar of stone, anointed with oil, in the place where he had talked with GOD.

Jacob left Bethel and went toward Bethlehem. On the way Rachel gave birth, and she had hard labor.

When her labor was at its hardest, the midwife said to her, "Don't be afraid. This one also is a son."

But Rachel's life was running out. As she was dying, she named her son Benoni, meaning Son of My Sorrow. But his father called him Benjamin, meaning Son of the Right Hand.

Rachel died and was buried along the way to Bethlehem. Jacob set up a pillar to mark her grave.

Then Jacob came to his father Isaac at Hebron. Isaac breathed his last and died, old and full of years. His sons Esau and Jacob buried him.

Esau took his three wives and seven sons and went to the land of Edom. He settled there, and his sons became chieftains of twelve tribes.

Jacob took his four wives and twelve sons and settled in the land of Canaan—the land where his father, Isaac, had once been a stranger.

THE STORY OF JOSEPH AND HIS BROTHERS

Of all his sons, Jacob loved Joseph the best because he was the child of his old age. Jacob made him a woven robe of many colors, and this made Joseph's older brothers jealous.

Joseph served his brothers, attending to their flocks, but he brought back bad reports about his brothers to their father, so his brothers hated him. They wouldn't speak a peaceful word to him.

When Joseph was seventeen, he dreamed a dream and told it to his brothers.

"Listen!" he said to them. "Let me tell you my dream. We were out in the field, tying up bundles of wheat, and mine stood up straight. Your sheaves were circled around and bowing down to my sheaf."

His brothers said to him, "Are you going to be king? Are you going to rule over us?" They hated him all the more for his dreams and for his words.

Joseph dreamed another dream and told it to his father and brothers.

"Listen!" he said. "I dreamed another dream. The sun and the moon and eleven stars were bowing down to me."

Joseph's father scolded him.

"What kind of dream is this?" he asked. "Am I and your mother and brothers going to bow down before you?"

His older brothers were jealous of him, while his father reflected on the dream's meaning.

One day, after his brothers had gone to feed their father's flock at Shechem, Jacob said to Joseph, "Please go and see how your brothers are and how the sheep are, and bring word back to me."

Joseph went out to Shechem, and a man found him wandering in the fields.

"What are you looking for?" the man asked.

"I'm looking for my brothers," Joseph said. "Please tell me where they are feeding the sheep."

"They were here," the man said, "but I heard them say they were going to Dothan."

Joseph went after his brothers and found them at Dothan. They saw him coming, and before he arrived, they plotted against him to put him to death.

"Here comes the lord of dreams!" they said to each other. "Come on, let's kill him and throw him into one of these pits. We'll say a vicious beast ate him. Then we'll see what happens to his dreams."

Reuben heard this and tried to rescue Joseph. "We mustn't take his life. Don't shed blood. Throw him into a pit, but don't lay a hand on him," he said, thinking he could rescue Joseph later and return him to his father.

When Joseph came close to his brothers, they stripped off the colorful robe that Jacob had made for him. Then they threw him into an empty pit. There was no water in it, but it was very deep.

The brothers sat down to eat their lunch. When they looked up, they saw a camel caravan of traders coming from the east. The traders were taking perfume and spices and medicine down to Egypt.

Judah said to his brothers, "What do we gain by killing our brother and covering up his blood? Let's sell him to the traders so our hand won't be against him. After all, he's our brother, our own flesh."

His brothers agreed. They pulled Joseph up out of the pit and sold him to the traders for twenty pieces of silver.

When Reuben returned to the pit and did not find Joseph, he tore his clothes in despair. He went to his brothers and cried, "Joseph is not there! What am I to do? What do I tell our father?"

Then his brothers killed a baby goat and dipped Joseph's robe in the blood. They gave the bloodstained robe of many colors to their father, saying, "We found this. Do you recognize it? Is it your son's robe, or not?"

"My son's robe!" cried Jacob. "A vicious beast has eaten him. Joseph has been torn to pieces!"

Jacob tore his own clothes in sorrow and put sackcloth around his waist and mourned his son for many days. All his sons and daughters tried to comfort him, but he refused to be comforted.

"I will go down to my grave mourning for my son," he cried.

The traders took Joseph down to Egypt, and Joseph was sold to Potiphar, an Egyptian official at Pharaoh's court.

The LORD was with Joseph, and he became successful in the house of his Egyptian master.

The LORD blessed the Egyptian's house because of Joseph. Potiphar saw that the LORD was with Joseph and so he put Joseph in charge of his house and all his possessions, entrusting everything to Joseph.

Now, Joseph was very handsome. His master's wife cast her eyes upon him and loved him. But Joseph did not love her, for he was a moral, upright man.

"Behold," he said to her, "my master trusts me with everything in his house. He has put everything he owns in my hands. He has held nothing back from me, except you, his wife. How could I love you and do such wickedness and offend GOD?"

Potiphar's wife spoke to Joseph day after day, but he wouldn't listen to her or be with her.

One day Joseph came into the house to do his work, and no other men were around. Potiphar's wife grabbed his shirt and said, "Come with me!" But Joseph tore himself away, leaving his shirt in her hand, and ran outside.

"Look!" the wife cried out to the men of the house. "My husband brought us a Hebrew man to mock us. He came to me, but I cried out, and he left his shirt beside me and ran outside."

She kept Joseph's shirt beside her until her husband returned home. She told him, "The Hebrew slave you brought us has mocked us. When I cried out, he left his shirt beside me and ran outside."

When Potiphar heard his wife's words, his anger flared up at Joseph, and he threw him into the dungeon where the king's prisoners were held.

But while Joseph was in the dungeon, the LORD was with him. The LORD caused the warden to look at Joseph with favor, and the warden put Joseph in charge of all the other prisoners. The warden trusted Joseph, and whatever Joseph did, the LORD made it to prosper.

THE DREAMS OF THE CUPBEARER AND THE BAKER

It came to pass that the chief cupbearer and the chief baker of Egypt had offended their master, the Pharaoh. Pharaoh was so furious, he threw them into the dungeon where Joseph was. Joseph was assigned to look after them, and they stayed several months under Joseph's watch.

One night, the two of them dreamed, each his own dream.

When Joseph came to them in the morning, he saw that they were frowning. "Why do you look so sad?" he asked.

They each said to him, "We have each dreamed a dream, and there is no one to interpret these dreams."

Joseph said to them, "Are not interpretations from GOD? Please, tell me your dreams."

The chief cupbearer said, "In my dream I saw a vine, and on the vine were three branches. Buds formed on the branches, blossoms came out, and the clusters ripened into grapes. I picked the grapes and squeezed them into Pharaoh's cup and put the cup in Pharaoh's hand."

Joseph said, "This is the interpretation: The three branches are three days. In three days, Pharaoh will call you before him and restore you to your place. When it goes well for you, please think of me. Show kindness, I pray you, and mention me to Pharaoh. Bring me out of this dungeon; for indeed, I was stolen away out of my homeland, and I have done nothing to deserve this prison."

When the chief baker heard the good interpretation of the cupbearer's dream, he said to Joseph, "In my dream, there were three baskets of white bread on my head. In the top basket were all kinds of baked goods for Pharaoh, and birds were eating them from this top basket."

Joseph said, "This is the interpretation: The three baskets are three days. In three days Pharaoh will call you before him, but he will hang you on a tree, and the birds will eat your flesh."

On the third day, which was Pharaoh's birthday, Pharaoh gave a party for all his servants. He called forth from the dungeon the chief cupbearer and the chief baker. He restored the cupbearer to his place, and he hanged the chief baker, just as Joseph had said.

But the chief cupbearer did not remember Joseph; he forgot him.

PHARAOH'S DREAM

Two years passed, and it happened that Pharaoh had an unusual dream. He dreamed that he was standing by the Nile River. He saw seven cows coming up out of the Nile. They were fine, fat animals, and they grazed on the reed grass. He saw another seven cows come up out of the Nile after them. They were ugly, skinny animals, and they stood beside the other cows on the bank of the Nile. The ugly, skinny cows ate up the seven fine, fat cows. Then Pharaoh woke up.

He slept again and dreamed a second dream. He saw seven ears of grain growing on one stalk, fat and full. Then he saw seven thin ears of grain, dried up by the desert wind, growing beneath them. The thin ears swallowed the full, fat ears. Then Pharaoh woke up.

In the morning, Pharaoh was very troubled. He sent for all the magicians and wise men of Egypt and told them his dreams. None of them could interpret the dreams for Pharaoh.

Then the chief cupbearer said to Pharaoh, "I remember something that happened two years ago, when Pharaoh had thrown me and the chief baker into the dungeon. The baker and I each dreamed a dream on the same night. A young Hebrew man, a slave, was with us in the dungeon. We told him the dreams and he interpreted them. All turned out just as he said. I was restored to my place, and the chief baker was hanged."

Pharaoh sent for Joseph, and he was hurriedly brought out of the dungeon. Joseph shaved his face and changed his clothes and came to Pharaoh.

ugly cows ate up the seven fat cows. They took them into their bellies, but you couldn't tell, because they looked just as skinny. Then I woke up.

"In my second dream, I saw seven ears of grain coming up on one stalk, fat and good. Then I saw seven thin ears, dried by the desert wind, growing up beneath them. The thin ears swallowed the seven fat ears. I told my dreams to my magicians, but none of them could tell me what they mean."

Joseph said, "Pharaoh's dreams are one. GOD has told Pharaoh what HE is about to do. The seven good cows and the seven good ears of grain are seven years of plenty. The seven skinny, ugly cows and the seven thin ears of grain are seven years of famine. Seven years of plenty are coming to all the land of Egypt. But seven years of famine will come after them. All the plenty in the land of Egypt will be forgotten, and the famine will destroy the land.

Pharaoh said to Joseph, "I dreamed two dreams that no one can interpret. I've heard that you are a man who can interpret dreams."

"Not I," said Joseph. "GOD will answer what is good for Pharaoh."

So Pharaoh said, "In my first dream, behold, I was standing on the bank of the Nile. I saw seven fine, fat cows coming out of the Nile, and they grazed on the reed grass. Then I saw another seven cows coming up after them—very ugly and skinny. I never saw such ugly cows in all the land of Egypt! The skinny,

"The dream was repeated two times because it indeed will happen, and soon. Now let Pharaoh find a wise man and set him over the land of Egypt. Let Pharaoh appoint overseers to collect food during the seven good years. Let them pile up grain in the cities and keep it under guard. Store the food, so that the land will not perish during the seven years of famine."

This seemed good to Pharaoh and his servants. "We'll never find a man like him," said Pharaoh. "The Spirit of GOD is in him."

Pharaoh said to Joseph, "Since GOD has shown all this to you, there is nobody wiser than you. You will be over my house. All my people will submit to your orders. Only I on my throne will be greater than you. See! I have set you over all the land of Egypt."

Pharaoh took off his royal ring and put it on Joseph's hand. He had him clothed in fine linen robes and placed a golden chain around his neck. He had Joseph ride in a royal chariot as second-in-command, and the people called out before him, "Bow down!"

Pharaoh made Joseph governor over the land of Egypt, saying, "I am Pharaoh! No one will raise a hand or foot in all the land of Egypt without your permission." He gave Joseph an Egyptian name meaning GOD Speaks and Lives, and he gave him an Egyptian wife, Asenath, the daughter of a priest.

Joseph was thirty years old when he stood before Pharaoh king of Egypt. And Joseph went out from Pharaoh's presence and went throughout all the land of Egypt.

JOSEPH RULES OVER THE LAND OF EGYPT

For seven years the land produced bountiful crops. Joseph collected all the extra food from those years and stored it in the cities.

Two sons were born to Joseph and Asenath before the famine. Joseph named the first child Manasseh, meaning Forget, for, he said, "God has made me forget my troubles and my father's family." He named his second son Ephraim, meaning Fruitful, and said, "God has made me fruitful in the land of my troubles."

The seven years of plenty ended, and the seven years of famine began, as Joseph had said. There was famine in all the lands, but food was stored in the land of Egypt. All Egypt felt the famine, and they cried out to Pharaoh for food.

Pharaoh said, "Go to Joseph and do whatever he says."

Joseph opened the storehouses and sold food to the Egyptians.

The famine grew greater. All the earth came to Egypt to buy food from Joseph.

When Jacob in Canaan heard that there was food in Egypt, he said to his sons, "Why are you afraid? There's food in Egypt. Go down and buy food, so we will live and not die."

Joseph's ten brothers made the long journey to Egypt to buy food—all except Benjamin, the youngest. Jacob didn't send Benjamin because he was his only remaining son by Rachel, and he was afraid that harm might befall him.

Jacob's sons went to Egypt, along with a crowd of hungry people from the land of Canaan. They went to Joseph, governor over the land and provider to all the people.

When they came into his presence, Joseph's brothers bowed down to him with their faces to the ground. Joseph recognized his brothers, but he acted like a stranger to them. He spoke harshly to them in the Egyptian language. "Where do you come from?"

"From the land of Canaan, to buy food," they said.

Joseph's brothers did not recognize him; and Joseph remembered the dreams he had dreamed about them. Just as the sheaths of grain had bowed, just as the sun, moon, and stars had bowed, so, too were his brothers now bowing before him. He said to them, "You are spies! You came to Egypt to see the weakness of the land."

"No, sir," they said. "We, your servants, have come to buy food. We're all the sons of one man. We're honest men, not spies."

"No!" said Joseph. "You came to see the weakness of the land."

"We are twelve brothers," they said. "We are the sons of one man in the land of Canaan. The youngest is home with our father, and another is no more."

Joseph said, "If you are honest men, this shall be the proof: You will send one of you to fetch your youngest brother and bring him here. If you don't, I will know you are spies." Then he put them under guard for three days.

On the third day he said, "If you do as I say, you will live, because I fear GOD. I'll keep one of you in the guardhouse. The rest can take food back to your families. Return with your youngest brother. That will prove that you've told the truth, and you won't die."

The brothers turned to each other and said, "We're being punished because we saw our brother Joseph suffer. We didn't listen when he pleaded with us to pull him out of the pit. That's why this is happening to us."

Reuben said to his brothers, "Didn't I tell you not to hurt the boy? But you didn't listen. Now we must pay for what we did to him."

They didn't know that Joseph understood, for they spoke to him through a translator between them. Joseph turned away with tears in his eyes.

When he had regained his emotions and was able to return, Joseph had Simeon taken and put in chains. Then he gave orders for the brothers' baggage to be filled with grain and supplies for the journey. He told his servant to take the silver they had used to pay for the grain and hide it in their bags.

The brothers loaded their donkeys and set out. When they camped for the night, one of them opened his bag to get feed for his donkey and found his silver in the mouth of his bag. "My silver has been put back!" he said to his brothers. "Look! It's in my bag!"

"What is GOD doing to us?" the brothers cried, trembling.

The brothers returned to Jacob in the land of Canaan and told him everything that had happened, and that they were to take Benjamin to Egypt. As they were emptying their bags, each one found his silver. When they saw it, they and their father were afraid.

Jacob said to them, "You've left me all alone. Joseph is no more. Simeon is no more. And now you want to take Benjamin! Oh, how I suffer!"

Reuben said to his father, "You can put my two sons to death if I don't bring Benjamin back. Put him in my hands, and I will bring him back."

"No!" cried Jacob. "My son won't go down with you. His brother is dead, and he alone is left. If anything happens to him, you'll send my gray hairs down in sorrow to the grave."

JOSEPH TESTS HIS BROTHERS

The famine grew worse, and Jacob's family had eaten all the food they had brought from Egypt. Jacob said, "Go back and buy more."

Judah said, "We can't go unless you let us take Benjamin. The man said he wouldn't see us unless we brought our brother."

"Why did you do this to me?" said Jacob. "Why did you tell the man you had another brother?"

"He kept asking us about our family," they said. "He kept saying, 'Is your father still alive? Do you have another brother?' How could we know?"

Judah said, "Send the boy with me. We must go so that we and you and our little ones will live and not die. I'll take the blame if Benjamin doesn't come back. Now let's get going."

Jacob said, "If that's what we must do, then go, and take a gift to the man—some perfume and spices, a little honey, some pistachio nuts and almonds. Take double the amount of silver along with the silver that was put back in your bags. Perhaps it was a mistake. May GOD Almighty have mercy on you, and let the man free your brother Simeon—and Benjamin. As for me, if I must mourn, I will mourn."

They took the gifts and silver and Benjamin and went down to Egypt.

When Joseph saw Benjamin with them, he said to his chief servant, "Bring them to the house and prepare some meat. They will eat with me at noon."

The servant did as Joseph ordered, and when he brought the men to Joseph's house, they were afraid.

"We've been brought here because of the silver," they said. "They're going to attack us and make us their slaves and take our donkeys."

They spoke to the steward at the entrance of the house. "Please, sir, when we came down to buy food, we found our silver in our bags. We've brought it back, and we've brought more silver to buy more food. We don't know who put the silver in our bags."

"It's all right," the steward said. "Don't be afraid. Your GOD put treasure in your bags for you."

Then the steward brought Simeon to them and took them all into Joseph's house. The steward gave them water and they washed their feet. He gave them feed for their donkeys.

The brothers unpacked the gifts and waited for Joseph. When Joseph arrived, they gave him the gifts and bowed down on the ground before him.

Joseph asked them how they were, and then he said, "Is your old father at peace? Is he still alive?"

"Our father is at peace," they said. "He's still alive." They knelt down before him.

Joseph looked up and saw his brother Benjamin, his mother's son. "Is this the youngest brother, the one you told me about?" Then he said, "GOD be gracious to you, my son."

Joseph hurried away. His feelings for his brother were so warm, he wanted to cry. He went into a private room and cried, and then he washed his face and came back.

He got control of himself and said, "Serve the food."

The servants served Joseph and the brothers at separate tables, and the Egyptians ate apart from them, for by law the Egyptians wouldn't eat with Hebrews.

Joseph's brothers were seated in front of him in age order, from the firstborn to the youngest. They stared at each other in amazement. Joseph had portions of food passed to them from his own table, and Benjamin's portion was five times greater than the others.

The brothers stayed all night and drank with Joseph.

In the morning, Joseph said to his servant, "Fill their bags with as much food as they can carry. Put each man's silver in his bag, and put my silver goblet in the bag of the youngest."

The servant did as Joseph said and sent them off in the early morning light. They were just outside the city when Joseph sent the servant after them with a message.

"Why have you repaid evil for good?" the servant demanded upon reaching the brothers. "Why have you stolen my lord's goblet? You have done evil!"

The brothers said to him, "Why do you say this? We brought back the silver we found in our bags. Why would we steal from your master's house? If you find the goblet, let whoever has it die, and make the rest of us your slaves."

"Just as you say. Whoever has it will become my slave. The rest of you will go free."

They hurried and set their bags on the ground, and each one opened his bag. The servant searched their bags, beginning with the oldest and ending with the youngest. He found the goblet in Benjamin's bag.

The brothers tore their clothes in sorrow. Each man loaded his donkey, and they returned to the city. They came into Joseph's house and threw themselves on the ground before him.

"What have you done?" said Joseph. "Didn't you know I would find out?"

Judah said, "What can we say, sir? How can we defend ourselves? GOD has found out our crime. All of us will be your slaves, not just the one who had your cup."

Joseph said, "The one who had the goblet will be my slave. The others may go back to your father."

"Please," said Judah, coming closer, "let me speak to you, my lord. Please don't be angry. The boy's brother is dead, and he's the only one left of his mother's sons. His father loves him. His

The brothers came close.

"I *am* Joseph, your brother, whom you sold into Egypt. Don't be upset with yourselves. GOD sent me here ahead of you to preserve life. This is only the second year of the famine, and there are five more years to come. It wasn't you that sent me here, but GOD. Now, hurry! Get my father and bring him down here. You'll stay near me, in the land of Goshen, and I'll take care of all of you."

He put his head on Benjamin's shoulders and cried, and Benjamin cried on his shoulders. Then he kissed all his brothers and cried over them. After that, his brothers relaxed and spoke with him.

When Pharaoh heard the news, he said to Joseph, "Tell your brothers to load their animals and return to the land of Canaan. Tell them to get your father and their families and come back to me. I'll give them the best of the land of Egypt. I'll give them wagons for their little ones and their wives. The best of all the land of Egypt is theirs."

Joseph did as Pharaoh ordered, and gave them wagons and supplies for the journey. He gave each one a set of new clothes. He gave Benjamin three hundred pieces of silver and five sets of new clothes. He sent his father twenty donkeys carrying the best provisions of Egypt, and ten she-donkeys carrying grain and food.

They went up from Egypt and came to their father in the land of Canaan. "Joseph is alive!" they said. "He is governor over all the land of Egypt!"

Jacob's heart stopped. He didn't believe them. Then they told him everything Joseph had said. When he saw the wagons that Joseph had sent, his spirit revived. "Enough," he said. "My son Joseph is still alive. Let me go and see him before I die."

whole life is wrapped up in the boy. If the boy leaves him, his father—our father—will die. Please, sir, take me instead. Make me your slave and let the boy return with his brothers. I can't bear to see my father suffer."

Joseph could no longer control his emotions. "Clear out!" he cried to his servants.

No servants were with him when he made himself known to his brothers.

"I am Joseph," he said. "Is my father still alive? Please come close to me."

JACOB'S FAMILY GOES DOWN TO EGYPT

Jacob left for Beersheba with all that he owned, and offered sacrifices to the GOD of his father Isaac.

GOD spoke to him in a dream, saying, "Jacob, Jacob."

"Here I am," said Jacob.

GOD said, "I am the GOD of your father. Do not be afraid to go into Egypt. I will go with you, and your family will become a great nation in Egypt. Then I will lead your family back to Canaan, the land I have promised you."

Jacob's sons carried him and their little ones and their wives in Pharaoh's wagons. Jacob's whole family of seventy men, women, and children came to Egypt.

Joseph jumped into his chariot and raced out to meet his father. He appeared before Jacob and threw his arms around him. He cried on his father's shoulder a long time.

Jacob said, "Now I can die, for I've seen your face. You're still alive."

Joseph took his brothers to meet Pharaoh. When Pharaoh learned that they were shepherds, he gave them good pasture land in Goshen and hired them to take care of his animals.

Joseph took his father to Pharaoh, and Jacob spoke with Pharaoh and

and he blessed his twelve sons—the children of "Israel," the name GOD had given Jacob. Then Jacob breathed his last and died.

Joseph wept over his father. Then he commanded the Egyptians to embalm Jacob's body. And, when the mourning time had ended, Joseph asked Pharaoh for permission to take his father's body to the land of Canaan. Pharaoh sent his officials and chariots and horsemen to go with Joseph and his brothers. They buried Jacob in the cave of Machpelah, as they had promised.

After Joseph and his brothers had returned to Egypt, his brothers said to each other, "What if Joseph holds a grudge against us? He might pay us back for all the evil we did to him."

They sent a message to Joseph, saying, "Before your father died, he said you should forgive us. Please forgive the crimes and evil we did."

Joseph cried when he heard the message.

His brothers went to him and bowed down before him. "We're your slaves," they said.

"Don't be afraid," said Joseph. "I'm not GOD. You meant to do me evil, but GOD meant it for good, to keep many people alive. I will provide for you and your little ones."

Joseph lived in Egypt with his father's family for many years. Before he died, he said to his brothers, "GOD will take notice of you and bring you up out of this land and take you to the land HE promised to Isaac and Jacob. Now I want you to swear to me: When GOD brings HIS people, the children of Israel, up out of Egypt, you will carry my bones up from this place."

When Joseph died, they embalmed his body and put it in a coffin in Egypt.

blessed him. Then Joseph settled his father and his brothers in the best part of the land of Egypt. He provided for their care and fed them.

Jacob lived in the land of Egypt for seventeen years. Then he called Joseph and said, "Promise that you won't bury me in Egypt. When I die, carry me out of Egypt and bury me with my fathers. GOD will be with you and bring you back to the land of Abraham and your ancestors."

Jacob adopted Joseph's two sons, Ephraim and Manasseh, as his own,

GOD RESCUES HIS PEOPLE
THE BABY IN THE ARK

These are the names of the sons of Jacob: Reuben, Simeon, Levi, Judah, Issachar, Zebulun, Benjamin, Dan, Naphtali, Gad, Asher, and Joseph. Jacob adopted Joseph's sons Ephraim and Manasseh and counted them as his own sons.

Joseph and all his brothers and that whole generation died. But the children of Israel were fruitful and multiplied. They became so numerous that the land of Egypt was filled with them.

Then a new Pharaoh, who knew nothing of Joseph, came to power in Egypt. He said to his people, "There are too many of these Hebrews. Think—if there were a war, they might join our enemies and attack us. Come, let's do something to stop them from increasing."

So the Egyptians set taskmasters over the children of Israel to oppress them with forced labor. They made them build treasure cities for Pharaoh. But the more the Hebrew people were oppressed, the more they multiplied and spread. They became so numerous, the Egyptians dreaded them and forced them into cruel slavery. The taskmasters made life bitter for the Israelites with hard labor, in mortar and brick and field work.

And Pharaoh feared the great numbers of the Israelites. He called for two midwives, Shiphrah and Puah, who helped the Hebrews with childbirth, and said to them, "When you help the Hebrew women give birth, watch carefully. If the baby is a boy, put him to death. But if it's a girl, let her live."

But the midwives feared GOD, and they did not do as the king of Egypt commanded them. They let the boys live.

Pharaoh called them in and said, "Why have you let the boys live?"

The midwives said to Pharaoh, "Hebrew women aren't like Egyptian women. They're so lively they give birth before the midwife arrives."

GOD was pleased with the midwives. HE rewarded them with homes and families of their own. And the Israelites continued to increase in number.

Then Pharaoh said to his people, "Take every newborn Hebrew boy and throw him into the Nile, but let the girl babies live."

Pharaoh's daughter came down to bathe at the Nile. While her maids were walking along the bank of the river, she saw the little ark among the reeds, and she sent one of the maids to fetch it. When Pharaoh's daughter opened the basket, there inside she found a baby boy, and he was crying.

"Look," she said. "This is one of the children of the Hebrews."

Just then the baby's sister came up and said to Pharaoh's daughter, "Shall I go find a Hebrew woman to nurse the baby for you?"

"Yes, go," Pharaoh's daughter replied.

The girl went and called her mother. And Pharaoh's daughter said to the mother, "Take this baby and nurse him for me, and I will pay you."

So the baby's natural mother took him home and nursed him. The child grew. After he was weaned, his mother brought him to Pharaoh's daughter, who adopted him as her son. She named him Moses, which means Drawn Out, because, she said, "I drew him out of the water."

Like Noah's ark, the little ark of Moses was part of God's plan to save his people.

It came to pass that a woman from the family of Levi gave birth to a beautiful baby boy, and she hid him for three months. When she could no longer hide him, she made him a little basket ark from papyrus straw. She covered the ark with clay and tar to make it waterproof and put him in it. Then she placed the ark in the reed grass along the banks of the Nile. The baby's sister, Miriam, stayed near the river to see what would happen to him.

Moses Escapes from Pharaoh

Moses grew to manhood in the palace. It came to pass that he went out among his Hebrew relatives and noticed how they suffered in their labor. He saw an Egyptian man beating a Hebrew, one of his people. Moses looked around, and, seeing no one, he struck down the Egyptian and buried him in the sand.

The next day, Moses saw two Hebrew men fighting. He demanded of the man who had started the fight: "Why did you strike the fellow?"

"Who made you prince and judge over us?" the man replied. "Do you intend to kill me the way you killed the Egyptian?"

Moses was afraid. "They know!" he said to himself.

Pharaoh heard about Moses' crime and tried to have Moses killed, but Moses fled from Pharaoh and settled in the land of Midian.

Moses was sitting beside a well one day, when the seven daughters of Jethro, the priest of Midian, came to water their father's sheep. Shepherds arrived and tried to drive the daughters away, but Moses stepped forward and helped them draw water to fill the troughs for their sheep.

When the daughters went home, their father Jethro said, "Why are you home so early today?"

"An Egyptian rescued us from the hands of the shepherds," they said. "He drew water for us and filled the troughs to water the sheep."

"Where is he? Why did you leave him behind? Go. Invite him to eat with us."

Moses was content to dwell with Jethro's family, and Jethro gave his daughter Zipporah to Moses as a wife. She gave birth to a son, and Moses named him Gershom, meaning Resident Stranger, for, he said, "I have been a stranger in a foreign land."

When she gave birth to a second son, Moses named him Eliezer, meaning God Is My Helper. "God has been my helper," he said. "He saved me from the sword of Pharaoh."

Many years later, the king of Egypt died. But the new king was just as cruel. The children of Israel groaned and cried out in their slavery, "Save us! Rescue us!"

Their cry went up to God, and God heard their despair. God remembered His covenant with Abraham and Isaac and Jacob. God took notice of the children of Israel.

The Voice from the Burning Bush

While the cries of the children of Israel were lifted up to GOD, Moses was herding the flock of Jethro, his father-in-law, priest of Midian. Moses led the flock through the wilderness and came to Sinai, the mountain of GOD.

There an angel of the LORD appeared to him in a flame of fire out of the middle of a bush. Moses looked in awe, for the bush burned with fire yet was not consumed by the fire. "What a sight!" Moses said to himself. "Let me go over there and see why the bush is not burnt."

And GOD called to Moses from the middle of the bush:

"Moses, Moses."

"Here I am."

"Do not come any closer. Take off your sandals, for you are standing on holy ground. I am the GOD of your father, the GOD of Abraham, Isaac, and Jacob."

Moses hid his face, for he was afraid to look upon GOD.

GOD said, "I have seen the suffering of MY people in Egypt. I have heard their outcry because of their taskmasters. I know of their sorrows. I have come down to deliver them from the Egyptians and to bring them out of that land to a good and spacious land, a land flowing with milk and honey. Now, go. I am sending you to Pharaoh to bring MY people out of Egypt."

"Who am I," said Moses, "that I should go to Pharaoh, and that I should bring the children of Israel out of Egypt?"

And GOD said, "I will be with you. This is the sign that I have sent you: After you bring the people out of Egypt, you will serve GOD upon this mountain."

Moses said to God, "If I go to the children of Israel and tell them the God of their fathers has sent me, they'll ask, 'What is his name?' What should I say?"

God said to Moses, "I AM THAT I AM. Tell the children of Israel, *I AM has sent me to you: the LORD, the GOD of your fathers, the GOD of Abraham, Isaac, and Jacob, sends me to you.*

"Now go and gather the elders and tell them you have seen the LORD, the GOD of their fathers. Say I have taken notice of them. Tell them I have decided to bring them up from the affliction of Egypt to a land flowing with milk and honey.

"They will listen to you, and you and the elders will go to the king of Egypt. Tell him that the LORD, the GOD of the Hebrews, has met with you. Ask him to let you go on a three-day journey into the wilderness to offer sacrifices to the LORD your GOD. He won't let you go, so I will strike Egypt, and then he will let you go. And when you go, you will not be empty-handed, for you will strip Egypt of silver and gold."

"But the elders will not believe me," said Moses.

The LORD said to him, "What is that in your hand?"

"A shepherd's rod."

"Throw it to the ground."

Moses threw the rod to the ground, and it became a snake, and he retreated from it.

The LORD commanded, "Stretch out your hand and seize it by the tail."

Moses took hold of the snake, and it became a rod.

"Now put your hand inside your robe," said GOD.

Moses put his hand in his robe. When he took it out, it was as white as snow.

"Put your hand back inside your robe!"

Moses put his hand back inside his robe, and when he took it out, his hand was restored to health.

The LORD said, "If they will not trust you and will not heed the first sign, they will trust the second sign. If they will not trust these two signs, pour some Nile water onto the dry land, and the water will become blood upon the dry land."

"Please," said Moses, "don't send me.

I am not a man of words. My speech is slow."

The LORD said to him, "Who put a mouth in human beings? Who gives a person speech and hearing, sight or blindness? It is I, the LORD. Now, go. I will be with your mouth, and I will tell you what to say."

"Please, send somebody else!"

The LORD's anger flared up against Moses, and HE said, "You have a brother, Aaron. He speaks very well. I will send him to meet you. You will speak to him and put the words in his mouth to be your spokesman. I will be with your mouth and his mouth, and I will tell you what to do. Take this rod in your hand to perform the signs and wonders."

Moses put his wife and his sons on a donkey to return to the land of Egypt, and he took the rod of GOD in his hand.

The LORD said to Moses, "When you go back to Egypt and perform the signs and wonders, I will harden Pharaoh's heart, so he will not let the people go. Then say to Pharaoh, 'The LORD says, MY son, MY firstborn, is Israel. I told you to let MY son go, so he can serve ME, but you refused. Therefore I will kill your son, your firstborn.' "

Then the LORD said to Aaron, "Go meet Moses in the wilderness."

Aaron went and met Moses at the mountain of GOD and kissed him, and Moses told Aaron everything the LORD had said. Then Moses and Aaron went and called the elders of the children of Israel together. Aaron spoke all the words the LORD had said to Moses, and Moses performed the signs before their eyes.

When the people heard that the LORD had taken notice of them and seen their sorrow, they bowed down and worshiped.

MAKING BRICKS WITHOUT STRAW

Moses and Aaron went to Pharaoh and said, "The LORD, the GOD of Israel, says, *Let MY people go, so they can worship ME in the wilderness.*"

"Who is the LORD?" said Pharaoh. "Why should I listen to him? I don't know the LORD, and I won't let the people go."

Aaron said, "The GOD of the Hebrews has met with us. Please let us journey three days into the wilderness to offer sacrifices to the LORD our GOD."

"Moses and Aaron," said Pharaoh, "why would you take the people from their work? Your people, the Hebrews, keep increasing in number, and now you want to take a three-day rest. Get back to your work!"

That day Pharaoh commanded the taskmasters, "Stop giving straw to the people for the brick-making. From now on, let them go and gather straw themselves. Yet order them also to make the same number of bricks as before. Not one brick less, for they are lazy. That is why they keep crying out and asking to go offer sacrifices to their GOD. Make them work harder. Keep the slaves busy and they won't have time to listen to lies."

The taskmasters gave the orders, and the people scattered throughout the land of Egypt looking for straw, for without chopped straw to mix in with the wet clay, they couldn't make bricks. "What's the matter with you?" the taskmasters said to the Hebrew foremen. "Why aren't your people making as many bricks as before?" Then they whipped the foremen with their lashes.

The foremen cried out to Pharaoh, "Why do you treat us like this? The taskmasters don't give us any straw, but

they order us to make as many bricks as before. It's impossible, and they beat us for not doing it. We haven't done anything wrong."

"You are lazy," said Pharaoh. "That is what's wrong. You talk about going to offer sacrifices to the LORD because you don't want to serve me. Return to your work!"

As the foremen were leaving Pharaoh, they met Moses and Aaron. "May the LORD punish you," the foremen said. "You've made Pharaoh and the taskmasters hate us."

Moses returned to the LORD and said, "Why did you send me here? Ever since I spoke to Pharaoh, he has been treating the Hebrews worse. You haven't done anything to rescue your people."

The LORD said to Moses, "Watch what I do to Pharaoh to make him let MY people go. He will drive them out.

Tell the children of Israel I will bring them out of slavery in Egypt, and they will know that I am the LORD their GOD. I will bring them into the land I promised to Abraham, Isaac, and Jacob."

Moses and Aaron spoke GOD's words to the children of Israel, but they were so spirit-broken they didn't listen.

Then the LORD said to Moses, "Go speak to Pharaoh, and tell him to let the children of Israel go."

"The children of Israel won't listen to me," said Moses. "Why would Pharaoh listen?"

"I am the LORD!" GOD said. "Speak to Pharaoh, as I command. I will harden his heart, and though I multiply MY signs and wonders in the land of Egypt, he won't listen. Then I will set MY hand against him and bring MY people out of the land of Egypt. And the Egyptians will know that I am the LORD."

"Let My People Go!"

The LORD said to Moses, "When Pharaoh asks for a sign, tell Aaron to take his rod and throw it down in front of Pharaoh. It will become a snake."

Moses and Aaron went to Pharaoh and did as the LORD commanded. Aaron threw down his rod and it became a snake.

Pharaoh called for his wise men and magicians, and they threw down their rods. Their rods became snakes, but Aaron's rod swallowed up their rods.

But Pharaoh's heart was hard, and he did not listen, just as the LORD had said.

THE PLAGUE OF BLOOD

The LORD said to Moses, "At daybreak, go meet Pharaoh by the bank of the Nile. Take your rod in your hand and say, 'The LORD, the GOD of the Hebrews, has sent me to say, *Let MY people go, so they can serve ME in the wilderness*.' Then strike the water in the Nile with the rod. The water will change to blood. The fish in the Nile will die, and the Nile will stink, and the Egyptians will not be able to drink the Nile water. Tell Aaron to take his rod and stretch his hand over all the waters of Egypt, over their streams and canals, their ponds and lakes; they too will turn to blood. There will be blood all over the land of Egypt—even in the wooden buckets and stone jars."

Moses and Aaron did as the LORD commanded. In the sight of Pharaoh and his servants, Aaron raised the rod and struck the water in the Nile. All the water in the Nile turned to blood. The fish in the Nile died and the Nile stank. The Egyptians couldn't drink the Nile water, and blood was all over the land of Egypt.

The magicians of Egypt performed the same feat through their own spells, so Pharaoh's heart remained hard. He did not listen, just as the LORD had said. He went back into his house and gave no thought to the bloodied water. All the Egyptians dug holes along the bank of the Nile to find water to drink. For seven days the water was blood.

THE PLAGUE OF FROGS

Then the LORD said to Moses, "Go to Pharaoh and say, 'The LORD says, *Let* MY *people go, so they can serve* ME.' Tell him that if he refuses to let them go, I will plague his whole land with frogs. Say, 'The Nile will swarm with frogs. They will come into your house, into your bedroom, up onto your couch, into your servants' houses, in among your people, into your ovens, and into your bread pans. The frogs will come up onto you, your people, and all your servants!' Tell Aaron to stretch out his hand with his rod over the streams and Nile canals and the ponds, and the frogs will come up onto the land of Egypt."

Aaron stretched out his hand over the waters of Egypt, and hordes of frogs came up and covered the land of Egypt. The magicians did the same thing with their spells and brought up more frogs onto the land of Egypt.

Pharaoh sent for Moses and Aaron and said, "Plead with the LORD to take these frogs away from me and my people. Then I'll let the Hebrew people go so they can offer a sacrifice to the LORD."

"And when do you wish this to take place?" said Moses.

"Tomorrow."

"Just as you say. Tomorrow the frogs will be gone, and you will know that there is none like the LORD our GOD. The frogs will be removed from you and your houses, from your servants and your people. They will remain only in the Nile."

Moses and Aaron went out, and Moses pleaded with the LORD to rid the land of frogs.

The LORD did as Moses asked. The frogs died out of the houses and court-yards and fields. The people piled them up in great heaps, and the land was filled with the stench of rotten frogs.

But as soon as Pharaoh saw that there was relief, his heart was hardened, as the LORD had said.

THE PLAGUE OF INSECTS

The LORD said to Moses, "Tell Aaron to stretch out his rod and strike the dust of the ground and turn it into biting insects all over the land of Egypt."

Aaron stretched out his hand with his rod and struck the dust of the ground, and fleas, lice, and ticks plagued humans and animals all over the land of Egypt.

The Egyptian magicians tried to do the same thing with their spells, but they could not. "This is the finger of GOD!" they said to Pharaoh.

But Pharaoh's heart remained hard, and he did not listen.

THE PLAGUE OF FLIES

The LORD said to Moses, "At day-break, go to Pharaoh and tell him, 'The LORD says, *Let* MY *people go, so they can serve* ME. *If you do not, I will send swarms of flies onto you and your ser-vants, your people and your houses. The houses of Egypt will be full of flies and so will the ground. But I will set apart the land of Goshen, where* MY *people are. In Goshen there will be no flies, so you can know that I am the* LORD *over all the earth.*' "

The LORD sent thick swarms of flies

The Lord did as Moses asked and took the flies and mosquitoes away from Pharaoh and his servants and his people. Not one fly remained.

But Pharaoh hardened his heart this time also, and he didn't let the people go, just as the Lord had said.

THE PLAGUE UPON LIVESTOCK

The Lord said to Moses, "Go to Pharaoh and tell him, 'The Lord, the God of the Hebrews, says, *Let* MY *people go, so they can serve* ME. If you refuse and still hold them, the hand of the Lord will strike your cattle, horses, donkeys, camels, oxen, and sheep with a deadly disease. But the Lord will set Israel's cattle apart from Egypt's cattle. Nothing will die that belongs to the children of Israel.' "

The next day, all the Egyptians' livestock died, but the animals of the children of Israel were spared. Pharaoh sent a scout, and, behold, not one of the animals of the Israelites was dead.

But Pharaoh's heart was hardened, and he did not let the people go.

THE PLAGUE OF SORES

The Lord said to Moses and Aaron, "Get handfuls of ashes from a furnace and throw it into the air in front of Pharaoh. A fine powder will fall on the people and animals, and blistering sores will break out all over the land of Egypt."

They took ashes from a furnace and stood in front of Pharaoh, and Moses threw the ashes into the air. Sores broke out on the skin of the people and the animals. The magicians could not face Moses because of their sores.

But the Lord made Pharaoh's heart very hard, and he didn't listen, as the Lord had said.

and mosquitoes into Pharaoh's house and the houses of his servants all over the land of Egypt. The land was ruined by the flying swarms.

Pharaoh called for Moses and Aaron and said, "Go! Sacrifice offerings to your God here in Egypt."

"No, not here," said Moses. "The Egyptians will be offended if they see us sacrificing the animals they worship. Let us go a three days' journey into the wilderness to worship the Lord our God."

"Very well," said Pharaoh. "I will let you offer sacrifices to the Lord your God in the wilderness. But do not go far. Plead for me, and make these flies and mosquitoes go away."

"I'll plead for you," said Moses. "Tomorrow the swarms will go away from Pharaoh and his servants and his people. But do not deal falsely with us."

THE PLAGUE OF HAIL

The LORD said to Moses, "Go out early in the morning and meet Pharaoh and say, 'The LORD, the GOD of the Hebrews, says, *Set* MY *people free, so they can serve* ME. *Tomorrow I will cause heavy hail to fall, such as has never been seen in Egypt. Bring all your animals into shelter. The hail will come down on every person and animal in the fields, and they will die.*'"

Those of Pharaoh's servants who feared the word of the LORD brought everything inside. Those who didn't listen to the word of the LORD left everything outside.

Then the LORD said to Moses, "Stretch your hand out toward heaven, so hail will fall all over the land of Egypt, on humans and animals and every plant."

Moses stretched his rod toward heaven, and the LORD sent thunder and hail; and lightning came down upon the earth. It was the heaviest hail that had ever been in Egypt. It struck down everything in the fields, both man and beast; it struck every plant and broke every tree. Only in Goshen, where the children of Israel lived, was there no hail.

Pharaoh sent for Moses and Aaron. "This time I've sinned," he said. "The LORD is right, and I and my people are wrong. Plead with HIM. We can't stand any more of this thunder and hail. I'll let you go. You won't have to stay here any longer."

Moses went out of the city and stretched out his hands to the LORD. The thunder and hail ceased, and the rain no longer poured upon the earth.

But when Pharaoh saw that the hail and thunder had ceased, he and his servants sinned again. He hardened his heart and did not let the children of Israel go, as the LORD had said.

THE PLAGUE OF LOCUSTS

Moses and Aaron went to Pharaoh and said, "The LORD, the GOD of the Hebrews, says, *How long will you refuse to humble yourself before* ME? *Let* MY *people go, so they may serve* ME. *If you refuse, tomorrow I will bring locusts into your country, and they will cover the face of the land. They will eat what is left over from the hail. They will eat your trees and fill your houses and the houses of your servants and all the Egyptians like nothing you have ever seen.*"

After Moses and Aaron left, Pharaoh's servants said to him, "How long will this man be a danger to us? Why don't you let just the men go? Can't you see that Egypt is being ruined?"

Moses and Aaron were brought back to Pharaoh, and Pharaoh said to them,

"Go serve the LORD. But tell me, just who needs to go with you?"

"Young and old, men and women, sheep and cattle. All of the Hebrew people must go to worship the LORD."

"No!" said Pharaoh. "I will never let all of you go, for I sense evil in your plans. Go, take just the men and serve the LORD, if that's what you really want."

Then servants drove Moses and Aaron out of the presence of Pharaoh.

The LORD said to Moses, "Stretch out your hand over the land of Egypt, so that locusts come and eat every plant left over from the hail."

Moses stretched his rod over the land of Egypt, and the LORD brought a wind from the east. It blew on the land all day and all night, and with the wind came millions of locusts. They covered the whole land, and the ground was dark with them. They ate all the plants and fruit left over from the hail. Not a single green leaf remained in the land of Egypt.

Pharaoh called Moses and Aaron to come quickly. "I've sinned against the LORD your GOD and against you," he said. "Now, I pray you, forgive my sin just this once, and plead with your GOD to take this death from me."

Moses pleaded with the LORD, and the LORD sent a strong west wind, and it lifted up the locusts and drove them into the Red Sea. Not one locust was left in Egypt.

But the LORD hardened Pharaoh's heart, and he did not let the children of Israel go.

THE PLAGUE OF DARKNESS

Then the LORD said to Moses, "Stretch out your hand toward heaven, so darkness will come over the land of Egypt— a darkness so thick it will be felt."

Moses stretched out his hand toward heaven, and there was thick darkness in all the land of Egypt for three days. It was so dark that people couldn't see each other, and nobody left his home for three days. But there was light where the children of Israel lived.

Pharaoh called Moses and said, "Go, serve the LORD. Your women and children can go with you. Just leave your flocks and herds behind."

Moses said, "You must let us have the animals so we can offer a sacrifice to the LORD. All the animals must go with us. We can't leave a single hoof behind."

But the LORD hardened Pharaoh's heart, and Pharaoh wouldn't let them go.

"Get away from me!" Pharaoh said to Moses. "Never come into my presence again. The day you see my face, you will die!"

THE PLAGUE UPON THE FIRSTBORN

Moses said to Pharaoh, "At midnight, the LORD will go through Egypt. All the firstborn in the land of Egypt will die, from the firstborn of Pharaoh to the firstborn of the servants and the firstborn of the animals. There will be a cry throughout all the land of Egypt —louder than anyone has ever heard. But not even a dog will bark against the children of Israel, and you will know that the LORD sets them apart from the Egyptians. Then your servants will come and bow down to me and tell me and my people to get out. Then I will go."

Moses went out from Pharaoh in hot anger, and the LORD said to Moses, "Pharaoh will not listen to you, so that MY wonders may be multiplied in the land of Egypt. When he lets you go, he will drive you out."

THE BLOOD OF THE LAMB

The LORD gave Moses and Aaron instructions for the people's last night in Egypt. First, they must take a perfect young lamb and kill it at sundown without breaking its bones. The LORD said, "Take some of the blood of the lamb and put it over the tops and sides of the doors of your houses. Roast the meat and eat it with unleavened bread and bitter herbs. Eat it quickly, with your belts tied and your sandals on your feet and your staffs in hand. You must be ready at a moment's notice to leave for a long, long journey. The blood will be a sign. When I see the blood, I will pass over you, and no plague will fall on you."

The blood set them apart from the

Egyptians. Moses told them that every year after this, the children of Israel were to keep the Passover and eat the same meal they were eating this night. The Passover feast would remind them that the LORD had set them apart from the Egyptians.

The people went home and did as the LORD commanded. They stayed indoors, dressed in their traveling clothes, ate the lamb, and waited.

At midnight, the LORD struck down all the firstborn in the land of Egypt, from the firstborn of Pharaoh on his throne to the firstborn of the prisoner in the dungeon, and all the firstborn of the animals, too. There was a great cry in Egypt, because there wasn't a house where someone wasn't dead. But death passed over the houses of the Hebrews.

85

While it was still dark, Pharaoh sent for Moses and Aaron.

"Get away from my people!" he said. "Go serve the LORD, as you have said. Take your flocks and herds, and go!"

As Moses was leaving, Pharaoh called after him, "Before you go, ask your LORD to bless me, too."

The LORD did not want the children of Israel to leave Egypt empty-handed, so HE told Moses they should ask the Egyptians to give them fine clothing and gold and silver jewelry. The Egyptians let them have whatever they wanted. "Just go from here!" they cried.

The Israelites marched victoriously out of Egypt, carrying great wealth with them. Thousands of men, women, and children followed Moses out of the city. Some of the Egyptians joined them, along with many sheep and cattle.

"Never forget this day," Moses told the people. "Celebrate this day forever with a Passover feast. When the LORD brings you into the land HE promised, remember that you came out of slavery in Egypt. When your children ask what Passover means to you, tell them how the LORD passed over the houses of the children of Israel in Egypt. Tell them the LORD brought you out with HIS mighty hand!"

Four hundred and thirty years after Jacob's family went into Egypt, the children of Israel came out.

And Moses took the bones of Joseph with him, as had been sworn to Joseph: "When GOD brings HIS people, the children of Israel, up out of Egypt, you will carry my bones up from this place."

CROSSING THE SEA ON DRY GROUND

The shortest way from Egypt to the land of Canaan was along the main road beside the shore of the Great Western Sea. But the Philistines had forts on the seacoast; so when Pharaoh let the people go, GOD did not lead them in that direction, for GOD said, "What if the people see war and repent of leaving? They may become full of fear and doubt, and turn back to Egypt." So HE led them south through the wilderness toward the Red Sea.

The LORD went before them to lead the way. By day, HE went in a pillar of cloud; and by night, HE went in a pillar of fire to give them light. With GOD's help, they could travel both day and night.

The LORD said to Moses, "Tell the people to set up camp between the mountains and the Red Sea. Pharaoh will think you are trapped in the wilderness. I will harden his heart, and he will come after you. Then I will defeat Pharaoh and his army, and the Egyptians will know that I am the LORD."

When Pharaoh heard that the people had fled, he and his servants changed their minds. "What have we done?" they said. "Why did we let those slaves go from us?"

Pharaoh made ready his chariot and took six hundred of his best war chariots and horses and drivers and went out in pursuit of the children of Israel. He caught up with them near their camp beside the Red Sea.

When the children of Israel saw the Egyptian army coming toward them, they were terrified. They said to Moses, "Weren't there enough graves in Egypt? Why did you bring us to the wilderness to die? We told you to leave us alone and let us serve the Egyptians. It is better to serve the Egyptians than die in the wilderness."

"Don't be afraid," said Moses. "Stand firm and see the salvation of the LORD. You will never see the Egyptians again. The LORD will fight for you."

The pillar of cloud in front of them moved behind them between the two camps. It brought darkness to the Egyptians, yet gave light to the Israelites, separating the two camps all night.

The LORD said to Moses, "Tell the children of Israel to go forward. Lift up your rod and stretch your hand over the sea and divide it, so the children of Israel can go through the midst of the sea on dry ground."

Moses stretched out his hand over the sea, and the LORD drove back the sea with a strong east wind. It blew all night, dividing the waters and turning the sea into dry land.

The children of Israel went into the midst of the sea on dry ground with a wall of water on their right side and on their left. All of Pharaoh's horses, chariots, and horsemen rode into the midst of the sea after them.

Just before sunrise the pillars of fire

walked on dry ground through the sea with a wall of water on each side.

Moses and the children of Israel sang a song of praise to the LORD for saving them:

"YOUR right hand shattered the enemy.
YOU blew with YOUR breath,
    and the sea covered them.
Let the LORD be king for ever and ever!"

The prophet Miriam, sister of Moses and Aaron, took a timbrel in her hand, and all the women went out after her with timbrels and dancing. Miriam sang to them:

"Sing to the LORD,
    for HE has triumphed gloriously!
The horse and its rider HE has thrown
    into the sea!"

and cloud came down onto the army of the Egyptians and threw them into a panic. Their chariot wheels came off in the mud, and they could not move. "Let us flee from here!" they cried. "The LORD is fighting against us!"

The LORD said to Moses, "Stretch out your hand over the sea, so that the waters will come back upon the Egyptians, their chariots, and their horsemen."

Moses stretched out his hand over the sea, and just as the sun was rising, the waters returned. It covered the chariots and the horsemen, and the whole Egyptian army that had followed the Israelites into the sea. Not one Egyptian remained. But the children of Israel

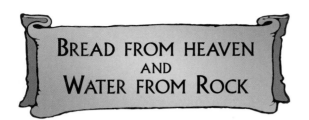

BREAD FROM HEAVEN
AND
WATER FROM ROCK

Moses led the people from the Red Sea into the rough and rocky wilderness. They journeyed for three days without finding water. And when they came to a place called Marah, they could not drink the water, for it was bitter. And the people murmured against Moses, saying, "What are we going to drink?"

Moses cried out to the Lord, and the Lord showed him a piece of wood, which Moses then cast into the water. And, lo, the water was made sweet.

The Lord said, "Hearken to my voice and do what is right in my sight, for I am the Lord that heals you."

They camped in Elim beside twelve springs of water, and rested in the shade of seventy palm trees. Then they moved on, into the wilderness.

After a month away from Egypt, the people began to grumble against Moses and Aaron. "The Lord should have killed us in the land of Egypt," they said. "When we were slaves, we could sit around our cooking pots and eat as much meat and bread as we wanted. You've brought us into this wilderness to starve!"

Then the Lord said to Moses, "Behold, I will rain bread from heaven, and the people are to go out every day and gather one day's supply only, so I can test them to see if they will obey me. I will give them bread every day for six days. Tell them to gather one day's supply on each of the first five days, two days' supply on the sixth day, and nothing on the seventh day."

Moses and Aaron told the people, "The Lord will give you all the bread you can eat every morning. He has heard your complaints. Your grumblings are not against us—who are we?—but against the Lord."

While they were still speaking, the glory of the Lord suddenly appeared in a cloud in the wilderness.

"I've heard the grumbling of the children of Israel," the Lord said to Moses. "Tell them, *You'll eat meat in the evening and bread in the morning, and you'll know*

that I am the LORD your GOD."

That evening, as the sun was going down, flocks of quail came and covered the camp. The people gathered them for meat. And in the morning, as the sun was coming up, a layer of dew lay all around the camp. When the dew dried, there on the surface of the wilderness lay something small and white, like frost, but round and thin.

When the children of Israel saw it, they said to each other, "Manna?" meaning "What is it?"

"It's the bread from heaven," said Moses. "It's the food the LORD is giving you. HE says to take enough for one day's supply, each man according to his fill."

The people gathered the manna and filled their baskets with it. Some gathered more, some less, but when they measured it, all the people had just as much as they needed.

The manna tasted sweet, like honey bread, and they ground it up, and boiled it, and made it into cakes and ate it with milk and cheese.

"Do not keep any for tomorrow," said Moses.

But some of the people didn't listen. They stored part; and the next morning it was filled with maggots and had a rotten smell.

After that, the people gathered only as much as they needed. Later in the day, when the sun was hot, what was left on the ground melted away.

On the sixth day, Moses told the people to gather twice as much. "The LORD has commanded that tomorrow be a day of rest," he explained. "It is the Sabbath, a day set apart to honor the LORD. Do no work tomorrow, but cook and bake enough today to eat on the Sabbath."

The people did what Moses said, and this time the manna kept overnight did not spoil.

They moved on through the wilderness to Rephidim. Every morning they found manna on the ground, but there was no water for the people to drink.

"Give us water to drink!" they cried.

"Why are you quarreling with me? Why are you testing the LORD?" said Moses.

But the people were thirsty, and they grumbled against Moses. "Why did you bring us out of Egypt to kill us and our children and our animals with thirst?"

"What should I do with these people?" Moses cried out to the LORD. "They're so angry, they're ready to stone me."

The LORD said, "Take some of the elders of Israel and go to the people. Take in your hand the rod you used to strike the Nile. I'll stand before you on the rock at Sinai. Strike the rock, and water will come out, enough for all the people and their animals to drink."

Moses did as the LORD said. He found the rock and struck it with his rod. Immediately, water poured out of the rock and over the ground.

While the Israelites were still camped at Rephidim, tired and faint, the Amalekites attacked them.

Moses said to his assistant, Joshua, "Choose some men and go out and fight the Amalekites. Tomorrow I'll stand on the top of the hill with the rod of GOD in my hand."

While Joshua fought the Amalekites, Moses and Aaron and Hur went up to the top of a nearby hill to watch the battle. Whenever Moses held up his hand, the children of Israel won, and whenever he lowered his hand, the Amalekites won.

But Moses' hands felt heavy, so Aaron and Hur got a large stone and put it under Moses, and he sat on it. Then Aaron and Hur held up his hands, one on each side. His hands were steady until the sun went down, and Joshua defeated the Amalekites.

On the first day of the third month after the children of Israel went out of the land of Egypt, they came to the wilderness of Sinai and camped in front of the mountain. Moses left the people in the camp and went up the mountain to GOD.

The LORD called to him from the mountain:

"Say to the children of Israel, *You saw what I did to the Egyptians. You saw how I carried you on eagles' wings and brought you to MYSELF. Now, if you listen to MY voice and keep MY covenant, you will be MY treasure among all nations. All nations are MINE, but you will be MY kingdom, set apart from all others.*"

Moses told the people these things, and all the people answered, "We will do everything the LORD says."

Moses went back and told the LORD what the people had said, and the LORD said to Moses, "I will come to you in a thick cloud so the people can hear when I speak with you and trust you. But first they must get ready. Tell them to wash themselves and their clothes. On the third day, I will come down on Mount Sinai in the sight of all the people. They must stay away from the mountain until they hear a long blast on a trumpet. Then they must come near the mountain; but warn them not to touch it, for it is holy ground."

Moses went down from the mountain to the people and told them to get ready to meet the LORD. On the morning of the third day, they heard loud thunder rolling and crashing on the mountain.

They looked up and saw flashes of lightning, and then a huge, dark cloud came down and covered the mountaintop. Suddenly they heard a long, loud blast of a ram's-horn trumpet.

They were trembling with fear as they left their tents and followed Moses to the foot of Mount Sinai. The whole mountain was wrapped in smoke, for the LORD was descending upon it in fire. Smoke was rising up like a giant furnace.

YOU MUST NOT HAVE ANY OTHER GODS BESIDES ME.

YOU MUST NOT MAKE IDOLS and bow down to them or serve them. For I, the LORD your GOD, am a jealous GOD.

YOU MUST NOT USE MY NAME WITH DISRESPECT.

REMEMBER THE SABBATH DAY AND KEEP IT HOLY. For six days you are to do all your work. But the seventh day is a Sabbath for the LORD your GOD. You are not to do any kind of work. For, in six days the LORD made heaven and earth, the sea and all that is in it; and HE rested on the seventh day. Therefore, the LORD gave the seventh day HIS blessing, and HE set it apart.

HONOR YOUR FATHER AND MOTHER, so that you may live many years on the land that the LORD your GOD is giving to you.

YOU MUST NOT KILL.

YOU MUST NOT BE UNFAITHFUL to the person you marry.

YOU MUST NOT STEAL.

YOU MUST NOT FALSELY ACCUSE YOUR NEIGHBOR.

YOU MUST NOT DESIRE YOUR NEIGHBOR'S HOUSE or wife or servant or ox, or anything that belongs to your neighbor.

The mountain quaked, and the sound of the trumpet grew louder and louder.

Moses spoke, and GOD answered him in thunder. The LORD descended upon Mount Sinai, and called Moses to the top of the mountain.

Moses went up to the top of the mountain, and then he came down to the people and told them the words of the LORD, the Ten Commandments:

I AM THE LORD YOUR GOD WHO brought you out of Egypt, out of the house of slavery.

When the people heard the thunder and the loud trumpet blasts, and saw the fiery lightning and the mountain smoking, they trembled with fear and backed away and stood far off. "You speak to us, and we'll listen," they said Moses, "but don't let GOD speak to us, or we'll die!"

"Do not be afraid," said Moses. "GOD has come to test you, so that you will be in awe of HIM and not commit sin."

But the people kept their distance, and Moses went up alone in the thick dark cloud where GOD was.

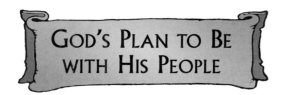
The LORD told Moses to say to the people, "The LORD says, *Serve only* ME, *and I will be with you, and I will bless you.*"

The LORD gave Moses many rules and instructions for the people. They were to treat each other with justice and be kind to foreigners. They were to help everyone and give generously to the poor.

Moses wrote down all the words of the LORD, and then he built an altar at the foot of the mountain and offered oxen as sacrifices. He took the blood of the animals and put half of it into bowls and sprinkled the other half on the altar. Then he read aloud to the people what the LORD had said.

"We will do everything the LORD has commanded," the people promised. "We will listen to the LORD!"

Moses took the bowls and sprinkled the rest of the blood onto the people.

"This is the blood of the covenant," Moses said. "The blood seals the agreement that the LORD has made with you."

Moses went back up the mountain. This time, Aaron and his two oldest sons, and seventy of the elders of the people, went with him. On their way up, they saw, under GOD's feet, a structure paved with sapphire stones, as pure and clear as heaven. It was a vision of the base of the footstool of the throne of GOD.

The LORD told Moses, "Come up to ME in the mountain, and I will give you stone tablets on which I have written the law and commandments, that you may teach the people."

"Wait here for us until we return," Moses said to the elders, and he and his minister Joshua went up into the mountain. The glory of the LORD settled on Mount Sinai, and a cloud covered it for six days.

On the seventh day, the LORD called to Moses out of the midst of the cloud. And the sight of the glory of the LORD was like a great fire on the top of the mountain in the eyes of the children of Israel. Moses went up into the midst of the cloud. And he was on the mountaintop forty days and forty nights.

Up on the mountaintop, the LORD gave Moses HIS plan to be with HIS people. He wanted the Israelites to build a special tent, the Tabernacle, where the people would gather to worship the LORD and see that GOD was with them. The worship services would be times to sing and praise the LORD. Priests would make sacrifices so the people's sins could be forgiven.

"Tell them to take up an offering for me," God said. "Receive from everyone whose heart is willing."

The Lord gave Moses a list of what was needed for the Tabernacle: gold, silver, and bronze; fine linen cloth of blue and purple and scarlet; goat hair and ram skins; acacia wood; oil for lamps, spices for anointing oil, and fragrant incense; gemstones for priests' clothing.

God said, "I'll show you the plan of the Tabernacle, and all its furnishings, so you can construct it."

The plan was very detailed. The most sacred part was a small wooden box called the Ark of the Covenant. It would be covered with pure gold and have a golden lid called the Mercy Seat, with cherubim of gold on the ends. These great winged creatures would face each other with their wings spread out above the Mercy Seat.

"Put the Mercy Seat on the top of the Ark," said the Lord, "and put the Tablets of the Law inside the Ark. I will meet you there and speak with you from above the Mercy Seat."

The Ark was to be set in the Holy of Holies, the innermost room of the Tabernacle. The Tabernacle was to be set within a large courtyard in the middle of the camp.

The Lord gave Moses directions for making furnishings for the Tabernacle. He also described in detail the clothing for the priests who would offer sacrifices on a small altar inside the Tabernacle and on a large altar in the courtyard.

When he was finished speaking on Mount Sinai, the Lord gave Moses the two stone Tablets of the Covenant, written by the finger of God.

THE GOLDEN CALF

Down at the foot of the mountain, the people began to wonder if Moses was lost in the thick cloud on Mount Sinai, or if he was dead. Weary of waiting, they gathered before Aaron and demanded, "Come! Make gods to lead us! As for this Moses who led us out of Egypt—we do not know what has happened to him."

"Very well," said Aaron. "If you need an image of GOD, then take off your golden earrings and bring them to me."

The people took off their earrings and brought them to Aaron. He melted them down in the camp fire and formed the gold into the shape of a young bull, and engraved it.

"These are your gods, O Israel!" shouted the people. "These are the gods who brought you up out of the land of Egypt!"

Aaron built an altar in front of the golden calf and said, "Tomorrow we will have a feast to honor the LORD."

Early the next morning, the people brought animals to offer as sacrifices to the golden calf. They sat down to eat and drink, and then rose up in revelry, playing and dancing.

The LORD said to Moses, "Go down to your people, whom you brought up out of the land of Egypt, for they have corrupted themselves. They have been quick to turn from the way I taught

HIS people out of Egypt only to kill them in the wilderness'? Turn from YOUR hot anger. Remember Abraham, Isaac, and Jacob, whom YOU call Israel, and YOUR promises to them that YOU would multiply their children like the stars of heaven, and give them land to inherit forever."

And the LORD repented of HIS plan to punish the people.

Moses turned and went down the mountain, carrying with him the two stone Tablets of the Covenant. The tablets were the work of GOD, and the writing was the writing of GOD.

Partway down the mountain Moses met Joshua.

"Listen!" cried Joshua. "I hear the sound of war in the camp!"

"No," said Moses. "It is not the shout of victory nor the cry of defeat, but the sound of singing that I hear."

As he neared the camp, Moses saw the golden calf and the dancing, and his anger flared up. He threw the stone tablets from his hands and they shattered on the rocks below.

He took the calf which they had made and threw it into the fire. He ground the gold into a fine powder, mixed it with water, and forced the children of Israel to drink it.

He turned to Aaron and said, "What have these people done to you, that you've led them into such great sin?"

Aaron said, "You know how the people are set on mischief. They wearied of waiting for you and asked me to make gods to lead them. So I took their gold jewelry and threw it into the fire, and out came this calf."

The next day, Moses told the people, "You have committed a great sin, but I will go back up to the LORD. Perhaps I can obtain forgiveness for you."

them. They have made a golden calf for themselves, and have bowed down to it and sacrificed to it, and said, 'These are your gods, O Israel! These are the gods who brought you up out of the land of Egypt!'

"I have seen how stubborn these people are. Now, therefore, leave ME alone, so that MY anger may flare up against them and consume them. Then I will make of only you a great nation."

But Moses pleaded with the LORD, saying, "O LORD, why does YOUR anger flare up against YOUR people, whom YOU brought out of the land of Egypt by great power and a mighty hand? Shall the Egyptians say, 'HE brought

GOD'S PEOPLE GET A SECOND CHANCE

Moses returned to the LORD and said, "O LORD, the people have committed a great sin. They've made themselves gods of gold. But now, if YOU will, please forgive them. And if not, I beg YOU, erase my name from the book YOU have written."

"Whosoever has sinned against ME, him will I erase out of MY book," said the LORD. "Go now, and lead the people to the land I promised to Abraham, to Isaac, and to Jacob: a land flowing with milk and honey. But I will not go with you, for you are a stubborn people, and MY wrath may consume you. Behold, MY angel will go before you. Even so, I will punish the people for their sins."

And the LORD sent a plague to punish the people because they had made the golden calf with Aaron.

When the people heard that the LORD would no longer be with them, they mourned and stripped off their jewelry as a sign of their sorrow.

Moses pitched a tent far outside the camp and called it the Tabernacle of the Congregation. And anyone who sought the LORD went out to the Tabernacle.

It came to pass that whenever Moses went out into the Tabernacle, all the people watched him until he was gone inside; then the pillar of cloud would descend and stand at the door, and the LORD would speak with Moses, face to face, as a man speaks to a friend. Moses then returned to camp, and his servant Joshua remained in the Tabernacle.

And Moses spoke unto GOD, "YOU told me to lead the people, but I don't know how. If I've found favor in YOUR eyes, go with us. If YOU're not with us, then we're just like all the other nations in the world. Please forgive our sins. Please take us to be YOUR people."

The LORD said, "Because you have found grace in MY sight, Moses, I will do as you ask."

"I pray YOU, LORD, show me YOUR glory."

"No man may see MY face and live," said GOD. "But come before ME on the mountaintop where you shall stand

upon a certain rock. As I pass by, I will put you in a cleft of the rock and cover you with MY hand. Then will I remove MY hand so that you may see MY back after I have passed by, but not MY face.

"Bring with you two tablets, cut from stone, and write upon these the words that were on the first tablets which you broke."

So Moses cut two stone tablets and went up Mount Sinai at daybreak.

The LORD came down in the cloud, and allowed Moses to see HIS glory after HE had passed by.

GOD called out HIS name, I AM, and said, "I am the LORD GOD, merciful and gracious, slow to anger, full of steadfast love and faithfulness, forgiving evil and sin, but I do not let evil go unpunished."

Moses bowed down to the ground and worshiped the LORD.

The LORD said, "I will forgive the people and give them MY covenant again, the covenant they broke. If they listen to ME, I will do great things for them, things that have never been seen in this world. All other nations will see what I do for MY people. I will drive out their enemies and give them the land. But you must keep MY commandments and worship only ME, according to MY laws."

Moses spent another forty days and forty nights with the LORD. During this time, he neither ate nor drank. Upon the tablets he wrote the laws and commandments of the LORD.

When Moses came down from Mount Sinai with the two Tablets of the Covenant in his hand, he did not know that his face shone from having been with GOD. Aaron and all the children of Israel looked at his face, and they were afraid to go near him.

Moses called out to them, and Aaron and the leaders of the people came near to him. Then the rest of the people gathered around him, and Moses gave them GOD's rules and commandments and told the people everything that GOD had said.

When he finished speaking to the people, Moses put a veil over his face. From then on, whenever he talked to the LORD, Moses took off the veil, and his face would shine. Upon each return, he would tell the people what the LORD had said. Then he would put the veil back over his face until it was time to talk to the LORD.

WORSHIPING THE LORD

Moses called all the people together and told them about the LORD's plan for a Tabernacle in the wilderness.

"Everyone who is willing, give what you can to the LORD," he said. "Bring gold, silver, and copper; colored yarn and cloth; goat hair and skins; wood and leather; oil, spices, perfume, and jewels. If you're a skilled craftsman, come help make the Tabernacle. We need a tent and furniture, an altar, and special clothing for the priests."

The people brought to Moses the cloth and treasures that the Egyptians had given them: gold pins and rings and necklaces, fine cloth, leather, silver, copper, wood, precious gems, and expensive spices and oils. They gave their most valuable possessions for the Tabernacle.

"Look," said Moses. "The LORD has called Bezalel and Oholiab to make the Tabernacle and everything in it. GOD gave me HIS plan, with the exact measurements, and HE has given these two

men skill in designing, gem cutting, woodcarving, weaving, and embroidering. HE has given them the ability to teach others these things, and HE has filled them with HIS Spirit."

All the engravers, seamstresses, and weavers came forward and offered their skills for the LORD's work. Moses gave them the things the people had brought, and they got to work, following GOD's plan.

Every morning, the craftsmen were interrupted by people bringing more offerings. Finally, the craftsmen told Moses, "The people are bringing more than we need."

Moses told the people not to bring anything else. They had already given more than enough to complete the work.

When the work was completed, the LORD said to Moses, "Set up the Tabernacle and put the Ark of the Covenant behind the veil. Bring in the furnishings, set up the altar and the courtyard, and anoint everything with oil. Then

bring Aaron and his sons to be MY priests."

They set up the Tabernacle in the middle of the camp with the courtyard around it and an altar in the middle of the courtyard.

The Tabernacle was larger than the other tents in the camp, and more beautiful. The outside was covered with goatskins, and the inside walls were covered with gold. The roof was made of layers of cloth and leather.

The outer room was the Holy Place, and the smaller, inner room was the Holy of Holies. Inside the Holy Place stood a golden table with golden dishes holding bread and wine.

A thick linen veil separated the Holy Place from the Holy of Holies. Inside the Holy of Holies were a golden altar for burning incense and the Ark of the Covenant.

Moses took the two stone Tablets of the Covenant, Aaron's rod, and a jar of manna, and placed them inside the Ark. He called the people together for a service to ordain Aaron and his sons as priests. He poured oil on the priests' heads as a sign that GOD's Spirit was in them, and gave them the priestly robes made by the craftsmen.

Moses poured anointing oil on the Tabernacle and the table, the lampstand, the altar of incense, the Ark of the Covenant, the great altar, and the basin in the courtyard.

Aaron offered sacrifices on the altar, and then he raised his hands and blessed the people, saying, "May the LORD bless you and keep you. May the LORD make HIS face to shine upon you and be gracious to you. May the LORD look kindly on you and give you peace."

After this, the priests, of the tribe of Levi, offered sacrifices and prayers every day at the great altar in the courtyard and at the golden altar in the Tabernacle. Other Levites helped the priests in the Tabernacle and carried the furniture and the Tabernacle when they moved camp.

Only the priests were allowed inside the Tabernacle, and only the high priest was allowed inside the Holy of Holies. Aaron was the high priest, and he was allowed into the Holy of Holies only one day a year. Every year on the Day of Atonement, the high priest entered the Holy of Holies and offered blood on the Mercy Seat. The blood of the sacrificed animals made the people pure, and then GOD would forgive their sins.

The people brought two goats to the high priest, and he took the animals to

the entrance of the Tabernacle. One goat was marked for the LORD, and was sacrificed on the altar. The other goat was marked as the scapegoat. The high priest took the blood of the goat from the altar, covered it with incense, and took it into the Tabernacle, behind the veil, inside the Holy of Holies. He burned the incense and sprinkled the Mercy Seat with blood. Then he took the scapegoat, put his hands on its head, and confessed the sins of the people. The people drove the scapegoat into the wilderness, and all their sins with it. The goat wandered away, and the people's sins were gone forever.

Moses gave the people a new calendar with annual feasts of GOD, which differed from calendars of other nations.

The seventh day of each week was the Sabbath day, a day of rest for the people. Every seventh year was a Sabbath year, a year of rest for the land. After seven times seven years was the year of Jubilee, when land, money, and slaves were given back to their original owners. The Jubilee reminded the people that the earth belongs to the LORD, and should be treated well and shared fairly.

Every year, the people were to celebrate special feast days. The most important was Passover, when they would eat lamb and flat bread and hear the story of how GOD brought them out of slavery in Egypt.

Moses told the people, "If you listen to the LORD your GOD, and follow HIS teachings, HE will bless you and give you everything you need. If you don't go after idols, you will live in the land forever, and the LORD will be with you.

"But if you go after other gods and do evil things like the other nations, the LORD will drive you out of the land."

THE GRAVES OF GREED

After the Tabernacle was set up, the pillar of cloud covered the Tabernacle. But one morning the people woke up and saw that the cloud had lifted. It was time to move out across the wilderness into the land of Canaan.

The priests took down the Tabernacle and wrapped everything up in leather and cloth. The people folded up their tents and left Mount Sinai, following the pillar of cloud by day and the pillar of fire by night. They stayed camped as long as the cloud stayed over the Tabernacle, but when the cloud lifted, they set out for a new place.

The Ark of the Covenant was set in the middle of the people, reminding them that the LORD their GOD was with them. Each time they made camp, they first set up the Tabernacle, with the courtyard around it and the altar in front of it. Then they set up their own tents.

Soon after they left Mount Sinai, the children of Israel began to complain. "Oh, if we could just have some meat to eat!" they cried. "Remember how we ate all the fish we wanted in Egypt? Remember the cucumbers and melons, the leeks and the onions and the garlic? But now there's nothing but this same manna to eat, day after day."

When Moses heard their complaints, he said to the LORD, "Why have YOU been so hard on me, YOUR servant? Why did YOU burden me with the charge of all these people? Am I their mother? Are they my babies to feed and carry to Canaan? They pester me with their complaints for meat. Where can I find enough meat for so many people?"

The LORD said to Moses, "Tell the people I've heard their complaints and I'll send them meat. I'll give them so much meat they'll eat it not just for one day, or two days, but for a whole month—until it comes out their nostrils and is loathsome to them."

Moses said to the LORD, "There are too many people to give them a month's supply of meat. Where would we get enough sheep and cattle?"

The LORD said, "Is MY hand too short? You'll see whether I can do what I say."

The LORD sent a wind that brought an enormous flock of quails into the camp. The small fat birds flew in and rested on the ground in and around the camp for miles in every direction. There were so many, they piled up three feet deep.

All that day, all that night, and all the next day, the people were busy catching quails. They roasted the meat and feasted on it.

But while the meat was still between their teeth, the anger of the LORD was kindled against the people, and the LORD struck them with a terrible sickness, and many died.

The Israelites named that place "Graves of Greed," because they dug graves there to bury the greedy people who died because they weren't satisfied with what the LORD had given them.

THE SPIES WHO WERE AFRAID OF GIANTS

The LORD said to Moses, "Send men to spy out Canaan, the land that I am giving to the children of Israel."

Moses chose twelve men, one leader from each tribe, and he gave them these orders: "Go by way of the wilderness of southern Canaan, and then into the hill country. See what the land is like, whether it's good or poor for planting, and whether forests grow there. See whether the cities are open or surrounded by strong walls. Find out how many people live there and whether they're weak or powerful. Be of good courage, and bring back some of the fruit of the land."

It was the season of the first ripe grapes when the twelve men went to spy out the land. They crossed the wilderness of southern Canaan and entered the city of Hebron, where the Anakim lived. They reached a river valley, and there they cut a large branch with a cluster of grapes and carried it between them on a pole. They also picked figs and pomegranates.

After forty days of exploring, the twelve spies returned and reported to Moses and Aaron and the people.

"We explored the land from one end to the other," they said. "It flows with milk and honey, and this is its fruit. But the people who live in the land are

strong, and their cities are large and well defended, with walls that reach the sky. We saw the Anakim, and they are giants. We saw other powerful people— the Amalekites, who live in the south; the Hittites, the Jebusites, and the Amorites, who live in the hill country; and the Canaanites, who live by the sea and along the River Jordan."

"Silence!" said Caleb, who was one of the spies. "Look at this fruit. Have you ever seen such grapes? Canaan is truly a land of milk and honey, as the LORD said. We should go up there right now and take the land. We can do it!"

"No, we can't," said all the other spies except Joshua. "We can't attack them. They are powerful giants! We looked like grasshoppers next to them."

The people stayed up all night weeping and fretting about the bad report of the ten frightened spies. They disregarded Caleb's good report. They heeded not the words of Moses: that the LORD would go ahead of them and fight for them.

"Oh, if only we had died in Egypt or in the wilderness!" they said. "Why is the LORD taking us into this land? We will be killed in battle, and our wives and children will be taken prisoners. Let's go back to Egypt without Moses and Aaron."

When Moses and Aaron found out what the people were saying, they bowed down in prayer in front of all the people.

Caleb and Joshua joined Moses and Aaron and said, "The land we spied out is a very good land. Don't rebel against the LORD! The people of the land have no protection, and the LORD is with us. Don't be afraid of them."

But the people picked up stones to throw at Caleb and Joshua. Suddenly the glory of the LORD appeared as a bright light over the Tabernacle.

The LORD said to Moses, "How long will these people refuse to trust ME? After all I've done for them, after all the signs I've shown them, they still treat ME without respect. I will strike them with a deadly disease and disinherit them, and I will make of you alone a nation, greater and mightier than they."

"Please, LORD," said Moses. "These are the people YOU brought out of Egypt. The nations know YOU'RE guiding us. If YOU kill YOUR people in the wilderness, the nations will say that YOU were not able to give YOUR people the land YOU promised. Please be patient with YOUR people, LORD.

Please forgive them, I beg YOU! YOU have forgiven so much already."

"Very well, Moses," said the LORD. "I will forgive them, as you have asked. But none who have seen MY glory and the signs that I did, and tested ME ten times yet listened not to MY voice— none of these will see the land I promised to give to their ancestors. Caleb and Joshua will see it, but none of the others will ever see it.

"Tomorrow they must leave this place and return to the wilderness! Tell them, *You will wander in the wilderness for forty years—one year for each day the spies explored the land. Your dead bodies will fall in this wilderness as you feared, because you did not trust ME. But your little ones will know the land that you despised. You will wander until the last of your dead bodies lies in the wilderness.*"

Angry Rebels

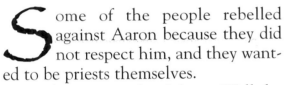

Some of the people rebelled against Aaron because they did not respect him, and they wanted to be priests themselves.

So the LORD said to Moses, "Tell the leader of each tribe to bring a rod and write his name on it. Tell Aaron to write his name on the rod of Levi. Take all the rods and put them in front of the Ark of the Covenant. The rod of the man I choose will sprout like a live branch. Thus will I end the grumbling of the children of Israel against Aaron."

All the leaders and Aaron gave rods to Moses, and Moses put the rods in front of the Ark of the Covenant. The next day, Moses went into the Tabernacle. There was Aaron's rod, sprouting like a live branch with buds and blossoms and ripe almonds.

Moses brought all the rods out to show the people. Each leader took back his rod, and Moses placed Aaron's rod in the Tabernacle in front of the Ark of the Covenant.

The LORD said to Moses, "Keep Aaron's rod as a sign for the rebels, to put an end to their grumbling, so they will not die."

Then the LORD said to Aaron, "I give the priesthood to you as a gift to you and your sons and your descendants."

And it came to pass that Moses himself rebelled against the holiness of GOD.

grapes, or pomegranates grow here, and there's no water to drink."

Moses and Aaron prayed and the LORD said to Moses: "Take the rod, call the people together, and speak to the rock in front of their eyes. It will send forth its water for all the people and their animals to drink."

Moses and Aaron called the people to come and stand in front of the rock.

"Listen to me, you rebels!" said Moses, raising his hand. "Do we have to get water out of this rock for you?"

He lifted up his hand; but, instead of speaking to the rock, he struck it twice with his rod. Water gushed forth abundantly onto the ground; and the thirsty people and animals came to drink.

The LORD said to Moses and Aaron: "You struck the rock in anger without honoring ME in the eyes of the people. Because you did not trust ME, you shall not bring these people into the land I have given them."

These were the waters of Meribah, a name meaning Quarrel, because the people quarreled there with the LORD, and HE showed himself holy among them.

When they came to Mount Hor, the LORD said to Moses and Aaron, "Aaron won't enter the land that I have given to the children of Israel because he rebelled against MY command at the waters of Meribah. Take Aaron and his son Eleazar up to the top of Mount Hor. Strip Aaron of his priestly robes and put them on Eleazar."

They went up Mount Hor in the sight of all the people. Moses stripped Aaron of his priestly robes and put them on Aaron's son Eleazar. Aaron died there on the top of the mountain. Then Moses and Eleazar came down from the mountain. And the people mourned for Aaron thirty days.

The people were encamped at Kadesh, on the border between the wilderness and the land of Canaan. There was no water, and the people were grumbling again.

"We wish we were dead!" they cried. "Why did you take us into this wilderness to die? Why did you bring us out of Egypt to this evil place? No grain or figs,

Balaam's Blessing

The children of Israel went down into the valley of Moab and set up camp on the border between the land of the Moabites and the land of the Amorites. The LORD gave them victory over the Amorites, and they took the land and spread their tents in the plains of Moab.

Balak king of Moab was terrified of the children of Israel, for they were numerous, and Balak saw that the LORD was fighting for them. All the Moabites and their neighbors, the Midianites, were overcome with fear.

So Balak sent a message to Balaam, a holy man who lived near the Euphrates River, saying, "A nation has come out of Egypt, and they're spreading everywhere. They've settled in the plains of Moab, and they're threatening to take my land. Come, curse this people for me. Perhaps with your help I can defeat them and drive them out of the land. I know that if you bless someone, they stay blessed, and if you curse someone, they stay cursed."

The leaders of Moab and Midian went to Balaam with Balak's message and money in their hands.

Balaam saw the money and said, "Stay here tonight. Tomorrow I'll bring back the word the LORD speaks to me."

That night GOD came to Balaam and said, "Who are these men?"

"They're messengers from Balak king of Moab," said Balaam. "Balak wants me to curse a people come out of Egypt."

"Don't go with them," GOD said. "You must not curse the people, for they are blessed."

The next morning, Balaam said to Balak's men, "Go home. The LORD has refused to let me go with you."

The elders went back to Balak and said, "Balaam refuses to come with us."

Once again Balak sent messengers to Balaam. This time he sent a large number of his nobles and a larger amount of

money. They told Balaam, "Balak says, 'Let nothing stop you from coming to me. I'll pay you and do whatever you say. Just come; curse this people for me.' "

Balaam answered, "Even if Balak were to give me all the silver and gold in his house, I could not disobey the command of the LORD my GOD to do anything, small or great. But, please, stay here tonight while I find out what the LORD says."

GOD came to Balaam at night and said, "If these men ask you to go, then go, but do only what I tell you."

The next morning Balaam rose up and, without the nobles asking him, he saddled his donkey and went with the nobles of Moab. GOD's anger was kindled because Balaam went with them, and HE sent an angel to stand in the way to oppose Balaam as he traveled with his two servants on the road to Moab.

Balaam's donkey saw the angel of the LORD standing in the road with a drawn sword in his hand, and she turned away from the road and went into the field. Balaam struck the donkey to turn her back into the road.

The angel of the LORD stood in a narrow path between two vineyards, with a wall on each side. When the donkey saw the angel of the LORD, she thrust herself against the wall, crushing Balaam's foot against the wall, and he struck her again.

The angel of the LORD went ahead of them and stood in a narrow place where there was no way to turn right or left. When the donkey saw the angel, she lay down under Balaam. Balaam's anger was kindled, and he struck the donkey with his staff.

The LORD opened the mouth of the donkey, and she said to Balaam, "What have I done to you that you hit me three times?"

"You've been making a fool of me!" said Balaam. "If I had a sword in my hand, I'd kill you."

"But I'm your donkey, the one you've ridden ever since you've owned me. Did I ever do anything like this to you?"

"No," responded Balaam; and the LORD opened Balaam's eyes, and he saw the angel of the LORD standing in the way with his sword in his hand. Balaam bowed his head and fell flat on his face.

The angel of the LORD said to him, "Why have you hit your donkey these three times? Behold, I came out to oppose you because your way is wrong. The donkey saw me and turned away from me three times. If she hadn't turned away, I would have killed you and let her live."

"I have sinned!" cried Balaam. "I did not know you were standing on the road to oppose me. If this journey be evil in your eyes, I'll go back."

"Go with the men," said the angel, "but speak only the word I tell you."

So Balaam went with Balak's nobles, and Balak came out to meet him at the border of Moab.

"What took you so long?" Balak said. "Why didn't you come the first time I sent for you? Did you think I couldn't pay you?"

Balaam said, "I've come, but I have no power to tell you anything. I can speak only the words that GOD puts in my mouth."

And Balaam went with Balak.

The next morning, Balak took Balaam to a high place where they could look out and see the edge of the Israelite camp.

Balaam said, "Build me seven altars and bring me seven bulls and seven rams."

Balak did as Balaam said, and they offered a bull and a ram on each altar, and Balaam looked for omens in the offerings.

Then Balaam said to Balak, "Stand beside your offering while I go to find out if the LORD has a message for me."

Balaam went to a high place and told GOD about the seven altars and the offerings. Balaam fell into a trance and the LORD put words in his mouth. "Now return to Balak and speak," said GOD.

Balaam returned and saw Balak standing with the nobles of Moab beside the offering. Then Balaam spoke:

"Balak brought me from Syria to curse Israel. How can I curse people God hasn't cursed? From the top of the mountain I see Israel, living apart from other nations. They will become so many, no one will be able to count them."

"What have you done!" cried Balak. "I brought you here to curse my enemies, and you blessed them."

"What can I do?" said Balaam. "The Lord puts the words in my mouth."

"Let's go somewhere else," said Balak. "Let's go where you can see more of them. Curse them for me there."

He took Balaam to a field on the top of Mount Pisgah and again he built seven altars. Balak sacrificed a bull and a ram on each altar, and Balaam looked for omens in the offerings. Balaam then went again to be alone with God.

The Lord met Balaam and put words in his mouth, and said, "Now return to Balak and speak."

Balaam returned to Balak, who was standing beside his offering with the nobles of Moab. "What does the Lord say now?" asked Balak.

"God has commanded me to bless," Balaam said. "He has blessed, and I can't undo it. God sees no trouble for the future of Israel. He is with them as their king. They will rise up like a lion, and they won't lie down until they devour their prey."

Balak said, "If you can't curse them, don't bless them!"

"Didn't I tell you?" said Balaam. "I must do what the LORD says."

Balak said, "I'll take you to another place. Perhaps it will please GOD to let you curse them from there." He took Balaam to the top of Mount Peor, overlooking the wilderness. Again Balak built seven altars and offered a bull and a ram on each altar.

But when Balaam saw that it pleased the LORD to bless Israel, he didn't look for omens. He looked at the wilderness and saw Israel camped tribe by tribe. Then the Spirit of GOD came upon him, and Balaam spoke:

"How beautiful are the tents of the family of Jacob. Their king will be greater than all kings. Whoever blesses them will be blessed, and whoever curses them will be cursed."

Balak's anger was kindled against Balaam, and he shook his fists at him. "I called you here to curse my enemies, and you've blessed them these three times! Get out of here! Go back where you came from. I was going to honor you, but the LORD has denied you honor."

Balaam said, "Didn't I tell your messengers, 'Even if Balak were to give me all the silver and gold in his house, I could not disobey the command of the LORD my GOD'? What the LORD speaks, I will speak. Now I'm going home. But first I'll let you know what this people will do to your people in days to come."

Then Balaam spoke, saying, "There shall come a Star out of Jacob, and a Scepter shall rise out of Israel and crush all Israel's enemies."

MOSES TEACHES THE PEOPLE

It came to pass, after forty years of wandering, that no one remained from the original children of Israel who had left Egypt, except for Moses, Joshua, and Caleb, just as the LORD had said. The LORD told Moses to count the people in order to divide the land of Canaan fairly, for they were soon to enter the Promised Land.

Moses knew that he was not to see the Promised Land, so he gathered the people one last time before GOD took him away. He taught them the stories of their ancestors, who stopped worshiping idols and began worshiping the LORD. He taught them the stories of their parents, who had escaped from slavery in the land of Egypt. He taught them about GOD.

"Listen, Israel!" said Moses. "The LORD our GOD is the only GOD. Love the LORD your GOD with all your mind and all your heart and all your strength. Write these words on your heart. Remember GOD's instructions and teach them to your children and grandchildren. Speak to your children about the LORD when you're at home and when you're traveling away from home. Teach your children about the LORD when you get up in the morning, during the day, and when you put them to bed at night.

"If you follow the teachings of the LORD your GOD, you and your children will live in the land as long as the heavens are above the earth. HE will drive out stronger nations and give you the land. You must destroy the altars and images of the gods of those nations. You must not worship where they do. Instead, you must worship in the place that your God will choose. When you cross the Jordan, the Lord will give you rest from all your enemies, and you will live in safety.

"The Lord set you apart from all the peoples on the earth to be his treasured possession. He didn't do this because you are great in number, for indeed you are not. Yet he has set you apart so that he may bless all the people of the earth through you.

"All those years in the wilderness, God was preparing your hearts to understand his ways. He was teaching you how to live in the land. Now you're ready.

"God's teaching is clear. You don't have to go up to the sky and bring it down. You don't have to cross the sea to find it. God's word isn't far away. It's right here, in your mouth and in your heart.

"Today you have a choice between good and evil, between life and death. If you listen to the Lord, he will bless you, and you'll be a great nation. If you don't listen to him, if you serve other gods, you will be destroyed. You have a choice today between God's blessing and God's curse, a choice between life and death. Choose life."

Then Moses said, "I'm an old man, too old to lead you. But don't be afraid. The Lord your God will destroy your enemies and give you the land. He will be with you, and some day, many years from now, he will send you another prophet like me; listen to him."

Moses called Joshua to come forward and said, "The Lord has chosen Joshua to lead you. God's Spirit is in him."

Moses laid his hands on Joshua. "Be strong and brave," he said to Joshua. "The Lord will be with you."

Moses blessed the people one last time and said, "Remember, the words of the Lord are your life."

Then he walked away from the Israelite camp and climbed up to the top of Mount Nebo. At the top of the mountain the Lord showed Moses all the land he was giving to each tribe of Israel. "This is the land I promised to Abraham, to Isaac, and to Jacob. I have let you see it with your eyes, but you shall not go over into this land."

Moses died on the top of Mount Nebo, and the LORD buried him in a valley in the land of Moab.

The children of Israel mourned and cried for Moses for thirty days.

And never again did a prophet arise in Israel like Moses, whom the LORD knew face to face, and who had performed all the signs and wonders the LORD had sent him to do in the land of Egypt, with such a mighty hand, in the sight of all Israel.

RAHAB AND THE SPIES

The LORD said to Joshua, "My servant Moses is dead. Rise up, cross over the Jordan, and enter the land I am giving to you. Every place the sole of your foot steps on is yours, as I promised Moses. Be strong and brave, and do what MY servant Moses commanded you. Don't be afraid, for the LORD your GOD is with you wherever you go."

Joshua said to the leaders of the children of Israel, "Go through the camp and tell the people to prepare food for a journey. In three days you will cross over the River Jordan and take the land the LORD has given you."

Then he sent two young men to go and spy out the land. "Go look at the land, especially Jericho," he said.

The two men found a place where they could wade across the river. In Jericho, they came to the house of a woman named Rahab and spent the night there.

But the king of Jericho was warned of the spies, and he sent a message to Rahab, saying, "Bring out the men who have come into your house. They're here to spy on the land."

The woman had hidden the two men, and she said, "True, men stayed at my house, but I didn't know they were spies. They left at sundown, just before the city gate was closed for the night. I don't know where they went. If you hurry, maybe you can catch them."

The king's men left the city, searching for the spies, and the city gate was shut behind them. But the spies were up on the roof where Rahab had hidden them among some stalks of flax she had laid out.

She said to them, "Everyone in Jericho is terrified of your people. We heard how the LORD your GOD dried up the water of the Red Sea before you. We heard how HE defeated the Amorites, and our courage melted away. The LORD your GOD is the GOD of heaven and earth. I know HE has given you this land, and that is why I am taking care of you. Now promise that you will deal kindly with my father and mother and my brothers and sisters, as I have dealt kindly with you. Spare them! Save us from death!"

The men said to her, "If you don't tell anyone what we're doing here, we'll deal kindly with you and your family when the LORD gives us the land."

Rahab's house was built upon the city wall, so she tied a cord to a window and let the spies slide down the cord to get safely out of the city.

As the men left, she said, "Go to the hills and hide there for three days until the king's men give up looking for you."

"We will return," they answered. "But before then, you must tie this scarlet cord in this same window. Bring your father and mother, your brother and sisters, and your whole family inside the house. When we come into this land, do not go out of your house!"

Then the spies climbed down the cord and went out into the darkness. After they left, Rahab tied the scarlet cord in her window.

The spies went into the hills and stayed there while the king's men searched along the road. After three days, the king's men returned to the city and the spies traveled back to Joshua. They told him what had happened, and then they said, "Truly the LORD has given all the land into our hands! Everyone is terrified of us!"

CROSSING THE JORDAN ON DRY GROUND

"Come here," Joshua said to the people, "and hear the words of the LORD your GOD! Behold, the Ark of the Covenant of the LORD of all the earth is about to cross over the Jordan River! When the soles of the feet of the priests who carry the Ark of the LORD rest in the waters of the Jordan, the waters will be cut off from flowing and the waters coming down from above will stand in a heap!"

The people set out, and the priests carrying the Ark went in front of them until they reached the edge of the river.

When the priests' feet touched water, the waters flowing from the hills stood and rose up in a heap far off, and the water flowing down toward the Salt Sea was cut off, leaving a path of dry riverbed that led across the river to Jericho. The priests stood in the middle of the dry ground as all the people crossed over to the other side.

After the whole nation with their belongings had finished crossing, the LORD said to Joshua, "Take twelve men, one from each tribe, and tell them, *Take twelve stones from the place where the priests*

The twelve men did as Joshua commanded. They took up twelve stones out of the middle of the Jordan and carried them to the place they were staying and laid them down.

Then the LORD said to Joshua, "Command the priests who carry the Ark of the Covenant to come up out of the Jordan."

Joshua commanded the priests to come out, and when they came out, the waters of the Jordan returned to their place and overflowed the banks.

The Israelites set up camp at Gilgal, on the edge of Jericho. And Joshua took the twelve stones from the Jordan and set them up, saying to the people:

"When your children ask what these stones mean, tell them that Israel crossed over the Jordan on dry ground. The LORD your GOD dried up the waters of the Jordan until you crossed over, just as HE dried up the waters of the Red Sea until you crossed over. HE did this so that all the nations of the earth will know that the hand of the LORD is mighty, and so that you will be in awe of the LORD your GOD forever."

are standing in the middle of the Jordan. Carry the stones over with you and put them down in the place you stay tonight."

And Joshua did as the LORD commanded and called the twelve men who would gather the stones.

"In times to come," Joshua told them, "when your children ask what these stones mean, tell them that the waters of the Jordan were cut off in front of the Ark of the Covenant of the LORD, and the Ark crossed over the Jordan while the waters were cut off. These stones will forever be a memorial to this event."

THE WALLS OF JERICHO

The kings of the Amorites who lived on the west bank of the Jordan, and the kings of the Canaanites, who lived by the sea, heard that the Lord had dried up the waters of the Jordan for the children of Israel, and their courage melted away.

Jericho was securely shut up inside and out because of the children of Israel. No one went out, and no one came in.

And it came to pass, when Joshua was walking near Jericho, he saw a man standing in front of him holding a drawn sword in his hand.

Joshua asked him, "Are you with us or our opponents?"

The man said, "I have come as the commander of the army of the Lord."

Joshua fell down in worship and said, "I am your servant. What is your command?"

"Take off your sandals," the man said. "You are standing on holy ground."

Then the Lord said to Joshua:

"I've given Jericho and its king and its mighty people into your hand. Have your people gather outside the city. Have the armed men march once all the way around the city. Behind them have priests carry the Ark, led by seven priests with trumpets of rams' horns. Behind the Ark will follow the rest of the people. Do this for six days. On the seventh day, march around the city seven times, with the priests blowing the trumpets. When the priests give a long blast on the trumpets, and you hear that signal, all the people must shout. The wall of the city will collapse, and the people will go in and take the city."

Joshua went back to the camp and assembled the people. He ordered priests to pick up the Ark of the Covenant, and ordered seven priests to go before the Ark, carrying seven trumpets. He commanded the armed men to march before the priests and lead the way to Jericho. The rest of the people followed the Ark.

They went forward, with the trumpets sounding as they marched. But Joshua had commanded the people, "Don't shout or make any sound with your voice until the day I give the order."

They went to Jericho and circled the city once, and then they returned to camp for the night.

The next day they lined up in the same order and marched around Jericho again. And again they returned to camp for the night.

They did this for six days. On the seventh day, the Israelites rose early and marched around the city seven times. As they marched, the priests blew the trumpets. After the seventh time around, the priests sounded one long blast on their trumpets, and Joshua said to the people:

"Shout! For the LORD has given you the city! The city with everything in it belong to the LORD. Don't take anything for yourselves, but take the treasures as an offering to the LORD! Only Rahab and her family are to be spared, because she hid the messengers we sent."

So the people shouted with a great shout while the priests blew the trumpets—and the wall of Jericho fell down!

The children of Israel marched straight over the rubble and entered the city, destroying everything in the houses.

But Joshua had said to the two men that had spied out the land, "Go get Rahab. Bring her and her family out, as you promised."

The young men went in and brought out Rahab and her father and mother and brothers and sisters and all their belongings. They led them to a safe place just outside the camp of the Israelites.

Joshua and his army gathered the silver and gold and the bronze and iron things for the treasury of the LORD. Then they set fire to the city and burned it to the ground.

Jericho was destroyed. Only Rahab and her family were saved. She dwelled with the children of Israel for the rest of her days, and was the great-great grandmother of King David.

GOD GIVES THE LAND

After the battle of Jericho, the Israelites fought and won another battle against the city of Ai. And all the cities around Jordan came to fear Joshua and the Israelites.

Joshua led the children of Israel to a place in the hills near Shechem. There he built an altar with great stones and wrote upon the stones the words of the Law of Moses. Then he offered sacrifices to the LORD on the altar.

Everyone listened as Joshua read GOD's teaching aloud. Men, women, and children heard how the LORD wanted them to live, never to worship idols.

Joshua told half the people to stand together, facing north, toward Mount Ebal. He read GOD's warnings to them: *If they did not follow GOD's teaching, GOD would let their enemies defeat them, and HE would drive them out of the land.*

Then Joshua had the other half of the people stand at a place facing south, toward Mount Gerizim. He read GOD's blessings to them: *If they obeyed GOD's teaching, GOD would give them everything they needed, and HE would let them stay in the land forever.*

After they heard GOD's teaching and the warnings and blessings, the people of Israel came down from the hills. They found that the news about them was spreading. Five kings were gathering an army to attack the Israelites and their allies, the Gibeonites.

The LORD said to Joshua, "Do not be afraid. I have given your enemies into your hand."

The people of the land had great armies, but the LORD fought for the children of Israel. HE threw the enemy armies into a panic and cast hailstones from heaven upon them.

Then Joshua spoke unto the LORD, saying:

"Sun, stand still over Gibeon; and, Moon, stay above the valley of Ajalon."

And the sun stood still, and the moon stayed until the people had avenged themselves on their enemies. And there was no day like that, before it or after it, that the LORD obeyed the voice of a man—for the LORD fought for Israel.

Joshua made war a long time with many other cities, making peace with none except the people of Gibeon. So Joshua took the whole land, according to

Covenant inside. The priests offered sacrifices on the altar to thank GOD for giving them the land.

Many years later, Joshua called all of Israel together and said, "I am old now and stricken in age. You've seen everything the LORD your GOD has done to the nations for your sake. If you follow HIS teachings, HE will drive out the nations that remain and you will possess their land, as the LORD your GOD has promised you.

"Therefore, be courageous to do all that is written in the Law of Moses. Love the LORD your GOD. Do not mix with the nations among you. Do not mention the names of their gods, or serve them, or bow down to them. If you do, you will lose the good land that the LORD your GOD has given you."

Then Joshua said to the people, "Choose, this day, whom you will serve —the gods of other nations or the LORD. You make your choice; but as for me and my household, we will serve the LORD."

The people answered, "We will never leave the LORD to serve other gods!"

"Be careful," said Joshua. "You cannot serve the LORD and other gods. HE is a holy GOD. HE is a jealous GOD. If you leave HIM and serve other gods, HE will turn from you."

"We will serve the LORD our GOD!" said the people. "We will obey HIS voice!"

Joshua let the people depart, every man to his inheritance. And it came to pass that Joshua, the servant of the LORD, died, and they buried him on his own property in the hill country of Ephraim.

And the bones of Joseph, which the children of Israel had brought up from Egypt, were buried in Shechem in the plot of ground Jacob had bought.

all that the LORD had said to Moses; and Joshua gave the land as an inheritance to Israel, according to their division by tribes. And the land rested from war.

Joshua divided the land fairly among the twelve tribes, with the larger tribes getting more land, and the smaller tribes less. The tribes were separated by rivers and mountains and valleys, and by the Canaanite cities among them.

The tribe of Levi received no land because they were set apart to serve as priests. The Levites were scattered among the people so they could teach them GOD's ways.

The people set up the Tabernacle at Shiloh, and placed the Ark of the

THE JUDGES
THE LEFT-HANDED JUDGE

Many years after the death of Joshua, the Israelites did evil in the sight of the LORD. They left the LORD and began serving the gods of the nations around them.

The angel of the LORD came to the people with GOD's warning. "I brought you out of Egypt and into this land that I promised to your ancestors. I swore to them that I would never break MY covenant with them. But you have not listened to ME. Because of this, I will not drive out the inhabitants of this land. They will attack you, and their gods will trap you."

The Israelites served the Canaanite god Baal and the goddess Asherah, and the anger of the LORD was kindled against them. He handed the Israelites over to raiders who robbed them. Whenever the Israelites fought their enemies, the hand of the LORD was against them.

Yet the LORD pitied them when HE heard their groans, and HE raised up leaders called judges to save them from the power of their enemies. But they didn't listen to the judges, and went on serving other gods and doing evil.

attacked and defeated the Israelites. They served Eglon the king of Moab for eighteen years.

When the Israelites cried out to the LORD, the LORD raised up Ehud, a left-handed man from the tribe of Benjamin.

The Israelites sent Ehud with gifts of tribute to Eglon, king of Moab. Ehud presented the tribute to Eglon at his palace among the palm trees near Jericho, and then Ehud and his men left to return home.

But after a short distance, Ehud went back to the palace. The guards recognized him and, seeing that he had no weapon on his left side, they let him in to see the king.

"I have a private message for you, O King," he said.

"Depart!" said Eglon; and his servants left the room.

Ehud went up to the king, sitting by himself in the upper room, and said, "I have a message from GOD for you."

Quickly, Ehud reached with his left hand and took a dagger that he had hidden on his right thigh, and plunged it into Eglon's belly.

Ehud escaped to the hill country of Ephraim. He sounded the trumpet, and shouted to the people, "Follow me! The LORD has given the Moabites into your hand!"

When the Moabites reached the Jordan, they found Ehud and the Israelites waiting for them. The Israelites had blocked all the shallows of the Jordan so that the Moabites could not cross over to escape. The Israelites were victorious and struck down all the Moabite soldiers. Not one escaped.

Ehud was judge in Israel until he died; and the land was at rest for eighty years, and the people lived in safety.

So the LORD delivered them into the hand of the king of Edom, and they served that king for eight years. Then the Israelites cried out to the LORD.

The Spirit of the LORD came upon a man named Othniel, and Othniel went out to fight the king of Edom, and the LORD gave the king of Edom into his hand. The land was at rest for forty years, and the people lived in safety.

After Othniel died, the Israelites again did what was evil in the sight of the LORD, and the LORD strengthened Eglon, king of Moab, against them. Eglon gathered a great army and

DEBORAH AND BARAK

Again the Israelites did what was evil in the sight of the LORD, and the LORD delivered them into the hand of Jabin, king of Canaan. Sisera, the commander of Jabin's army, had nine hundred chariots of iron; and for twenty years Sisera cruelly oppressed the children of Israel.

Deborah, a prophet, was one of the judges in Israel at that time. She dwelt under a palm tree between Ramah and Bethel in the hill country of Ephraim, and the Israelites came to her for wise judgments.

One day, Deborah sent for a man named Barak to come from Naphtali, and she said to him:

"The LORD GOD of Israel commands you to take armed men from the tribes of Naphtali and Zebulun and gather at Mount Tabor. The LORD will bring Sisera, the general of Jabin's army, to meet you by the river Kishon with his chariots and his troops. The LORD will give him into your hand."

Barak answered, "If you go with me, I will go. But if you won't go with me, I won't go."

"I will go with you," said Deborah, "but the road you're on won't lead to your glory, for the LORD will deliver Sisera into the hand of a woman."

Deborah rose and went with Barak to Naphtali. Barak called out the men of Naphtali and Zebulun, and they all went on to Mount Tabor.

When Sisera heard that Barak had gone up to Mount Tabor, he called out his nine hundred iron chariots and his men and took them to the river Kishon.

The river ran through the Valley of Jezreel, but when Sisera arrived, the riverbed was dry. The horses and chariots rode right through the dust in the middle of it.

From the top of Mount Tabor the Israelites looked down and saw Sisera's army.

"Up!" said Deborah to Barak. "This is the day the LORD is giving Sisera into your hand. He will go out ahead of you."

Barak and his men charged down the mountainside, taking Sisera's army by surprise. The LORD sent down great rains, turning the dry ground into mud and swelling the stream into a mighty, rushing river. The water came roaring over the horses and chariots and swept the soldiers away. The horses stamped the ground with their hooves, but they couldn't pull the chariot wheels out of the mud.

Sisera was so frightened, he jumped down from his chariot and ran out of the valley on foot. His soldiers tried to run up the valley toward the mountain, but were trapped by the flood.

Sisera escaped. He reached Kedesh and stopped at the tent of Jael, the wife of Heber the Kenite. The Kenites were at peace with Jabin, so Sisera thought this would be a safe place to hide. But the Kenites were relatives of Moses' father-in-law and were allies of the Israelites.

Jael came out to meet Sisera and said to him, "Come in, sir. Come into my tent. Do not be afraid."

Sisera went into the tent to rest, and Jael covered him with a small rug.

"Give me a little water to drink," Sisera said, "for I am thirsty."

Jael opened a leather bag of goat's milk. She poured some into a fine bowl and gave it to him, then covered him again with the rug.

Again he spoke to her, saying, "Stand at the entrance of the tent. If anybody comes and asks if someone is here, say 'No.'"

Then, being weary, he fell asleep.

Jael took a wooden tent peg in her left hand and a mallet in her right, and she crept softly up behind Sisera. As he lay sleeping, she smote him in his temple with the peg, and he died.

Jael looked out of the tent and saw Barak, who was pursuing Sisera. She went out to meet him, saying, "Come! I'll show you the man you're looking for!"

Barak went into her tent, and there lay Sisera on the ground, dead.

Back at Sisera's house, the Canaanite women were waiting for the soldiers to return. Sisera's mother leaned out the window, watching for him.

"Why is his chariot so late?" she asked. "Why are the horses so slow?"

One of her maids answered, "They've stopped to steal some presents for us! An embroidered scarf for me! Two scarves for the head of Sisera!"

In Naphtali, Deborah and Barak were singing a song of victory:

"*Praise the LORD, for HE has won
the victory! And blessed be Jael,
who has killed the enemy!*"

After this, the land had rest for forty years, and the people lived in safety.

Over time, the Israelites returned to their wrongdoing and began to worship Baal and other foreign gods. So the LORD handed them over to the Midianites.

The Midianites stole from the Israelites all that they had. Before each harvest, the Midianites rode in from the east on their camels to attack the people, steal the animals, and plunder the land. Like a swarm of locusts they came, and then left with everything they could carry, leaving nothing behind for the Israelites.

With no land or homes, the Israelites resorted to hiding in dens and caves in the hills; and they cried out to the LORD. Thus they lived under the rule of the Midianites for seven years.

And there came an angel of the LORD, who sat under an oak tree in Ophrah which belonged to Joash the Abiezrite. Joash's son, Gideon, was threshing wheat nearby in a winepress, hiding from the Midianites.

The angel appeared to him and said, "The LORD is with you, mighty warrior."

"But, sir," replied Gideon, "if the LORD is with us, why have all these things happened to us? Where are the miracles our parents told us about? The LORD brought us out of Egypt, but now the LORD has gone away and left us to the Midianites."

The LORD looked upon him and said, "I will give you the strength to save Israel from the hand of Midian. Have I not chosen to send you?"

"Please, sir," said Gideon, "how can I save Israel? My family is the poorest in Manasseh, and I am the youngest in my family."

"I will be with you," said the LORD. "You will defeat the Midianites as easily as if they were one man."

"Sir," said Gideon, "if I have found favor in YOUR eyes, show me a sign that it is really YOU speaking. Please don't go away until I come back with a gift for YOU."

Gideon went and prepared a young goat and unleavened cakes. He put the meat in a basket and the broth in a pot and presented them to the angel of GOD under the oak.

The angel said, "Take the meat and cakes and put them on this rock, and pour the broth over them."

And Gideon did so.

The angel of the LORD put forth the tip of the staff that was in his hand. When it touched the meat and cakes, fire sprang up out of the rock and consumed them. Then the angel vanished from sight.

"O LORD GOD!" said Gideon in fear. "I have seen the angel of the LORD face to face."

The LORD said unto him, "Peace be unto you. Fear not. You shall not die."

That same night the LORD told Gideon to tear down his father's altar to Baal and cut down the sacred pole of the goddess Asherah that stood beside the altar. Gideon went out with ten of his servants and tore down the altar and cut down the Asherah. In their place he built an altar to the LORD. He took his father's prize bull and offered it as a sacrifice to the LORD, using the wood of the Asherah as firewood. He did this at night, fearful of his family and the people of the town.

The next morning the townspeople saw that the altar of Baal was destroyed, and that the pole of Asherah had been cut down. They saw the ashes of the bull on the new altar, and said to one another, "Who did this?"

Someone answered, "Gideon, the son of Joash!"

Then the men of the city said to Joash, "Bring your son out to us! He must die because he has torn down the altar of Baal and cut down the Asherah!"

But Joash said, "Are you going to defend Baal? Does he need you to rescue him? If he's a god, he can take care of himself. It was his altar that was torn down—let Baal defend himself."

Meanwhile, the Midianites and the Amalekites and other tribes from the east had joined forces and had crossed the Jordan. They were camped in the Valley of Jezreel, ready to attack the Israelites.

The Spirit of the LORD came upon Gideon, and Gideon sounded the trumpet; and all the men of the land gathered at his side, prepared for battle.

Gideon said to the LORD, "If you will save Israel by my hand, give me a sign. Behold! I will lay a fleece of wool on the threshing floor. Tomorrow morning, if there is dew on the fleece while the ground around it is dry, then I will know that YOU will save Israel by my hand."

And it was so, for the next morning Gideon squeezed the fleece and was able to wring out enough dew to fill a bowl with water.

Then Gideon said to GOD, "Please don't let your anger burn against me, but let me make one more trial with the fleece. Please let the fleece be dry, while the ground is wet with dew."

GOD did so that night, for in the morning only the fleece was dry, and the ground was wet with dew.

THE LORD SHRINKS GIDEON'S ARMY

Gideon took his army and camped on the side of Mount Gilboa, for the Midianites were camped in the valley below.

The LORD said to Gideon, "The people with you are too many. If I hand the Midianites over to them, then Israel will boast, saying, 'We have saved ourselves.' Go tell your men that everyone who is afraid must go home."

Twenty-two companies went home, and ten companies stayed, numbering several thousand men.

"The people are still too many," said the LORD. "Take them down to the water, and I will test them and watch how they drink. I will tell you which ones to take with you and which ones to send home."

Gideon took the men down to the water and told them to drink. On one side he put all the men who drank standing up, lapping the water, as dogs lap, from their cupped hands. On the other side he put all those who kneeled down to drink. Only three hundred drank while standing. All the others kneeled down to drink.

The LORD said to Gideon, "I will save Israel with the three hundred. Send the others home."

That night the LORD said to Gideon, "Arise, go down to the valley and attack the camp of the enemy, for I have given it into your hand. If you are afraid, take your servant Purah down with you to the camp. Listen to what the Midianites are saying about you, and your hands will be strengthened for the battle."

Gideon went down with his servant in the darkness to the edge of the enemy camp. The tents of the Midianites and the Amalekites and the tribes of the East were spread out along the valley as thick as locusts, and there were more camels than sand on the seashore.

When Gideon drew near, two guards were talking. "I dreamed a dream," one of them said. "A little loaf of barley bread came rolling into our camp and hit one of the tents so hard the tent fell down and overturned and lay flat."

The other man said, "That can only be the sword of Gideon, a man of Israel. GOD has given Midian and our whole army into his hand!"

When Gideon heard the dream and its interpretation, he bowed down to the LORD. Then he went back to his camp and said, "Rise up! The LORD has given the army of Midian into your hand."

He divided the three hundred men into three groups and gave them trumpets and empty clay jars with torches inside.

"Watch me and do likewise," Gideon said. "When we get to the edge of the Midianite camp, do as I do. When I blow the trumpet, you blow your trumpets and shout, 'The sword of the LORD and of Gideon!' "

Gideon and one group went to the edge of the camp in the darkness. They blew their trumpets and smashed their jars. Then the other two groups sounded their trumpets and broke their jars. They stood every man in his place, all around the camp; and, holding their flaming torches in their left hands and their trumpets in their right, they shouted:

"The sword of the LORD and of Gideon!"

The army of Midian awoke and cried out. The three hundred blew on their trumpets, and the LORD brought confusion and terror into the camp. The Midianites stumbled over each other in the dark and swung their swords at each other, and many of them were killed. The rest fled toward the Jordan, but all the men of Israel rose up and gathered against them, capturing and killing many. And Gideon pursued two Midian kings and smote them.

The Israelites were so grateful to Gideon, they came to him and said, "Rule over us, you and your son and your son's son, for you have saved us from the hand of Midian."

"No," answered Gideon, "I will not rule over you, nor will my son rule over you. The LORD will rule over you."

After Midian was defeated, the land had rest for forty years, and the people lived in safety.

THE OUTLAW CHIEF AND HIS TERRIBLE VOW

After Gideon, Tola and Jair judged Israel. Then the Israelites again began to serve Baal and Asherah, the gods of Syria, the gods of Sidon, the gods of Moab and the Ammonites, and the gods of the Philistines.

The anger of the LORD was kindled against them, and HE handed them over to the Philistines and the Ammonites. For eighteen years they oppressed and crushed the tribes of Israel who lived beyond the Jordan in Gilead. Then the Ammonites crossed the Jordan and attacked the tribes of Judah, Benjamin, and Ephraim.

Israel was besieged, and they cried out to the LORD, "We've sinned against YOU! We've left our GOD and served Baal!"

The LORD said, "I rescued you from the Egyptians and the Amorites, from the Ammonites and the Philistines. The Sidonians and the Amalekites and the Maonites oppressed you, and you cried out to ME, and I rescued you from their hand. But you left ME and served other gods. I will rescue you no more. Go cry out to the gods you have chosen. Let them rescue you."

"We've sinned," said the Israelites. "Do whatever YOU wish, but please, please save us!"

They put away the foreign gods and served the LORD, and the LORD was grieved for the misery of HIS people.

The Ammonites were gathering a great army in Gilead, and the Israelites said to each other, "Whoever leads the fight against the Ammonites will be head over all the inhabitants of Gilead."

Now, Jephthah the Gileadite was a mighty warrior with a loyal band of men, but he was an outlaw, driven out of his home by his own brethren. When the Ammonites attacked Israel, the elders of Gilead went to Jephthah and said, "Come and be our leader so we can fight the Ammonites."

"Why are you coming to me?" he said. "You're the same men who drove me out of my father's house. You've come to me now because you're in trouble."

"Please," they said, "come with us to fight the Ammonites, and be chief over all of Gilead."

"If you bring me home again to fight the Ammonites," responded Jephthah, "and the LORD gives them over to me, I will be your chief?"

"May the LORD be our witness, yes," they said. "We will do whatever you say."

Jephthah went with the elders of Gilead, and they made him head and leader over them.

Jephthah took command and sent messengers to the king of the Ammonites, saying, "Why are you gathering an army to invade my land?"

The king of the Ammonites answered, "Because Israel came from Egypt and took the land away from us. Now give back the lands peaceably."

Jephthah sent a message in return: "Israel didn't take the land of Moab nor the land of the Ammonites. The LORD, the GOD of Israel, took the land and gave it to Israel to possess. You possess whatever your god Chemosh gives to you, and we possess whatever the LORD our GOD gives to us. We've been here for three hundred years. If your cause is just, why did you wait so long? The LORD, the Judge, will decide today between the Israelites and the Ammonites."

But the king of the Ammonites paid no heed to Jephthah's message. So the Spirit of the LORD came over Jephthah and had him gather an army in Gilead and Manasseh.

And Jephthah made a vow to the LORD, saying, "If you give the Ammonites into my hand, then it shall be that when I return home in peace, whatever creature first comes out to meet me, that will I give unto YOU, and it will become the LORD's."

Sheep or goat or prize bull, Jephthah would offer the creature to the LORD to thank HIM for the victory. The vow was foolish and terrible.

Jephthah led the Israelites against the Ammonites, thoroughly defeating them, and the LORD gave them into his hand.

After the battle, Jephthah returned to his home. And, behold, as he approached his door, his only child, his daughter, ran out to meet him with timbrels and dances.

When he saw her, he tore his clothes in sorrow and said, "Oh, my daughter! You're breaking my heart! I made a promise to the LORD, and I can't take back my vow."

And he told her of his vow.

"My father," she said, "if you have made a promise to the LORD, you must honor the vow, for the LORD has defeated your enemies. But, please, let me be alone with my closest friends for two months, to wander on the hills and mourn that I will never marry and have children."

So Jephthah sent her away for two months, and she went with her friends and cried on the hilltops.

At the end of two months, she returned to her father, who gave her up unto the LORD's service, never to marry nor have children.

THE BIRTH OF A STRONG MAN

Jephthah judged six years, and then he died and was buried in Gilead. After him Ibzan, Elon, and Abdon judged Israel. But then the Israelites again did what was evil in the sight of the LORD, and the LORD gave them into the hand of the Philistines for forty years.

In those days there was a man from the tribe of Dan whose name was Manoah. His wife was barren and had no children.

The angel of the LORD appeared to the woman and said to her, "You are barren, but you will soon give birth to a son. Be careful and drink no wine nor strong drink, and eat no impure food. No razor must ever touch your son's head, for he will be dedicated to GOD from the time of his birth, and he will begin to deliver Israel from the Philistines."

The woman went to her husband and said, "A man of GOD came to me, and his face was as awesome as the face of the angel of GOD! I didn't ask him where he came from, and he didn't tell me his name, but he said to me, 'You will give birth to a son. Drink no wine nor strong drink, and eat no impure food, for the boy will be set apart for GOD from birth to the day of his death.'"

Manoah pleaded with the LORD, saying, "Please, LORD, let the man of GOD YOU sent come again to us and teach us what to do with the boy who will be born."

The LORD listened to Manoah, and the angel of GOD came again to the woman as she sat alone in the field. She ran quickly and told her husband, "The man who came to me the other day has reappeared to me."

Manoah rose up and went with his wife to the man and said to him, "Are you the man who spoke to this woman?"

"I am."

"Well, then, when your words come true, how should the boy be raised? What should we do?"

The angel of the LORD said to Manoah, "The woman must do everything I commanded and not drink wine nor strong drink, and eat no impure food."

Manoah said, "Please stay and let us prepare a young goat for you."

"If I stay," replied the angel, "I won't eat your food, but you may prepare a sacrifice to offer to the LORD." (For Manoah did not know that this was the angel of the LORD.)

"Tell us your name, so when your words come true, we can honor you," said Manoah.

The angel of the LORD replied, "Why do you ask my name, seeing as it is WONDERFUL?"

Then Manoah took the young goat and some grain and offered them on a rock to the LORD, and the angel worked wonders. For, as the flame went toward heaven from the altar, the angel went up in the flame while Manoah and his wife looked on; and they fell on their faces to the ground.

"We will surely die," said Manoah, "because we have seen GOD!"

But his wife said, "If the LORD intended to kill us, HE would not have accepted our offerings, nor shown us and told us these things."

And it came to pass that the woman gave birth to a son and named him Samson. The boy grew and the LORD blessed him and gave him great strength, and the Spirit of the LORD stirred within him.

SAMSON'S RIDDLE

One day Samson went down to Timnah and saw a Philistine woman, and, in his eyes, she was the right one to marry. But his father and mother said to him, "Is there no woman among our people, that you must go get a wife from the Philistines?" For they did not know that this marriage was part of GOD's plan to destroy the Philistines who ruled over Israel.

"She's the right one in my eyes," Samson said to his father. "Get her for me."

Samson went on ahead of his parents to Timnah and came to a vineyard. There a young lion came roaring at him. The Spirit of the LORD came upon Samson with power, and he tore the lion asunder with his bare hands. But he didn't tell his father or mother what he had done.

Then he went down to Timnah and talked with the woman; and she was, in Samson's eyes, the right one. He and his parents returned home to make wedding plans.

When Samson traveled again with his parents to Timnah for the wedding, he turned off the road to look at the carcass of the lion. There inside the body he saw a swarm of bees and honey. He took the honey into his hands and went on, eating as he walked. He offered some to his father and mother, but he did not tell them he had taken the honey from the carcass of the lion.

Samson's father arranged the marriage. After the wedding, Samson held a feast that lasted seven days. Thirty Philistine men came to join the feast.

Samson said to them, "Let me ask you a riddle. If you can tell me the answer within the seven days of the feast, I'll give each of you thirty linen robes and thirty changes of fine clothes. But if you can't tell me, then you will give me thirty linen robes and thirty changes of fine clothes."

"Tell us your riddle," they said. "Let's hear it."

"Out of the eater came something to eat. Out of the strong came something sweet," said Samson. "What is it?"

After three days the men had not solved the riddle.

On the fourth day, they said to Samson's wife, "Did you invite us here to rob us? Tease the answer out of your husband, or we'll set your father's house on fire and burn you alive!"

Samson's wife went to him in tears and said, "You don't really love me. You told my countrymen a riddle, and you didn't tell me the answer."

"I have not told even my father or my mother," said Samson. "Why should I tell you?"

But she went on weeping through the rest of the wedding feast. On the seventh day Samson told her the answer, for she gave him no peace. Then she told her countrymen.

Just before sunset on the seventh day, the men of the city said to Samson:

"What is sweeter than honey? What is stronger than a lion?"

Samson replied, "If you had not plowed with my own cow, you would not have dug up the answer!" And he was angry with the woman he had married.

The Spirit of the LORD came upon Samson with power, and he went down to Ashkelon and killed thirty men of the town. He took their fine robes and gave these to the men who had answered the riddle. In hot anger he went back to his father's house, but there he found that his wife had been given to his best man at the wedding.

After a while, at the time of the wheat harvest, Samson went to visit his wife, taking a young goat to present to her as a gift.

But his wife's father wouldn't let him see her, saying, "I thought you hated her and were divorcing her, so I gave her to your friend. But she has a younger sister. See! Isn't she better looking? Please take her instead."

Samson said to him, "This time I won't be to blame when I injure the Philistines!"

He went out and caught three hundred foxes and tied them tail to tail and put torches in the knots. He lit the torches and drove the foxes into the Philistines' grain fields and burned the wheat in the fields and the wheat that was stacked up, and the olive orchards.

The Philistines cried, "Who did this?"

The reply came:

"Samson! Because his father-in-law gave his wife to his friend."

The Philistines went to the house where Samson's wife and father-in-law were, and they burned it to the ground.

"I will be avenged!" said Samson. And he struck with force, killing many; and then he left and hid in a cave at the Cliff of Etam.

The Philistines came up to Judah, looking for him. They raided a town, and the men of Judah said, "Why are you attacking us?"

"We are after Samson," said the Philistines. "We will make him pay for what he did to us."

Armed men from Judah went down to the cave and said to Samson, "Do you not know that the Philistines rule over us?

What have you done to us?"

"I was only doing to them what they did to me," he said.

"We're here to bind you," the men said, "and hand you over to the Philistines."

"Promise me one thing," said Samson. "Don't attack me yourselves."

"Very well," they said, "but we will bind you and hand you over to them."

They bound him with two new ropes and took him to the Philistine camp.

When the Philistines came out shouting, the Spirit of the Lord came upon Samson with power, and the ropes on his arms became like straw, and they fell off his hands. He found a fresh jaw-bone of a donkey and seized it with his hand and swung it like a club, killing a thousand men.

Then Samson sang, "With the jaw-bone of an ass, I have heaped them in a mass, and have slain a thousand men!" and then he cast away the bone.

He was very thirsty and called upon the Lord, saying, "You gave this great deliverance through the hand of your servant. Now will you let me die of thirst and fall into the hands of the Philistines?"

God split open a rock and water came out, so that Samson could drink, and his spirit and strength returned.

SAMSON AND DELILAH

Samson's great strength was feared by the Philistines. One day, when Samson went to the town of Gaza, the men of Gaza lay in wait for him all night at the city gate. "When he tries to leave in the morning," they said, "we will kill him."

But Samson came at midnight and took hold of the doors of the city gate and pulled up the two posts, bar and all. He put them on his shoulders and carried them to the top of the hill that faces Hebron, forty miles away.

The overlords of the Philistines heard that Samson was in love with a woman named Delilah, and they went to her and said, "Help us catch Samson. Tease out of him the secret of his great strength, and how we can overpower him, so we can tie him up and make him helpless. We'll each give you a hundred pieces of silver."

So Delilah said to Samson, "Tell me, please, the secret of your great strength, and how you could be bound and made helpless."

Samson said to her, "If seven fresh bowstrings were knotted round me, I'd be as weak as any other man."

The overlords brought Delilah seven fresh, undried bowstrings and she tied him up with them.

Now, she had an ambush waiting in her inner chamber, so she called out, "The Philistines are upon you, Samson!"

But Samson snapped the bowstrings, as a string snaps when it touches the fire. So the secret of his strength remained unknown.

Then Delilah said to Samson, "See, you have mocked me and told me lies. Now tell me, I beg you, how you can be made helpless."

He said to her, "If I were bound with new ropes that have never been used, I'd be as weak as any man."

So Delilah took new thick ropes and bound his arms tightly, and called out, "The Philistines are upon you, Samson!"

As before, an ambush lay in wait, but again Samson broke the bonds like thread.

"Until now you have been playing games with me," said Delilah, "and telling me lies. Tell me *now* how you might truly be bound."

"If you tightly weave the seven locks of my hair into the cloth on your loom," Samson told her, "then I will become weak and be like any other ordinary man."

While he was sleeping, Delilah took the seven locks of Samson's hair and wove them into the cloth on the loom. She made them tight with the pin and said to him, "The Philistines are upon you, Samson!"

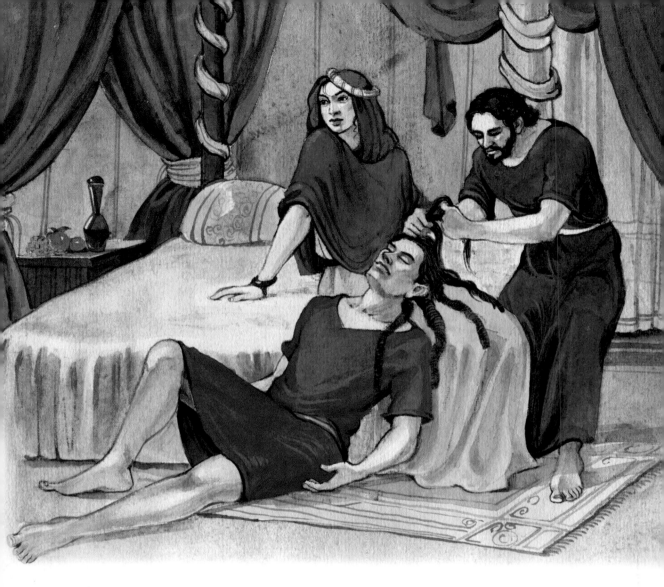

He woke up from his sleep and pulled away the pin, the loom, and the cloth.

"How can you say you love me," Delilah protested, "when your heart is not mine? You've mocked me three times, and you haven't told me the secret of your great strength."

Day after day she pestered him until Samson grew weary and he opened his heart to her.

"A razor has never touched my head," he said. "I've been dedicated to GOD since before I was born. If I were shaved, then my strength would leave me, and I would become weak and be like any other man."

When Delilah realized that he had told the truth, she sent for the overlords of the Philistines, saying, "Come at once! He has told me the truth." And the overlords of the Philistines came with the money in their hands.

Delilah lulled Samson to sleep with his head on her lap. She called for a servant to come and shave off the seven locks of Samson's hair. And this began to weaken him until his great strength left him.

When Samson heard Delilah cry, "The Philistines are upon you, Samson!" he woke up from his sleep, intending to shake himself free, for he didn't know that the strength of the LORD had left him.

147

The Philistines seized him and gouged out his eyes, and took him down to Gaza. They bound him with bronze chains and put him to work turning the millstone in the prison.

Over time Samson's hair began to grow back out.

And it came to pass that the overlords of the Philistines gathered to offer a great sacrifice to Dagon, their god. They rejoiced and sang, "Our god has given into our hand Samson, the enemy of our land!"

The people shouted praises and said, "Our god has handed over the enemy, the destroyer of our country, who killed many!"

During their merrymaking, they cried:

"Call Samson! Let him entertain us!"

Samson was brought up out of the prison. He was placed between the pillars of the state house and was made to entertain the crowd. He said to the boy who kept hold of his hand, "Let me lean against the pillars that hold up this house, and leave me while I rest."

The house was full of men and women. All the overlords of the Philistines were there, with three thousand men and women on the roof looking on while Samson entertained them.

Samson called to the LORD, "O LORD GOD, please remember me! Please, GOD, give me back my strength. Just this once. Let me be avenged of the Philistines for my eyes."

Samson grasped the two middle pillars that supported the building and threw his weight against them, his right arm on one pillar and his left arm on the other.

"Let me die with the Philistines!" Samson said; and he pushed forward with all his might.

The house came crashing down on the overlords and all the people who were in it. And those Samson killed at his death were more than he had killed during his lifetime.

Then his brethren and family came down and took him and brought him up to his homeland and buried him in the tomb of his father.

And Samson had judged Israel in the days of the Philistines for twenty years.

CIVIL WAR IN ISRAEL

In those days there was no king in Israel, and every man did what was right in his own eyes. They worshiped idols, they lied, they cheated, and they stole. They did not serve the Lord and they did not treat each other with kindness. They behaved like the nations who lived all around them. Because of this, the people and the land had no rest from their enemies, and no one lived in safety.

A Levite was traveling in the territory of Benjamin, and certain vile men of the town of Gibeah murdered his wife. The man sent messengers through all the territory of Israel and to all the tribes telling of this murderous deed at the hands of fellow Israelites.

"Such a thing has never happened before!" the people cried. "We must do something—but what?"

The leaders and the people gathered at Mizpah and heard from the Levite how the Benjaminites had murdered his wife. All the people arose as one and said, "We won't go home until we punish Gibeah for this crime."

Messengers were sent to the tribe of Benjamin to demand, "Give the criminals to us! Let us put them to death."

But the Benjaminites gathered an army and went out to fight the Israelites. In three days of fighting, the Israelites burned the city of Gibeah and killed all the Benjaminites.

The Israelites had made a vow that they would not allow their daughters to marry men from Benjamin. But after the civil war ended, they cried to the Lord,

"A whole tribe of Israel has died out!"

While they were praying, someone came and told them that six hundred Benjaminites had escaped and were hiding in the wilderness.

They said to each other, "What can we do about wives for those Benjaminites? We promised we wouldn't let our daughters marry them."

"Did all the towns join in the battle?" one asked.

Someone pointed out that when the roll had been called, no one had answered from the town of Jabesh.

Men were sent to Jabesh and they returned with four hundred young women. When the leaders sent an offer of peace to the six hundred Benjaminites who were hiding, the Benjaminites returned, and they were given the four hundred women of Jabesh. But two hundred Benjaminite men still had no wives.

"Go hide in the vineyards of Shiloh," the leaders told the two hundred, "for it is almost time for their yearly festival. When the young women of Shiloh come out to dance, seize them and take them back to the territory of Benjamin."

The two hundred Benjaminites hid in the vineyards, and when the young women came out to dance, they rushed out and seized them. They took them home and married them and rebuilt their cities, and the Israelites went back to their tribes.

Crime, war between tribes, kidnapping—these were some of the evil things that happened in those days. For there was no king in Israel, and every man did what was right in his own eyes.

THE STORY OF RUTH

Long ago, in the days of the judges, there was a famine in the land. A man from Bethlehem in Judah went with his wife and his two sons to live as strangers in the country of Moab. The man's name was Elimelech, his wife's name was Naomi, and the names of his two sons were Mahlon and Chilion. They came to the country of Moab and settled there.

Elimelech died, and Naomi was left with her two sons, who married two Moabite women, Orpah and Ruth. After ten years, both Mahon and Chilion died, and Naomi was left without her two sons and her husband.

Naomi heard that the LORD had taken notice of HIS people in Judah and given them food. So she set out to return to the land of Judah, and her daughters-in-law walked with her.

Naomi turned to her two daughters-in-law and said, "Go, return, each of you, to your mother's house. May the LORD treat you with loving kindness, as you have treated me and my sons. May the LORD reward you and give each of you security in the house of a husband."

She kissed them, and they wept, saying, "No! We will return with you to your people."

Naomi said, "Turn back, my daughters. What's the use of coming with me? I have no more sons to take care of you. No, my daughters. Turn back. Life is more bitter for me than for you. You are young enough to remarry and have sons, but I am too old. There is no one left to take care of me. Surely, the hand of the LORD is raised against me."

They wept again. Finally Orpah dried her tears and kissed her mother-in-law good-bye and went back to her own people. But Ruth stayed with Naomi, holding on to her tightly.

"Behold," said Naomi, "your sister-in-law has gone back to her people and her god. Return with her."

"Don't plead with me to leave you or to turn back from following you," said Ruth. "For, wherever you go, I will go. Wherever you stay, I will stay. Your people will be my people. Your GOD is now my GOD. Wherever you die, I will die, and there I will be buried. May the LORD punish me if even death separates me from you."

Naomi saw that Ruth was determined to go with her, so she said no more. The two of them went on until they came to Bethlehem. They arrived in early spring, at the beginning of the barley harvest, and they were greeted with excitement.

"Is it really you, Naomi?" the women asked.

"Call me Naomi no more," she said. "That name means Sweet. Call me Mara, which means Bitter, for God Almighty has made me truly bitter. I went away full, and the Lord has brought me back empty. Why call me Naomi, when the Lord has afflicted me, and God Almighty has punished me?"

RUTH GLEANS IN THE FIELD OF BOAZ

The fields around Bethlehem were full of ripe barley, ready to be cut and harvested. During the harvest, men went out to the fields to cut the grain. Women walked behind the reapers and tied the stalks of grain into sheaves. Other workers loaded the sheaves onto donkeys and took the grain to the threshing floor. There they beat the stalks of grain to separate the kernels of grain from the straw.

According to the teaching of Moses, poor people could go to the fields at harvest time and gather grain left on the ground.

Soon after they arrived in Bethlehem, Ruth said to Naomi, "Let me go out to the fields and glean barley. I will follow after someone in whose eyes I find favor."

"Go, my daughter," said Naomi.

Ruth went out and gleaned in the field after the reapers. She happened to come to the part of the field belonging to Boaz, a worthy man and relative of Elimelech, her father-in-law.

That same morning, Boaz himself happened to come out to the fields from Bethlehem. "The Lord be with you!" he said to the reapers.

"The Lord bless you!" they answered.

Boaz turned to the servant in charge of the reapers. "Who is that young woman?" he asked.

"She is a Moabite girl," the servant answered. "She is the one who came back with Naomi from the country of Moab. She asked if she could glean and gather among the sheaves after the reapers. She has been out here since early this morning without resting even for a minute."

Boaz went to Ruth and said, "Now listen, my daughter. Do not go to any other field to glean, or leave this one; but stay close to my servant girls. Keep your eyes on the field where they are reaping, and follow behind them. I am ordering the young men not to bother you. When you are thirsty, go over there to the water jars and drink what the young men have brought."

Ruth bowed low before Boaz, so low that her face touched the ground. "Why have I found favor in your eyes, that you have taken notice of me, a foreigner?"

He answered, "I've heard about everything you have done for your mother-in-law since your husband's death. You left your father and mother and your homeland and came to live among strangers for her sake. May the LORD reward you for what you have done. May the GOD of Israel give you shelter beneath HIS wings."

"You are very kind, sir," answered Ruth. "Your kind words have comforted me. I hope I continue to find favor in your eyes. I am at your service, sir, but, indeed, I am far beneath your servants."

When it was time to eat, Boaz said to Ruth, "Come and share our lunch. Have some of this bread. Here, dip your piece into the wine."

Ruth sat down next to the reapers, and Boaz gave her a large portion of food. She ate until she was satisfied and she had some left over.

When she rose to go back to the fields to glean, Boaz ordered his servants, "Let her glean even among the sheaves. Do not bother her. When you are reaping and binding the sheaves, pull out some of the stalks of grain from

the bundles and let them fall to the ground in front of her."

Ruth gleaned in the field until evening. Then she pounded out the stalks to separate the grain from the straw and weighed it carefully. She had more then twenty-five pounds of barley. She returned to the city and showed Naomi what she had gleaned, and also gave her the food she had left from lunch.

Her mother-in-law said to her, "Where did you glean today? Where have you worked? Blessed be the man who took notice of you."

"The man's name is Boaz," said Ruth.

"May the LORD bless him!" said Naomi. "The LORD has not forgotten the living or the dead. This man is related to us. He is one of our circle of redeemers."

According to the law of Moses, should a married man die without children, it was the duty of his family to support and protect the man's widow. It was the duty of the nearest male relative to marry the widow to keep the man's property in the family and to carry on his name. The relative who fulfilled this duty was called the Redeemer.

"There is more," said Ruth. "Boaz told me to stay close to his workers and glean in his field until the end of the harvest."

"Yes," agreed Naomi, "it would be better for you to go with his servants than to some other field where someone might bother you."

Each morning Ruth went out to glean in the fields of Boaz. She kept close to his servant girls, gleaning until the barley and the wheat were harvested. In the evenings she returned home to her mother-in-law.

Naomi said to Ruth, "My daughter, I want to see that you are settled. Tonight, Boaz and his workers are celebrating the festival of the grain harvest. Wash and put on perfume, dress in your best clothes, and go down to the threshing floor. Don't make yourself known to the man until he has finished eating and drinking. But when he lies down, notice the place where he lies. Then go and uncover his legs and lie down near him. He will tell you what to do."

"I will do everything you say," Ruth answered.

Ruth went down to the threshing floor and hid until Boaz was finished with eating and drinking and his heart was merry. She waited while he settled down to sleep at the far end of the threshing floor by the pile of grain. Then she quietly went and uncovered his legs and lay down nearby.

In the middle of the night Boaz felt cold and reached for his cover. He sat up and looked around and saw a woman lying nearby. "Who are you?" he asked.

"I am Ruth, your servant. Spread your wing over me and take me under your protection. You are one of our redeemers."

"May the LORD bless you," he said. "First you were kind to Naomi by coming to Bethlehem. Now, instead of looking for a young man to marry, you are asking me. Fear not. Everyone in Bethlehem knows you to be a worthy woman. Yes, it is true that I have the right of redemption, but there is another man who is a closer relative. Wait here tonight, and in the morning I will speak to him. If he wants to be your redeemer, well, let him. But if not, why then, as the LORD lives, I'll redeem you myself."

In the early morning, Boaz filled Ruth's cloak with barley. She went back into the city and was greeted by Naomi.

"What happened, my daughter?" she asked.

Ruth told her everything Boaz had said. "He gave me these six measures of barley, and he told me, 'Don't go back empty-handed to your mother-in-law.'"

"Now let us sit here and wait to see what happens," said Naomi. "Boaz won't rest until he settles the matter, and I think he will settle it today."

While Naomi and Ruth waited at home, Boaz went up to the city gate where the men of the city conducted business, and there he sat on the bench inside the gate. Just then, the relative he was looking for came by.

"Come, man," said Boaz. "Sit down here."

The young man sat down by Boaz.

Then Boaz picked out ten of the town leaders as they came through the gate. "Sit down here," he told them.

Then he said to the young man, "Naomi, who has returned from Moab, is selling the parcel of land that belonged to our cousin Elimelech. I thought I should tell you about it, and give you the chance to buy it, for you have the right to redeem the land now, in front of these men. If you don't want to, tell me, for I am the only other person who can do it. The land should stay in the family, but you are the closer relative, so you decide."

"I'll redeem it," the young man said.

"Wait, there's more," said Boaz. "If you buy the field, you are responsible for Naomi's daughter-in-law, Ruth, the Moabitess, who is a widow. You must marry her so the property will stay in her husband's family and his name won't die out."

"If that is so," said the man, "I cannot do it. I have enough responsibilities. You redeem her yourself."

"You are witnesses today," said Boaz to the people there. "I am buying what belonged to Elimelech and his sons. And, more important, I am taking responsibility for Ruth, the widow of Mahlon. I am going to marry her and keep his name alive among our people."

"We are witnesses," said the people.

The leaders of the town blessed Boaz and Ruth, saying, "May the LORD give Ruth many children to build up your family. May they make a name for you in Bethlehem."

Boaz and Ruth were married, and the LORD caused Ruth to give birth to a son.

Naomi's friends came to celebrate with her.

"Praise the LORD!" they said. "Today HE has given you a redeemer, to keep your family's name alive in Israel. He has made your life sweet again. This child will take care of you when you are old. Your daughter-in-law, who loves you, is worth more to you than seven sons."

Naomi took the boy and held him in her arms.

"A son has been born for Naomi," said the neighbor women.

They named the boy Obed. And Obed was the father of Jesse, the father of King David.

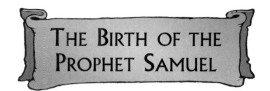

THE BIRTH OF THE PROPHET SAMUEL

There was a man from the tribe of Ephraim whose name was Elkanah. He had two wives, Hannah and Peninnah. Peninnah had children, but Hannah had no children.

Year after year Elkanah went to Shiloh to worship and offer sacrifices at the house of the LORD, where Eli and his sons, Hophni and Phinehas, were priests.

At the yearly festival, Elkanah gave portions of the sacrifice to Peninnah for herself and all her sons and daughters. He gave Hannah a double portion, because he loved her and because the LORD had prevented her from having a baby. And year after year Hannah went to the house of the LORD, and she wept and wouldn't eat.

It came to pass that one year Eli the priest was sitting on a chair by the doorpost of the LORD's Temple when Hannah came to pray. She prayed to the LORD, crying bitterly. She vowed:

"LORD, if you see my troubles and remember me and give me a son, I will dedicate him to you all the days of his life."

Eli could see her lips move, but he couldn't hear her voice. He thought she was filled with wine.

"How long will you act this way?" he said. "Put your wine away!"

"No, sir, I am a woman of sorrow," said Hannah. "I have had no strong drink. I have been pouring my heart out to the LORD."

Then Eli said, "Go in peace, and may the GOD of Israel give you what you have asked of HIM."

Hannah went back to her family and ate, and her face was no longer sad. And the next day Elkanah's household returned to the town of Ramah.

The LORD remembered Hannah, and she gave birth to a son. She named him Samuel, meaning Asked of GOD, because, she said, "I asked the LORD for him."

When it was time for Elkanah to go to Shiloh to offer the yearly sacrifice, Hannah didn't go with him.

"This year I am staying home," she said. "When the boy is weaned, I'll bring

him to the LORD, and he'll stay there always."

"Do what you think best," said Elkanah. "May the LORD help you keep your promise."

Hannah stayed home and nursed her son. When he was weaned, she took him with her, along with a bull and some flour and wine as offerings, and brought him to Eli in the house of the LORD. He was still a little boy.

"Pardon me, sir," Hannah said to Eli. "I am the woman who was standing here

in your presence, praying to the LORD. I prayed for this boy, and the LORD gave me what I asked of HIM. Now I am granting him to the LORD for all the days of his life."

She bowed down to the LORD and said, "My heart rejoices in the LORD! There's no one like the LORD. HE judges the ends of the earth and strengthens HIS anointed king."

Elkanah and Hannah went home to Ramah, and Samuel served in the presence of the LORD with Eli the priest.

GOD CALLS SAMUEL

Now, Eli's sons Hophni and Phinehas were dishonorable fellows who didn't know the LORD. Priests were permitted to take some of the meat offerings, but Eli's sons took the best pieces for themselves and scorned the LORD's offering.

At the same time, Samuel wore a priest's robe, serving and learning from Eli. Every year his mother made a little cloak for him and brought it to him when she came with her husband to offer the yearly sacrifice. Then Eli would bless them and say, "May the LORD give you more children in place of the one she has granted to the LORD."

The LORD took notice of Hannah and she gave birth to three sons and two daughters. And the boy Samuel grew up in the presence of the LORD.

When Eli was very old, he heard what his sons were doing.

"Why do you do such things?" he said to them. "If a man sins against man, GOD will plead for him. But if a man sins against the LORD, who can plead for him?"

Meanwhile, the boy Samuel was growing in height and in favor with the LORD and with men.

A man of GOD came to Eli and said:

"The LORD says, *I chose Aaron and your family to be MY priests and bring the people's offerings to MY altar. But your sons are fattening themselves with the best pieces of MY offering. Therefore, I will cause your family to die by the sword. Your two sons will die on the same day, and in days to come I will raise up a new family of priests.*"

The word of the LORD was rare in those days, and visions were not common.

It came to pass that Eli was lying down inside the Tabernacle near where the Ark was kept. The lamp of GOD had not yet gone out, but Eli's eyesight was growing dim and he couldn't see.

The LORD called to Samuel in another room, and Samuel said, "Here I am!"

Samuel ran to Eli and said, "Here I am, for you called me."

But Eli said, "I didn't call. Lie down again."

So he went and lay down.

The LORD called again, "Samuel!"

Samuel got up and went to Eli and said, "Here I am, for you called me."

"I didn't call you, my son," said Eli. "Lie down again."

Samuel didn't yet know the LORD, and the word of the LORD hadn't yet been revealed to him.

When the LORD called him a third time, he got up and went to Eli and said, "Here I am, for you called me."

Then Eli understood that the LORD was calling the boy, and he said, "Go lie down. If HE calls you, say, 'Speak, LORD, for YOUR servant is listening.'"

Samuel went and lay down. Again the LORD called, "Samuel! Samuel!"

Samuel said, "Speak, for YOUR servant is listening."

The LORD said to Samuel, "Behold, I am going to do something in Israel! All ears that hear of this will tingle! On an appointed day, I will punish Eli and his household, for I have passed judgment on his family. His sons have scorned ME, and Eli did not stop them."

Samuel lay down until morning, and then he opened the doors of the house of the LORD. He was afraid to tell Eli about the vision.

"Samuel, my son!" called Eli.

"Here I am!"

"What did HE tell you? Don't hide it from me."

Samuel told Eli everything he had heard, and Eli said, "HE is the LORD. Let HIM do what is good in HIS eyes."

Samuel grew, and the LORD was with him. All of Israel knew that Samuel was to be a prophet of the LORD.

And the word of the LORD was revealed to Samuel, and Samuel spoke to all Israel.

THE ARK IS TAKEN AWAY

Now, the Israelites went out to fight the Philistines, and the Philistines defeated them. The elders of Israel said, "Why did the LORD let the Philistines defeat us? Let us bring the Ark of the Covenant of the LORD from Shiloh to be with us here and save us from our enemies."

They sent a message to Shiloh and Eli's sons Hophni and Phinehas brought the Ark. When the Ark came into the camp, all Israel gave a mighty shout, and the earth shook.

The Philistines heard, and they said, "What's that shouting in the Hebrew camp?"

When they learned that the Ark had come into the camp, they were afraid, for they thought, "GOD has come into their camp!"

"Woe to us," they said. "Who can save us from the hands of these mighty gods? These are the gods that struck the Egyptians! Be brave and fight like men, Philistines, or you'll become slaves of the Hebrews."

The Philistines fought, and Israel was defeated. They were struck hard and many were killed. The Ark was captured, and Eli's sons Hophni and Phinehas died in the battle.

A messenger ran from the battle to Shiloh with his clothes torn and soil upon his head. When he arrived, he saw Eli sitting in a chair by the road, his heart trembling over the Ark of GOD. When the man told the news, the whole city cried out.

Eli said, "What's that sound?" Eli was ninety-eight years old, and he was blind.

The man hurried to Eli. "I've come from the battle," he told Eli.

"What happened, my son?" said Eli.

"Israel ran away from the Philistines, and there has been a great slaughter. Your two sons are dead, and the Ark of God has been taken."

The moment the Ark of God was mentioned, Eli fell over backward from his chair. His neck was broken and he died.

His daughter-in-law, the wife of Phinehas, was about to give birth. When she heard that the Ark was captured and her father-in-law and her husband were dead, she went into labor and gave birth.

The midwives said to her, "Don't be afraid, for you have a son."

But she didn't answer.

She named the boy Ichabod, meaning Glory Has Been Taken Away. She said, "Glory has been taken away from Israel, for the Ark of God has been captured."

The Philistines took the Ark of God to the city of Ashdod and brought it into the house of Dagon, their god, and set it up beside him.

When the people of Ashdod got up the next day, they saw Dagon, fallen face down on the ground in front of the Ark of the LORD. They took him and set him back up in his place.

The next morning they saw Dagon, fallen face down on the ground in front of the Ark of the LORD. His head and both his hands were broken off and lying in the doorway. Only his trunk was left.

The people were terrified by the LORD's power over their god Dagon.

Then the LORD caused rats to swarm from ships docked in the Philistine ports. The rats carried fleas that were infected with plague. The fleas bit the Philistines, and their skin broke out in sores. Many of them died from the tumors.

The people of Ashdod cried out, "The GOD of Israel mustn't stay among us, for HIS hand is hard upon us and Dagon our god!"

They sent for the overlords of the five Philistine cities and said, "What should we do with the Ark of the GOD of Israel?"

"Take it to Gath," they said.

They took the Ark to Gath. But the hand of the LORD was against the city, striking the people, young and old, with tumors.

They sent the Ark to Ekron. But when the Ark came to Ekron, the people of Ekron cried out, "They have brought the Ark of the GOD of Israel to kill us!"

They sent for the Philistine overlords and said to them, "Send the Ark of the GOD of Israel back to its place before it kills us all!"

The Ark was in the country of the Philistines seven months, moving from city to city, bringing death and destruction wherever it went.

Finally the Philistines called for their priests and sought advice on how to send the Ark back to the Israelites.

They harnessed cows to the cart that carried the Ark of the Covenant. The cows went straight toward Israelite territory, lowing as they went, turning neither to the right or the left. The Philistine rulers went with them as far as the border at Beth-shemesh.

The people of Beth-shemesh were harvesting wheat in the valley when they looked up and saw the Ark. They rejoiced as the cart came into a field. When the five Philistines overlords saw it, they returned to Ekron.

The Ark of the LORD was taken to Kiriath-jearim and placed in the house of Abinadab, and his son Eleazar was consecrated to watch over the Ark of the LORD. The Ark stayed at Kiriath-jearim for twenty years.

THE PEOPLE ASK FOR A KING

Samuel judged Israel all the days of his life. He traveled around from year to year, settling disputes and teaching the people the ways of the LORD. At the top of a hill above Ramah he built an altar to the LORD.

When Samuel was an old man, he set up his sons, Joel and Abijah, as judges. But his sons did not follow in his ways. They took bribes and twisted justice. The elders of Israel came to Samuel and said:

"You're old, and your sons aren't following your ways. So now set a king over us to rule us, so we can be like all the other nations."

This thing was evil in Samuel's eyes, and he prayed to the LORD.

The LORD said to Samuel, "Listen to the people and do what they ask. It is not you they have rejected. They have rejected ME as their king. Listen to them, but tell them what their king will do to them."

Samuel said to the people:

"Your king will take your best fields and vineyards and olive trees and give them to his officials. He will take your servants and your cattle and donkeys. He will take some of your sons to be soldiers, and make others plow his fields and harvest his crops, and make his chariots and weapons of war. He will take your daughters to be his cooks and bakers. After he takes your children, he will take you to be his slaves. When you cry out to the LORD for help, it will be too late."

The people refused to listen to Samuel. They said, "We must be like other nations, with a king to rule over us and lead us in war and fight our battles."

Samuel listened to the people and told the LORD how they wanted a king to rule over them.

The LORD said, "Give them what they ask for. Appoint a king to rule over them."

THE MAN WHO LOOKED FOR DONKEYS AND FOUND A KINGDOM

There was a wealthy man, Kish, from the tribe of Benjamin. He had a handsome son named Saul. There wasn't a better-looking man in Israel than Saul. He was a head and shoulders taller than everyone else.

Some donkeys that belonged to Kish were lost. So Kish said to his son Saul, "Take one of the servant boys and go look for the donkeys."

They went through the hill country but didn't find them. When they came near Ramah, Saul said to the servant, "Come, let us turn back, so my father doesn't stop worrying about the donkeys and start worrying about us."

The servant boy said, "There's a man of GOD in this town, and everything he says comes true. Let us go into town. Perhaps he can tell us where to look for the donkeys."

"What gift can we bring the man?" asked Saul. "The bread in our sacks is gone, and we have nothing to give the man of GOD."

The boy answered, "Here! I have a small piece of silver. I'll give it to the man of GOD to tell us our way."

"Good!" said Saul. "Let us go."

They went to the town of the man of GOD. They were going up the hill when they met some young women coming down to draw water from the well.

"Is the prophet in town?" they asked.

"Yes," the women answered. "He is here today for a sacrificial feast on the hill. The people won't eat until he

comes to bless the food. If you hurry, you can see him."

The men were just coming into the town when Samuel came out toward them on his way to the hill above the town. The LORD had shown Samuel the day before that Saul was coming. He had said, "At this time tomorrow I will send to you a man of Benjamin, and you will anoint him king." When Samuel saw Saul, the LORD said to him:

"Here is the man I told you about. He is the one who will rule over MY people."

Saul went up to Samuel and said, "Tell me, please, where is the prophet's house?"

"I am the prophet," Samuel said. "Come with me to the hill, for you are to eat with me today. Don't worry about those donkeys you've been looking for these three days—they've already been found. Don't worry about such things anymore, for the treasure of Israel belongs to you and your father's family."

"Why do you speak to me this way?" said Saul. "I'm from the tribe of Benjamin, the smallest tribe in Israel, and my clan is the least in the whole tribe."

Samuel led Saul and the servant to a hall where thirty guests were already seated, and he put Saul in the place of honor at the head of the table. Then he said to the cook, "Bring the special piece of meat, the one I told you to save."

The cook brought an enormous piece of meat—the best piece—and placed it in front of Saul.

"Here!" said Samuel. "This is the piece we saved for you. Eat."

Saul ate with Samuel. Then he went back into town and found a place prepared for him to spend the night.

Early the next morning, Samuel came and woke Saul. "Get up," he said. "It is time for you to go home."

Saul got up and the two of them went outside. When they came to the edge of town, Samuel said, "Tell your servant to go on ahead of us. When he has gone on, you stay here and I'll make the word of GOD known to you."

Samuel took a small jar of olive oil and poured the oil on Saul's head. He kissed him and said, "The LORD has anointed you prince over HIS people Israel. You will reign over the people of the LORD and save them from the hand of their enemies."

When Saul arrived home, his uncle said, "Where did you go?"

"To look for the donkeys," Saul replied. "When we couldn't find them, we went to Samuel."

"Tell me what Samuel said."

"He told us that the donkeys had been found." But Saul didn't tell his uncle about the kingdom or anything else that Samuel had said.

Samuel called the people to meet at Mizpah and said, "The LORD brought Israel up out of Egypt and rescued you from all your enemies. Only HE is your Savior, but you have asked for an earthly king. Well, I have found your king."

He asked the people to stand in groups of tribes and families while he cast lots to discover GOD's will. The lot fell to the tribe of Benjamin.

The Benjaminites stepped forward, and Samuel cast lots again. This time the lot fell to the family of Kish.

The family of Kish came forward, one by one, and the lot pointed to Saul. But when they looked for him, he couldn't be found.

"Where is he?" they asked the LORD.

The LORD said, "He is hiding in the baggage."

They ran and brought him out. When he stood in the middle of the people, he was head and shoulders taller than everyone else.

Samuel said to the people, "Do you see the one the LORD has chosen? There's no one like him among all the people."

"Long live the king!" they shouted.

Everyone went home, and Saul worked in his father's fields until the people came to him and asked for help against the Ammonites. The Spirit of

GOD came upon him with power, and he ordered all the tribes of Israel to send men to him for an army. They went out and defeated the Ammonites, and the people accepted Saul as king.

Samuel called the people to come to Gilgal to crown Saul king. He said to the people, "I've listened to you and set a king over you. Now you have your king! Your king will lead you, and I'll go home.

The LORD your GOD brought you from Egypt into this land. HE gave you everything you need, but you turned away from HIM to serve other gods. When you put away your idols, the LORD forgave you and saved you from your enemies. But now you're rejecting the LORD, your Savior. You want a king instead. Well, here's your king! You are getting what you asked for."

GOD REJECTS SAUL

The Philistines gathered an army of chariots and horsemen and ground troops and marched toward the Israelites. Many terrified Israelites ran away and hid among rocks and in caves or escaped across the Jordan. Excepting Saul and his son, the Israelite troops had no swords or spears because of restrictions placed by the Philistines. The Israelites brought axes, pickaxes, and sickles for the battle.

Saul was at Gilgal with his fearful troops. He received a message telling him to wait seven days for Samuel to come and offer a sacrifice to the LORD. Samuel didn't come after seven days,

and the troops were slipping away. So Saul offered the sacrifice himself. As he finished, he saw Samuel coming.

"What have you done?" said Samuel.

Saul said, "I saw the troops slipping away, and you didn't come and I thought the Philistines would attack before I pleaded with the LORD. So I forced myself to offer the sacrifice without you."

"You've been very foolish," said Samuel. "If you had kept the LORD's command, HE would have established your kingdom forever. But now your kingdom will not stand. The LORD has found someone else, because you

I made Saul king, for he has turned his back on ME and has not kept MY commandments."

Samuel was angry and he cried out to the LORD all night. The next morning he went out to Saul.

Saul said to him. "I've kept the LORD's commandment!"

Samuel said, "Then, what is this sound of sheep in my ears? This sound of cattle that I hear?"

"They brought them from the Amalekites," Saul said. "The people spared the best of the sheep and oxen to sacrifice to the LORD your GOD. We've destroyed everything else, and—"

"Stop!" said Samuel. "I will tell you what the LORD said to me last night."

"Speak."

"The LORD sent you to destroy all the Amalekites. Why didn't you listen to the voice of the LORD? Why did you pounce on the loot?"

"I did listen to the voice of the LORD!" protested Saul. "I did what the LORD sent me to do. I brought back the king of the Amalekites, but I destroyed the Amalekites. The people took the best part of the sheep and cattle to sacrifice to the LORD your GOD."

Samuel said, "Do you really think the LORD enjoys sacrifices as much as obedience? Listening to the voice of the LORD is better than any sacrifice."

"I have sinned," said Saul. "I was afraid of the people, and I listened to their voice. Please forgive me."

Samuel said, "You rejected the word of the LORD, and now the LORD rejects you as king."

As Samuel turned to go, Saul grasped the hem of Samuel's cloak and it tore.

Samuel said, "Today the LORD has torn the kingdom away from you and given it to a better man."

haven't done as the LORD commanded."

Later on, Samuel returned to Saul and said, "Listen to the voice of the LORD! He wants you to punish the Amalekites for their sneak attack against us when our people came up out of Egypt. Go now and completely destroy them. Put to death every man, woman, and child; every ox and sheep, camel and donkey."

Saul attacked and defeated the Amalekites, but he didn't destroy them all. Instead, he and his people brought back the Amalekite king and the best sheep and cattle. They kept what was good and destroyed what was worthless.

The LORD said to Samuel, "I am sorry

GOD CHOOSES DAVID

The LORD said to Samuel, "Take some oil and go to Bethlehem. I am sending you to Jesse, for I have seen MY king among his sons."

"How can I go?" said Samuel. "If Saul hears, he will kill me."

"Take a calf," said the LORD, "and say you've come to offer a sacrifice, and invite Jesse to the feast. You will anoint for ME the one that I name to you."

Samuel went to Bethlehem and the elders of the city came out to meet him. They were trembling because they were afraid of Saul.

"Do you come in peace?" they said.

"In peace," he said. "I've come to sacrifice to the LORD."

Samuel invited Jesse and his sons to the feast. When they arrived, he looked at Eliab, the firstborn, and thought, "Surely this is the LORD's anointed king."

The LORD told Samuel, "Look not at his appearance or his height. I have rejected him. The LORD does not see as people see. People look on the outward appearance, but the LORD looks into the heart."

Jesse called Abinadab, his second son, and Samuel said, "Neither has the LORD chosen this one."

Jesse brought Shammah, the third son, to him, and Samuel said, "Neither has the LORD chosen this one."

Jesse brought seven of his sons to Samuel.

Samuel said to Jesse, "The LORD has not chosen any of these. Are these all you have?"

Jesse said, "There's still the youngest, but he's watching over the flock."

"Send for him," said Samuel. "We won't eat until he comes."

Jesse sent for him, and they brought in a fresh-faced, bright-eyed, handsome youth.

"This is the one," said the LORD. "Anoint him."

Samuel took the oil and anointed him as he stood in the midst of his brothers.

The Spirit of the LORD came upon David with power from that day on. But the Spirit of the LORD turned away from Saul, and an evil spirit from the LORD tormented him.

Saul's servants said to him, "Let us help you. Just say the word, and we'll look for a man who can play the lyre. When the evil spirit is upon you, he'll play and you'll be well."

"See to it," said Saul. "Go find someone who plays well and bring him to me."

One of the servants said, "I have seen a son of Jesse of Bethlehem who plays well upon the lyre. He is a young shepherd, brave and tactful. He is a good-looking man, and the LORD is with him."

Saul sent messengers to Jesse and said, "Send me your son David, who is with the flock."

Jesse sent David to Saul and David entered Saul's service. Saul loved him greatly, and David became his armor-bearer.

Saul sent a message to Jesse, saying, "Let David stay in my service, for he has found favor in my eyes."

Whenever the evil spirit was upon Saul, David would take the lyre and play for him. Then Saul would be soothed by the music, and the evil spirit would leave him.

DAVID AND GOLIATH

Now, the Philistines gathered their army and went into Judah. Saul and the Israelites gathered and camped in the Valley of Elah, preparing for the battle. The Philistines took their stand on the hill on one side, and the Israelites took their stand on the hill on the other side, with the valley between them.

There came a champion out from the Philistine camp. He name was Goliath of Gath, and he was over eight feet tall. He wore a bronze helmet and a coat of armor that weighed one hundred and twenty-five pounds. He had bronze armor on his legs and between his shoulder blades. His carried a heavy bronze sword and a thick spear with a heavy iron point. A shield bearer walked before him.

Goliath shouted to the troops of Israel, "What are you doing here, all lined up for battle? I'm a Philistine, and you are Saul's slaves! Choose a man and send him down to fight with me! If he kills me, we'll be your slaves. But if I kill him, you'll be our slaves! I dare you, Israelites! Give me a man and let us fight!"

The three oldest sons of Jesse were serving in Saul's army, and David was going back and forth from the camp to Bethlehem, taking care of the sheep.

Jesse said to David, "Take these ten loaves of bread to your brothers in the camp right now. See how they are, and bring me back some word."

David left the flock with a keeper and took the food and went, as Jesse had commanded. When he came to the camp, the Israelites and the Philistines were lined up for battle, army against army. David left his things with the baggage keeper and ran to the battle lines.

As soon as David arrived and had talked to his brothers, the champion—Goliath, the Philistine of Gath—came out from the Philistine lines and roared his same challenge.

David heard him and he saw the Israelites running away in terror.

"Have you seen this man?" they said to David. "He comes out to insult Israel. The king will give a rich reward to the man who kills him."

"What will be given to the man who kills that Philistine?" asked David. "Who is this heathen Philistine to insult the army of the living GOD!"

Eliab, his oldest brother, overheard David talking with the soldiers, and his anger was kindled.

"Why are you here?" he said. "Who's taking care of that small flock in the wilderness? You rascal! You have just come here to see the fighting!"

"What did I do?" said David. "I was only talking."

David went to another part of the camp and talked to more soldiers. They all told him the same thing.

When Saul heard what David had said, he sent for him, and David said to Saul, "Tell your men not to be afraid. I'll fight with this Philistine."

"You can't fight him!" said Saul. "You're only a boy, and he's been a man of war all his life."

David said, "I've been a shepherd. When a lion or a bear would come and take a lamb from the flock, I would go after it and kill it and rescue the lamb from its mouth. If it attacked me, I would seize its beard and kill it!"

Saul looked doubtful, so David said, "I've killed lions and bears. This Philistine will be like one of them, for he has insulted the army of the living GOD! The GOD WHO rescued me from the paw of the lion and the paw of the bear will rescue me from the hand of this Philistine."

"Go," said Saul, "and may the LORD be with you."

Saul clothed David in his own battle gear and put a bronze helmet on his head and gave him a suit of armor. David put his sword over his clothes and tried to take a few steps in Saul's armor.

"I can't walk in this," he said. "I'm not used to it."

David took off the armor and picked up his shepherd's staff. Then he went out to the little stream in the valley and selected five smooth stones and put them in his shepherd's pouch. His sling was in his hand, and he went out toward the Philistine.

The Philistine was coming close to David, with a man in front of him carrying his shield. When he saw David, he called out:

"Am I a dog, that you come at me with sticks?" He cursed David and said, "Come to me, and I'll give your flesh to the birds of the air and the beasts of the field!"

David said, "You come to me with a sword and a spear and a lance, but I come to you with the NAME of the LORD GOD of the armies of Israel, WHOM you have insulted! Today the LORD will deliver you into my hand, and I will strike you down and cut off your head! I'll give the dead bodies of the Philistines to the birds of the air and the wild beasts of the field! All the earth will know that there is a GOD in Israel! All the people here will know that the LORD saves, but not with swords and spears! The battle is the LORD's, and HE will give you into our hand!"

When the Philistine came near to meet David, David ran quickly toward him. He put his hand into his pouch and took out a stone and slung it—and struck the Philistine on his forehead. The stone sank into Goliath's forehead, and he fell on his face to the ground.

David had defeated the mighty giant with a sling and a stone.

David ran and stood over the Philistine. He took Goliath's sword, drew it out of its sheath, killed the Philistine, and cut off his head with it.

When the Philistines saw that their champion was dead, they fled. The Israelites shouted and pursued them and looted their camp.

SAUL TURNS AGAINST DAVID

Saul was so pleased with David he would not let him go back to his father's house. Saul made him an officer and sent him out with the army. David was successful wherever Saul sent him. This was good in the eyes of all the people and Saul's servants.

Saul's son Jonathan loved David as his own brother. He gave him his cloak and his battle garb and his sword as a vow of friendship.

But as David and his troops were returning from a victory, women came out from all the towns of Israel, dancing and singing to greet Saul the king with tambourines and songs of joy. The women sang to each other as they made merry:

"Saul has killed his thousands,
and David his ten thousands!"

Saul was very angry, and he said, "The next thing you know, David will have the kingdom!"

From that day on, Saul kept his eye on David.

One day an evil spirit seized Saul and he ranted and raved like a lunatic while David was playing the lyre. Saul had his spear in his hand, and he threw it at David, thinking, *I'll pin him to the wall!*

But David ran from the point of the spear.

Saul was afraid of David because the LORD was with David but had left Saul. So Saul sent David away and made him commander of a thousand men. David

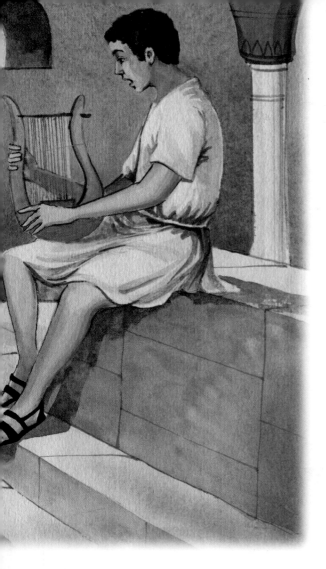

Michal loved David, and he thought, *I'll give her to him as a trap, so the hand of the Philistines will be against him.*

For the second time Saul asked David to be his son-in-law.

"This is a great honor," said David. "But I'm a poor man and not worthy of becoming the king's son-in-law."

Saul sent his servants to tell David, "The only bride-price the king wants is a hundred dead Philistines."

It pleased David to be the king's son-in-law. He went right out with his men and killed two hundred Philistines and brought the trophies back to the king.

So Saul gave David his daughter Michal to be his wife.

But when Saul saw that the LORD was with David and that all of Israel loved him, he was still more afraid of David. He sent men to David's house to watch and kill him when he came out in the morning.

David's wife, Michal, told David, "Don't wait! If you don't get away tonight, tomorrow you will be dead!"

Michal let David down through the window, and he ran away. Then she took the household gods and put them in the bed with a goat-hair pillow at its head. She covered them with clothes to look like a man asleep in the bed.

When Saul's men came to take David, she said, "He is sick."

The men went back to Saul and he sent them again, saying, "Bring him to me in the bed, so I can kill him!"

Saul's men came and discovered the household gods in the bed with the goat-hair pillow at its head. They reported to Saul, and Saul said to Michal, "Why did you deceive me and let my enemy get away?"

Michal lied, "He threatened to kill me if I didn't let him go."

was successful in everything he did, for the LORD was with him. When Saul saw David's success, he was even more afraid. But all of Israel and Judah loved David.

Then Saul said to David, "Here is my oldest daughter, Merab. I'll give her to you as a wife. Just be my mighty warrior and fight the LORD's battles." Saul was thinking, *My hand won't be against him, but let the hand of the Philistines be against him!*

David said to Saul, "Who am I, and who is my father's family, that I should be the king's son-in-law?"

But when it was time to give Merab to David, she was given to someone else.

Then Saul heard that his daughter

DAVID THE OUTLAW

David escaped to Ramath and told Samuel everything that Saul had done. Then he went to his dear friend Jonathan for help and advice, saying, "Why is your father trying to kill me?"

Jonathan told him, "I will do all that I can to save you. I will speak to my father about you, and I promise to warn you of danger."

And they made a covenant of love and friendship.

Now, Saul's anger was kindled against Jonathan when Jonathan questioned him about David. Saul feared that his own son was helping David.

"If David lives," Saul told him, "you won't be king after me. He must die!"

"Why?" said Jonathan. "What has he done?"

Saul raised his spear at Jonathan, and Jonathan left in fierce anger. He told David what had happened, and David went to Ahimelech the priest at Nob.

Ahimelech trembled when he saw David, saying, "Why are you here all alone?"

"The king has sent me on a secret mission," David answered, "and my men are waiting in a hiding place. Now, do you have anything to eat? Give me whatever is here."

"I have no ordinary bread," said Ahimelech. "I have only the holy bread in the presence of the LORD. The priests are replacing it today with fresh bread. You may have five loaves."

Now, one of Saul's men was there that day, watching—Doeg the Edomite.

David said to Ahimelech, "Do you have a spear or a sword? I was in such a hurry about the king's business, I didn't bring mine with me."

The priest said, "The sword of Goliath the Philistine, whom you killed, is here, wrapped in a cloth. If you want it, take it. It's the only one we have."

"There's none like that," said David. "Give it to me."

A few days later, Saul was sitting under a tree in Gibeah, with his spear in his hand and his servants standing around him.

"I know you're all plotting against me!" he ranted. "You think the son of Jesse is going to reward you. Nobody tells me anything or helps me find him!"

Doeg the Edomite was standing with Saul's servants, and he said, "I saw the son of Jesse at Nob a few days ago. Ahimelech prayed for him and gave him food and the sword of Goliath the Philistine."

The king sent for Ahimelech and all the priests at Nob and said to them, "Why are you and David plotting against me? Why did you give him food and a sword and pray for him? You helped him rebel against me!"

Ahimelech said, "David is your loyal servant. He's your own son-in-law. Of course I prayed for him. My family and I don't know anything about plots against you."

"You must die, Ahimelech!" said the king. "You and your whole family!"

Saul turned to his palace guards. "Go, kill all the priests of the LORD!" he commanded. "They knew David was running away, and they didn't tell me! They are helping my enemy!"

Saul's servants wouldn't lift their daggers against the priests of the LORD, so he said to Doeg, "You, then! Slay the priests!"

Doeg the Edomite slew the priests and killed eighty-five of them. Then he went to Nob and put the whole city to the sword. He killed men, women and children; cattle, donkeys, and sheep.

But Abiathar, one of Ahimelech's sons, got away. He ran to David and told him how Saul had killed the priests of the LORD.

"I knew Doeg was at Nob," said David. "It is my fault that your father's family was killed. Stay with me. The one who wants to kill me wants to kill you, too. Don't be afraid. I'll watch over you."

David went out into the wilderness of Judah and hid in a cave. When his brothers heard, they went out to him, and so did many people with debts and other troubles. There David gathered a band of four hundred outlaws.

While David was in the wilderness, Saul gave Michal to a man named Palti. David also started a new life. He remarried and had many children.

One day, Saul went out to the wilderness with a band to men, looking for David. David and his men were sitting in the back of a cave when Saul went into the cave to rest.

David's men whispered, "The LORD has given your enemy into your hands. You can do whatever you want to him."

"We mustn't strike the LORD's anointed," said David. Then he sneaked up behind Saul and cut off the hem of his cloak.

As Saul left the cave, David went after him, bowed low, and held up the piece of cloth.

"Behold!" he said. "The LORD gave you into my hand, but I didn't kill you, because you are the LORD's anointed. You can see there's no disloyalty in me. I haven't hurt you, yet you are trying to kill me. The LORD will judge between us, but my hand won't be against you."

Saul said, "Is that your voice, my son David?" Then he began to weep, saying, "You are righteous. You were good to me, and I wronged you. The LORD will reward you. Now I know that you will be king, and the kingdom will be established in your hand. Promise you won't kill my family and wipe out my name."

Saul returned home, but David and his men went back into hiding.

It came to pass that Samuel died, and all Israel gathered and mourned for him. They buried him at his home in Ramah.

David and his men and their families moved near the border between the Philistines and Judah. Many experienced soldiers joined him—the best and the bravest warriors.

David went to Achish, king of Gath, and he settled in the country of the Philistines. He and his men raided the desert tribes and brought back sheep, cattle, donkeys, camels, and clothing. When Achish asked him about the raids, David said he was attacking Judah. Thus Achish trusted David and believed that he was loyal to the Philistines.

A Ghost Story

Saul camped with his troops in the Valley of Jezreel, at Gilboa. The Philistines camped across the valley at Shunem. When Saul saw the Philistine army, he trembled and his heart pounded with fear. He asked the LORD for help, but the LORD didn't answer him, either through dreams or priests or prophets.

The LORD had commanded HIS people not to deal in fortune-telling, omen readings, or seeking mediums to call up spirits of the dead. Saul himself had sent all the fortune-tellers and mediums out of the land. But now Saul was desperate. He didn't know where to turn for help.

"Go find a medium for me," he said to his servants. "I want to consult someone who can talk to a ghost."

They said, "There's a medium at Endor."

Saul took off his royal robes and put on different clothes to disguise himself. He took two men with him and went to the woman at night.

"Bring up a ghost for me," he said. "Call up the one I name to you."

"No, sir," she answered. "Surely you know that Saul sent all the mediums and fortune-tellers out of the land. It is against the law to consult the spirits of the dead." She looked keenly at the stranger. "Are you setting a trap for me? I will be put to death if anyone finds out."

"It's all right," he said. "I promise, you won't be punished."

"Whom shall I call up for you?"

"Call up Samuel."

The woman saw Samuel and she screamed in a loud voice, "Why did you deceive me? You are Saul!"

The king said to her, "Don't be afraid. What do you see?"

"I see a god rising up from the earth!"

"What does he look like?"

"An old man is rising up, and he's wrapped in a cloak."

Saul knew it was Samuel, and he bowed with his face to the ground.

"Why have you disturbed me?" said Samuel.

"I'm in great trouble!" said Saul. "The Philistines are fighting against me, and GOD has turned away from me. HE won't answer me through prophets or dreams. I've called you to tell me what I should do."

Samuel said, "Why do you ask me, when the LORD has turned away from you and become your enemy? The LORD has done what I told you HE would do. HE has torn the kingdom from your hand and given it to David. He has done this because you didn't listen to HIS voice. Tomorrow HE will give Israel and you and the army of Israel into the hands of the Philistines. Then you and your sons will join me here."

Saul immediately threw himself full length on the ground. He was filled with fear because of Samuel's words. He had no strength, for he hadn't eaten anything all day and all night.

The woman saw that Saul was very upset and said, "I listened to you and risked my life and did what you asked. Now please listen to me, and let me give you a little food so you'll have strength when you go on your way."

"I won't eat," he said; but his servants and the woman urged him, and he got up and sat on the couch.

The woman hurried out and prepared a fatted calf and baked flat bread and set the food in front of Saul and his servants. They ate and then went off into the night.

SAUL'S LAST BATTLE

The Philistines were gathered at Aphek, and the Israelites were camped in the Valley of Jezreel. When the Philistine commanders reviewed the troops, they saw David and his men with Achish. "What are those Hebrews doing here?" they asked.

"This is David, the servant of Saul, king of Israel," said Achish. "He has been with me ever since he deserted from Saul. I find no fault in him."

But the commanders said, "Send the man back lest he turn against us during the battle. Isn't this the one about whom they sing 'Saul has killed his thousands, and David his ten thousands'?"

Achish said to David, "You've been trustworthy, but the lords of the Philistines don't approve of you. Go back now in peace."

And David took his men back to the wilderness.

A great battle was fought that day in the Valley of Jezreel. The Philistines attacked and the Israelites scattered. Many of them fell dead on Mount Gilboa, including Saul's son Jonathan and two of his other sons.

The battle raged on with heavy fighting around Saul. When some Philistines found him, he shook with fear. The archers shot him with their arrows and wounded him in the stomach.

Saul said to his armor-bearer, "Draw your sword and run it through me, or the Philistines will come and kill me and abuse my body."

But the fearful armor-bearer didn't want to do it. So Saul took the sword and fell upon it. When the armor-bearer saw that Saul was dead, he fell upon his own sword and died with him.

The next day, the Philistines found Saul's body on Mount Gilboa. They cut off his head and stripped off his armor. They put Saul's armor in the temple of Asherah, and they fastened his body to the wall of the city of Beth-shan.

When the people of Jabesh heard what the Philistines had done to Saul, all the brave men rose up and traveled that night. They sneaked into Beth-shan and took Saul's corpse and the corpses of his sons down from the wall. They brought them home and buried their bones under a tree in Jabesh.

When David learned that Saul and Jonathan were dead, he tore his clothes in mourning, and so did all the men with him. They cried and wailed and fasted until evening for Saul and his son Jonathan and the LORD's people.

David wrote a song about the death of Saul and Jonathan. He lamented:

Saul and Jonathan, the warriors we loved!
Their swords are gone;
their shields are covered with blood!

After consulting the LORD, David took his wives and his men and their families and settled in Hebron. The people of Judah came to Hebron and anointed David as king over Judah.

Meanwhile, Abner, Saul's cousin and commander, took Ish-bosheth, the only living son of Saul, and made him a king. First he was king over Gilead, and then he was king over all the northern tribes of Israel. He declared war on David and Judah.

Abner went out with Ish-bosheth's men. Joab, David's cousin and commander, led David's men. The two armies met at a pool near the city of Gibeon and took up their positions on opposite sides of the pool. Fierce fighting broke out, and Abner's men were defeated by David's men, and they ran away.

Joab's brother Asahel ran after Abner. Abner turned around and said, "Is that you, Asahel?"

"Yes!"

"Turn aside and chase someone else!"

But Asahel kept running after Abner, and Abner said:

"Turn aside! If I kill you, there will be trouble between me and your brother Joab!"

He refused, and Abner struck him in the belly with the butt of his spear, and he fell down dead.

Joab and Abishai, his other brother, pursued Abner all day. Just as the sun was setting, they reached a hilltop. Abner's men gathered behind him and

called down, "Must the sword devour forever? Surely you know the end will be bitter. How long will it be before you order your men to turn away from chasing their fellow Israelites?"

"As GOD lives," said Joab, "it is a good thing you spoke when you did. My men were prepared to chase you all night." Then he sounded the trumpet, and all the troops gave up the chase and the fighting ended.

Abner went back to Gilead, and Joab returned to Hebron.

The fighting between Saul's family and David's family went on a long time. David grew stronger and stronger, while Saul's people became weaker and weaker.

Abner saw that he couldn't defeat David, so he sent messengers to David, saying, "Make a treaty with me, and I'll bring all the northern tribes Israel to you."

David said, "First you must return my wife, Saul's daughter Michal."

Abner took Michal to David, and said, "Let me bring the leaders of the tribes here to make a treaty with you, and you can reign over all your heart desires."

David sent Abner away in peace.

When Joab found out, he went to David and said, "What have you done? Abner came to spy on you, and you sent him away in peace!"

Without telling David, Joab had Abner brought back to Hebron. Then Joab killed Abner, in revenge for the blood of Joab's brother, who had been killed by Abner.

When David heard, he ordered all his people, including Joab, to mourn for Abner. Abner was buried in Hebron, and David cried loudly over his grave. The people noticed, and it was good in their eyes. Everything the king did was good in the eyes of the people.

Now, Saul's son, Ish-bosheth, knew his life was in danger, too. And indeed, two of his own servants, Baanah and Rechab, went to his house when he was resting in the heat of the day. They sneaked past the doorkeeper and entered his bedroom and killed him and cut off his head.

The men traveled through the night to Hebron and brought Ish-bosheth's head to David, expecting a reward.

"Behold the head of Ish-bosheth, son of your enemy!" they said. "Today the LORD has given you revenge on Saul and his family!"

David said, "You wicked men have killed an innocent man in cold blood! I will avenge his blood and rid the land of you!" And David ordered that the servants be killed.

They took Ish-bosheth's head and buried it in Abner's grave.

The leaders of the northern tribes of

Israel came to Hebron and anointed David king over Israel. He was now king over all the tribes, both Israel and Judah.

It came to pass that David took his soldiers to Jerusalem, and the Jebusites who lived in the land said to him, "You will never enter our city!"

They thought they were safe in their strong fortress on top of Mount Zion. But David knew about a tunnel that brought water from outside the city wall.

"Crawl through the tunnel," he said to his men.

The soldiers squeezed up through the tunnel under the wall, and came out in the middle of the city. They defeated the Jebusites and captured Jerusalem.

David moved into the fortress. He rebuilt it and called it the City of David.

When the Philistines heard that David had been anointed king over all Israel, they sent an army to capture him.

Seeing the Philistine army camped outside the walls of Jerusalem, David asked the LORD:

"Should I attack the Philistines? Will you give them into my hand?"

"Go!" said the LORD. "I will give the Philistines into your hand! Go up behind them, opposite the aspen trees. As soon as you hear the sound of marching in the treetops, move boldly. The LORD will be going in front of you to strike the Philistines."

David did as GOD commanded. He waited for the sound of the wind rustling in the treetops, then he struck down the Philistines and drove them from Jerusalem to the border of their own territory.

DAVID BRINGS BACK THE ARK

David gathered his troops and went to bring the Ark of GOD back from Kiriath-jearim, where it had been for twenty years. They put it on a new cart and carried it away from the house of Abinadab. Uzzah and Ahio, the sons of Abinadab, were driving the cart, and Ahio was walking in front of the Ark.

David and all Israel were celebrating in the presence of the LORD with all their might, singing and playing lyres and tambourines and castanets and cymbals. As they came to the threshing floor of Nacon, the oxen stumbled, and Uzzah reached out his hand and touched the Ark. The LORD's wrath flared up against Uzzah, and GOD struck him down. He died there in front of the Ark.

David was angry because the LORD had burst out against Uzzah, and he was afraid of the LORD. "How can the Ark of the LORD come to me?" he said.

He wasn't willing to bring the Ark into the City of David, so he had it taken to the house of Obed-edom. The Ark stayed in the house of Obed-edom three months, and the LORD blessed Obed-edom and his whole family.

When David heard that Obed-edom and his family had been blessed because of the Ark, he went and brought the Ark up to the City of David with rejoicing. He and the whole house of Israel were bringing up the Ark with shouts and the sound of the trumpet.

They brought the Ark of the LORD and set it up in its place inside the tent that David had set up for it. David offered sacrifices to the LORD, and then he blessed the people. He gave a loaf of bread, a date cake, and a raisin cake to every man and woman in Israel. Then all the people went home, and David went to bless his own family.

David was living in a beautiful palace with his wives and children. The LORD had given him rest from his enemies, and all was well. He sent for Nathan the prophet and said:

"Here I am, sitting in a house of cedar, while the Ark of GOD is in a tent of cloth."

Nathan said to the king, "Go, do whatever is in your heart, for the LORD is with you."

The word of the LORD came to Nathan, saying:

"Tell David, 'The LORD says, I do not need you to build a house for ME. Ever since I brought the Israelites out of Egypt, I have been moving from place to place in a tent. I never asked MY people to build ME a house of cedar.'

"Tell David, 'The LORD also says, I took you from the flock to rule over MY people Israel, and I have been with you wherever you have gone, and defeated all your enemies. I will make your name great. Now I declare to you that the LORD will make a house for you—a dynasty to rule after you. When you are dead, your son will build MY house. When he commits sin, I will punish him, but I will not take MY loving kindness from him, as I took it from Saul. The throne of David will be established forever.' "

Nathan told these words to David and David went to the tent where the Ark was and sat in the presence of the LORD.

"Who am I," he said, "and what is my house—my family—that YOU have brought me this far? You've done so much for me already, and now YOU're doing even more. How great YOU are, LORD GOD! There is no GOD like YOU, and no people like YOUR people. All nations have heard of YOU because of the great things YOU have done for YOUR people. Now, LORD GOD, I ask YOU to bless my house forever."

DAVID'S SIN

In the spring of the year, when kings go out to battle, David sent Joab and his army to attack the Ammonites. While the army was laying siege to the city of Rabbah, David sat in Jerusalem.

One afternoon David got up from his bed and walked around on the flat roof of his house, looking out onto the dwellings of the city. He chanced to see a woman bathing, and she was very beautiful. He asked about her and was told that she was Bathsheba, the wife of Uriah the Hittite, who was serving in the war.

David met with the woman and he fell in love with her, even though she was married to Uriah.

David sent a message to Joab, asking him to send Uriah to him. When Uriah came, David asked him how he was and how the troops were doing and how the fighting was going.

Then David told Uriah, "Go down to your house and bathe your feet."

Uriah went out from the king's house

good conscience go to my house to eat and drink in comfort with my wife? As the LORD lives, I won't do this thing."

David said, "Stay here today, and tomorrow I'll send you back."

Uriah stayed in Jerusalem that day and the next. David called him, and he ate and drank with him, but still Uriah would not be convinced to leave his post and go home.

In the morning David wrote a letter to Joab and sent it with Uriah. He wrote, "Put Uriah in the face of the fiercest fighting and leave him, so he will be struck down and die."

Joab put Uriah at a place where he knew the enemy would be strong. The Ammonite men of the city of Rabbah came out and fought with Joab, and some of David's troops fell, and Uriah the Hittite died.

Joab sent a message to David with news of the battle. He told the messenger, "When you finish reporting all the news about the battle to the king, if the king's anger rises and he says, 'Why did you get so near the city to fight? Didn't you know they would shoot from the wall?' then say, 'Your servant Uriah the Hittite is also dead.'"

The messenger went to David and told him everything Joab said.

The king said to the messenger, "Tell Joab, 'Don't let this thing seem evil in your eyes. You never know who's going to be killed in battle. Strengthen your attack on the city and destroy it."

Uriah's wife heard that her husband was dead, and she cried and lamented for him. When the mourning was over, David had her brought into his house and she became his wife and gave birth to his son.

But the thing David had done was evil in the eyes of the LORD.

and lay at the entrance with the palace guards, but he did not go down to his house as David had asked.

David was told that Uriah didn't go down to his house, and he said to Uriah:

"You've been away a long time. Why haven't you gone to your house?"

Uriah said, "The Ark and Israel and Judah are sitting in huts, and my master Joab and my master's servants are camped in the open field. How can I in

The LORD sent Nathan the prophet to David. Nathan came to him and told him a parable:

"There were two men who lived in the same city. One was rich and the other poor. The rich man had many flocks and herds. The poor man had nothing but one little lamb that he had bought. He took care of her and raised her with his children. She ate from his dish and drank from his cup and lay in his lap. She was like a daughter to this poor man.

"A traveler came to stay with the rich man, and the rich man was unwilling to take an animal from his own flock or herd to prepare for the traveler. But he took the poor man's lamb and prepared it for his visitor's meal."

David's anger flared hot against the rich man in the parable, and he said to Nathan:

"The man who has done this deserves to die! He should pay for the poor man's lamb four times because he did this thing and had no pity!"

"*You* are that man!" said Nathan. "The LORD GOD of Israel says, 'I anointed you king over Israel and I saved you from the hand of Saul. I gave you the house of Israel and Judah, and if that was too little, I would have given you more. Why did you despise the word of the LORD and do what is evil in HIS eyes? You killed Uriah the Hittite and took his wife. You struck him down with the sword of the Ammonites! Now the sword will never leave your house. I will raise up evil against you from within your own house!' "

"I have sinned against the LORD," moaned David.

"The LORD has put away your sin," assured Nathan. "You won't die. But because you have scorned the LORD by doing this thing, the child will die."

Nathan went to his house, and the LORD struck the child that Uriah's wife had born to David, and he became very sick.

David pleaded with GOD for the child. He fasted and spent the night lying on the ground. His officials tried to make him get up, but he refused, and he wouldn't eat.

David did this for seven days, and then the child died.

David's servants were afraid to tell him that the child was dead.

"While the child was alive, he wouldn't listen to us," they said. "Who knows what he'll do when he finds out that the child is dead!"

David saw them whispering together.

"Is the boy dead?" he asked.

"He's dead," they answered.

David got up and bathed and changed his clothes. He went into the house of the LORD and worshiped. Then he came back to his house and ate.

"What does this mean?" asked his servants. "You fasted and cried while the child was alive, but when the child died, you got up and ate."

David said, "While the child was still alive, I fasted and cried because I thought the LORD might be gracious to me and let the child live. But now that he's dead, why should I fast? Can I bring him back? Someday I'll go where he is, but he'll never come back to me."

David comforted his wife Bathsheba. She gave birth to another son and named him Solomon, and the LORD loved him.

ABSALOM REBELS

In all Israel there was no man so praised for his beauty as David's beloved son Absalom. He was without a blemish, from the sole of his foot to the crown of his head. Once a year he would cut his thick hair, and when he weighed the hair of his head on the king's scales, it weighed five pounds.

And David loved Absalom dearly, even though Absalom had often rebelled against his father the king, acting on his own accord.

Absalom had chariots and horses and fifty men to attend to him. He went out early every morning and stood by the gate near the place of judgment, and when anyone came up who was taking a legal matter to the king, he would say, "You have a good case, but there's no one in the king's service to hear you. But now, if *I* were judge, everyone with a case could come to me, and I would give them justice."

Whenever people came and bowed down to him, he would reach out his hand and take hold of them and kiss them. He acted thus toward all Israelites who came to the king for justice, and he

stole the hearts of the people.

He did this for four years, building up support for himself and plotting against David.

At the end of four years Absalom said to his father the king, "Please let me go to Hebron to worship. When I was staying in Syria, I had promised the LORD that if HE brought me back to Jerusalem, I would worship HIM."

"Go in peace," said the king.

So Absalom went to Hebron. There, he invited two hundred guests from Jerusalem to a sacrificial feast. Then he

sent secret agents to all the tribes of Israel to tell the people, "When you hear the sound of trumpets, say, 'Absalom is king in Hebron!' "

A messenger came to David, saying, "The hearts of the people of Israel have gone after Absalom."

David said to his servants, "We must run away while we can. Hurry, before Absalom overtakes the city."

"We will do whatever the king decides," said his servants.

Then David and the people with him went out on foot.

All the land was crying loudly as King David and his people walked out of the city, crossed the Brook Kidron, and went out toward the wilderness. Zadok and Abiathar the priests and all the Levites were with him, carrying the Ark of the Covenant.

After they crossed over the Brook Kidron, they set the Ark down, and the king said to Zadok, "Take the Ark back to the city. If I find favor in the eyes of the LORD, HE'll bring me back and let me see it again. If not, well, here I am. Let the LORD do whatever is good in HIS eyes. You go back to the city, and I'll wait in the wilderness until I hear from you."

Zadok and the other priests took the Ark back to Jerusalem, and David went up the Mount of Olives, crying as he went. His head was covered and he was barefoot. All the people with him covered their heads, and they went up with him, weeping as they went.

David was told that Ahithophel, his chief advisor, was with Absalom, and he prayed, "O LORD, turn around Ahithophel's advice!"

When David reached the top of the hill, he saw his friend Hushai coming toward him with his shirt torn and soil upon his head.

David said, "If you go with me, you will be a burden. But if you return to the city, you can help me. When Absalom arrives in Jerusalem, he'll have my advisor Ahithophel with him. Ahithophel will give him good advice. I want you to turn that advice around. Go to Absalom and say, 'I'll be your servant, O King. As I have been your father's servant in the past, so now I will be your servant.' Then you can advise Absalom and overturn Ahithophel's advice. When you find out what Absalom is going to do, go to Zadok and Abiathar the priests and have them send their sons to me with everything you hear."

Hushai went back to the city, and David and his people walked on.

They met a man from Saul's family named Shimei, who cursed David and threw stones at him and the people.

"Get out of here, you man of blood!" cried Shimei. "The LORD is punishing you because you spilled the blood of the house of Saul. The LORD has given the kingdom to your son Absalom! You are ruined, because you are a man of blood!"

Abishai, Joab's brother, said to David, "Why should this dead dog curse my lord the king? Let me go over and take off his head!"

But the king said, "My own son is trying to kill me. Leave this man alone and let him curse. The LORD has allowed this. Perhaps the LORD will see my troubles."

So David and his men went on the road, while Shimei went along on the hillside opposite and cursed and threw stones and tossed dirt at them.

By the time the king and all the people with him reached the Jordan River, they were exhausted.

BAD ADVICE FOR ABSALOM

Hushai arrived in Jerusalem just as Absalom was entering the city. Hushai went to him and said, "Long live the king!"

"Where's your loyalty to your friend?" said Absalom. "Why didn't you go with him?"

"I will be loyal to the one the LORD has chosen," said Hushai. "I served your father, and I will serve you."

Then Absalom turned to Ahithophel and said, "Give *your* advice. What should we do?"

Ahithophel said, "David and his people are exhausted. Let me take some men and go after him tonight. I'll surprise him and throw his men into a panic. They'll all run away and we'll be able to kill him. It's only necessary to kill one man."

Absalom turned back to Hushai, saying, "Should we do what Ahithophel says? Or do you have a better idea?"

Hushai said, "This time Ahithophel's advice isn't good. Your father and his men are mighty warriors. Don't attack now when they're as angry and fierce as a wild bear robbed of her cubs. Besides, your father is an expert man of war. He won't spend the night with his people. He's probably already hiding in a cave. As soon as his men kill some of yours, everyone who hears about it will say you've been defeated, and your supporters will panic.

"Here is my advice: Gather an army from all Israel, and you yourself lead the troops into battle. Think of the great victory! If David is in the countryside, you will surprise him like dew falling on the ground. If he is in a walled city, you can drag it down with ropes until no stone is left."

Absalom liked the idea of leading the troops himself. It seemed much better than sending Ahithophel.

Absalom announced, "Hushai's advice is better than Ahithophel's!"

And everyone agreed. They didn't know that the LORD had decided to overturn Ahithophel's good advice in order to bring evil upon Absalom.

Hushai went to Zadok and Abiathar, the priests, and told them to send a message to David immediately.

When David and his people heard the message, they quickly crossed the Jordan. David organized his troops and sent them in three groups under three commanders.

"I'll march out with you," David said to the three commanders.

"Don't come with us," the commanders said. "It will matter little if we were to flee or be killed. But you are like ten thousand of us. It is better that you lead us from inside the city."

David stood beside the city gate while the troops marched out. He ordered his commanders, "For my sake, deal gently with young Absalom."

The battle took place in the forest of Ephraim. The troops of Israel were defeated by David's men, and the slaughter was great. The battle spread out over the countryside, and the forest devoured more people than the sword.

Absalom happened to come upon David's men just as the mule he was riding went under the tangled branches of a great oak tree. Absalom's head of long, thick hair caught in the tree, and there he dangled between heaven and earth while the mule went on without him.

A man saw him and told Joab, "I have seen Absalom dangling from an oak."

"Why didn't you strike him?" demanded Joab. "I would have given you ten pieces of silver."

The man said to Joab, "Even if I felt in my palm the weight of a thousand pieces of silver, I would not reach out my hand against the king's son, for we heard what the king said to you about Absalom."

"I will not waste my time with you," said Joab, and he took three wooden barbs and plunged them into Absalom's heart, still alive in the branches of the oak. Joab's ten armor-bearers surrounded

Absalom and struck him and killed him.

Joab sounded the trumpet, and David's troops came back from chasing Israel. They took Absalom and threw him into a great pit in the forest and heaped a pile of stones over it.

Ahimaaz, son of Zadok the priest, said, "Let me run and take the good news to the king that the LORD has delivered him from his enemies."

"No," said Joab. "Today is not the day for you to take news. Another day, perhaps. The king's son is dead."

Then Joab turned to his Ethiopian servant, Cushi, and said, "Go, tell the king what you have seen."

The Ethiopian bowed to Joab and ran off.

Ahimaaz said to Joab again, "Please, let me run after your servant."

"No," said Joab. "Why should you go? Your news isn't welcome."

"Whatever happens, I want to go," said Ahimaaz.

"Run, then," said Joab.

Ahimaaz ran down the road.

And it happened that he caught up to and then ran past Cushi.

BAD NEWS FOR DAVID

David was sitting between the two gates of the city. There was a lookout on the roof of the gate by the wall, and he saw a man running alone and told David.

"If he's alone, he has good news in his mouth," said David.

The runner came closer, and the lookout saw another man running.

"Look!" he called to the gatekeeper. "There's another man running alone!"

"This one also brings good news," said David.

"The first one is Ahimaaz!" called the lookout. "I can tell by the way he is running."

"He is a good man," said David. "He must be bringing good news."

Ahimaaz called out to the king, "All is well!"

He bowed down to the king and said, "Praise the LORD your GOD, WHO has delivered the men who raised their hand against the king."

The king said, "Is it well with young Absalom?"

Ahimaaz said, "I saw a great commotion, and I do not know what it was about."

"Stand over there," said David.

Then Cushi came and said, "Good news! The LORD has delivered you today from the hand of all the rebels."

The king said, "Is it well with the young man Absalom?"

Cushi answered, "May all the enemies of my lord the king, and all who rebel against you, be as Absalom is now."

David staggered up the steps of the city wall, crying:

"O my son Absalom! My son, my son Absalom! If only I had died instead! O Absalom, my son, my son!"

The victory that day turned into mourning for all the people, because they heard that the king was grieving for his son. They stole into the city like men

ashamed who have run from a battle.

The king covered his face and cried out in a loud voice, "My son Absalom! Absalom, my son, my son!"

Joab went to David and said, "You are behaving as if your men mean nothing to you. They saved your life. You love those who hate you and hate those who love you. Would you be happy if we were all dead and Absalom alive? Now, get up and speak to your servants. If you don't, no one will be left, and it will be worse for you than ever."

David went and sat by the city gate, and all the people heard and gathered around him as he spoke. Then he returned to Jerusalem and ruled as king over Israel and Judah.

THE SWEET SINGER OF ISRAEL

The people loved David because he was a great warrior and saved them from their enemies. But David knew that his greatness came from GOD. David loved the LORD, and the LORD loved David, even though David had sinned.

David knew much joy and much sorrow in his long life. He wrote songs of praise and songs of sorrow and joy. He was known as "the sweet singer of Israel," and his songs were written down for all generations.

PSALM 23

The LORD is my Shepherd; I shall not want.
HE maketh me to lie down in green pastures.
HE leadeth me beside the still waters.
HE restoreth my soul.
HE leadeth me in the paths of righteousness
    for HIS name's sake.
Yea, though I walk through the valley
    of the shadow of death, I will fear no evil,
    for THOU art with me.
THY rod and THY staff, they comfort me.
THOU preparest a table before me in
    the presence of mine enemies.
THOU anointest my head with oil.
My cup runneth over.
Surely goodness and mercy shall follow me
    all the days of my life,
And I will dwell in the house of the LORD
    for ever.

FROM PSALM 47

O clap your hands, all ye people.
Shout unto GOD with the voice of triumph.
For the LORD most high is awesome.
HE is a great King over all the earth.

PSALM 100

Make a joyful noise unto the LORD, all ye lands.
Serve the LORD with gladness.
Come before HIS presence with singing.
Know ye that the LORD, HE is GOD.
It is HE that hath made us,
    and not we ourselves.
We are HIS people, and the sheep of HIS pasture.
Enter into HIS gates with thanksgiving,
And into HIS courts with praise.
Be thankful unto HIM, and bless HIS name.
For the LORD is good, HIS mercy is everlasting.

FROM PSALM 27

The LORD is my light and my salvation;
    whom shall I fear?
The LORD is the strength of my life;
    of whom shall I be afraid?

FROM PSALM 18

A Psalm of David when the LORD delivered
him from the hand of Saul

I will love THEE, O LORD, my strength.
The LORD is my rock, and my fortress,
    and my deliverer.

ᴄ·ᴐ

I will call upon the LORD, WHO is worthy
    to be praised;
So shall I be saved from mine enemies.

FROM PSALM 51

A Psalm of David when Nathan came
to him after he had married Bathsheba

Have mercy upon me, O GOD,
    according to THY loving-kindness:
According unto the multitude of THY tender
    mercies blot out my transgressions.
Wash me thoroughly from mine iniquity,
    and cleanse me from sin.
For I acknowledge my transgression,
    and my sin is ever before me.

ᴄ·ᴐ

Create in me a new heart, O GOD;
    and renew a right spirit within me.

FROM PSALM 3

A Psalm of David when he fled
from Absalom his son

LORD, how are they increased that trouble me!
Many are they that rise up against me.
Many there be which say of my soul,
    "There is no help for him in GOD."
But THOU, O LORD, art a shield for me;
My glory and the lifter up of my head.

FROM PSALM 22

My GOD, my GOD, why hast THOU forsaken me?
Why art THOU so far from helping me,
    and from the words of my roaring?
O my GOD, I cry in the daytime,
    but THOU hearest not;
And in the night season, and am not silent.
But THOU art holy, O THOU THAT inhabitest
    the praises of Israel.

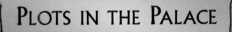

PLOTS IN THE PALACE

King David was very old, and he grew feeble. His servants wrapped him in bedclothes, but still he felt cold, for his strength was leaving him.

Adonijah, David's oldest son, plotted to become king in his father's place. He bought some chariots and horsemen and hired fifty men to run ahead of him as he drove through the city.

David his father never questioned him.

Everyone in the city noticed the prince. Like his brother Absalom, he was very handsome, and some people thought he looked like a king.

Adonijah met with Joab the com- mander and Abiathar the priest, and they agreed to help him. But Zadok the priest, Benaiah, the captain of the palace guard, Nathan the prophet, and some of David's warriors refused to sup- port Adonijah.

Adonijah held a great feast at the well of En-rogel, just outside the city. He invited all the king's sons and all the royal officials. But he did not invite Nathan the prophet, Benaiah, the war- riors, or his own brother Solomon.

Nathan the prophet said to Bath- sheba, Solomon's mother, "Haven't you heard that Adonijah has named himself king, and David doesn't know it? Let me give you some advice, so you can

Now Adonijah has become king, and you don't even know it. He held a great feast and invited all the king's sons, Abiathar the priest, and Joab the commander. But he did not invite Solomon. Now the eyes of all Israel are on you to tell them who will sit on your throne after you. If you do not name someone, I and my son Solomon will be in danger when you are sleeping with your ancestors."

She was still speaking when Nathan came in. He bowed before the king and said, "My lord, did you say Adonijah will reign after you and sit on your throne? Today he went and sacrificed many sheep, oxen, and bulls, and invited all the king's sons, Joab the commander of the army, and Abiathar the priest. They are eating and drinking with him and saying, 'Long live King Adonijah!' But I, your servant, and Zadok the priest, and Benaiah and Solomon were not invited. Did you do this and not tell us who would sit on your throne after you?"

David called for Bathsheba to draw near, and he said, "I will keep my promise. Your son Solomon will reign after me and sit on my throne. I will appoint him today."

Bathsheba bowed low and said, "May my lord King David live forever."

"Bring Zadok the priest, Nathan the prophet, and Benaiah!" ordered David.

When they came, King David said to them, "Take my servants with you and put my son Solomon on my own mule, and take him down to the spring at Gihon. Have Zadok the priest and Nathan the prophet anoint him king over Israel. Then blow the trumpet and shout, 'Long live King Solomon!' Bring him here to sit on my throne. I have appointed him to rule over Israel and Judah."

save your own life and the life of your son Solomon. Go to King David right now and say to him, 'Hasn't the king sworn to me that my son Solomon would reign after you and sit on your throne? Then why has Adonijah become king?' While you are still speaking, I will come in and say the same thing."

Bathsheba went to the king in his bedroom, where, Abishag, his handmaid, was caring for him.

Bathsheba bowed low, and David said, "What is the matter?"

"My lord," said Bathsheba, "you swore to me that my son Solomon would reign after you and sit on your throne.

"So be it," said Benaiah. "May the LORD be with Solomon as HE has been with my lord the king. May HE make his throne even greater than the throne of my lord King David."

Zadok the priest, Nathan the prophet, Benaiah, and the palace guards had Solomon ride on King David's mule to the spring of Gihon just outside the city. Zadok took holy oil and anointed Solomon. They blew the trumpet, and all the people shouted, "Long live King Solomon!" Then the people followed him back up to the city, playing on pipes and rejoicing so loudly that the earth was split by their noise.

Adonijah and all his guests heard the sound as they were finishing their feast. Joab heard the trumpet and said, "What's the meaning of this uproar in the city?"

While he was still speaking, a messenger arrived and said, "King David has made Solomon king! Zadok the priest and Nathan the prophet anointed him king at Gihon. The entire city is rejoicing. That is the noise you heard. What is more, Solomon is now sitting on the throne. What is more, the king's servants are congratulating King David and saying 'May your GOD make Solomon's name more famous than yours, and his throne greater than your throne.' What is more, the king bowed on his bed and said, 'Blessed be the LORD, the GOD of Israel, WHO has let one of my sons sit on my throne, and let me see it with my own eyes.' "

Adonijah's guests trembled with fear, and they all got up and hurried away. Adonijah ran to the great altar and put his hands on the horns at the corners of the altar, the holiest place he could touch.

Solomon was told, "Adonijah is afraid of you. He's holding onto the horns of the altar, saying, 'May King Solomon swear to me that he won't kill me with the sword!'"

Solomon said, "If he proves to be trustworthy, not a hair will fall from his head. But if evil is found in him, he must die."

King Solomon sent for Adonijah, and they brought him down from the altar. He came and bowed to the king, and Solomon told him, "Go to your house."

When it was time for David to die, he said to his son Solomon:

"I go the way of all the earth. Therefore,

be strong and show yourself to be a man. Follow the teachings of the LORD our GOD and walk in HIS ways. Be wise in all that you do. As for Joab, you know that he deserted me for Adonijah. You are a wise man. You will know how to deal justice to Joab. Deal kindly with those who were loyal to me."

And these were the last words of David:

"He that rules over men must be just, ruling in the fear of GOD. And he shall be like the light of the morning without clouds when the sun rises, and like the tender grass springing out of the earth in clear sunshine after rain."

David died and slept with his fathers and was buried in the City of David. He had ruled as king for forty years.

And Solomon sat on the throne of David his father.

He dealt with a swift hand against those who had not remained loyal to his father. When Adonijah dared to ask for one of David's young wives to be his own, Solomon declared, "He might as well ask me to give him the kingdom! This will cost Adonijah his life."

Solomon ordered the death of Adonijah. He also ordered the death of Joab, and he made Benaiah commander of the army in Joab's place. He banished Abiathar the priest, and made Zadok the high priest in place of Abiathar. Solomon put to death or sent away everyone who had injured David, and everyone who threatened the throne of Solomon.

And the kingdom was firmly established in Solomon's hand, just as the LORD had promised through Nathan the prophet to David:

The throne of David will be established forever.

THE WISDOM OF SOLOMON

Solomon loved the LORD and offered great sacrifices to HIM at the altar in Gibeon. The LORD appeared to Solomon in a dream at Gibeon and said, "Ask ME what you want ME to give you."

Solomon said, "You have shown great loving kindness to my father David, and given him a son to sit on his throne. O LORD, YOU've made me YOUR king, and I am so young. I don't know what to do. Give me an understanding mind to govern YOUR people."

GOD said to Solomon, "You have made a good choice. Instead of asking for long life or riches or the defeat of your enemies, you have asked for understanding to discern what is right. Now I give you what you have asked for. I give you a wise and discerning mind, greater than anyone has ever had or ever will have. I also give you what you have not asked for. I give you more riches and honor than any other king. If you follow MY ways and keep MY laws and commandments, I will give you a long life."

Then Solomon woke up and knew he had dreamed. He went back to Jerusalem and stood before the Ark of the Covenant. He offered burnt offerings and peace offerings and prepared a feast for all those who served him.

Then there came two women to the king, and they were brought to stand before him.

The first woman said, "My lord, this woman and I live in the same house. I gave birth to a child while she was in the house. Then three days later, this woman also gave birth. We were alone. There was nobody else in the house except the two of us. This woman's son died one night, because she rolled over on him. While I was sleeping, she got up and took my son from my side and carried him to her bed and laid her dead son next to me. When I got up the next morning to nurse my child, I saw that he was dead! But when I looked closely at him, I saw it was not my son."

"No!" cried the second woman. "The living child is mine, and the dead child is yours."

The first woman said, "No! The dead child is yours, and the living child is mine."

And they continued to argue in this way before the king.

Then the king said:

"One says, 'This is my son that is alive, and your son is dead,' and the other says, 'No, your son is dead, and my son is the living one.' " The king motioned to a servant and said, "Bring me a sword."

A sword was brought to the king, and the king said, "Divide the living child in two, and give half to the one and half to the other."

Then the heart of the true mother ached for her son, and she said, "O my lord king, give her the living child. Don't kill him!"

But the other said, "Let it not be mine *or* yours. Divide it!"

Then the king gave his answer:

"Give the child to the first woman, and do not kill it. She is the mother."

All Israel heard about Solomon's wise decision, and they were in awe of him. They understood that the wisdom of GOD was in him to do justice

Solomon ruled from the Egyptian border to the Euphrates River, from the Great Western Sea to the eastern desert. He was at peace with all his neighbors, and Judah and Israel lived in safety all the days that Solomon was king.

GOD gave Solomon wisdom and understanding beyond measure. His wisdom was greater than the wisdom of the people of the east and all the wisdom of Egypt. He was wiser than anyone, and his proverbs and songs were known throughout the lands. People and kings came from all nations to hear his wisdom.

SOLOMON BUILDS THE HOUSE OF GOD

Hiram king of Tyre sent messengers to Solomon when Solomon became king, for Hiram loved David.

Solomon sent back this message:

"My father David couldn't build a house for the LORD his GOD because he was busy fighting his enemies. But now the LORD my GOD has given me rest on every side. I am planning to build a house for the LORD. I need some of the cedar wood that grows in the mountains of Lebanon. Please ask your lumbermen to cut down the trees. I'll send workers to help them, and I'll pay your people whatever you ask."

When Hiram received Solomon's message, he rejoiced and said, "Praise the LORD, WHO has given David a wise son to rule over this great people!"

Hiram ordered his lumbermen to cut down cedars of Lebanon, and Solomon sent workers to help them. They trimmed the logs and dragged them down to the seacoast and tied the logs into rafts and floated them behind ships.

In return, Solomon sent Hiram wheat and oil and food for his household.

Solomon forced the people of Israel to work on his building project. He sent some to Lebanon, and other workers went to the hill country of Judah and mined huge blocks of limestone for the foundation of the house.

When it was completed, the house of the LORD stood on the top of the highest hill in Jerusalem, facing east toward the rising sun. It had a large courtyard outside and a Holy Place and Holy of Holies inside for the Ark of the Covenant.

Solomon gathered the people to come to a great service to dedicate the Temple to the worship of the LORD. They sacrificed sheep and oxen, and the priests brought the Ark of the Covenant to its place.

As the priests came out of the Holy Place, a cloud filled the house of the LORD, and the glory of the LORD filled it with a bright, unearthly light.

Solomon blessed the people and raised his hands toward heaven, and he prayed, "O LORD GOD of Israel, hear my prayer. Watch over this house night and day. Teach us to do what is right. Listen to us when we ask YOU for help and when we confess our sins. Bless YOUR priests and help them in their work. For the sake of YOUR love for David, don't reject YOUR anointed kings. May one of David's family sit on the throne of Israel forever."

He then went to the front of the altar and cried out in a loud voice:

"Thanks be to GOD, WHO helps HIS people! May HE always be with us. And may we always be faithful to HIM, so all the people on earth will know that the LORD, and only the LORD, is GOD!"

The LORD appeared to him and said:

"This will be MY house. MY name and MY eyes and MY heart will be here for all time. If you follow MY ways and MY teachings, I will establish your royal throne over Israel forever, as I promised your father David.

"But if you or your children turn away from MY ways and go after other gods, I will cut the people off from the land and destroy this house. Those who pass by the ruins of this house will be shocked. Some will ask, 'Why did the LORD do this to this land and this house?' Others will answer, 'Because the people left the LORD their GOD and served other gods.' "

Solomon spent seven years building the house of the LORD and thirteen years building his own house. His palace was made of white limestone and cedar wood and stood on a hill just below the Temple. The main building of Solomon's palace had so many cedar pillars, it was called "the House of the Forest of Lebanon."

Solomon built fortresses across the land. He kept thousands of horses and chariots in the fortresses, and built storage cities for his chariots and horsemen. He forced the people to build his fortresses and to send food to his household and pay taxes of grain and crops.

He built a fleet of ships on the shore of the Red Sea. Hiram sent his seamen with Solomon's servants, and they brought gold from Orphir to King Solomon.

Solomon and the Queen of Sheba

When the Queen of Sheba heard about Solomon's power and wisdom, she came to test him with hard questions. She arrived in Jerusalem with many servants and camels bearing spices and much gold and precious stones.

She posed questions to Solomon on many subjects, and Solomon answered all her questions. There was nothing he could not explain to her.

The Queen of Sheba witnessed the wisdom of Solomon, and saw the house he had built, the food on his table, the furniture of his officials, the clothing of his servants, and the offerings he sacrificed at the house of the LORD. It astounded her and took her breath away.

"I had heard many things about you in my own country," she said, "but I did not believe them until I came and saw with my own eyes. Everything I heard is true—and I only heard half of it. You are richer and wiser than they say. How happy are your wives! How happy are your servants, who stand in your presence and hear your wisdom every day! Praise the LORD your GOD, WHO delights in you and Israel so much. Your GOD has made you king to do justice and righteousness."

Then she gave him great quantities of gold and spices and precious jewels.

King Solomon gave the Queen of Sheba all that she desired, whatever she asked. Then she returned to her own land with her servants.

Solomon had so much gold that the furniture in his palace was made of gold and the palace guards carried golden shields. He made a great ivory throne and covered it with the finest gold. The throne had six steps, and at the back of the throne was a calf's head, and on either side of the seat were arm rests with two lions standing beside them. Carved lions stood beside the six steps. No one ever saw such a throne in any kingdom.

All of King Solomon's drinking cups were made of gold, and all the dishes in the House of the Forest of Lebanon were made of pure gold.

Every three years, Hiram's fleet of ships sailed from Tarshish to Orphir and came back with gold, silver, ivory, apes, and peacocks.

King Solomon exceeded all the kings of the earth in riches and in wisdom. And all the earth came to him to hear the wisdom that God had put in his heart. Everyone who came brought a gift: goblets and dishes of silver and gold, clothing and armor, perfume, spices, horses and mules.

Solomon had fourteen hundred chariots and twelve thousand horsemen. He made silver as common in Jerusalem as stone, and cedar as plentiful as sycomore-fig trees. He grew even richer by buying horses from Egypt and Cilicia and selling them to the kings of the Hittites and the kings of Syria.

THE FOOLISHNESS OF SOLOMON

Early in his reign, King Solomon made an alliance with the Pharaoh of Egypt by marrying Pharaoh's daughter. Then Solomon married Moabite, Ammonite, Edomite, Sidonian, and Hittite women. The LORD had said, "Do not marry the women of other nations, for they will turn your heart to their gods." But Solomon loved them all.

He had a thousand wives. When he was old they turned his heart to their gods. He made a place for Asherah, goddess of the Sidonians, and Milcom, god of the Ammonites. He built a high place

for Chemosh, god of Moab, and for Molech, god of the Ammonites. He did this for all his foreign wives, who burned incense and sacrificed to their gods.

The LORD was angry with Solomon, for his heart had turned away. So HE said to Solomon, "Because you did this, I will tear the kingdom from you and give it to one of your servants. But for the sake of your father David, I will not do this in your lifetime, and I will not tear away the whole kingdom. I will tear the kingdom from your son's hand, but I will leave him one tribe."

It came to pass that Solomon went

out to check some repair work on the walls of Jerusalem. He noticed a hard-working young man named Jeroboam and sent him to be in charge of the workers in the north.

As Jeroboam was leaving Jerusalem, the prophet Ahijah found him on the road. Ahijah was wearing a new cloak, and the two of them were alone in the open country.

Ahijah took the cloak and tore it into twelve pieces. Then he said:

"Take ten pieces for yourself. The LORD says, *I'm about to tear the kingdom from Solomon's hand. I will give Jeroboam ten tribes, and leave only the tribe of Judah and little Benjamin to Solomon's son, because Solomon has left ME to worship the gods of other nations. If you listen to ME, Jeroboam, and follow MY ways, and do what is right, I will be with you and build you a firm house, as I did for David."*

Solomon learned of this and tried to kill Jeroboam. But Jeroboam escaped to Egypt and stayed there until Solomon died.

Solomon was king in Jerusalem and over all Israel for forty years. When he died, his son Rehoboam reigned in his place.

THE FOOLISHNESS OF REHOBOAM

Rehoboam went to Shechem, where all Israel was gathered to make him king. Jeroboam heard about this, and so he returned from Egypt and joined the people at Shechem.

The leaders of Israel said to Rehoboam, "Your father, King Solomon, burdened us with taxes and forced us to work on his building projects. If you lighten the load your father put on us, we will serve you."

Rehoboam was wealthy, spoiled, and still fairly young. He had not paid attention when his father was king, and he did not know anything about government.

"Give me three days," he said. "I'll have an answer for you then."

Rehoboam went to the old men who had been Solomon's advisers and said, "How should I answer the people?"

They said, "Speak kindly to them, and they will serve you forever."

Rehoboam did not understand this as good advice. He did not think he should serve the people. He thought they should serve him.

So he went to his friends, young men like himself who also knew nothing about government. He said to them, "How should we answer the people who told me to lighten the burdens my father put on them?"

The young men told Rehoboam to say to the people, "My little finger is thicker than my father's waist! My father

laid heavy burdens on you, and I will add to your burdens. My father disciplined you with whips, but I will discipline you with bullwhips!"

On the third day, Jeroboam and all the people came to Rehoboam, as he had said. The king did not follow the old men's advice, but spoke to the people harshly, as the young men had advised.

He said, "My little finger is thicker than my father's waist! My father laid heavy burdens on you, and I will add to your burdens. My father disciplined you with whips, but I will discipline you with bullwhips!"

When the people saw that the king paid them no heed, they cried, "What do we care about David's family? The son of Jesse means nothing to us! Go to your tents, Israel! Look after your own house, David!"

The people went home, and Rehoboam sent a taskmaster to go after them. But the people picked up stones and stoned him to death. Rehoboam hurried to his chariot and escaped to Jerusalem before they attacked him.

When the people heard that Jeroboam had returned from Egypt, they sent for him and made him king over all Israel. No one followed Rehoboam except the tribe of Judah.

In Jerusalem, Rehoboam gathered the men of Judah and Benjamin to fight against Jeroboam.

Then the word of the LORD came to Shemaiah, a man of GOD. The LORD said, "Tell Rehoboam and all the people of Judah and Benjamin, 'You mustn't fight against your relatives, the people of Israel. Go home, everyone, for this is of the LORD.' "

They listened to the word of the LORD and went home.

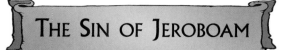

THE SIN OF JEROBOAM

Jeroboam said in his heart, "If the people go to Jerusalem to offer sacrifices at the Temple, their hearts will turn to Rehoboam, and they'll kill me."

So he made two golden calves and said to the people:

"You have gone to Jerusalem long enough. Here are your gods, O Israel, who brought you up out of the land of Egypt!"

He set one calf up in Bethel and the other in Dan. This thing became a great sin, because the people went to worship at Bethel and Dan instead of the house of the LORD in Jerusalem. When they stopped worshiping in the house of the LORD, they stopped following the ways of the LORD. They left the LORD and began to live like other nations instead of like a people set apart.

A man of GOD came out of Judah, sent by the word of the LORD, to Bethel, where Jeroboam was standing by the altar. The man of GOD cried against the altar:

"O altar! The LORD says, *A son will be born to the house of David named Josiah. On you, O altar, Josiah will sacrifice the priests who burn incense on you! Human bones will be burned on you!*"

Then he said, "This is the sign that the LORD has spoken: The altar will fall apart, and the ashes will be scattered to the ground."

When Jeroboam heard this, he stretched out his hand and said:

"Seize him!"

Immediately Jeroboam's hand withered, and the altar fell apart and the ashes scattered to the ground.

Jeroboam said to the man of GOD, "Plead with the LORD our GOD to restore my hand!"

The holy man pleaded with the LORD, and the king's hand was restored.

But Jeroboam didn't turn away from evil. He continued to worship idols and lead the people into sin. For that reason, the house of Jeroboam was destroyed from the face of the earth.

Jeroboam's son Abijah grew ill, and Jeroboam said to his wife, "Disguise yourself and go to Shiloh. Find Ahijah, the prophet who told me I would be king. He will tell you what will happen to the child."

Jeroboam's wife got up and went to Ahijah's house in Shiloh.

Ahijah was old and blind. The LORD said to him, "Jeroboam's wife is coming to ask you about her son, who is sick. I will tell you what to say to her."

When Jeroboam's wife came to his house, Ahijah heard the sound of her feet, and he said:

"Come in, wife of Jeroboam. Why are you pretending to be someone else? I must give you bad news to tell Jeroboam. The LORD says, *I raised you up and made you king, but you have done more evil than anyone who came before you. You have provoked ME to anger by making other gods and turning your back on ME. Because of that, I will punish the house of Jeroboam and destroy every male in your family. Anyone belonging to Jeroboam who dies in the city will be eaten by dogs. Anyone who dies in the fields will be eaten by the birds of the air.*

"Now go home. When your feet enter the city, the child will die. All Israel will mourn for him and bury him. He will be the only one of Jeroboam's family to have a decent burial. What's more, the LORD will raise up a king who will destroy the house of Jeroboam. The LORD will uproot Israel from this good land and scatter the people far away, beyond the great river Euphrates, because they made idols and provoked the LORD to anger. The LORD will abandon Israel because of the sin of Jeroboam, and the sins he caused Israel to sin!"

Jeroboam's wife went home. As soon as she came to the entrance of the house, the child died. All Israel buried him and mourned for him.

Jeroboam reigned for twenty-two years, and then he died. His son Nadab reigned in his place.

After the kingdom of Solomon was divided, there was constant war between Israel and Judah.

The people of Judah did what was evil in the sight of the LORD. They built altars on the hilltops and images of Asherah. They did shameful things like the other nations.

Rehoboam took away the treasure of the house of the LORD, and his son Abijam followed the sins of his father.

Some of the kings, like Asa, followed the ways of the LORD, and some did evil. None of them tore down the altars to Baal and Asherah.

But the LORD preserved the royal house of Judah, because of his promise to David that his throne would be established forever.

The LORD did not preserve the royal house of Israel, because of the sin of Jeroboam. Each of the kings of Israel after Jeroboam was worse than the one before. Each one followed the example of Jeroboam and the sins he caused Israel to sin.

Jeroboam's son Nadab was murdered by a man named Baasha, who became king in his place. Baasha destroyed the whole house of Jeroboam, killing everyone, as the LORD had said. Baasha also did what was evil in the sight of the

LORD and followed the example of the sin of Jeroboam.

Baasha's son Elah was murdered by Zimri, the captain of the chariot drivers. Zimri made himself king and killed the whole house of Baasha. This happened because Baasha and Elah followed the example of the sin of Jeroboam.

The army made Omri, the commander, king, and Omri led the army against Zimri. Then Zimri set the king's house on fire and died in the flames. This happened because Zimri also followed the example of the sin of Jeroboam.

Omri ruled as king over Israel from Samaria, the city he built with a fortress on a hill. He did more evil in the sight of the LORD than everyone before him. He followed the example of the sin of Jeroboam and provoked the LORD to anger.

Omri's son Ahab married Jezebel, the daughter of the king of Sidon. Ahab and Jezebel served Baal and worshiped him as lord of the weather, master of rain and thunder. Ahab built a great altar and temple for Baal in Samaria.

Following the example of the sin of Jeroboam was the least of Ahab's evil deeds.

THE PROPHET ELIJAH

It came to pass that the prophet Elijah appeared as if from nowhere, wearing an unusual cloak, a mantle of animal hair, and a leather belt around his waist. When Elijah heard the word of the LORD, he would come and speak, and then he would disappear. No one knew who his father was or where he lived.

One day Elijah said to Ahab, "As surely as the LORD lives, WHOM I serve, there will be neither dew nor rain for years, except by my word!"

The word of the LORD came to Elijah, saying, "Get out of here and go to the Brook Cherith, east of the Jordan River. There you will drink from the brook, and I have commanded the ravens to feed you."

Elijah went as the LORD said, and lived beside the Brook Cherith. The ravens brought him bread and meat in the morning and evening, and he drank from the brook.

After a while the brook dried up, because there was no rain in the land.

The word of the LORD came to Elijah, saying, "Get up and go to Zarephath, outside of Sidon. I have commanded a widow there to feed you."

Elijah got up and went to Zarephath, and when he came to the gate of the city, he saw a widow gathering sticks. He called to her and said:

"Bring me a little water in a cup, so I can drink."

As she was going to get it, he called after her, "Bring me a little piece of bread, too."

She said, "As the LORD your GOD lives, I have nothing but a handful of flour in a jar and a little oil in a pitcher. I am gathering just a few sticks so I can go in and prepare a last small meal for myself and my son, so we can eat it, then die."

"Do not be afraid," said Elijah. "Go and do what you said, but first make me a little roll and bring it to me. Afterward make some for yourself and your son. For the LORD GOD of Israel says, *The flour jar won't be empty, and the pitcher won't run out of oil, until the day the LORD sends rain upon the earth.*"

The widow went and did as Elijah said. She and Elijah and her son ate for many days. The flour jar never became empty, and the pitcher never ran out of oil, as the LORD had spoken by Elijah. And the widow invited Elijah to stay at their house.

It happened that the woman's son became ill, and his sickness was so serious that there was no breath left in him.

The woman said to Elijah, "What do you have against me, man of GOD? You have come to remind me of my sins and cause the death of my son!"

"Give me your son," said Elijah.

He took the boy from her lap and carried him into the upstairs room where he stayed and laid him on his own bed.

Then Elijah cried to the LORD, "O LORD, my GOD! Are YOU going to bring disaster on the widow, too, and kill her son?" He stretched himself out on the child's body three times and cried. "O LORD, my GOD, let this child's life return to him!"

The LORD heard Elijah, and the child's life came into him again, and he revived.

Elijah picked up the child and took him downstairs and gave him to his mother.

"See!" he said. "Your son is alive!"

The woman said, "Now I know that you are a man of GOD, and the word of the LORD in your mouth is truth."

ELIJAH'S CONTEST WITH THE PROPHETS OF BAAL

In the third year of the drought, the word of the LORD came to Elijah, saying, "Go show yourself to Ahab. I will send rain upon the earth."

Elijah went to show himself to Ahab.

The drought was severe in Samaria, and Ahab called Obadiah, his servant in charge of the palace.

Now, Obadiah was very faithful to the LORD. When Ahab's wife Jezebel was slaughtering the prophets of the LORD, Obadiah hid a hundred of them in a cave and fed them with bread and water.

Ahab said to Obadiah, "Go all over the land, to all the springs of water and all the valleys. Perhaps we'll find grass and keep the horses and mules alive, and not lose all the animals."

They divided the land between them. Ahab went in one direction and Obadiah in another.

As Obadiah was on the way, Elijah appeared. Obadiah bowed down to the ground and said, "It that you, my lord Elijah?"

"Yes," Elijah said. "Go tell your master I am here."

"What sin have I committed," asked Obadiah, "that you ask me to put my life in danger? My master has sent me everywhere to look for you. As soon as I leave you, the Spirit of the LORD will carry you off somewhere. If I tell Ahab I found you and you disappear, he will kill me!"

"As the LORD lives," promised Elijah, "I will show myself to him today."

Obadiah went and told Ahab, and Ahab went to meet Elijah. When he saw Elijah, Ahab said, "Is that you, you troublemaker in Israel?"

"I am not the troublemaker," said Elijah. "You are the troublemaker—you and your father's family. You have abandoned the commandments of the LORD and followed the Baal gods. Now call Israel to meet me at Mount Carmel, and bring the four hundred and fifty prophets of Baal and the four hundred prophets of Asherah that Jezebel supports."

Ahab sent for all the people of Israel and gathered the prophets together at Mount Carmel.

Elijah went close to the people and said, "How long will you hop back and forth on one foot and then the other, not choosing either side? Make up your minds! If the LORD is GOD, follow HIM. But if it be Baal, then follow him!"

The people did not say a word.

Then Elijah said, "I, only I, am left of the prophets of the LORD. But Baal's prophets are four hundred and fifty men! Bring us two bulls. Let the other prophets choose one bull to prepare for sacrifice and lay it on the wood—but do not light the fire. I will prepare the other bull and lay it on the wood, but not light the fire. You call on the name of your god, and I will call on the name of the LORD. The one who answers with fire is GOD!"

All the people answered, "That's a fair contest!"

Elijah said to the prophets of Baal, "Choose for yourselves one bull and prepare it first, for you are many. Call on the name of your god, but do not light the fire."

They took the bull and prepared it and called on the name of Baal from morning to noon, saying, "O Baal, answer us!"

But there was no sound, and no one answered.

They hopped around the altar that they had made, first on one foot and then the other.

At noon Elijah made fun of them, saying, "Call louder—he is a god! Perhaps his mind is on other matters. Perhaps he is on a journey, or he is asleep and you must wake him up!"

They called louder and cut themselves with swords and lances until their blood ran. They raved on and on until it was time to sacrifice the offering, but there was no sound. No one answered. No one paid any attention.

Then Elijah said to the people, "Come near me."

All the people went near him.

Elijah repaired the altar of the LORD, which had been torn down. He took twelve stones, one for each of the tribes of Israel, and built it in the name of the LORD. He dug a trench around the altar and arranged the wood on it and cut the bull in pieces and laid it on the wood.

"Fill four jars with water," he ordered the people, "and pour it over the offering and on the wood."

Then he said, "Do it a second time."

They did it a second time.

"Do it a third time," he said.

They did it a third time, and the water flowed down the sides of the altar and filled up the trench.

When it was time to offer the sacrifice, Elijah went up to the altar and said,

"O LORD GOD, let it be known today that YOU are GOD in Israel, and that I am YOUR servant and have done all these things at YOUR word. Answer me, LORD! Answer me so these people will know that YOU, LORD, are GOD, and YOU have turned their hearts back to YOURSELF!"

Then the fire of the LORD fell, and it consumed the offering and the wood and the stones and the dust and licked up the water that was in the trench.

When the people saw the lightning, they fell on their faces and said:

"The LORD, HE is GOD! The Lord, HE is GOD!"

Elijah said to them, "Seize the prophets of Baal! Don't let one of them escape."

They seized them, and Elijah took them down to the Brook Kishon and killed them.

Then Elijah said to Ahab, "Get up. There's a sound of the rushing of rain."

Elijah went to the top of Mount Carmel and bowed down on the ground and put his face between his knees.

Then he said to a servant, "Go up now, and look toward the sea."

The servant went and looked, and said, "There is nothing."

"Go again seven times," said Elijah.

At the seventh time the servant said, "I saw a little cloud like a man's hand, rising out of the sea."

"Be off!" said Elijah. "Tell Ahab to harness his chariot and go, before the rain comes."

Before long, the heavens grew black with clouds and the wind blew and heavy rains began to pour down. Ahab harnessed his chariot and rode to Jezreel.

The hand of the LORD was on Elijah. He tucked his hairy mantle into his leather belt and ran in front of Ahab all the way to the gate of Jezreel.

ELIJAH ON THE MOUNTAINTOP

Ahab told Jezebel everything Elijah had done, and how he had killed all the prophets of Baal.

Jezebel sent a messenger to Elijah, saying, "May the gods punish me if you are not as dead as my prophets by this time tomorrow!"

Elijah was so frightened, he ran away to save his life. He went south, as far as Beersheba, and left his servant there. Then he went by himself a day's journey into the wilderness and sat down in the shade of a small tree. He was exhausted.

"It's too much, LORD," he said. "Take my life! I'm no better than my ancestors."

Then he lay down and went to sleep under the tree.

Suddenly an angel touched him and said, "Get up and eat."

He looked around and saw beside his head a warm loaf of bread and a jar of water. He ate and drank and lay down again.

The angel came a second time and touched him and said, "Get up and eat, or the journey will be too much for you."

He got up and ate and drank and went on the strength of that food for forty days and nights, all the way to Sinai, the mountain of GOD.

He came to a cave and spent the night there. The word of the LORD came to him and said to him, "What are you doing here, Elijah?"

"I have been concerned for the LORD," responded Elijah, "for the people of Israel have abandoned YOUR covenant and torn down YOUR altars and killed YOUR prophets. I, only I, am left, and they are looking for me, to kill me."

The LORD said, "Go out and stand on the mountain in the presence of the LORD."

The LORD passed by, and a mighty wind tore the mountain and broke the rocks to pieces in the presence of the LORD. But the LORD was not in the wind.

After the wind, an earthquake—but the LORD was not in the earthquake.

After the earthquake, a fire—but the LORD was not in the fire.

After the fire, a quiet sound, a still small voice, and the LORD was there.

When Elijah heard it, he wrapped his face with his cloak and went out and stood at the entrance of the cave.

A voice came to him and said, "What are you doing here, Elijah?"

"I've been concerned for the LORD, for the people of Israel have abandoned YOUR covenant, torn down YOUR altars, and killed YOUR prophets. I, only I, am left, and they are looking for me, to kill me."

The LORD said to him, "Go and return through the wilderness of Damascus. When you arrive, anoint Hazael to be king over Syria. Anoint Jehu to be king over Israel. Anoint Elisha to be prophet in your place. Anyone who escapes from the sword of Hazael will be killed by Jehu. Anyone who escapes from the sword of Jehu will be killed by Elisha. I will leave seven thousand in Israel—all the knees that have not bowed to Baal, and every mouth that has not kissed him."

Elijah went from there and found Elisha plowing with a team of oxen. Elijah went up to him and threw his haircloth cloak on him.

Elisha left his plow and ran after Elijah, saying, "Let me kiss my father and my mother good-bye, and then I'll follow you."

"Go, and return to me," said Elijah.

And Elisha arose and followed Elijah and served him.

Ahab and Jezebel Steal Naboth's Vineyard

Ahab, king of Israel, owned hundreds of horses and camels that he kept in great stables at the city of Megiddo. He owned a beautiful palace in Jezreel and another one in Samaria, the city his father Omri had built. His palaces were filled with expensive ivory furniture. The LORD gave Ahab victory over the Syrians, and he gained more territory for his kingdom. But Ahab wasn't satisfied. He wanted more.

Next to Ahab's palace in Jezreel was a vineyard that belonged to a man named Naboth.

Ahab said to Naboth, "Give me your vineyard. It is near my house, and I can use it for a vegetable garden. I'll give you a better vineyard for it. Or, if you prefer, I'll pay you a fair price for it."

But Naboth said to Ahab, "May the LORD prevent me from giving you the inheritance of my ancestors."

Ahab went into his house, irritated and depressed because of what Naboth had said. He lay down on his bed, turned his face to the wall, and refused to eat.

His wife Jezebel went to him and said, "Why are you so depressed that you aren't eating?"

Ahab said, "I want Naboth's vineyard, and he won't sell it to me."

"Is this how you run the country?" said Jezebel. "Come on, cheer up and eat. I will get Naboth's vineyard for you."

According to the Law of GOD, land was to stay in the same family, so each family could earn a living from the land. Jezebel knew the law, but she had no respect for it. She also knew that the king could legally take over the property of a criminal who was condemned to death. But how could Naboth be condemned to death? A serious crime had to be witnessed by two people. That was the law.

Jezebel wrote letters in Ahab's name and he sealed them with his seal and sent them to the leaders of Naboth's city. She wrote in the letters:

"Proclaim a fast and set Naboth up in front of the people. Set two sons of Belial opposite him and have them bring a charge against him, saying, 'You have cursed GOD and the king.' Then take him out and stone him to death."

The elders and nobles did as Jezebel had said. They proclaimed a fast and set Naboth up in front of the people. Two men came in and sat opposite him and said falsely, "Naboth has cursed GOD and the king!"

The leaders took Naboth outside the city and stoned him to death. Then they sent a message to Jezebel, saying, "Naboth has been stoned. He is dead."

As soon as Jezebel heard that Naboth had been stoned to death, she said to Ahab, "Get up, and take possession of Naboth's vineyard, which he refused to sell to you. Naboth is dead."

And Ahab got up to go down to the vineyard and take possession of it.

The word of the LORD came to Elijah, saying, "Get up and go meet Ahab, king of Israel. He has gone to Naboth's vineyard to take possession of it. Tell him, 'The LORD says, *Have you killed and also taken possession?*' Then say to him, 'In the place where dogs licked up the blood of Naboth, dogs will lick your blood!'"

Elijah confronted Ahab, and Ahab said to him, "Have you found me out, O my enemy?"

Elijah answered, "I've found you out because you have sold your soul to do what is evil in the sight of the LORD. Hear what the LORD says: *I will bring evil on you. I will completely destroy you and every male of your family. I will make your house like the house of Jeroboam and the house of Baasha, because you have provoked ME to anger and caused Israel to sin.*

"Hear what the LORD says of Jezebel:

The dogs will eat Jezebel in the city of Jezreel. Anyone belonging to Ahab who dies in the city will be eaten by dogs. Anyone of his who dies in the fields will be eaten by the birds of the air."

When Ahab heard those words, he tore his clothes and put on sackcloth. He refused to eat. He walked humbly and depressed through his palace, wearing sackcloth and ashes.

The word of the LORD came to Elijah, saying, "Have you seen how Ahab has humbled himself before ME? Because he has humbled himself, I will not bring evil in his lifetime."

It came to pass that Ahab made a treaty with Jehoshaphat, son of Asa, king of Judah. The two kings led their armies against the Syrians, and Ahab was killed in battle. His body was brought to Samaria and buried. When they washed his chariot by the pool in Samaria, dogs licked up his blood.

After Ahab died, his son Ahaziah ruled as king over Israel. He also did what was evil in the sight of the LORD. He served Baal and provoked the LORD to anger, in every way that his father had done.

Ahaziah fell through the lattice on the balcony of his palace in Samaria and died. He had no son, and his brother Joram became king of Israel.

235

When it came to pass that the LORD had decided to take Elijah up to heaven in a whirlwind, Elijah and Elisha were on their way from Gilgal.

Elijah said to Elisha, "Please wait here. The LORD has sent me as far as Bethel."

Elisha said, "As the LORD lives and as you live, I will not leave you."

They went on to Bethel, and some men from a community of prophets who lived there came out to Elisha.

"Do you know that the LORD is going to take your master away from you today?" they asked.

"Yes, I know," said Elisha, "but keep silent."

Elijah said, "Please wait here, Elisha. The LORD has sent me to Jericho."

But Elisha said, "As the LORD lives and as you live, I will not leave you."

They went on, with fifty prophets following them. When they reached the Jordan, they stopped, and the fifty prophets stopped a little way behind them.

Elijah took off his mantle and rolled it up and struck the water with it. The water divided in two, and the two of them crossed over on dry ground.

After they crossed the river, Elijah said to Elisha, "Ask me what I should do for you before I am taken up."

Elisha said, "Please let me inherit a double share of your spirit."

"You have asked a hard thing," said Elijah. "But if you see me as I'm being taken from you, it will be so. If you don't see me, it will not be so."

As they went on and talked, a chariot of fire and horses of fire suddenly appeared between the two of them and swept them apart.

And Elijah went up in a whirlwind into heaven.

Elisha saw it and cried out:

"My father! My father! The strength of Israel! The chariot of Israel and its horsemen!"

Then Elijah disappeared.

Elisha took his own robe and tore it in two. Then he picked up Elijah's mantle and went back and stood on the bank

of the Jordan. He took Elijah's mantle and struck the waters and said, "Where is the LORD, the GOD of Elijah?"

The water divided, and Elisha crossed over to the other side.

The prophets who were watching him said, "The spirit of Elijah rests on Elisha."

They bowed down to him, saying, "There are fifty of us, all strong men. Send us to look for your master. Perhaps the Spirit of the LORD threw him onto a mountaintop or into a valley."

"No," said Elisha.

They kept urging him and then he let them go. Fifty men looked for three days, but they found no trace of Elijah.

"Didn't I tell you?" said Elisha.

He knew that Elijah was no longer on this earth.

And Elisha lived with the community of prophets and worked signs and wonders as Elijah had. He made bad water wholesome, he brought a dead child back to life, and he fed a hundred men with twenty loaves of barley bread. Everyone in Israel knew that he was a man of GOD with power over life and death.

Naaman's Cure and Gehazi's Punishment

In those days the kings of Israel were at war with the kings of Syria, and Elisha gave advice and worked signs and wonders to save Israel.

Naaman, the commander of the Syrian army, was a great warrior, but he was a leper. He could defeat armies, but he was helpless against the disease that had turned his skin white.

On one of their raids, the Syrians had carried off a little girl from the land of Israel, and she waited on Naaman's wife. One day the little girl said to her mistress, "I wish my master would go to the prophet in Samaria. He would cure him of his leprosy."

Naaman told the king what the little girl had said, and the king of Syria said, "Go now, and I will write a letter for you to take to the king of Israel."

Naaman took the letter and set out for Israel. He and his servants rode in chariots, bringing gifts of six thousand pieces of gold, thirty thousand pieces of silver, and ten beautiful robes.

The letter he was carrying said, "I am sending my commander Naaman to you, that you may cure him of his leprosy."

When the king of Israel read the letter, he tore his clothes and said, "I am not God! I have no power over life or death! Why is this man asking me to cure a man of leprosy? He must be looking for an excuse to start a war!"

Elisha heard about this, and he sent a message to the king, saying, "Send him to me, so he will know that there is a prophet in Israel."

Naaman came with his horses and chariots to the door of Elisha's house.

Elisha sent a messenger to him, saying, "Go wash yourself in the Jordan seven times, and your skin will be restored."

But Naaman was angry and went away, saying, "I thought he would come out to me and pray to his God and wave his hand over my skin and cure me. Surely, the rivers of Damascus are better than all the waters of Israel! I could have stayed at home and washed in them."

He turned and went away in a rage.

But his servants went to him and said, "Sir, if the prophet had commanded you

to do something difficult, wouldn't you do it? Why don't you just go wash yourself as he says?"

Naaman went down and dipped himself seven times in the Jordan, as Elisha had said. And, behold! His skin became as smooth as the skin of a little child. He was completely cured.

He went back with all his servants, and this time the prophet came out to meet him.

Naaman said, "Now I know there is no GOD in all the earth except in Israel! Please, sir, accept a gift from me."

"No," said Elisha. "As the LORD lives, WHOM I serve, I won't accept a thing."

Naaman insisted, but Elisha refused.

Then Naaman said, "If you won't accept my gift, then please let me have two mule-loads of earth to take home with me. From now on I won't offer sacrifices to any god but the LORD. When I go with my master the king to the temple of his god and bow down before the idol, I hope the LORD will forgive me."

"Go in peace," said Elisha.

When Naaman had gone just a short distance, Elisha's servant Gehazi said to himself, "My master has let this Syrian go without taking anything from him.

I'll run after him and get something!"

Naaman saw someone running after him, and he got down from his chariot and said, "Is everything all right?"

"All is well," said Gehazi. "My master has sent me to say that two of the servants of the prophets have just arrived. He would like you to give them three thousand pieces of silver."

"Please take six thousand pieces," said Naaman, and he tied up the silver in two bags with two beautiful robes and put them on his servants to carry.

When Gehazi came to the hill, he took the bags from them and hid them in the house. Then he sent the men away and went in and stood before his master.

"Where have you been, Gehazi?" said Elisha.

"Nowhere," he said.

Elisha said, "Didn't I go with you in spirit when the man got down from his chariot to meet you? Was this your chance to accept money and robes and buy olive groves and vineyards, sheep and oxen, and slaves? Because you did this, Naaman's leprosy will cling to you and your descendants forever."

And Gehazi went out from Elisha a leper, his skin as white as snow.

ELISHA AND THE ARMY OF THE LORD

When the king of Israel was at war with the king of Syria, Elisha would tell the king of Israel where the Syrians would strike, and the Israelites would be ready when they attacked.

The king of Syria said to his officers, "Which one of you is betraying us to the king of Israel?"

One of his servants said, "None of us, my lord. Elisha the prophet, who is in Israel, tells the king of Israel the words you speak in your bedroom."

"Go get Elisha!" said the king.

They heard that Elisha was at Dothan, and they sent horses and chariots and a great army, who came by night and surrounded the city.

Elisha's servant got up the next morning and saw the army around the city.

"Oh, master!" he cried. "What should we do?"

"Fear not," said Elisha. "There are more with us than with them."

Then Elisha prayed, "O LORD, please open his eyes so he can see."

The LORD opened the servant's eyes, and he saw. The mountain was covered with horses and chariots of fire all around Elisha.

When the Syrians came toward him, Elisha prayed, "Strike them with blindness."

The LORD struck them with blindness, as Elisha asked. Then Elisha said to them, "This is not the way, and this is not the city. Follow me, and I will take you to the man you are looking for."

And Elisha led them to Samaria.

As soon as they entered Samaria, Elisha said, "O LORD, open their eyes so they can see."

The Syrians saw that they were in the middle of Samaria, with Israelite soldiers all around them.

When the king of Israel saw the enemy soldiers, he said to Elisha, "My father, should I kill them?"

"No," said Elisha. "Do not kill them. Would you kill those you have taken captive with your sword and your bow? Set bread and water in front of them, and let them eat and drink and go to their master."

The king of Israel prepared a great feast, and when the captives had eaten and drunk, he sent them away, and they went to their master.

The Syrian raiding parties never invaded Israel again.

THE SWORD OF JEHU

Elisha sent for one of the young prophets and said to him, "Take this jar of oil and go to the army of Israel at Ramoth-gilead. When you arrive, find Commander Jehu, and ask him to go with you to a private room. Take the oil and pour it on his head, and say, 'The LORD says, *I anoint you king over Israel.*' Then open the door and flee as fast as you can."

The young prophet went to Ramoth-gilead and found all the commanders of the army meeting together. He went up to them and said, "I have a message for you, O Commander."

Jehu said, "For which one of us?"

"For you, O Commander."

Jehu got up and went into the private room.

The young man poured the oil on his head and said, "The LORD GOD of Israel says, *I anoint you king over the people of the LORD, over Israel. You must strike down the house of Ahab, to pay Jezebel for the blood of MY servants the prophets and the blood of all the servants of the LORD. Ahab's whole family will perish. I will make the house of Ahab like the house of Jeroboam and the house of Baasha. The dogs will eat Jezebel in Jezreel, and no one will bury her.*"

Then he opened the door and ran away.

When Jehu returned to the officers, they said to him, "Is everything all right? Why did that mad man come to you?"

He said to them, "You know how those prophets babble."

They said, "Come, tell us what he said."

"Well," he said, "he told me that the LORD has anointed me king over Israel."

Immediately they all took off their cloaks and spread them out for Jehu to stand on. Then they blew the trumpet and proclaimed, "Jehu is king!"

Jehu said, "If that's what you think, then don't let anyone slip out of the city to go and tell the news in Jezreel."

Jehu got into his chariot and went to Jezreel.

Now, Joram, son of Ahab, was king of Israel. The king of Judah also belonged to the family of Ahab. Jehoram, king of Judah, had married Athaliah, the daughter of Ahab. They had a son, Ahaziah, and when Jehoram died, Ahaziah, Ahab's grandson, became king of Judah. Ahaziah had joined forces with Joram to fight the Syrians at Ramoth-gilead. Joram was wounded in battle and had returned to Jezreel to rest and recover.

Ahaziah went to visit his uncle Joram, and so he was there in Jezreel when Jehu arrived in his chariot.

The watchman in the tower of Jezreel saw Jehu's men as they approached, and he said, "I see soldiers!"

Joram was thinking about the battle at Ramoth-gilead, and he said, "Send a horseman to meet them and say, 'Is it peace?'"

A horseman went to meet Jehu, saying, "The king says, 'Is it peace?'"

Jehu said, "What have you to do with peace? Get behind me!"

The watchman reported, "The messenger reached them, but he isn't coming back."

Joram sent out a second horseman, who said to Jehu, "'Is it peace?'"

Jehu said, "What have you to do with peace? Get behind me!"

Again the watchman reported, "He reached them, but he isn't coming back.

The driving is like the driving of Jehu, who drives furiously!"

Joram said, "Prepare my chariot."

They prepared his chariot, and Joram king of Israel and Ahaziah king of Judah set out, each in his own chariot, to meet Jehu.

They met near Naboth's vineyard.

When Joram saw Jehu, he said, "Is it peace, Jehu?"

"What peace can there be, as long as your mother, Queen Jezebel, continues her sorcery and idolatry?"

Joram wheeled his chariot around and fled, warning Ahaziah, "It is treason, Ahaziah!"

Jehu drew his bow with his full strength and shot Joram between the shoulders. The arrow pierced his heart, and he sank down in his chariot.

Jehu said to his driver. "Pick him up and throw him into Naboth's vineyard, to avenge the blood of Naboth and the blood of his sons in the same field."

Ahaziah king of Judah saw this and tried to escape.

Jehu chased after him and said, "Shoot him, too!"

They shot arrows toward his chariot, wounding Ahaziah, but he escaped to Megiddo and died there.

When Jezebel heard that Jehu was in Jezreel, she put on eye make-up and arranged her hair. Then she went and stood by a window and looked out.

As Jehu came through the city gate, she cried out:

"Is it peace, you Zimri? Assassin! Murderer of your master!"

Jehu looked up at the window and called, "Who's on my side? Who?"

Two or three palace officials looked out at him.

"Throw her down!" he ordered.

So they threw her down and trod her underfoot.

Jehu went into the palace and ate and drank. Then he said, "Take that cursed woman and bury her, for she was the daughter of a king."

But when they went to bury her, they found no more of her than the skull and the feet and the palms of her hands, for the dogs had found her, as Elijah had prophesied.

Jehu ordered the leaders of Samaria to kill all the males in Ahab's family. He found and executed all the officials, friends, and priests of the royal family.

Then Jehu went to Samaria to rule as king. He called the people of the city together and said to them, "Ahab served Baal a little, but Jehu will serve him more! Now bring me all the prophets of Baal, all his worshipers, and all his priests. Don't leave anyone out, for I have a great sacrifice to offer to Baal!"

Jehu was scheming to destroy the worshipers of Baal. He proclaimed a great feast in honor of Baal. He sent messengers all over Israel to invite every Baal worshiper to come to the temple in Samaria.

When the worshipers of Baal arrived, there were so many, they filled the temple from one end to the other.

Jehu went into the temple and said to them, "Make sure that no worshiper of the LORD is in here. I want only worshipers of Baal here today."

Then he went outside and said to the guards, "Come in as soon as I finish the offering. Strike them all down. Don't let a single one get away."

As soon as he was finished, the guards entered the temple with their swords in their hands. They struck the prophets and priests and worshipers of Baal and killed every one. They pulled down the great image of Baal and burned it. They smashed the great altar and the building and turned the house of Baal into a sewer.

Jehu swept Baal out from Israel. But he didn't turn away from the sin of Jeroboam, or tear down the golden calves that were in Bethel.

Then the LORD said to Jehu, "Because you punished the house of Ahab, your sons will rule as kings of Israel for four generations."

But Jehu wasn't careful to follow the Law of the LORD. He didn't turn from the sin of Jeroboam.

Jehu reigned for twenty-eight years. He was buried in Samaria, and his son ruled upon his death.

THE LITTLE PRINCE
WHO HID IN THE TEMPLE

When Athaliah, daughter of Ahab, saw that her son Ahazah was dead, she gave orders that the rest of the royal family of Judah be killed, so that she and Ahab's family could take over the throne of David.

But Jehosheba, wife of the high priest, took Ahaziah's son Joash and hid him. He stayed with her for six years, hidden in the house of the LORD, while Athaliah ruled as queen over the land.

When Joash was seven years old, Jehoiada the high priest, sent for the guards. He showed them the king's son and told them his plan.

The next Sabbath day, while the people were going up to the house of the LORD to worship, Jehoiada ordered the soldiers and guards to take positions around the building. Some surrounded the house of the LORD, some guarded the palace, and others guarded little Joash. They all had their swords ready in their hands.

Jehoiada brought Joash and put the crown on his head and anointed him as king of Judah. The people clapped and shouted, "Long live the king!"

When Athaliah heard the shouting, she hurried to the Temple. But when she arrived, she was not able to get past the guards who were standing around the building with their swords and shields. Over the tops of the heads of the crowd she could see the little boy with the crown on his head. He was standing with Jehoiada the priest beside the great bronze pillars in front of the house of the LORD. The people were rejoicing and blowing trumpets.

"Treason! Treason!" cried Athaliah.

"Take her out!" ordered Jehoiada. "Guard her carefully so no one can rescue her. Don't let her be killed in the house of the LORD."

The soldiers led Athaliah past the line of armed men and away from the house of the LORD and put her to death.

Then Jehoiada spoke to the people about the LORD. The people and the king agreed to serve the LORD, and the people promised to obey GOD and the king. The king promised to rule Judah according to the LORD's teachings.

Jehoiada led Joash and the people from the house of the LORD to the king's house. Joash took his seat on the throne, and all the people rejoiced.

Joash reined for forty years. He did what was right in the sight of the LORD all his days, because Jehoiada the priest taught him. He told the priests to repair the Temple, and Jehoiada asked all the people to bring silver to pay for the repairs. They paid the carpenters and builders, the masons and stonecutters, and they bought timber and quarried stone to repair the house of the LORD.

THE STRENGTH OF ISRAEL

Elisha was sick with his last illness, and Jehoash, the grandson of Jehu who ruled as king of Israel, went to visit him. He saw that Elisha was dying, and he cried, "My father! My father! You are the strength of Israel! You are our chariots and horsemen!"

Elisha said, "Take a bow and arrows."

He took a bow and arrows.

Then he said, "Draw the bow."

He drew it.

Elisha laid his hands on the king's hands, and said, "Open the window toward the east."

He opened it.

Elisha said, "Shoot!"

He shot.

Elisha said, "The LORD's arrow of victory! The arrow of victory over Syria! You will fight the Syrians until you put an end to them!"

Then he said, "Take the arrows."

He took them.

"Strike the ground with them."

Jehoash struck three times and stopped.

Elisha was angry and said to him, "You should have struck the ground five or six times. Then you would have struck down the Syrians and put an end to them. But now you'll strike them down only three times."

Elisha died and was buried. Jehoash fought the Syrians three times and defeated them, as Elisha had said. But they continued to attack and weaken Israel. The time was soon coming when the LORD would put an end to both Syria and Israel.

It was never the power of the kings and their armies that saved Israel. The LORD saved Israel by the power of HIS prophets. The strength of Israel wasn't swords and spears. The strength of Israel was the word of the LORD.

THE LION ROARS

In the silence of the wilderness of Judah, Amos the shepherd heard the word of the LORD. It sounded like a mighty voice thundering across the land, like a roll of thunder before the breaking of a great storm, like the roar of a pouncing, attacking lion.

Amos trembled as the LORD spoke to him. He heard things no human being had ever heard. He saw visions no human being had ever seen.

Then the voice was gone, and Amos was alone again with the sheep. He was trembling with fear, but he left his sheep with a keeper and headed north, to the kingdom of Israel.

These were the days when Jeroboam II was king, and the kingdom of Israel was very rich. Amos saw the magnificent mansions that the wealthy landowners, officials, and merchants of Israel had built with their new riches. Some of these people were so successful, they owned two houses—one for summer and one for winter.

Amos reached Bethel on a feast day. Men, women, and children from all the towns and villages of Israel were coming to worship at the great national Temple.

Priests in fine robes were taking offerings and burning sacrifices on the altar. The smell of roasted meat hung in the air above the crowd as smoke from the altar rose into the clear sky and drifted across the rocky hills.

The Temple musicians played harps, lyres, and cymbals. The people sang hymns and prayed aloud to the LORD.

They were so busy with their sacrifices, music, and prayers, they didn't notice the shepherd from Judah.

Then Amos shouted:

"Hear the word of the LORD!"

The people stopped what they were doing and stared at the stranger.

Amos said, "The LORD is going to judge the nations for all their crimes! The crimes of the Syrians are so terrible, the LORD is going to send them into exile. He's going to destroy the Philistines and strike the king of Moab!"

The people liked Amos's words. They listened eagerly as he described the disasters the LORD was going to send to the nations. How pleasant it was to hear

about their neighbors' sins!

But then Amos said, "The LORD is going to punish Israel. He is angry because the rich people have been cheating the poor! They lie and steal and bribe judges! Merchants use false weights and overcharge their customers. They sell poor folks into slavery when they can't pay their debts.

"The rich men and women of Samaria anoint themselves with fine oil and lie on ivory couches, listening to music and drinking wine by the bowlful. They stuff their mansions with luxuries, but don't care a bit about the suffering of the poor."

The worshipers at Bethel didn't like Amos's message. They didn't believe a

houses will completely disappear. The LORD won't overlook your crimes anymore. HE will destroy your places of worship and attack your king's family!"

The people were shocked. What about their beautiful worship service—their offerings, their music, their prayers?

"Your worship means nothing to GOD!" cried Amos. "You pray to HIM while you cheat your neighbors. The LORD says to you: *I hate, I despise your feasts! I loathe your worship services! I reject your offerings! I refuse your sacrifices! I won't even look at them! Take the noise of your songs away from ME! I won't listen to your music! But let justice roll down like waters, and righteousness like an ever-flowing stream!*"

Amaziah the priest of Bethel sent a message to Jeroboam II, king of Israel, saying, "Amos is plotting against you right in the midst of the people. The land cannot stand the weight of his preaching! He says Jeroboam will die by the sword, and Israel will go into exile far away from the land."

Amaziah said to Amos, "Go away, prophet! Get out of here and go back to the land of Judah! Prophesy there. But never prophesy at Bethel again! It's the king's sanctuary—the national Temple!"

"I am not a prophet," said Amos. "I am just a shepherd and a tree trimmer. The LORD took me from watching the flock and said to me, 'Go prophesy to MY people, Israel.' When the lion roars, who isn't afraid? When the LORD GOD speaks, who can refuse to prophesy?"

Before he left Bethel, Amos gave the people some messages of hope:

"If you turn to the LORD, HE will save you. If you seek good, and not evil, if you do justice to your neighbors, then the LORD will really be with you, as you say HE is now."

word he was saying. How could the LORD punish them? They weren't like other nations. They were the nation GOD was blessing!

Amos said, "The LORD brought you out of Egypt and taught you how to live, but you disobeyed HIS laws. HE sent prophets to warn you, but you told them not to speak. When HE sent small disasters to get your attention, you ignored HIM. Now the LORD is preparing to send a great disaster. This time you will pay attention.

"HE is going to send an enemy nation to invade the land. The wealthy will be the first to be taken prisoner. The rich women of Samaria will suffer. Their

GOD SENDS ISAIAH

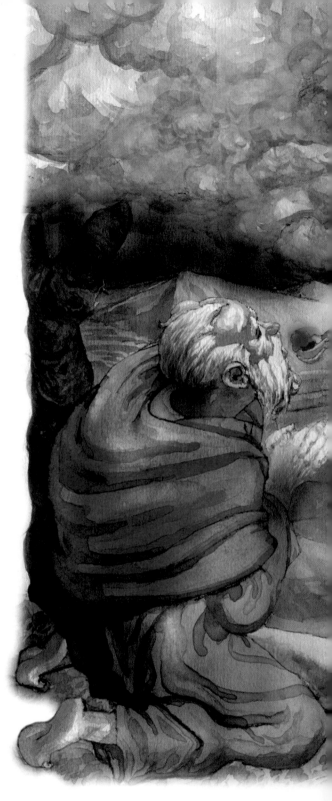

A prophet named Isaiah saw a vision of the LORD in the Temple. Later he described it to his disciples, saying:

"I saw the LORD sitting on a throne, high and lifted up. The train of HIS robe filled the Temple. Above HIM stood the fiery seraphim. Each of them had six wings. With two they covered their faces, with two they covered their feet, and with two they hovered in the air. They called to each other, 'Holy, holy, holy is the LORD of the Heavenly Armies! All the earth is filled with HIS glory!'

"At the sound of their voices, the frame of the door shook, and the house was filled with smoke.

"Then I said, 'Woe is me, I am doomed! For I am a man of unclean lips, living among a people of unclean lips. Yet my eyes have seen the King, the LORD of the Heavenly Armies!'

"Then one of the seraphim flew to me, with a burning coal in his hand that he had taken with tongs from the altar. He touched my mouth and said, 'This has touched your lips. Your guilt is taken away and your sin is forgiven.'

"I heard the voice of the LORD saying, *Whom shall I send? Who will go for us?* Then I said, 'Here I am! Send me!'

"Then HE said, *Go to the people and tell them what I say to you. If they understand, they'll turn from their wicked ways and be saved; they'll become healthy again. But it won't happen. The people will refuse to listen to you. They'll look, but they won't see. They'll hear, but they won't understand. The more you prophesy, the more stubborn they'll become.*

"I said, 'How long will this go on, LORD?'

"HE said, *Until their cities are ruined, their houses are empty, and the land is*

deserted, for I'm going to remove them from the land."

Isaiah went into the city and spoke to the people of Jerusalem. He said:

"The LORD is going to make this land a wasteland. HE looked for justice and saw bloodshed. HE looked for righteousness and heard the cry of the poor. The people will be carried away into exile because they are ignorant about the LORD. If they want to praise the LORD, they should do justice!"

SIGNS OF HOPE

Tiglath-Pileser king of Assyria and his army conquered, killed, looted, and destroyed many small nations. When Tiglath-Pileser sent his soldiers to Israel, Menahem the king of Israel collected thirty-eight tons of silver to give him as tribute. Tiglath-Pileser took the tribute and left without attacking. But every year after that, the kings of Israel had to pay tribute to the king of Assyria. Menahem's son Pekahiah, and Pekah, who became king after him, were subjects of the king of Assyria.

Rezin, king of Damascus, plotted with other Syrian kings to rebel against the king of Assyria. Pekah king of Israel joined them. They wanted Jotham king of Judah to join them, but he refused. Jotham's son Ahaz also refused to cooperate with Rezin and Pekah.

Then Pekah and Rezin said to each other, "Let's go and tear Judah apart and appoint one of our own people to be king of Judah!"

When Ahaz and his officials heard this, they trembled like trees blowing in the wind.

Pekah and Rezin attacked Jerusalem and killed many of the people. And this sent great fear into the heart of Ahaz king of Judah.

The LORD said to Isaiah, "Go to Ahaz and tell him, 'Don't be afraid of Pekah and Rezin. Their fire is going out, and their plans will fail. Pekah's kingdom will be crushed. But unless you stand firm and trust the LORD, the same thing will happen to you.' "

But Ahaz paid no attention to Isaiah's message.

The LORD sent Isaiah to Ahaz again, and he said, "You didn't pay attention before, so now ask the LORD for a sign. Go ahead, ask for anything at all."

Ahaz said, "I won't put the LORD to the test."

Then Isaiah said:

"Hear now, O House of David. Isn't it enough for you to try my patience? Now you are trying GOD's patience! The LORD HIMSELF will give you a sign:

"Behold, a maiden shall conceive and bear a son, and shall call his name Emmanuel, meaning GOD With Us. Before the child is old enough to refuse evil and choose good, the land of Rezin and Pekah will be deserted."

Ahaz gave no heed to Isaiah's signs of hope, and did not trust the LORD. Instead, he took silver and gold from the Temple and palace and sent it to Tiglath-Pileser with the message: "Come and rescue me from the king of Syria and the king of Israel!"

The king of Assyria attacked Damascus and captured it. He took the people away as captives.

Then Ahaz went to Damascus to meet Tiglath-Pileser, and he saw a great altar. He was so impressed, he sent a scale model back to the priests in Jerusalem and they built an exact copy. When he returned from Damascus, he moved the altar of the LORD and offered sacrifices on the new altar.

Ahaz died, and his son Hezekiah became king of Judah in his place.

WHAT DOES THE LORD REQUIRE?

In the days of Jotham, Ahaz, and Hezekiah, the word of the LORD came to Micah in Judah.

And Micah went into Jerusalem and said to the people:

"You ask what gift you should bring to the LORD. You ask if the LORD will be pleased with the offering of a thousand rams or ten thousand rivers of oil. You ask what sacrifice is great enough to take away your sin. But HE has already shown you what is good. What does the LORD require of you? Only this:

To do justice, to love mercy,
and to walk humbly with your GOD.

"The LORD says, *The summer fruit has been harvested, but there are no grapes. I hunger for ripe figs, but there are none. There is no justice or mercy in the land.*"

But the people listened not.

And it came to pass that the king of Assyria attacked and conquered the kingdom of Israel and the city of Samaria. The people were captured and taken away as captives to Assyria.

The ten tribes of Israel disappeared into the Assyrian empire, because they left the LORD and went after false gods, and they themselves became false.

The king of Assyria brought people from other parts of his empire and settled them in the land and cities of Israel. Then he commanded:

"Send back one of the priests of Israel that you carried away. Let him go and settle there and teach them the ways of the god of the land."

For the king of Assyria thought the god of each nation had power in his own land. But he didn't believe the LORD was greater than any other god.

One of the priests they had carried away came and lived in Bethel and taught the people how to worship the LORD. But they also served the gods of their own nations. These people became known as Samaritans, and the territory of the kingdom of Israel became known as Samaria.

THE BAREFOOT PROPHET

Hezekiah was a much better king than his father, Ahaz. He followed the ways of the LORD and smashed his father's idols and repaired the house of the LORD. He trusted the LORD, but not completely. He joined the king of Egypt and rebelled against the king of Assyria.

Isaiah the prophet came to Hezekiah and said, "You are making alliances without consulting the LORD. Instead of trusting in the LORD, you're putting your faith in warhorses, chariots, and soldiers. The Egyptians are mortals, not gods. Their horses are flesh, not spirit. Pharaoh's protection will shame you when the Egyptians will prove to be useless. They'll bring you disgrace, not help. The LORD is going to stretch out HIS hand to make them stumble. When they fall, you'll go down with them."

The LORD said to Isaiah, "Go, take off the sackcloth you are wearing, and remove the sandals from your feet."

Isaiah did as the LORD said and walked through the streets of Jerusalem barefoot and wearing only a loincloth.

He said to the people, "I'm walking naked and barefoot as a sign against Egypt. The king of Assyria will lead captives from Egypt, naked and barefoot. When that happens, you'll be ashamed that you trusted in Egypt. Everyone who sees their disgrace will say, 'Look what happened to those we hoped would save us from the king of Assyria!'"

Isaiah spoke of disaster while Hezekiah and the people of Judah rejoiced. They were certain that the rebellion would succeed.

Sennacherib king of Assyria was busy putting down revolts in the eastern part of his empire, and he didn't bother with the rebellion. The leaders of Judah boasted that they had brought peace and freedom with their clever politics and military strength. No one paid any attention to the barefoot prophet who wandered through Jerusalem, speaking of shame and defeat.

SENNACHERIB INSULTS THE LORD

After three years, Sennacherib king of Assyria gained control of the eastern part of his empire and turned his army westward, toward Egypt and Judah.

Hezekiah king of Judah prepared for a long siege. He sent men to cut off the water supply outside the city. They blocked up all the springs and channels in the countryside, saying, "Why should the Assyrians find water when they arrive?"

Jerusalem's water came from Gihon spring, which flowed down a channel to a pool just outside the city walls. Hezekiah ordered his workers to dig a long, winding tunnel underneath the city, so the water would flow from the pool outside into the Pool of Siloam, inside the walls.

While some men dug through the rock with pickaxes, others repaired the city walls and strengthened them with defense towers. Hezekiah checked his storerooms, counted the weapons and armor, and ordered more to be made.

Isaiah came to him and said, "You made all these preparations to defend the city against the Assyrians, but you forgot the LORD! You will not need your water tunnel or your walls and towers or your swords and arrows. The LORD can defend Jerusalem."

Sennacherib's army entered Judah

and captured all the towns except Lachish, the fortress that guarded the road to Jerusalem.

When Hezekiah realized that the Egyptians weren't going to help him, he sent a message to Sennacherib, saying, "I've done wrong. Please withdraw your troops! I'll pay whatever tribute you demand."

Sennacherib demanded a ton of gold and ten tons of silver. Hezekiah stripped the gold from the door of the Temple, took all the silver he could find in the storerooms, and sent it all to the town of Lachish.

Then Sennacherib sent three officials and a great army to Jerusalem. The three officials stood by the water tunnel on the road outside the city and called for Hezekiah and his officials to come out to meet them.

Hezekiah sent Eliakim, Shebna, and Joah.

One Assyrian official, called the Rabshakeh, stepped forward and said to them, "Tell Hezekiah that the great king, the king of Assyria says: 'What makes you so confident? Do you think mere words can win this war? You trusted in the Egyptians, and they turned out to be a broken reed that pierced the hand that leaned on it. Now you're trusting in the LORD your GOD. If I gave you two thousand horses, you wouldn't have enough men to put on them! So how do you think you can defeat even the smallest unit of our great army? What's more, your GOD told me to attack and destroy this land!' "

Eliakim, Shebna, and Joah said to the Rabshakeh, "Please speak to us in the Aramaic language, for we understand it. But don't speak in the language of Judah, for the people on the wall are listening."

The officials knew Aramaic, the international language, but the common people understood only Hebrew.

The Rabshakeh said to them, "Do you think my master sent me to speak only to you and your master, and not to the people sitting on the wall, who are doomed with you?"

Then the Rabshakeh stood up and shouted in Hebrew, "Hear the words of the great king, the king of Assyria! He says, 'Don't let Hezekiah deceive you! Don't believe him when he says the LORD will save you and this city won't be given into the hand of the king of Assyria. Don't listen to Hezekiah!'

"The king of Assyria says, 'Make peace with me, and every one of you will eat from his own vine and fig tree, and drink the water of his own well, until I come and take you away to a land like your own land, a land of grain and wine, a land of bread and vineyards. Don't let Hezekiah deceive you by saying the LORD will save you. Has any one of the gods of the nations saved his land from the king of Assyria? No, not one! What makes you think the LORD will save Jerusalem?' "

The people said nothing because King Hezekiah had commanded them not to answer.

Eliakim, Shebna, and Joah went to Hezekiah, their clothes torn in grief, and told what the Rabshakeh had said.

When Hezekiah heard it, he tore his clothes, covered himself with sackcloth, and went into the house of the LORD.

He sent Eliakim, Shebna, and the priests, now also clothed in sackcloth, to Isaiah. They said, "Hezekiah says, 'This is a day of suffering, punishment, and disgrace! Perhaps the LORD your GOD heard the words of the Rabshakeh, sent by the king of Assyria to mock the living GOD, and the LORD will punish him. Pray to the LORD to save Jerusalem!' "

Isaiah said to them, "Tell Hezekiah, 'The LORD says, *Do not be afraid because the servants of the king of Assyria insulted* ME. *I will cause the king of Assyria to listen to a rumor and return to his own land. I will make him fall by the sword in his own land.*' "

Sennacherib sent a letter to Hezekiah, saying, "Do not let your god deceive you by promising that Jerusalem will not be handed over to the king of Assyria. You have heard how the Assyrians have destroyed whole countries. Why should you be any different?"

Hezekiah read the letter and took it to the house of the LORD. He unrolled it in the presence of the LORD and prayed:

"O LORD of the heavenly armies! GOD of Israel! Maker of heaven and earth! Only YOU are GOD of all the kingdoms of the earth! Bend YOUR ear, O LORD, and hear! Open YOUR eyes, O LORD, and see! Hear the mocking words of Sennacherib! The kings of Assyria have destroyed whole countries and thrown their gods into the fire. But their gods weren't true gods, but just the work of human hands; and so they were destroyed. O LORD our GOD, save us, so all the kingdoms of the earth will know that only YOU are GOD!"

Isaiah sent a message to Hezekiah, saying, "The LORD has heard your prayer, and HE says to the king of Assyria: *Jerusalem despises you! She laughs at you behind your back! Whom have you insulted? The Holy One of Israel! You boasted that you conquered your empire because of your horses and chariots and your armed men. Have you not heard? I planned long ago that you would destroy whole countries. I know all about you. I heard your raging against* ME, *and I will send you back where you came from. The king of Assyria won't even enter the city. He won't shoot a single arrow against it. I will defend Jerusalem for* MY *own sake, and for the sake of* MY *servant David.*"

That night, the angel of the LORD went out and killed thousands of soldiers in the Assyrian camp. When the Assyrian troops arose the next morning, they found the dead bodies.

Sennacherib king of Assyria turned around and went back to Nineveh without even entering Jerusalem. He went to worship in the house of his god, and two of his own sons killed him with their swords.

Hezekiah king of Judah enjoyed success and peace and a long life. When he died, his son Manasseh reigned in his place.

YOUNG KING JOSIAH

Manasseh reigned for fifty-five years, longer than any other king of Judah. But he was a very wicked king. He was the worst king who ever reigned in Judah.

Manasseh rebuilt the altars that Hezekiah had smashed and built altars for Baal and made images of Asherah. He worshiped the sun and the moon and the stars. He persecuted the followers of the LORD and filled Jerusalem with the blood of innocent people.

After Manasseh died, his son Amon reigned in his place. Amon followed his father's example and served the idols his father served. Amon's servants plotted against him and killed him in his house. The common people were so outraged,

they turned on the assassins and killed them and crowned Amon's eight-year-old son Josiah as king.

When Josiah was still a little boy, the word of the LORD came to Zephaniah, a member of the royal family of Judah. Zephaniah said to the people:

"The LORD is coming to judge all the earth! He will strike Judah and all the people of Jerusalem! He will punish the rulers who misuse their authority and the wealthy who misuse their riches. Come, before you are driven away, and seek the LORD! Seek righteousness, seek humility, and perhaps you will be able to hide from the destruction that is surely coming!"

Some of the people of Judah, including King Josiah, listened to Zephaniah

and began to seek the LORD.

And it came to pass in the eighteenth year of King Josiah's reign that the king said to Shaphan, the scribe:

"Go and tell Hilkiah the high priest to melt down the silver that the people have donated to the Temple. Tell him to use it to pay builders and masons to buy timber and stones to repair the house of the LORD."

Shaphan went to the Temple and gave Hilkiah the king's message.

A short time later, Hilkiah came to Shaphan and said, "I have found the Book of the Law in the house of the LORD!"

For while Hilkiah was taking the silver out of the storerooms, he had found an old scroll that had been hidden away in the days of Manasseh and Amon. On the scroll was written part of the teaching of Moses.

Hilkiah gave the book to Shaphan, and he read it. Then Shaphan went to King Josiah and said:

"We've done as you commanded. We took the silver we found in the Temple and gave it to the workmen who are repairing the Temple. Now, look at this! Hilkiah has given me a book."

Shaphan read the book aloud to the king. When Josiah heard what was written in the book, he was so upset that he tore his clothes in grief, for the people of Judah had not been following the teachings of Moses.

Josiah said to Hilkiah and Shaphan and his other officials, "Go ask the LORD for me and the people of Judah about the words of this book. The LORD must be very angry, for our ancestors have not obeyed the words of this book."

The men went to Huldah the prophet and told her what had happened. She consulted the LORD and came back to them and said:

"The LORD says, 'Tell the king, *I will* bring disaster *on this place and all its people, as it says in the book, because they have left* ME *and have worshiped other gods and provoked* ME *to anger.* MY *wrath will be kindled against this place, and it will not be quenched.'*

"But also say to the king of Judah, *Because your heart was sorry and you humbled yourself before the LORD, and you tore your clothes and cried before* ME, *I have heard you. I will gather you to your*

people, and then made a covenant, promising to follow the ways of the LORD and do what was written in the book. And the people joined in the covenant.

Then Josiah commanded the priests and officials to cleanse the Temple of all the things that had been made for idols. He burned them in the city dump in the Kidron Valley. He sent away the mediums and wizards and destroyed the idols and images in Jerusalem and Judah.

Next Josiah went to Bethel and tore down the altar built by Jeroboam. He smashed the altar and burned the idols. He killed the priests and burned their bones on the altar. All these things happened just as the man of GOD had said to Jeroboam.

Then Josiah returned to Jerusalem and said to the people, "Celebrate the Passover in honor of the LORD our GOD, as it is written in this book."

Josiah turned to the LORD with all his heart and soul and might. He was the most righteous king to ever reign in Judah.

While Josiah was king of Judah, the Assyrian empire began to fall apart. Neco, Pharaoh of Egypt, went to help the Assyrians, for he feared that the Babylonians who were attacking the Assyrians would next attack Egypt.

Josiah was more afraid of the Assyrians than the Babylonians. He sent a message to Pharaoh Neco, telling him to stay home.

Neco answered, "This war is none of your concern, king of Judah!"

Josiah went out to battle against Neco. The armies met at Megiddo, near Jezreel, and Josiah was killed by an Egyptian arrow.

Josiah's servants took his body back to Jerusalem and buried him, and his son Jehoahaz reigned in his place.

ancestors and you will go down to your grave in peace. Your eyes won't see the disaster that I will bring on this place."

The men went back to Josiah and told him what Huldah had said. Josiah called together the leaders of Judah and Jerusalem and went with them to the house of the LORD. All the people of Judah and Jerusalem went with them, priests and prophets, rich and poor.

Josiah read the book out loud to the

Now, Jeremiah was about the same age as Josiah. When he was very young, the word of the LORD had come to him, saying:

"Before I formed you in the womb, I knew you. I set you apart and appointed you as a prophet to the nations before you were born."

Jeremiah said, "Ah, LORD GOD! I don't know how to speak. I am only a youth."

The LORD said to him, "Do not say you are only a youth. You must go where I send you, and speak what I command you. Fear not, for I am with you!"

The LORD put out HIS hand and touched Jeremiah's mouth and said, "I have put MY words in your mouth. Today I have set you over nations and kingdoms, to pluck up and tear down, to build and to plant."

Jeremiah began to speak to the people, warning them that the LORD was coming to destroy Jerusalem if the people did not change their behavior.

Jeremiah said, "The LORD is disappointed in you, people of Judah! He says, I want to harvest fruit, but there are no grapes on the vine, no figs on the fig tree. Even the leaves are withered."

But no one listened to him.

But the rich people were even worse than the poor. "Don't speak to us about the LORD!" they said. "HE won't do anything bad to us. You prophets are nothing but wind."

"Foolish people!" cried Jeremiah. "You have eyes, but you do not see. You have ears, but you do not hear. You grow fat by cheating the poor. You don't defend the rights of the needy. Why should the LORD not punish you?"

Upon Josiah's death, the prophet Jeremiah said to the people, "Don't cry for Josiah. Cry for Jehoahaz, who will never return to his native land. He will die a prisoner in a foreign country."

Josiah's son Jehoahaz was put in chains by Pharaoh Neco and taken as a captive to Egypt. He never returned to Judah, but died in Egypt, as Jeremiah had prophesied. Neco made Jehoahaz's brother Jehoiakim the new king of Judah.

The LORD showed Jeremiah visions of the Babylonians invading Judah and Jerusalem. Jeremiah loved his people, so it hurt him to see such things.

"I can't bear it!" he cried. "My heart is sick at the sight of so much misery. Oh, I wish my head were water and my eyes a fountain of tears so I could cry all day and all night for my people."

The LORD was also grieving, and he said to Jeremiah, "MY heart is wounded because of the wound of MY people. I mourn, because of what will happen to them."

But the people did not listen to Jeremiah, and they did not return to the LORD. They were sure that the LORD was with them and would bless them, no matter what they did. Even Jeremiah's family and the people in his hometown hated his message.

Then the LORD said to Jeremiah, "Go through the streets of Jerusalem. Search everywhere for someone who does justice and seeks truth. If you find one person, I will pardon the whole city."

Jeremiah went back and forth through the streets of Jerusalem, looking for one person who followed the ways of the LORD. But he found only liars, cheats, and thieves.

He said to himself, "I've only seen the poor people. They have no sense. They don't know what the LORD requires. I'll go speak to the rich people. They know GOD's Law."

"Everyone laughs at me!" complained Jeremiah. "When I speak, they criticize me. I am sorry I was born! I've done nothing wrong, but everyone hates me. I sit alone while they laugh and have a good time. I'm just trying to serve YOU, LORD. Please help me."

"Complain no more," said the LORD. "I will watch over you."

Jeremiah went back to the people and said, "The LORD said to me: *Go buy yourself a linen waistcloth. Wear it around your waist, and do not put it in water.* So I bought the waistcloth, as the LORD said, and put it on.

"Then the word of the LORD came to me a second time, saying, *Take the waistcloth and go to the Euphrates River and hide it under a rock.* So I went to the Euphrates and buried the waistcloth.

"After many days, the LORD said to me, *Go to the Euphrates and bring back the waistcloth.*

"I went to the Euphrates and took the waistcloth from the place I had hidden it. But the waistcloth was ruined. It was good for nothing.

"Then the LORD said to me, *I will spoil the pride of Judah and Jerusalem. The people refuse to hear MY words, and they have gone after other gods. They will be like this waistcloth—good for nothing. Just as a waistcloth clings to the body, I wanted the people of Israel and Judah to cling to ME. I wanted them to be MY people. But they would not listen.*"

TWO BASKETS OF FIGS

Jehoiakim king of Judah saw that the Babylonians were becoming powerful, so he changed sides and supported the Babylonians against the Egyptians. He paid tribute to Nebuchadnezzar king of Babylon for three years. Then the Egyptians seemed strong, and he changed sides again.

Nebuchadnezzar sent his troops to Judah. But before they arrived, Jehoiakim died and his son Jehoiachin became king. Nebuchadnezzar attacked and captured Jerusalem; and Jehoiachin and his family were taken prisoner and carried away to Babylon, along with the gold of the Temple and the treasures of the palace. The nobles and leading people of Judah were carried away into exile in Babylon.

Jehoiachin remained in Babylon for the rest of his life. Nebuchadnezzar put a third son of Josiah on the throne of Judah and renamed him Zedekiah.

And it came to pass that the LORD showed Jeremiah a vision of two baskets of figs placed in front of the Temple. In one basket were some very good figs. The ones in the second basket were so bad, they could not be eaten.

"What do you see, Jeremiah?" asked the LORD.

"Figs. The good ones are very good, but the bad figs are very bad. They are so bad, they cannot be eaten."

The LORD said to Jeremiah:

"The exiles I sent away to Babylon are like the good figs. I will watch over them and bring them back to this land. I will give them a new heart, and they will know that I am the LORD. They will be MY people, and I will be their GOD. But Zedekiah and his officials and the people remaining in this land are like the bad figs. I will send war, starvation, and disease until they are wiped out."

Jeremiah's message was not welcome in Jerusalem. The king and his officials believed that GOD was with them and not the exiles.

Many false prophets agreed with the king. They said, "The LORD will never let Jerusalem be destroyed, for HIS Temple is here. HE will never let the royal family of Judah die out, for HE made a promise to David. Do not worry. All will be well."

JEREMIAH IN THE PIT

The Pharaoh of Egypt plotted with other kings against Nebuchadnezzar, and Zedekiah joined the rebellion. Ambassadors came to Jerusalem to plan the rebellion.

Then the LORD said to Jeremiah, "Make some leather cords and a wooden yoke beam. Tie the yoke across the back of your neck, as a farmer puts a yoke on the neck of an ox. Then go see the foreign ambassadors and show them the yoke and speak to them as I tell you."

Jeremiah made the leather cords and the wooden yoke and tied the yoke to his shoulders. Then he went to the palace to see the ambassadors.

He said, "It is the LORD who has handed the nations over to Nebuchadnezzar, king of Babylon. You will be his subjects until the LORD destroys Babylon. Everyone who refuses to put his neck under the yoke of Nebuchadnezzar will be punished with war, starvation, and disease.

"Do not listen to the false prophets who tell you not to serve the king of Babylon. If you listen to them, you will be removed from your land. If you put your neck under the yoke of the king of Babylon and serve him, the LORD will leave you in your land."

Then Jeremiah left the ambassadors and went to the priests and the people. He kept the yoke on his neck and said, "Do not listen to false prophets. Serve the king of Babylon and live. The LORD is going to let the Babylonians come to Jerusalem and take everything that's left in the Temple and carry it to Babylon until the LORD brings them back!"

But the rebellion continued, for King Zedekiah had Jeremiah arrested and put into a dungeon.

Then the officials went to the king and said, "Put this man to death! He is discouraging our soldiers and our people. He doesn't care about Jerusalem. He wants us to be destroyed."

Zedekiah said, "He is in your hands. Do whatever you want to him."

They took Jeremiah and dropped him into a pit—a cistern in the court of the prison. There was no water in the cistern, only mud. As Jeremiah was let down with ropes, he sank into the mud.

A palace official, an Ethiopian named Ebed-Melek, heard what was going on, and he went to the king and said, "My lord king! The men who have thrown Jeremiah the prophet into the cistern have committed a great crime! They've left him down there to die!"

Zedekiah said, "Take three of my servants and go to Jeremiah and pull him out before he dies."

Ebed-Melek went to a room in the palace where clothing was stored and took some scraps and rags. He lowered these with ropes to Jeremiah in the pit.

"Put these rags under your arms," he said. "They will pad you against the ropes so they will not cut you."

Jeremiah did so, and Ebed-Melek and Zedekiah's servants pulled him up out of the pit with the ropes.

Zedekiah sent a message to Jeremiah to meet him in a private place outside the Temple, where no one could see or hear them.

"I want to ask you something," Zedekiah said. "Keep nothing from me."

Jeremiah answered, "If I speak openly, won't you have me put to death? And if I give you good advice, won't you ignore it?"

"I promise I won't have you put to death," Zedekiah said, "and I won't hand you over to your enemies."

"I will tell you exactly what the LORD has said. If you obey the LORD and surrender to the Babylonians, HE will let you live, and the city won't be destroyed. You'll die peacefully, with a proper funeral and burial. But if you don't surrender, the city will be burned down. You and your family will be handed over as prisoners to Nebuchadnezzar. You'll see him face-to-face, talk with him, and go with him to Babylon."

"I'm afraid!" cried Zedekiah. "If I surrender, they might torture me!"

"Do not worry," said Jeremiah. "That won't happen. If you listen to the voice of the LORD, all will be well. But if you refuse, you and your wives and children will be taken to the Babylonians and terrible things will happen."

"Tell no one of this secret meeting," said Zedekiah. "If my officials should ask, just say you were asking me not to send you back to prison."

Zedekiah did not trust in the LORD. Instead, he listened to his officials and went ahead with the rebellion. Nebuchadnezzar sent an army to Judah, and the Egyptians came to help.

Then Jeremiah said to Zedekiah and his officials, "The Egyptians will turn around and go home. Nothing can stop the Babylonians from destroying Jerusalem. If you strike them down and only the wounded are left, the LORD will raise them up from their beds and bring them back!"

The LORD gave Jeremiah a message for Ebed-Melek the Ethiopian. Jeremiah said to him, "The LORD will surely bring disaster to this city, but on that day HE will rescue you, for you have put your trust in the LORD."

The Last Days of Judah

The Egyptian army pulled out of Judah, and the Babylonians returned. They captured the last two fortresses outside of Jerusalem, and then they laid siege to the city.

During the siege the LORD said to Jeremiah, "Your cousin Hanamel is going to come and ask you to buy his field at Anathoth."

Hanamel came and said, "I have a field I want to sell, and you have the duty to buy it to keep it in the family."

Jeremiah knew this came from the LORD, and he bought the field for seventeen pieces of silver. He weighed the silver and signed a deed and sealed it in front of witnesses. He took the deed and gave it and a copy to his friend Baruch to put in a clay pot for safekeeping.

Jeremiah told his friends that buying a field was a sign of hope. Still he prayed:

"LORD GOD! See how the siege ramps are already in place to capture the city! The Babylonians will soon destroy Jerusalem! Why did YOU tell me to go and buy a field at a time like this? I don't understand."

The LORD said to Jeremiah, "Is anything impossible for ME? I am giving this city into the hand of Nebuchadnezzar because of the evil of the people and their kings. But someday I will gather MY people and bring them back to this place, and they will live in safety. They will be MY people, and I will be their GOD. Your deed to the field is a sign of these things. Someday they will buy fields in this place and draw up deeds and witness them. I am not rejecting MY people forever. I will restore them and have mercy on them."

The siege of Jerusalem lasted eighteen months. The Egyptians never arrived.

Nebuchadnezzar's army attacked the city with towers, ramps, and battering rams. They cut off supplies of food and water, so many people inside the city died of disease and starvation. When the Babylonians broke through the walls of Jerusalem, they killed many more with their swords. They set fire to the city, and the walls and the Temple collapsed into heaps of rubble.

Zedekiah ran away to Jericho and was captured and taken to Nebuchadnezzar's headquarters. Nebuchadnezzar killed Zedekiah's sons in front of his eyes. Then he killed all the nobles of Judah. He put out Zedekiah's eyes and bound him in chains to take him away as a prisoner to Babylon.

Nebuchadnezzar's commander burned the Temple and the palace and the mansions of the city. He set fire to the wood, and the heat of the fire cracked the stones. Jerusalem was a wasteland.

He carried into exile the rich people of Judah and left their fields and vineyards for the poor people of the land.

He smashed the pillars in front of the Temple and took all the gold and silver furnishings out of the Temple and took them to Babylon.

After the fall of Jerusalem, Jeremiah wrote a letter to the exiles in Babylon saying:

"The LORD says, *Build houses and become settled. Plant gardens. Marry, have children, and raise families. Seek the good of the city where I have sent you. Pray for its welfare, because your good depends on its good. I will bring you back in seventy years. I will take notice of you and bring you back to this place, because I have plans for you. MY plans are for good, not evil. I plan to give you a future.*"

A priest named Ezekiel was living in Babylon with the first group of captives, before Jerusalem was destroyed. In the fifth year of the exile, the word of the LORD came to him as he was standing in the valley beside the Chebar River. He saw a vision of a fiery chariot driven by four living creatures, and above the chariot he saw the glory of GOD. This is what Ezekiel said about his vision:

The faces in front were human faces, the faces on the right were lions' faces, the faces on the left were bulls' faces, and the faces in back were eagles' faces.

Each creature had two wings hanging down, with human hands underneath. The other two wings were spread out, touching the tips of the other creatures' wings.

In the middle of the creatures was something that looked like burning coals of fire, like torches moving back and forth among the creatures. The fire was bright, and lightning was coming out of it.

I saw four wheels on the ground, one beside each creature. Within each wheel was another wheel, so each could move in all four directions without turning. The wheels sparkled like jewels. They had rims and spokes, and around the rims were watching eyes.

When the creatures moved, the wheels moved beside them. Wherever the Spirit would go, they went, and the wheels rose along with them. The Spirit of the living creatures was in the wheels. When the wheels moved, they moved. When the wheels stood still, they stood still. They rose from the earth, and the wheels rose with them.

When they moved, I heard the sound of their wings like the roar of the ocean —like the thunder of the Almighty— like the sound of a battle! When they stood still, they let down their wings.

Spread out over their heads was something like a dome, shining like crystal.

Above the dome was something like a throne, looking like sapphire.

Sitting high above it was something that looked like a human being. Above the waist I saw what looked like shining bronze, surrounded by what looked like fire. Below the waist I also saw the fire,

The heavens were opened, and I saw visions of GOD.

I saw a wind coming out of the north, and a great cloud with brightness around it, and fire flashing out of it.

In the middle of the fire were four living creatures, golden and shiny, like polished bronze. They had the form of human beings, but each had four faces and four wings. They stood up on straight legs, but their feet were round like cattle.

surrounded by brightness. It was as bright as a rainbow in the clouds after the rain. It looked like the glory of the LORD, and when I saw it, I fell on my face.

A voice came from above the dome, and said:

"Son of man, stand on your feet, and I will speak with you."

When HE spoke, the Spirit entered into me and set me back up on my feet.

He said:

"Son of man, I am sending you to the Israelites, who are a stubborn people. Speak the word of the LORD. Whether or not they listen, they will know that a prophet has been among them. As for you, son of man, listen to what I say. Do not be rebellious like them. Now open your mouth and eat what I give you."

I saw a hand stretched out to me with a scroll in it. HE unrolled it in front me, and I saw writing on the front and the back. I saw words of sadness and mourning and cries of grief.

"Son of man," HE said, "eat this scroll. Then go and speak to the Israelites."

I opened my mouth, and HE gave me the scroll.

He said:

"Son of man, swallow this scroll."

I ate it, and it was as sweet as honey in my mouth.

He said:

"Son of man, go to the Israelites and speak MY words. You are not being sent to a people who speak a strange language to you. Yet, if I sent you to foreigners, they would listen—but the Israelites won't listen. They aren't willing to listen, because they are stubborn. So I am hardening your face against their faces, and I am making your head

as hard as a diamond, harder than flint. Do not be afraid of them, for they are a rebellious nation."

Then HE said to me:

"Son of man, receive all MY words in your heart. Go to the exiles and speak MY words to them, whether or not they listen to you."

Then the Spirit lifted me up, and the glory of the LORD rose from its place. I heard behind me the sound of a great earthquake. It was the sound of the wings of the creatures as they touched each other, and the sound of the wheels beside them.

The Spirit took me away, and I felt angry and bitter when I returned to the exiles who lived beside the Chebar River. I stayed in my house, exhausted, for seven days.

Seven days later the word of the LORD came to me, saying:

"Get up and go out into the valley. I will speak to you there."

I got up and went out into the valley. I saw the glory of the LORD, like the glory I had seen by the Chebar River, and I fell on my face.

The Spirit entered into me and lifted me back up on my feet. HE said to me:

"Go, shut yourself inside your house. I will make your tongue stick to the roof of your mouth so you will not be able to speak. But when I speak with you, I will open your mouth, and you will tell them what I have said. Let those who hear, hear. Let those who refuse, refuse. For they are a rebellious people."

I went home and locked myself inside my house. I spoke only when the LORD opened my mouth. When I tried to say anything else, my tongue stuck to the roof of my mouth.

The Lord Destroys the Temple

When God opened Ezekiel's mouth, Ezekiel spoke the word of the Lord to the exiles and told them about the terrible destruction coming to Jerusalem. He said the people in the city would die from starvation and be killed by the sword. Some would be scattered, and only a few would be saved and turn back to the Lord.

Ezekiel kept speaking the word of the Lord to the exiles. Then one day, in the ninth year of the exile, he heard very bad news. This is what he told the people.

The word of the Lord came to me, saying, "Today is the day that the king of Babylon is beginning the siege of Jerusalem. The city is doomed."

Then the word of the Lord came to me again and said, "Son of man, I am about to take the delight of your eyes away from you. But you must not mourn or cry nor let your tears run down. Sigh, but not out loud. Do not mourn for the dead. Tie on your turban and put your shoes on your feet. Do not cover your lips or eat the food of mourners."

I told this to the people in the morning, and in the evening my wife died.

The next morning I did as I was commanded, and the people said to me, "Won't you tell us what this means for us? Why are you behaving like this?"

I answered, "The Lord said to me, *Tell the Israelites I will destroy* MY *Temple, the pride of your power, the delight of your eyes, the desire of your soul. Your sons and daughters left behind in Jerusalem will fall by the sword. Then you must do what Ezekiel has done. You must not cover your lips or eat the food of mourning. Keep your turbans on your heads, and your shoes on your feet. Do not mourn or weep, but pine away in your sin and groan to one another.*"

Then the Lord said to me, "On the day that I take away the Temple, their joy and glory, the delight of their eyes and their heart's desire, and their sons and daughters, a fugitive will come to you to report the news. On that day your mouth will be open to the fugitive, and you will speak."

One evening in the twelfth year of our exile, the hand of the Lord was on me, and HE opened my mouth, and I could speak whenever I wished. The next morning a man who had escaped from Jerusalem came to me and said:

"The city has fallen."

The Valley of Dry Bones

After Jerusalem fell and the Temple was destroyed, the Israelites were depressed and afraid. The LORD sent prophets to give them hope about their future. The prophets said, "Nothing is impossible for the LORD. HE is the Creator of life, and HE loves HIS people. Do not be afraid."

Ezekiel told the people, "With GOD, death is not the end."

Then he told them about a vision.

⌒

The hand of the LORD was on me, and HE brought me out by HIS Spirit and set me down in the middle of a valley. It was full of bones—a great many dry bones.

HE said to me, "Son of man, can these bones live?"

I answered, "O LORD GOD, YOU know."

HE said to me, "Prophesy to these bones, and say to them, 'O dry bones, hear the word of the LORD. The LORD GOD says to these bones: *I will cause breath to enter you, and you will live. I will put muscles on you and cause flesh to come upon you and cover you with skin and put breath in you, and you will live. You will know that I am the LORD.*' "

I prophesied as I was commanded.

As I prophesied, I heard a noise of rattling, and the bones came together, bone to its bone. As I watched, there were muscles on them, and flesh had come upon them, and skin had covered them. But there was no breath in them.

Then the LORD said to me, "Prophesy to the breath! Prophesy, son of man, and say to the breath, 'The LORD GOD says: *Come, wind, from the four corners of the earth, and breathe on the bodies of these who have been killed. Let them live!*' "

I prophesied as HE commanded me, and the breath came into them, and they lived and stood on their feet. It was a very great army!

Then HE said to me:

"Son of man, these bones are the whole people of Israel. They say, 'Our bones are dried up, and our hope is lost. We are destroyed.' Prophesy and say to them, 'The LORD says: *I will open your graves and raise you from your graves, O* MY *people! I will bring you back home to the land, and you will know that I am the LORD. I will put* MY *Spirit in you, and you will live, and I will place you in your own land. Then you will know that I, the LORD, have spoken and I have done it.*' "

EZEKIEL'S VISION OF A NEW JERUSALEM

When the Temple was destroyed, the people were afraid that GOD had left them forever.

But it came to pass that GOD gave Ezekiel a vision of a new Jerusalem, and showed him that HE had plans for HIS people.

"Someday," GOD said to Ezekiel, "I will destroy the evil kingdoms of the world, and I will be with MY people in a new Jerusalem."

This is what Ezekiel told the people.

⌒

In the twenty-fifth year of our exile, the hand of the LORD was on me, and brought me in a vision to the land of Israel, and he set me down on a very high mountain, with a city opposite.

I saw a man who was like bronze with a linen string and measuring stick in his hand, and he was standing in the gateway of the city.

The man said to me, "Son of man, look with your eyes, hear with your ears, and set your mind on everything I will show you. Then go back and report everything to the Israelites."

He took me to a new Jerusalem, and showed me all through a new Temple. He carefully measured every part of the Temple, inside and out. He gave me detailed instructions for worship in the new Temple, and then he took me to the east gate.

I looked up and saw the glory of the LORD of Israel coming toward the Temple from the east. I heard a sound like many waters, and the earth was shining with the glory of the LORD. Then I fell down with my face on the ground.

The glory of the LORD entered the east gate of the Temple, and the Spirit lifted me up and took me to the inner courtyard. I saw the glory of the LORD filling the Temple, and I heard someone speaking to me from inside the Temple, saying:

"Son of man! This is the place of MY throne and the place of the soles of MY feet. I will live here among the Israelites forever. Never again will they disgrace MY holy name with their sins.

"Go to the people and tell them about the plan for a new Temple and let them know how to worship in this place."

Then HE said:

"The new Jerusalem will be called 'The LORD Is Here.'"

THE STORY OF JOB

Priests like Ezekiel and prophets like Jeremiah had warned the people that if they didn't change their behavior, Jerusalem and the Temple would be destroyed. They told them that the king, who sat on the throne of David, and the people of GOD would go into exile in a foreign land.

But the people didn't listen to the prophets, and they didn't change their behavior.

When these things happened, their hearts were broken. They felt ashamed and shocked that the LORD had allowed such horrible things to happen to them. They cried over the ruins of the city, and they struggled with GOD.

Some asked GOD, "Why did you do this to us, YOUR own people? Why us? Look at all those other nations whose sins were worse than ours!"

Others said, "If this is how the LORD treats us, why should we even bother with HIM?"

They wanted to know, "Why do we suffer? Where is GOD when we endure troubles?"

They looked for answers in the words of the prophets and the stories of GOD's people. The prophets and the stories didn't give them the answers to all their questions, but they revealed truths about GOD and HIS plan.

The *Story of Job* and his many sufferings is one such story.

Long ago in the land of Uz, there lived a man whose name was Job. He was a righteous man who honored GOD and turned from evil. He and his wife had seven sons and three daughters. He had seven thousand sheep, three thousand camels, five hundred pairs of oxen, five hundred donkeys, and many servants. He was the richest man in the East.

Job's sons used to take turns holding feasts in their houses, one after the other. They invited each other and their three sisters to eat and drink with them. After each of the seven parties, Job would rise early in the morning to pray and offer a sacrifice for each of his children, "Just in case," he thought, "one of them has sinned or offended GOD."

Then one day the heavenly beings came into the presence of the LORD, and Satan, the Accuser, was with them.

"Where have you been?" the LORD asked Satan.

"Roaming the earth," he answered. "Spying."

"Did you check on my servant Job?" asked the LORD. "There is no one on earth as righteous as Job. He honors ME and turns away from evil."

Then Satan said to the LORD, "Would Job honor YOU if YOU gave him no reward? You've put a fence around him and his family and everything he owns. You've blessed the work of his hands, and his possessions have increased in the land. But if YOU put out YOUR hand now and touched all that he has, he will curse YOU to YOUR face."

The LORD said to Satan, "We will see. All that he has is now in your power. But keep your hand off Job himself."

Then Satan went out from the presence of the LORD.

One day when Job's sons and daughters were eating and drinking wine in their oldest brother's house, a messenger came to Job and cried:

"The oxen were plowing and the donkeys were feeding beside them, when desert raiders from the south attacked them and took them away! They killed the servants with their swords! And only I am escaped to tell you."

While he was still speaking, another came and said:

"The fire of GOD fell from heaven and burned up the sheep and the servants and consumed them! And only I am escaped to tell you."

While he was still speaking, another came and said:

"Babylonian soldiers from the north raided the camels and took them and killed the servants with their swords! And only I am escaped to tell you."

And while he was still speaking, yet another came and said:

"Your sons and daughters were eating and drinking wine in their oldest brother's house. Suddenly a great wind came across the wilderness and struck the four corners of the house, and it fell down on the young people, and they are dead! And only I am escaped to tell you."

Then Job stood up and tore his robe and fell on the ground and worshiped. He said:

"I was naked when I came into the world, and I will return naked. The LORD gave, and the LORD has taken away. Blessed be the name of the LORD!"

In all this, Job did not sin or accuse GOD of wrong.

Again the heavenly beings came into the presence of the LORD, and Satan the Accuser was with them.

"Where have you been?" the LORD asked Satan.

"Roaming the earth," he answered. "Spying."

"Did you check on my servant Job?" asked the LORD. "There is no one on earth as righteous as Job. He honors ME and turns away from evil. He still holds on to his integrity, even though you moved ME against him to destroy him for no reason."

Then Satan said, "Skin for skin! A man will give all he has for his life. If YOU put out YOUR hand now and touch his bone and his flesh, he will curse YOU to YOUR face."

The LORD said to Satan, "We will see. He is in your power. But spare his life."

Then Satan went out from the presence of the LORD and afflicted Job with horrible sores from the top of his head to the bottom of his feet.

Job was so miserable, he took a pottery shard to scratch himself and went and sat on top of an ash heap.

His wife said to him, "Do you still hold on to your integrity? Curse GOD and die."

But he said to her, "You speak foolishness. All things, both good and bad, are gifts from GOD. If we receive the good, we must receive the bad."

Job's three friends, Eliphaz, Bildad and Zophar, heard about the evil that had come upon him, and they agreed to go together and comfort him. When they saw him from a distance, he looked so awful they didn't recognize him. Then they saw that it really was their friend sitting on the ash heap, and they cried aloud and tore their robes and threw dust up in the air over their heads.

Job's friends sat down on the ground beside him for seven days and seven nights, and no one said a word to him, for they saw that his suffering was very great.

Then Job opened his mouth and cursed the day of his birth.

He said, "I wish that I had never lived. Everything I was ever afraid of has happened to me. It is unfair!"

Eliphaz said to Job, "You used to help other people when they were in trouble.

Now let me help you. Here is my advice. It is known that GOD rewards the innocent and punishes the guilty. If you obey GOD, HE will reward you and make you rich and healthy. If you sin, HE will punish you with poverty and disease. That's the way it is, Job. That's what the wise men teach. If I were you, Job, I'd pray to GOD right now and confess my sins. Listen to me, Job. I know what I'm talking about."

"Your advice does me no good," answered Job. "What you say is senseless. I don't deserve this punishment. What terrible things have I done?"

Bildad said to Job, "GOD always rewards the righteous, and HE always punishes sinners. Obviously, if you haven't sinned, then your children have. That is

the answer! That is why you're being punished. Now go on and pray to GOD. If you're innocent, HE will reward you."

Job said, "I know my family is innocent—but I am miserable. I'll soon die and go down to the grave. Until that happens, I will go on complaining. I won't be quiet, for GOD is attacking me! I know I can't win an argument with GOD. HE's too powerful. I just wish someone would come between me and HIM. I know there must be someone who could redeem me. If not now, then after I die. Then I'll see GOD!"

Zophar said, "Don't speak that way, Job. You say you and your family are innocent, but it's not possible. If you're innocent, then GOD must reward you. GOD must bless the innocent and punish

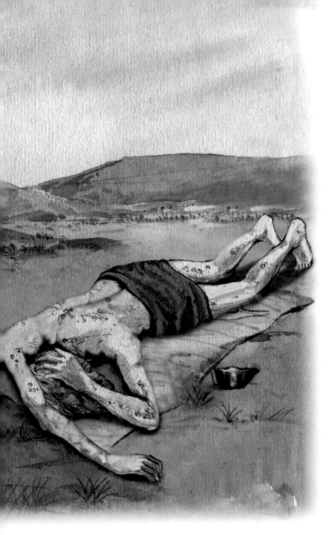

the guilty. That's the way it works, so you must be a sinner."

Job said, "I know the same things you know. But I want to argue my case with God."

Job's skin was covered with painful, oozing sores. He was so thin, his bones stuck out. He cried out to God, saying:

"It is unfair! If I'm guilty, then pardon me. I know I'm not perfect. I admitted my faults. Why don't you forgive me? Is there no justice?"

Eliphaz said to Job, "You're guilty! How dare you question God! You're a worse sinner than we ever knew!"

"Stop!" cried Job. "You criticize me for crying out to God, but you defend HIM with lies, you miserable comforters! Is there no end to your vain words?

You don't understand what I'm going through."

And Job thought deeply on matters, and he asked God, "Why do the wicked live to old age, and get rich? Why don't you punish evildoers?"

The longer he sat on the pile of ashes, the more he questioned his own thoughts on truth and justice.

He said, "Why do the poor suffer? The rich cheat them and steal their land. They push them off the road and take their possessions. The poor have to gather the castoffs of the rich. They have no blankets to cover them in the cold. It's not their fault. They are not greater sinners than the rich. They work hard and cry out, and yet God pays no attention."

Job's friends gave up in disgust.

Job said to himself, "I'm not guilty of any serious sin. I helped the poor. I was not proud. I gave hospitality to strangers. I admitted my faults. I didn't trust in riches. I didn't worship idols. I did not rejoice when my enemies suffered. I was kind to everyone. Oh, I was so happy in the old days! Everyone respected me then. Now they all laugh at me. I wish I could go back to the way things used to be."

Then Job said to God, "It is unfair! You punish the innocent and reward the guilty! Aren't we all the same? Aren't we all sinners?"

Then a young man named Elihu came to Job and said:

"Now it's my turn to speak. I may be young, but I know what I speak of. The reason God sends suffering is to teach us lessons and to keep us from sinning. Your suffering is part of the order that God has created. Wise people understand these things. You should be aware of this."

After Elihu finished speaking, the Lord answered Job from out of a whirlwind.

"Who are you to question ME?" HE said to Job. "Your words are empty and ignorant. Stand up like a man! I will ask the questions and you will answer.

"Where were you when I created the earth? Tell ME, if you know so much: Who decided on its measurements? Do you know? Who laid its foundations? Where were you then? Do you understand how the wild animals live? Tell ME about lions and mountain goats. They live without any help from you. You men think you can control everything. But I delight in the freedom of wild animals. You are not the reason for MY Creation. I made animals that are of no use to you. I send rain to places it does you no good. Do you know why? I created the sun and the moon and the stars. You think you can understand GOD! Do you know why

I created great sea creatures? Well, Job, do you give up? Does the critic of Almighty GOD have an answer?"

Job said, "My words have been small. How can I answer? I put my hand over my mouth. I won't say anything else. I've already said more than I should."

The Lord spoke again from the whirlwind:

"Stand up like a man! I will ask the questions and you will answer. You accuse ME of injustice to prove your innocence. Do you have an arm like GOD? Can you thunder with a voice like GOD's? Should I give humans the power to destroy evil? Would you destroy the sea monsters I created? Do you really think you understand these things?"

Job said, "I know that YOU can do all things, and nothing can stop YOUR purposes. I have spoken about things I did not understand. Before this, I knew YOU only from hearing what other people said about YOU. But now I have seen YOU with my own eyes. I am sorry. I take back everything I said."

The LORD turned to Job's comforters and said:

"I am angry with you, for you did not tell the truth about ME, as MY servant Job has done. Take seven bulls and seven rams and give them to Job to offer as a sacrifice. Job will pray for you, and I will listen to his prayers and forgive you."

The men did as the LORD commanded, and the LORD answered Job's prayer and forgave them.

Then the LORD restored Job's fortunes and gave him twice as much as before.

All Job's brothers and sisters and old friends came and feasted with him in his house. They showed him sympathy for all his past troubles. Each of them gave him a silver coin and a gold ring.

The LORD blessed the end of Job's life more than the beginning. Now he had fourteen thousand sheep, six thousand camels, a thousand pairs of oxen, and a thousand donkeys.

He also had seven sons and three daughters. And in all the land, there were none so fair as the daughters of Job. And Job gave them a full share of the inheritance with their brothers.

After this, Job lived long enough to see his grandchildren and great-grandchildren. He died an old man, full of days.

THE STORY OF DANIEL
REFUSING THE KING'S FOOD

When Nebuchadnezzar king of Babylon came to Jerusalem and besieged it, the LORD gave the king of Judah into Nebuchadnezzar's hand, along with some of the furnishings and vessels from the house of GOD. Nebuchadnezzar brought them to his land and placed them in the treasury of his god.

Then he commanded Ashpenaz, his palace master, to select some boys from the Jewish captives and bring them to the king's palace. He told him to teach the boys the language and literature of the Babylonians. He wanted youths without blemish—handsome and intelligent, healthy and well-educated.

The king directed his officials to give the youths a daily portion of the rich food that the king ate, and the wine that he drank. They were to be educated for three years, and at the end of that time they were to enter the service of the king.

Now, among these youths were some of the boys of Judah: Daniel, Hananiah, Mishael, and Azariah. The palace master gave them new names. Daniel became Belteshazzar, Hananiah became Shadrach, Mishael became Meshach, and Azariah became Abednego.

Daniel decided to keep the Jewish laws and not eat the king's rich food or drink the wine. When he asked the palace master to let him refuse the food, GOD caused the palace master to look at Daniel with favor and compassion. He said to Daniel:

"I fear what will happen if the king sees you and you don't look healthy. If you don't eat the food and drink the wine that the king has directed me to give you, I'll be in danger of losing my head."

Daniel went to the steward in charge of Daniel, Hananiah, Mishael, and Azariah, and said to him, "Test us for ten days. Give us peas and beans to eat and water to drink. Then see how we look compared to the youths who eat the king's food."

The steward agreed to do what Daniel asked, and he tested them for ten days. At the end of ten days, he saw that they looked better and fatter than all the youths who ate the king's rich food. So he took away their rich food and the wine and gave them peas and beans.

GOD gave the four youths knowledge and skill in all literature and science. Daniel also had understanding of visions and dreams.

At the end of the time that the king had set, the palace master brought the youths into the presence of Nebuchadnezzar, and the king spoke with them. Among them all, none compared to Daniel, Hananiah, Mishael, and Azariah, and they entered the king's service. Whenever the king asked them for wisdom and understanding, he found them ten times better than the magicians and enchanters in all his kingdom.

And Daniel stayed in the palace during his long life, even until the reign of King Cyrus.

NEBUCHADNEZZAR'S DREAM

In the second year of the reign of Nebuchadnezzar, Nebuchadnezzar had dreams. His spirit was troubled and he couldn't sleep.

He called for the magicians, the enchanters, the sorcerers, and the wise men to tell him his dreams. They came in and stood before the king, and the king said to them, "I had a dream, and my spirit is troubled. I must know what it means."

The wise men said, "O King, live forever! Tell us the dream, and we'll tell you what it means."

The king answered, "I hereby decree: If you do not tell me the dream and what it means, you'll be torn limb from limb, and your houses will be destroyed. But if you tell me the dream and what it means, I'll give you gifts and rewards and great honor. Tell me the dream and what it means!"

They answered a second time, "Let the king tell us the dream, and then we'll tell you what it means."

The king answered, "I know you're stalling for time, because you see that I really will punish you if you do not tell me what the dream means. If you can tell me the dream, I'll know that you can tell me what it means."

The wise men answered, "There is not a man on earth who can meet the king's demand. No great and powerful king has ever asked such a thing from any magician or wise man. That which the king asks is difficult, and no one can reveal it to the king except the gods, who don't live among human beings."

The king was enraged, and he commanded that all the wise men of Babylon be destroyed.

The decree went out that the wise men were to be killed, and the officials went looking for Daniel and his friends to kill them, also.

But Daniel responded carefully to Arioch, the king's chief executioner, who was about to kill the wise men of Babylon. He said, "Why is the king's decree so severe?"

Arioch told Daniel what had happened, and Daniel went in and asked for an appointment with the king so that he could tell him the meaning of his dream the next day.

Then Daniel went home and told Hananiah, Mishael, and Azariah (who were called Shadrach, Meshach, and Abednego) what had happened. He asked them to pray to the GOD of heaven so that they and the other wise men of Babylon would not perish.

The mystery was revealed to Daniel in a vision that night, and Daniel praised the GOD of heaven, saying, "GOD removes and sets up kings. HE gives wisdom and knowledge and reveals mysteries. I praise YOU, O GOD, for YOU have given me wisdom and power, and made known to me what we asked."

Then Daniel went to Arioch, the chief executioner, and said to him,

"Don't destroy the wise men of Babylon. Take me to the king, and I will reveal the meaning of the dream."

Arioch hurried and took Daniel to the king and said, "I've found among the exiles from Judah a man who can reveal the meaning of the dream to the king."

The king said to Daniel, "Are you able to tell me my dream and what it means?"

Daniel answered the king, "No wise men, magicians, or astrologers can reveal the mystery, but there is a GOD in heaven WHO reveals mysteries, and HE has shown to King Nebuchadnezzar what will be at the end of days. Your dream

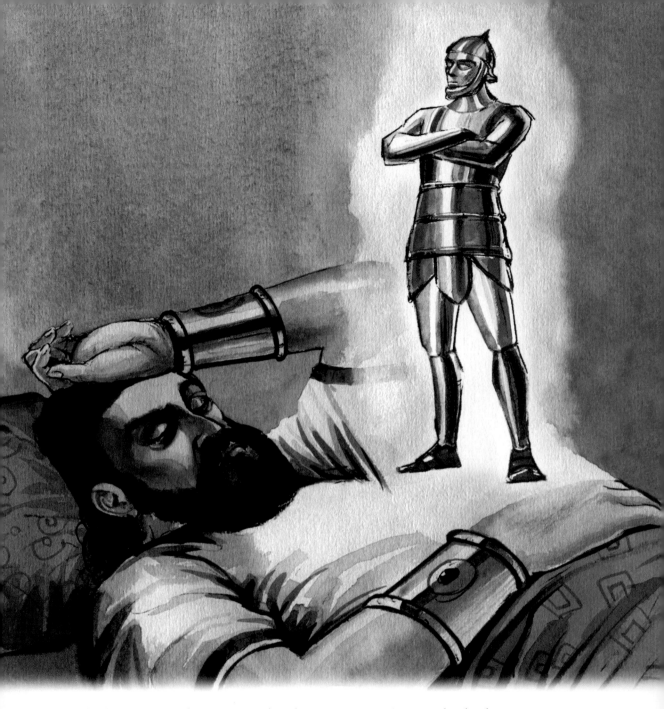

reveals the future. This mystery has been revealed to me, not because I have more wisdom than others, but so that the meaning may be revealed to the king.

"O King, you saw a great statue, and it was huge and very bright. It stood before you, and its appearance was frightening. The head of this statue was of fine gold, its chest and arms of silver, its belly and thighs of bronze, its legs of iron, and its feet partly of iron and partly of clay.

"As you looked, a stone was cut out, not by human hands, and it struck the statue on its feet of iron and clay, and broke them in pieces. Then the iron, the clay, the bronze, the silver, and the gold were all broken in pieces. They became like the chaff of the summer threshing floors, and the wind carried them away, leaving no trace. But the stone that struck the statue became a great mountain and filled the whole earth.

"This was the dream. Now we will tell the king what it means. O King, the king of kings! The GOD of heaven has given the kingdom, the power, and the glory! Into your hand HE has given men wherever they live, and the beasts of the field, and the birds of the air, making you ruler over them all. You, O King, are the head of gold.

"After you, another kingdom will rise up, inferior to you, and then a third kingdom of bronze, which will rule over all the earth. There will be a fourth kingdom, strong as iron, because iron breaks to pieces and shatters all things. Like iron which crushes, it will break and crush all these other kingdoms. As you saw the feet and toes partly of potter's clay and partly of iron, it will be a divided kingdom. As the toes of the feet were partly iron and partly clay, so the kingdom will be partly strong and partly brittle.

"While that last kingdom is still standing, the GOD of heaven will set up a kingdom that will never be destroyed. It will break all these kingdoms into pieces and bring them to an end, and it will stand forever. A great GOD has shown the king what will be. The dream is certain, and its meaning sure."

Then King Nebuchadnezzar fell upon his face and bowed down to Daniel and commanded that an offering be made to him. The king said to Daniel:

"Truly, your GOD is GOD of gods, King of kings, and revealer of mysteries, for you have been able to reveal this mystery."

The king gave Daniel high honors and many gifts. He made him ruler over the whole province of Babylon and head of all the wise men of Babylon.

Daniel made a request of the king, and he put Shadrach, Meshach, and Abednego in charge of the province of Babylon. But Daniel remained at the king's court.

THE FIERY FURNACE

King Nebuchadnezzar made a statue of gold, ninety feet high and nine feet wide. He set it up on the plain of Dura, in the province of Babylon.

Then King Nebuchadnezzar sent for the princes, the governors, the counselors, the treasurers, the judges, and all the officials of the provinces to come to the dedication of the statue that Nebuchadnezzar the king had set up.

Then the princes, the governors, the counselors, the treasurers, the judges, and all the officials of the provinces gathered for the dedication of the statue. They stood before the statue and the herald proclaimed:

"You are commanded, O peoples and nations, that when you hear the sound of the horn, pipe, lyre, harp, drum, and every kind of music, you must fall down and worship the golden statue that King Nebuchadnezzar has set up. Whoever does not fall down and worship will immediately be cast into a furnace of burning fire."

So as soon as the people heard the sound of the horn, pipe, lyre, harp, drum, and every kind of music, all the people from the various nations fell down and worshiped the golden statue that King Nebuchadnezzar had set up.

Then some astrologers came forward and accused the Jews. They said to King Nebuchadnezzar:

"O King, live forever! You, O King, have made a decree that everyone who hears the sound of the horn, pipe, lyre, harp, drum, and every kind of music, must fall down and worship the golden statue. Whoever does not fall down and worship will be cast into a furnace of burning fire. There are certain Jews whom you have put in charge of the province of Babylon: Shadrach, Meshach, and Abednego. These men, O King, pay no attention to you. They will not serve your gods or worship the golden statue that you have set up."

Then Nebuchadnezzar in a great rage ordered that Shadrach, Meshach, and Abednego be brought before him.

And Nebuchadnezzar said to them, "Is it true, O Shadrach, Meshach, and Abednego, that you do not serve my gods or worship the golden statue that I have set up? Now, if you are ready when you hear the sound of the horn, pipe, lyre, harp, drum, and every kind of music, to fall down and worship the statue that I have made, well and good. But if you do not worship, you will immediately be cast into a furnace of burning fire. Who is the god that will rescue you from my hand?"

Shadrach, Meshach, and Abednego answered King Nebuchadnezzar, "We don't have to answer you. If our GOD WHOM we serve is able to rescue us from the furnace of burning fire, HE will rescue us from your hand, O King. But if not, know for sure, O King, that we will not serve your gods or worship the golden statue that you have set up."

Then Nebuchadnezzar was full of fury, and his face was distorted with rage against Shadrach, Meshach, and Abednego. He ordered the furnace heated seven times more than was customary, and he ordered his strongest soldiers to tie up Shadrach, Meshach, and Abednego and cast them into the furnace of burning fire.

The three were tied up still wearing their trousers, their shirts, their hats, and their outer clothes, and they were thrown into the furnace of burning fire.

Because the king's order was strict and the furnace very hot, the flames of the fire killed the men who lifted up Shadrach, Meshach, and Abednego. But the three young men, Shadrach, Meshach, and Abednego, fell, tied up, into the furnace of burning fire.

Then King Nebuchadnezzar was astonished and got up quickly. He said to his officials, "Did we not throw three men tied up into the fire?"

"True, O King," they answered.

"But I see four men, untied, walking in the middle of the fire," said the king, "and they're not hurt. The fourth looks like a god!"

Nebuchadnezzar went near the door of the furnace of burning fire and said,

"Shadrach, Meshach, and Abednego, servants of the MOST HIGH GOD, come out! Come here!"

Then Shadrach, Meshach, and Abednego came out of the fire.

The princes, the governors, the judges, the officials, and all the king's counselors gathered together and saw that the fire had not had any power over the bodies of those men. The hair of

their heads wasn't singed, their clothes weren't burned, and they didn't smell like fire.

Nebuchadnezzar said, "Blessed be the GOD of Shadrach, Meshach, and Abednego! HE sent HIS angel and rescued HIS servants, who trusted in HIM. They disobeyed the king's command and surrendered their bodies rather than serve and worship any god except their own GOD.

Therefore I make a decree: Any people or nation that speaks anything against the GOD of Shadrach, Meshach, and Abednego will be torn limb from limb, and their houses will be destroyed. For there is no other god who is able to rescue like this!"

Then the king promoted Shadrach, Meshach, and Abednego in the province of Babylon.

THE HANDWRITING ON THE WALL

After the death of King Nebuchadnezzar, his son Belshazzar became king, and Daniel continued to serve in the king's court.

King Belshazzar made a great feast for a thousand of his lords, and drank wine in front of the thousand. Under the influence of the wine, Belshazzar sent for the gold and silver vessels that his father Nebuchadnezzar had taken from the Temple in Jerusalem, so the king and his lords and his wives and girlfriends could drink from them.

They brought in the golden and silver vessels that had been taken from the house of GOD in Jerusalem, and the king and his lords, his wives, and girlfriends drank from them. They drank wine and praised the gods of gold and silver, bronze, iron, wood, and stone.

Immediately the fingers of a man's hand appeared and wrote on the plaster wall of the palace, opposite the lamp stand.

The king saw the hand as it wrote. His face turned pale, and his thoughts terrified him. His limbs gave way and his knees knocked together.

He shouted for the enchanters, the wise men, and the astrologers, and he said to the wise men of Babylon, "Whoever reads this writing and tells me what it means will be clothed with purple and have a collar of gold around his neck, and he will be one of three rulers in the kingdom."

All the king's wise men came in, but they could not read the writing or tell the king what it meant.

King Belshazzar was terrified, and his face became pale. And his lords were bewildered.

When the queen mother heard what was going on, she came into the banqueting hall and said:

"O King, live forever! Don't let your thoughts terrify you or your face become pale. There's a man in your kingdom who has the spirit of the holy gods in him.

King Nebuchadnezzar, your father, made him chief of the magicians, enchanters, the wise men, and astrologers, because this man, Daniel, had an extraordinary mind, with knowledge and understanding to interpret dreams, explain riddles, and solve problems. Let Daniel be called, and he will tell you what it means."

Daniel was brought before the king, and the king said to him:

"You are that Daniel, one of the exiles of Judah, whom the king my father brought from Judah. I have heard that the spirit of the holy gods is in you, and that light and understanding and excellent wisdom are found in you.

"Now, the wise men and enchanters have been brought to read this writing, but they could not tell me what it means. I have been told that you can give interpretations and solve problems. If you can read the writing and tell me what it means, you will be clothed with purple and have a chain of gold around your neck, and will be the third ruler in the kingdom."

Daniel said to the king:

"Keep your gifts and give your rewards to another. But I will read the writing to the king and tell him what it means.

"Hear, O King! The Most High GOD gave Nebuchadnezzar your father the kingdom and the greatness and the glory and the majesty. Because of the greatness he received, all peoples and nations trembled in his presence. Whomever he wished, he killed. Whomever he wished, he kept alive. Whomever he wished, he raised up, and whomever he wished, he put down.

"But when his heart was lifted up and his spirit was hardened and he became proud, he was removed from his kingly throne, and his glory was taken from him until he learned that the Most High GOD rules the kingdom of men and sets over it whomever HE wishes.

"You his son, Belshazzar, have not humbled your heart, although you knew all this, but you have lifted up yourself against the LORD of heaven. The vessels of the LORD's house have been brought in before you, and you and your lords, your wives, and your other women have sipped wine from them. You have praised the gods of silver and gold, of bronze, iron, wood, and stone, that do not see or hear or understand; but you did not honor the GOD WHO holds your breath and your life in HIS hand.

"Then the hand was sent from HIS presence, and this writing was written.

"This is what was written: MENE, MENE, TEKEL, UPHARSIN.

"This is what it means:

"MENE means: *numbered*. GOD has numbered the days of your kingdom and brought it to an end.

"TEKEL means: *weighed*. You have been weighed in the balances and found wanting.

"UPHARSIN means: *and divided.* Your kingdom has been divided and given to the Medes and Persians."

Then Belshazzar commanded that Daniel be clothed with purple, and that a chain of gold be put around his neck. And he made a proclamation that Daniel, called Belteshazzar, should be the third ruler in the kingdom.

That very night Belshazzar the king was killed, and Darius of Media received the kingdom.

DANIEL IN THE LIONS' DEN

It pleased Darius to set over the kingdom a hundred and twenty princes, and over them three presidents, including Daniel. Daniel stood out among all the other chief ministers and princes because an excellent spirit was in him. The king planned to set him over the whole kingdom.

Then the chief ministers and the princes looked for a reason to complain against Daniel, but they could find no fault in him.

They said, "We won't find any reason for complaint against this Daniel unless we find something related to the law of his GOD."

These chief ministers and princes went in together to the king and said:

"O King Darius, live forever! All the chief ministers of the kingdom, the princes, the counselors and the governors, have agreed that the king should establish a rule that anyone who makes a request from any god or man for thirty days, except from you, O King, will be thrown into the den of lions.

"Now, O King, establish the rule and sign the document, so it cannot be changed, according to the law of the Medes and the Persians, which cannot be cancelled."

King Darius established the rule and signed the document. When Daniel learned about it he went into his house. It had windows in the upper room, facing Jerusalem, and three times a day he went down on his knees and prayed and offered praise to his GOD, just as he had done before this rule.

These men came and found Daniel praying to his GOD, and they went to the king and said, "Did you not sign a rule saying that anyone who makes a petition to any god or man within thirty days, except to you, O King, will be thrown into the lions' den?"

The king answered, "The rule is firm, according to the law of the Medes and Persians, which cannot be cancelled."

They said, "That Daniel, who is one of the exiles from Judah, pays no attention to you, O King, or the rule you have signed, but makes his request three times a day."

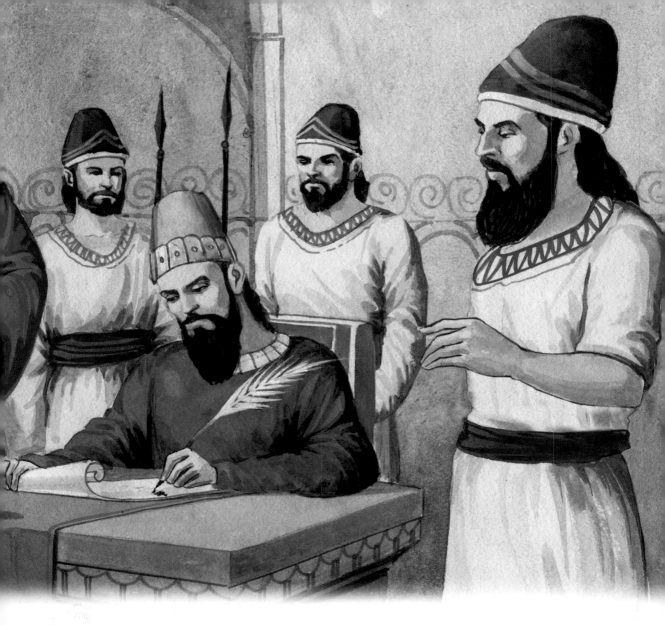

When the king heard these words, he was troubled and tried to save Daniel. He worked until the sun went down to rescue him.

Then these men went to the king, and said:

"Know, O King, that it is a law of the Medes and Persians that no rule or decree that the king establishes can be changed."

Then the king commanded, and Daniel was thrown into the lions' den.

The king said to Daniel:

"May your GOD, WHOM you faithfully serve, rescue you!"

A stone was brought and laid on the mouth of the den, and the king sealed it with his own ring and with the ring of his lords, so nothing could be done for Daniel.

Then the king went to his palace and spent the night fasting. No amusements were brought to him, and sleep fled from him.

Early the next morning, the king got up and hurried to the lions' den. When he came near, he shouted:

"O Daniel, servant of the living GOD, has your GOD, WHOM you faithfully serve, been able to save you from the lions?"

Daniel said to the king, "O King, live forever! My God sent his angel and shut the lions' mouths, and they have not hurt me, for God finds me innocent. O King, I have done no wrong."

The king was very glad, and he commanded that Daniel be removed from the den.

Daniel was taken up out of the den, and no harm was found on him, because he trusted in his God.

Then the king commanded, and the men who accused Daniel were brought and thrown into the den of lions. Before they reached the bottom of the den, the lions overpowered them and shattered their bones.

Then King Darius wrote to all the peoples and nations that live in all the earth:

"Peace be multiplied to you. I make a decree, that everywhere I rule, people will tremble before the GOD of Daniel, for HE is the living GOD, enduring forever. His kingdom will never be destroyed, and HIS rule will last to the end of time. HE saves and rescues, HE works signs and wonders in heaven and on earth, HE WHO has saved Daniel from the power of the lions."

Daniel prospered during the reign of Darius and the reign of Cyrus the Persian. He lived long enough to see his people return to Jerusalem after seventy years of exile.

CYRUS SETS THE EXILES FREE

The Babylonians, who came after the Assyrians, didn't know the LORD, and neither did the Persians, who came after the Babylonians. But the LORD's hand was on them for good and for evil.

One of the prophets said, "The LORD's hand is on Cyrus, king of Persia, and he will bring the exiles back to Judah. The LORD says, *Cyrus doesn't know* ME, *but I have anointed him to defeat nations. He is* MY *shepherd, and he will carry out* MY *plan. He will set* MY *exiles free. Jerusalem and the Temple will be rebuilt. The time of punishment for Jerusalem is ended. Her sin is forgiven.*"

In the first year of the reign of Cyrus, the LORD stirred up Cyrus's spirit to make a proclamation and send it in writing throughout the empire.

"Hear the word of Cyrus, king of Persia!" cried royal messengers. "Cyrus says: 'The LORD, the GOD of heaven, has made me ruler of all the kingdoms of the earth. HE has told me to build a house for HIM in the city of Jerusalem in Judah. HIS

Cyrus the king took the gold and silver bowls, cups, plates, and vessels that Nebuchadnezzar had removed from the house of the LORD, and he gave them to the exiles who were planning to return. Their Babylonian neighbors gave them gifts of silver and gold; food for the journey; mules, camels, and donkeys to carry their baggage; and offerings for the house of the LORD.

When they arrived in Jerusalem, the exiles found a ruined city in a barren land. The broken-down walls were black from the smoke of the fires that had destroyed the city. Jerusalem wasn't safe, so the returned exiles settled in nearby towns and villages.

Joshua the high priest and Zerubbabel led the people in rebuilding the altar of the LORD in front of the ruins of the Temple. As soon as the altar was finished, the people offered sacrifices to the LORD.

The people collected silver and gold to pay masons and carpenters. They sent grain and other food supplies to Lebanon in exchange for cedar wood to rebuild the Temple, just as Solomon had done hundreds of years before.

They built the foundation of the new Temple on the ruins of the old Temple. When the foundation was in place, they held a worship service to celebrate. The priests dressed in their best robes and blew their trumpets to call the people.

Everyone praised the LORD and sang:

"It is good to give thanks to the LORD, for HE is good; and HIS loving kindness endures forever."

The young people shouted with joy and praised the LORD for bringing them to Judah. But many of the old people who remembered the first Temple cried aloud. The sounds of joy and sadness mixed together, and the sound was heard a long way off.

people may go to Jerusalem and rebuild the house of the LORD, the GOD of Israel, WHO is in Jerusalem. My subjects are to help these people by giving them silver and gold, food, and pack-animals for the journey, and offerings for the house of GOD in Jerusalem.'"

GOD stirred the spirit of many of the exiles to answer the call and return to Jerusalem. But most of them stayed in Babylon, for they had built houses and planted crops and become successful farmers and merchants.

REBUILDING THE TEMPLE

It was during the years of exile in Babylon that the Israelites were called Jews, meaning people of Judah. When they returned to the territory of the old kingdoms of Israel and Judah, the Jews found a mixed people called Samaritans living in the land.

The Samaritans were descendants of the people who had come as captives of the Assyrians two hundred years earlier. The Jews and Samaritans were very suspicious of each other, for they had different ways of worshiping the LORD.

The Samaritans went to the leaders of the Jews in Jerusalem and said, "Let us join you in building the Temple. We've been worshiping your GOD ever since we came to this land."

"No," responded the Jews. "You shall have no part in building the Temple with us. We are the only ones who will build the house of the LORD, the GOD of Israel, as Cyrus king of Persia has commanded us."

Then the Samaritans and other people of the land began to work against the Jews. The Jews were so afraid of their enemies, they gave up the plan to rebuild the Temple. Instead, they settled in the land and the Temple was forgotten.

Some years later, in the second year of the reign of Darius II king of Persia, the word of the LORD came to a prophet named Haggai. Haggai said to the Jews and their leaders:

"Hear the word of the LORD! You say

it's not time to rebuild the Temple. Then is it time to live in your nice new houses while the LORD's house lies in ruins? Think about what's been going on. You have planted crops, but very little grows. You don't have enough to eat and drink. You are so poor, you don't have enough clothes to wear. You cannot support your families.

"Think on this: Why are these things happening? Why does the LORD ruin your crops? Because the LORD's house is in ruins! This is why there is no rain: the LORD HIMSELF has sent this drought! Now go up to the hills and gather timber. If you rebuild the Temple, the LORD will bless you, and the glory of the LORD will be among you."

The people gathered timber, prepared large blocks of stone, and organized the construction workers. In a few weeks, they were ready to rebuild the Temple.

Then Haggai said, "Is there anyone here who remembers the splendor of the first Temple, with its gold and silver? How does this building compare with it? Not much, is it? But don't be discouraged. Be strong!

"Now get to work! The LORD is with you. Take courage. All the silver and gold in the world belongs to the LORD. The treasure of all the nations will come to the Temple, and the LORD will fill it with HIS glory. The glory of this Temple will be even greater than the glory of the first Temple!"

The people listened to Haggai and began to rebuild the Temple.

But it came to pass that Tattenai, the governor of the Persian province of Judah and Samaria, came to Jerusalem and said to the Jews, "Who said you could rebuild this Temple?"

The Jews said, "Cyrus king of Persia commanded us to rebuild the Temple."

Tattenai sent a report to Darius king of Persia, to find out whether this was true. While he was waiting for an answer from Darius, he allowed the Jews to go on with their work.

Darius read the report from Tattenai and told his officials to look in the archives of Babylon, to find out whether the Jews were telling the truth. When they looked, the officials found a scroll with the words of Cyrus concerning the Temple. Darius read Cyrus' proclamation, and wrote to Tattenai:

"Leave the Jews alone. Let them finish their Temple, and give them whatever they need from the royal treasury. Tell them to pray for me and my sons. If anyone disobeys this command, pull down his house and have him whipped. May the GOD of Jerusalem strike anyone who dares to disobey my order! I, Darius, have spoken!"

Silver and gold from the treasury of Persia went to buy offerings for the Temple of GOD, as the LORD had said through the prophet Haggai.

It took the Jews four and a half years to rebuild the Temple, and when it was finished, they held a great worship service to celebrate. This happened seventy years after the destruction of the first Temple, as the LORD had said through the prophet Jeremiah.

315

NEHEMIAH BUILDS THE WALL

In the days of Artaxerxes king of Persia, the governors of Judah and Samaria wrote to the king and complained about the Jews. They said if Jerusalem gained strength, the Jews would rebel against the king. So Artaxerxes the king of Persia ordered the Jews to stop rebuilding Jerusalem.

Then the LORD raised up Nehemiah, an exile who was the cupbearer of the king of Persia. This is his story.

⁓

One day, visitors from Judah arrived at Susa, at the winter palace of Artaxerxes king of Persia. I asked them about the exiles who had returned to Jerusalem. They said:

"The Jews are in great trouble and disgrace. The wall of Jerusalem is broken down, and its gates were ruined by fire."

When I heard the news, I sat down and cried. I mourned and fasted and prayed to GOD. After four months I said to the LORD:

"O LORD GOD of heaven, please hear my prayer. You are the great GOD WHO keeps HIS promises to those who love HIM and keep HIS commandments. We have sinned against YOU, and YOU have scattered us among the nations. But YOU said if we turn back to YOU, YOU will bring us back and be with YOUR people, the ones YOU saved with YOUR great power and YOUR strong hand.

"O LORD, please hear my prayer! Give me success today when I speak to the king. Let him be merciful to me."

Then I went to the king and gave him his cup of wine.

The king had never seen me look sad before, and he said, "Why is your face so sad? You aren't sick. This is a sadness of the heart."

I was very afraid of the king, especially because he had given the order to stop the rebuilding of Jerusalem. I chose my words very carefully.

"May the king live forever!" I said. "Why shouldn't my face be sad when the city where my ancestors are buried is in ruins and its gates have been destroyed by fire?"

"What do you want?" asked the king.

I prayed silently to the LORD before I answered. Then I said, "If it pleases the king, and if I have found favor in your

sight, send me to Judah, to the city where my ancestors are buried, so I may rebuild the city."

The king said, "How long will your mission take, and when will you return?"

I answered his questions, and he agreed to send me. Then I said, "If it please the king, give me letters for the governors of the province, so they will give me safe passage through their territory. Please also give me a letter to the king's forester, so he'll give me timber to build the gates of the Temple and the wall of the city, and a house for me to live in."

The good hand of my GOD was with me, and the king gave me everything I asked for. He also gave me a military escort and letters to the Persian governors in Judah and Samaria. When I arrived in their territory, I went to the governors and gave them the letters from the king.

Sanballat, governor of Samaria, Tobiah, governor of Ammon, and Geshem, governor of Edom, were very displeased that someone had come to help the Jews.

Then I went on to Jerusalem, but I didn't tell anyone about my mission.

I waited for three days, and then I took a few men and went out in the middle of the night. I rode around the outside of the city on the back of a donkey, inspecting the ruins of the wall and the gates. I went back into the city without anyone knowing where I had been and what I had been doing.

Then I went to the leaders of the Jews and said, "You see the trouble we're in. Jerusalem is in ruins, and its gates have been destroyed by fire. Come, let's rebuild the wall and put an end to this disgrace!" I told them how GOD had helped me, and what the king had said to me.

The leaders said:

"Let us rise up and build."

But Sanballat, Tobiah, and Geshem scorned the Jews, saying, "What do you think you're doing? Are you rebelling against the king?"

I answered, "The GOD of heaven will give us success. We will rebuild, but you have no claim to anything in Jerusalem."

We organized the people into forty groups of families, and divided the wall into sections. Each group repaired and rebuilt one section of the wall. Everyone helped—from the priests and rich merchants to the humble farmers—to lay beams, set doors in the gates, and repair the wall. We used the old stones that were lying in the heaps of rubble.

As we worked, Sanballat jeered at us, saying, "What do these feeble Jews think they're doing? Will they repair a wall for themselves in a day? Will they turn piles of burnt rubbish into building stones?"

Tobiah added, "See what a flimsy fence they're building! If a fox went up on their wall, he'd break it down!"

But we kept building. We filled in the gaps and built the wall up to half its old height.

When the Samaritans and others heard that we were making progress on the wall, they said to each other, "Let's sneak up and attack them before they know what's happening. Let's strike them down and put an end to Nehemiah's plans."

Some Jews heard them plotting together and came to warn us. I put armed guards behind the wall and passed out swords and spears and bows and arrows to the workers. Then I said to the people:

"Don't be afraid of your enemies. Remember the LORD! Fight for your brothers, your sons and daughters, your wives, and your homes!"

I divided the workers into two groups. Half worked on construction and half held the swords and spears and bows and arrows. All the workers carried swords in

their belts. The Jews kept working, with half the people holding spears all day. They worked from the time the sun rose in the morning until the stars came out at night.

And the wall was finished in fifty-two days.

When the nations around us heard that the wall was finished, they were afraid. They saw that this work had been done with the help of the LORD.

We held a great celebration to dedicate the wall. We sang and made music with cymbals, harps, and lyres.

I brought the princes of Judah onto the wall in two groups. One group walked in one direction around the wall, and the other group walked in the opposite direction. The singers and musicians and priests followed behind them. When they reached the Temple, the two groups joined and all the people praised the LORD with loud singing.

We offered great sacrifices that day, and all men, women, and children rejoiced. There was no sound of sadness in Jerusalem that day, and the sound of joy was heard a long way off.

ESTHER IS CHOSEN QUEEN

The story of Esther tells how GOD can bless HIS people even when they live in a foreign land, under the law of a foreign king. Sometimes GOD's people, like Esther, had to choose which law or which king to obey.

In the third year of the reign of Xerxes, called Ahasuerus, king of Persia, who reigned from India to Ethiopia over one hundred and twenty-seven provinces, Ahasuerus gave a banquet at his winter palace in Susa. He invited all his princes and officials, the army chiefs and nobles, and the governors of the provinces. For a hundred and eighty days he showed them the riches of his kingdom and the splendor of his majesty.

When these days were completed, the king gave another banquet for all the people in Susa, both rich and poor. The banquet lasted for seven days in the court of the garden of the king's palace.

Queen Vashti gave a banquet for the women inside the palace.

On the seventh day, when the heart of the king was merry with wine, he commanded his seven personal servants to bring Queen Vashti to him, wearing her royal crown, to show her beauty to his guests.

But Queen Vashti refused to come at the king's command. The king was enraged, and his anger burned within him. He said to his seven advisors:

"What does the law say I can do to punish Queen Vashti for not obeying the king's command?"

Memucan, one of the king's advisors, said, "Queen Vashti has done wrong, not only to the king, but also to all the officials and all the men in all the provinces of the empire! When the women hear about this deed, they will look with contempt at their husbands. They will say, 'King Ahasuerus commanded Queen Vashti to appear before him, and she didn't come.'

"Therefore," said Memucan, "if it please the king, let him send out a royal order, and let it be written into the laws so it can never be changed. Let it say that Vashti may never again appear before the king. Let the king give her royal position to another who is better than she. When the king's decree is proclaimed throughout the vast kingdom, all women will give honor to their husbands, both rich and poor."

This advice pleased the king and his officials, and the king did as Memucan advised. He sent letters to all the royal provinces, to every province in its own writing and to every nation in its own language, so that every man would be lord in his own house.

And it came to pass that the king's advisers said to the king, "Let the king choose officials to find all the beautiful young women in all the provinces of his kingdom. Let them be brought to the women's house in Susa to receive beauty treatments. Then let the young woman who pleases the king become queen instead of Vashti."

This pleased the king, and he did so.

Now, there was a Jew in Susa whose name was Mordecai. His family had been carried away from Jerusalem in the first group of exiles. He had raised Esther, the daughter of his uncle. The girl was beautiful and graceful, and when her father and mother died, Mordecai adopted her as his own daughter.

When the king's order was proclaimed, many young women were found in Susa, and Esther was taken into the king's palace. She was put in the custody of Hegai, the official in charge of the women's house. He was pleased with her, so he quickly provided her with her

beauty treatments and her portion of food and seven maids from the king's palace. He advanced Esther and her maids to the best part of the women's house.

Esther didn't let anyone know about her people or her family, for Mordecai had ordered her not to tell. Every day, Mordecai walked in front of the courtyard of the women's house to find out how Esther was doing.

The young women spent twelve months receiving beauty treatments, six months with oil of myrrh and six months with spices and ointments. They were given costly clothes and jewelry. When it was each woman's turn to go before King Ahasuerus, she was given whatever she desired to take with her from the women's house. When it was Esther's turn, she asked for nothing except what Hegai advised. Esther found favor in the eyes of all who saw her.

When she was taken to King Ahasuerus in his royal palace, the king found more favor in Esther more than all the other women, and he fell in love with her. He set the royal crown on her head and made her queen instead of Vashti.

Then the king gave a great banquet for all his officials in Esther's honor. He decreed a tax holiday throughout the empire and gave generous gifts.

Esther had not told anyone about her family or her people, as Mordecai had ordered. She obeyed Mordecai just as she had when she was growing up.

Now, Mordecai worked as a royal official. One day, as he was sitting at the king's gate, he overheard the two officials who guarded the royal bedchamber. They were angry with the king and were plotting to harm him. Mordecai told what he knew to Queen Esther. Esther reported it to the king and told him that Mordecai had given her the information. The king ordered an investigation and found the report to be true. The guards were both hanged on the gallows, and the matter was recorded in the official records in the presence of the king.

HAMAN'S DECREE

After these things, another royal official named Haman was promoted by the king above the other royal officials. All the king's officials at the gate kneeled and bowed down to Haman. But Mordecai didn't kneel and bow down—for it happened that Haman was a descendant of King Agag, an ancient Amalekite enemy of Mordecai's tribe, the Benjaminites.

When Haman saw that Mordecai did not kneel and bow down to him, he was filled with rage. The other officials told Haman that Mordecai was a Jew. In his anger, Haman decided to find a way to destroy all the Jews in all the kingdom.

At the start of the new year, Purim, or lots, were cast before Haman. The lots fell on the twelfth month. This, Haman decided, would be the time of the Jews' destruction. He went to the king and said:

"There's a people scattered among the other peoples in all the provinces of your kingdom. Their laws are different and they don't keep the king's laws. It is not in the king's interest to tolerate these people. If it please the king, let it be decreed that these people be destroyed. If you do this, I'll put ten thousand pieces of silver into the king's treasury."

The king took off his signet ring and gave it to Haman and said, "The money and the people are yours. Do with them as it seems good to you."

Haman sent for the royal scribes and dictated a decree to the king's agents and the governors over all the provinces. It was written in the name of King Ahasuerus and sealed with the king's ring.

Letters were sent to the king's provinces to destroy and kill all Jews, young and old, women and children, in one day, the thirteenth day of the twelfth month, and to take all their possessions. It was proclaimed to all the people to be ready for that day.

In every province, wherever the king's decree arrived, there was great mourning among the Jews.

When Mordecai found out what had been done, he tore his clothes and put on sackcloth and ashes. He went out into the city of Susa, wailing with a loud and bitter cry, and up to the entrance of the king's gate, for no one could enter the king's gate clothed in sackcloth.

When Esther learned of Mordecai's condition, she was very upset. She sent clothes out to Mordecai, but he refused them. Then she sent her servant Hathach to go to Mordecai and find out why he was mourning.

Hathach went out to Mordecai in front of the king's gate, and Mordecai told him the news. He told him the exact amount of money that Haman had promised to pay into the king's treasury for the destruction of the Jews. He also gave him a copy of the decree issued in Susa for their destruction. He told him to show it to Esther and explain it to her, and to tell her to go to the king to plead for her people.

Hathach went back to Esther and told her what Mordecai had said.

Esther gave him a message for Mordecai, saying, "All the king's subjects know that if any man or woman goes to the king inside the inner courtyard without being called, that is grounds to be put to death, unless the king holds out his golden scepter. I haven't been called to come in to the king for thirty days."

Mordecai told Hathach to say to Esther, "Do not think that you'll be safer in the palace than all the other Jews. If you remain silent at a time like this, salvation will come for the Jews from elsewhere, but you and your father's family will perish. Who knows? Perhaps you have come to the kingdom for such a time as this!"

Then Esther told Hathach to say to Mordecai, "Go, gather all the Jews in Susa and hold a fast for my sake. Don't eat or drink for three days, night or day. My maids and I will keep the same fast. Then I will go to the king, although it's against the law. If I perish, I perish."

Mordecai went and did as Esther ordered.

ESTHER'S REQUEST

On the third day, Esther put on her royal robes and stood in the inner courtyard of the king's palace. When the king saw Queen Esther standing in the courtyard, she found favor in his sight, and he held out to her his golden scepter.

Esther went close to him and touched the tip of the scepter.

"What is it, Queen Esther?" said the king. "What's your request? I will give it to you, even if it's half my kingdom."

"If it please the king," said Esther, "let the king and Haman come today to a dinner that I have prepared for the king."

The king turned to his servants and said, "Bring Haman at once, so we may do as Esther desires."

So the king and Haman went to the dinner that Esther had prepared.

As they were drinking wine, the king said to Esther, "What is your petition? It will be granted."

Esther said, "If I have found favor in the sight of the king, and if it please the king, let the king and Haman come tomorrow to dinner, and then I will do as the king has said."

Haman went out that day joyful and glad of heart. But when he saw Mordecai at the king's gate, and Mordecai didn't stand up or tremble before him, Haman was filled with anger against Mordecai.

Haman went home and boasted to his wife Zeresh and his friends that he had been invited to a banquet with the queen and king. "Yet all this does me no good," he added, "as long as I see Mordecai the Jew sitting at the king's gate."

His wife Zeresh said to him, "Have a gallows made, seventy-five feet high, and in the morning tell the king to have Mordecai hanged on it. Then go merrily with the king to the dinner."

This advice pleased Haman, and he had the gallows made.

THE KING HONORS MORDECAI

That night the king couldn't sleep. He ordered his servants to bring the book of records of memorable deeds, and they read the book to the king. They happened to read the part where it was recorded how Mordecai had reported the plot against the king.

The king said, "What honor has been given to Mordecai for this?"

"Nothing," said the king's servants.

"Who is in the palace now?"

Haman had just entered the outer courtyard to speak to the king about having Mordecai hanged on the gallows. So the king's servants told the king:

"Haman is standing in the courtyard."

"Send him in," said the king.

Haman came in, and the king said to him, "What should be done to the man whom the king delights to honor?"

Haman said to himself, *Whom could the king delight to honor more than me?*

"If the king delights to honor someone," said Haman, "let royal robes and a royal horse be handed over to one of the king's most noble princes. Let him clothe the man, and lead him on horseback through the open square of the city, proclaiming before him, 'See what's done for the man the king delights to honor!'"

The king said to Haman, "Hurry, take the robes and the horse, as you have said, and do these things for Mordecai, the Jew who sits at the king's gate. Don't leave out anything you've mentioned."

So Haman took the robes and the horse and clothed Mordecai and led him on horseback through the open square of the city, proclaiming:

"See what is done for the man the king delights to honor!"

Then Mordecai returned to the king's gate, but Haman hurried to his house, covering his head in shame. He told his wife Zeresh and all his friends what had happened to him.

Just then, the king's servants arrived and took Haman quickly to the banquet that Esther had prepared.

ESTHER'S BANQUET

The king and Haman went in to feast with Queen Esther. On the second day, as they were drinking wine, the king said to Esther again, "What's your petition, Queen Esther? It will be granted. What's your request? Even if it's half my kingdom, it will be fulfilled!"

Queen Esther answered, "If I have found favor in your sight, O King, and if it please the king, let my life be given me at my petition, and my people at my request. For my people and I have been sold to be destroyed, to be killed, and to be exterminated. If we had merely been sold as slaves, men and women, I would have held my peace. For our affliction is

not to be compared with the loss of money to the king's treasury."

Then King Ahasuerus said to Queen Esther, "Who is responsible for this? Where is he? Who dares to plot such evil?"

"An enemy!" cried Esther. "A persecutor! This wicked Haman!"

Haman was in terror before the king and queen. The king stood up in a rage and went into the palace garden, but Haman stayed to beg Queen Esther for his life, for he saw that the king had decided to do evil against him.

The king returned from the palace garden just as Haman was falling on the couch where Esther was sitting.

The king said, "Will this man actually attack the queen in my presence in my own house?"

As soon as the king's words left his mouth, the king's servants covered Haman's face, for he was a man condemned to death.

Then one of the king's attendants said, "That's not all. Look at the gallows that Haman has prepared for Mordecai, the man who saved the king's life—the gallows that stand at Haman's house, seventy-five feet high."

"Hang him on that!" said the king.

So they hanged Haman on the gallows he had prepared for Mordecai. Then the king's anger cooled down.

On that day King Ahasuerus gave to Queen Esther the house of Haman, the enemy of the Jews.

Then Mordecai came into the king's presence, for Esther had told how he was related to her. The king took off his signet ring, which he had taken from Haman, and gave it to Mordecai, and Esther set Mordecai over the house of Haman.

Esther spoke again to the king. She threw herself at his feet, crying and pleading with him to stop the evil plan of Haman the Amalekite and the plot he had made against the Jews. The king held out his golden scepter, and Esther stood up.

"If it please the king," she said. "If I have found favor in your sight, and if it seems right to the king, and I am pleasing in his eyes—let an order be written to cancel the letters of Haman the Amalekite, that he wrote to destroy the Jews in all the provinces of the king. How can I bear to see the disaster that is coming to my people or the destruction that is coming to my relatives?"

Now, a decree that had been sealed by the king could not be revoked. Therefore, the king sent a new decree: that every Jew throughout his kingdom was permitted to defend his own life and the lives of the women and children against any who attacked the Jews on the thirteenth day of the twelfth month. Letters were drawn up and sent by couriers on swift hoses from the king's own stables.

A copy of the letter was proclaimed as a decree in every province to all peoples, telling them that the Jews would be ready on that day to avenge themselves on their enemies. The decree was issued first in Susa, and the people of Susa shouted with joy.

THE REJOICING OF THE JEWS

When Mordecai left the king's presence, he was wearing royal robes of blue and white, with a great golden crown and a cloak of fine linen and purple. He went out into the city of Susa, and found the people shouting with joy, and the Jews overcome with gladness.

In every province and in every city, wherever the king's decree came, there was gladness and joy among the Jews, and a feast and a holiday. Many people of the country claimed to be Jews, because they were afraid of the Jews.

The thirteenth day of the twelfth month was the day that the enemies of the Jews hoped to overpower them, but now it was changed to a day when the Jews could overpower their enemies. On that day the Jews gathered in their cities throughout all the provinces of King Ahasuerus to harm anyone who tried to harm them.

The Jews in the king's provinces gathered to defend their lives and to get relief from their enemies. They killed thousands of those who hated them, but they didn't take their possessions.

The next day they rested and feasted and celebrated.

Mordecai recorded these things and sent letters to all the Jews in all the provinces, telling them to celebrate every year on the thirteenth and fourteenth days of the twelfth month. These were the days the Jews found relief from their enemies. This was the month that had been turned from sorrow into gladness, from mourning into a holiday. He told them to make them days of feasting and gladness, days for sending fine food to each other and gifts to the poor.

Every year after that, the Jews celebrated on those days, and they called the holiday Purim, because Haman had cast Purim to destroy them.

Queen Esther and Mordecai sent a second letter, telling all the Jews in the hundred and twenty-seven provinces of the kingdom of Ahasuerus to observe these days of Purim. The command of Queen Esther made the celebration of Purim an official law of the Persians.

King Ahasuerus filled his treasury with gold and silver from taxes on the land and the coastlands. Mordecai the Jew was next to the king in power. He was popular with his people, who respected him highly, for he saw that they were treated well, and he saw that they lived in safety.

THE STORY OF JONAH

Jonah was an unusual prophet. He wasn't sent to speak GOD's word to his own people, but to the enemies of GOD's people.

The word of the LORD came to Jonah, saying, "Get up and go to Nineveh, that great city, and cry out against it, because their wickedness has come up to MY presence."

Jonah got up and ran away to Tarshish, away from the presence of the LORD. He went down to Joppa and found a ship going to Tarshish. He paid the fare and went on board, to flee from the presence of the LORD.

But the LORD threw a great wind onto the sea, and there was a great storm on the sea, so that the ship was in danger of falling apart.

The sailors were afraid, and each of them cried out to his own god. They threw the cargo that was in the ship into the sea, to lighten the ship.

Jonah had gone down into the inner part of the ship to lie down, and he was sound asleep.

The captain went to him and said, "Why are you sleeping? Get up, call on your god! Perhaps the gods will give a thought to us, so we don't perish."

Up on the deck the sailors were saying to each other, "Come, let us cast lots, to find out who is to blame for this evil that has come up on us."

They cast lots, and the lot fell on Jonah.

They said to him, "Tell us, who is to blame that this evil has come on us? What is your business? Where do you come from? What is your country?"

He said to them, "I'm a Hebrew. I fear the LORD, the GOD of heaven, WHO made the sea and dry land." Then he admitted that he had run away from the LORD.

The men were very afraid, and they said to him, "What have you done?"

Now, the sea was growing more and more stormy, and the men said, "What must we do to you so the sea will quiet down for us?"

Jonah said to them, "Pick me up and throw me into the sea, and the sea will quiet down for you. I know that I am to blame for this great storm that has come upon you."

Still, the men rowed hard to bring the ship back to land; but they could not, for the sea was growing more and more stormy against them.

Then they cried out to the LORD:

"We beg YOU, O LORD, don't let us perish for taking this man's life! Don't accuse us of shedding innocent blood. It is YOU, O LORD, WHO has done what pleased YOU."

Then they picked Jonah up and threw him into the sea, and the sea stopped its raging. The men were filled with fear of the LORD, and they offered a sacrifice to HIM and promised to serve HIM.

The Lord directed a great fish to swallow Jonah, and Jonah was in the belly of the fish for three days and three nights.

Then Jonah prayed to the Lord his God from the belly of the fish, saying:

"I called to the Lord for help, and He heard my prayer! You threw me into the deep water, away from Your presence. I went down to the roots of the mountains, but You brought my life up out of the pit. I'm not like people who

worship idols and leave YOU. I will offer a sacrifice to YOU, I promise. Salvation belongs to the LORD!"

The LORD spoke to the fish, and it spat Jonah out onto the dry land.

The word of the LORD came to Jonah a second time, saying:

"Get up and go to Nineveh and proclaim to that great city the message that I tell you."

Jonah got up and went to Nineveh, as the LORD had said.

Nineveh was a very great city, three days' journey across.

Jonah started into the city, and he went a day's journey and cried out:

"In forty days Nineveh will be overthrown!"

The people of Nineveh believed GOD. They proclaimed a fast and put on sackcloth, from the greatest to the least of them.

When news reached the king of Nineveh, he got up from his throne, took off his robe, covered himself with sackcloth, and sat in ashes.

The king made a proclamation and sent it throughout Nineveh, saying:

"By the decree of the king and his nobles: Let neither man nor beast, herd nor flock, taste anything. Let them not feed or drink water, but let man and beast be covered with sackcloth, and let them cry out mightily to GOD. Let everyone turn from his evil ways and from the violence that is in his hands. Who knows? Perhaps GOD will change HIS mind and turn from HIS fierce anger, and we won't perish."

GOD saw how the people repented, and how they turned from their evil ways. And when HE saw this, HE turned from the evil punishment HE had planned for Nineveh.

This displeased Jonah and made him angry. He prayed to the LORD, saying:

"I knew it, LORD! Isn't this what I said when I was still in my country? That's why I hurried to run away to Tarshish. I knew that YOU are a gracious GOD and merciful, slow to anger, and abounding in steadfast love. I knew YOU would change YOUR mind about doing evil. Therefore, LORD, I beg YOU, take my life!

It's better for me to die than to live."

The LORD said, "What reason do you have to be angry?"

Jonah went out of the city and sat down in a place east of the city and made a shelter for himself. He sat under it in the shade and waited to see what would happen to the city.

The LORD directed a gourd plant to grow up over Jonah, to be shade over his head and save him from discomfort. And Jonah was very glad because of the plant.

Early the next morning, GOD directed a worm to attack the plant, and it withered and died. Later that day, when the sun rose high in the sky, GOD directed a scorching east wind to beat on Jonah's head until he felt faint.

Then Jonah asked that he might die, saying, "It's better for me to die than to live."

But GOD said to Jonah "What reason do you have to be angry about the plant?"

Jonah said, "I have reason to be angry—angry enough to die!"

Then the LORD said, "You pity the plant, but you did not labor for it or make it grow. It came into being in a night, and perished in a night.

"Should I not, then, pity and spare Nineveh, that great city, with all its cattle and all its hundred and twenty thousand persons who do not know their right hand from their left?"

GOD'S PLAN

A hundred years after the return of the exiles, Ezra, a priest, led a second group of exiles out of Babylon back to the land of Judah.

After the people were settled, they came and gathered in the square in front of the Temple. And Ezra brought the book of the Law of Moses to all the people, both men and women. He faced the square and read from early morning until the middle of the day, and said:

"Praise the LORD, the great GOD!"

All the people said, "Amen, Amen," and lifted up their hands.

And Ezra read to them from the teachings of Moses.

When the people understood how GOD wanted them to live, they began to cry, for they realized that they had been disobeying the LORD's commandments.

"Don't mourn and cry," said the men standing with Ezra. "Today is a holy day. Go celebrate and feast. Eat rich food and drink sweet wine, and send portions to the needy. This day is holy to our LORD. Don't grieve, for the joy of the LORD is your strength."

All the people went to eat and drink and share with the poor. They rejoiced, because they had heard and understood the teaching of the LORD.

Many times GOD's people left the LORD and went after the gods of other nations. But GOD had a purpose in mind when HE separated HIS people from other nations. It wasn't just for their sake. GOD brought a remnant back to the land, because HE had a great plan for them and for the whole world.

As one prophet had said:

"The LORD says, *It is too small a thing to restore the remnant of Israel. I want Israel to be a light to the nations, so MY salvation will reach the end of the earth.*"

And the Spirit of the LORD
shall rest upon him…

Isaiah 11: 1–6

And there shall come forth a rod out of the stem of Jesse, and a Branch shall grow out of his roots.

And the Spirit of the LORD shall rest upon him, the spirit of wisdom and understanding, the spirit of counsel and might, the spirit of knowledge and of the fear of the LORD; and shall make him of quick understanding in the fear of the LORD.

And he shall not judge after the sight of his eyes, neither reprove after the hearing of his ears: but with righteousness shall he judge the poor, and reprove with equity for the meek of the earth: and he shall smite the earth with the rod of his mouth, and with the breath of his lips shall he slay the wicked.

And righteousness shall be the girdle of his loins, and faithfulness the girdle of his reins.

The wolf also shall dwell with the lamb, and the leopard shall lie down with the kid; and the calf and the young lion and the fatling together; and a little child shall lead them.

CYPRUS

GREAT SEA
(MEDITERRANEAN SEA)

Sidon

SYRIA
Damascus

Tyre

GALILEE

Capernaum
Cana

Sea of Galilee
Gerasenes Region

Nazareth

Caesarea

Jordan River

Sychar

SAMARIA

Jericho

Jerusalem

Dead Sea

Bethlehem

Gaza

JUDEA

PALESTINE

EGYPT

SINAI

BABYLON

Tigris River

Euphrates River

THE HOLY LAND
OF THE NEW TESTAMENT

ARABIAN
DESERT

GABRIEL BRINGS GOOD NEWS

G OD's chosen people, the family that began with Abraham and Sarah so long ago, lived in their own land, Judea, but foreign kings ruled over them. The Jews longed to be free, but they had no one to lead them. The Greek kings gave way to the Roman kings, but still the Jews were not free.

GOD sent prophets to comfort HIS people. "When the time is right," the prophets said, "GOD will send us a new King, one who is anointed with the holy oil. This anointed one, the Christ, will bring about GOD's kingdom here on earth."

Their empire was so large that the Romans appointed kings to govern the many peoples under their rule. It came to pass that the Romans chose a man named Herod as king of the Jews.

In those days, there was a priest named Zechariah who had a wife named Elizabeth. They were both right-eous in the sight of GOD and followed all of HIS teachings. They had no chil-dren, because Elizabeth was barren. They were both quite old.

One day while Zechariah was serving in the Temple, it was his turn to enter the Holy Place and burn the incense. He went in alone while everyone else prayed outside.

An angel of the LORD appeared, standing on the right side of the altar, and Zechariah was frightened.

"Don't be afraid, Zechariah," said the angel. "Your prayer has been heard. Your wife Elizabeth will give birth to a

son, and you will name him John. Many people will rejoice when he is born. He will be great in the eyes of the LORD. From the moment of his birth he will be filled with the Holy Spirit, and he will help people get ready for the coming of the Christ."

Zechariah asked, "How can I be sure of this? My wife and I are too old to have children now."

"I am Gabriel," said the angel. "I stand in the presence of GOD. I was sent to bring you this good news. Because you did not believe me, you will be silent and unable to speak until my words come true."

The people outside wondered why Zechariah had stayed so long in the Temple. When he came out, he could not speak, and they realized that he had seen a vision. Zechariah made signs to them with his hands, but remained speechless.

When Zechariah's time of service at the Temple was over, he went home. Soon his wife Elizabeth became with child.

"The LORD has shown me favor," she said, "and taken away my disgrace among the people."

In the sixth month after that, GOD sent HIS angel Gabriel to Nazareth, a town in Galilee. The angel appeared to a young woman named Mary. She was engaged to Joseph, who was a descendant of King David.

Gabriel said to Mary, "Greetings, favored one! The LORD is with you!"

Mary was troubled by these words and wondered what the angel meant.

"Don't be afraid, Mary," said the angel. "You are special in GOD's eyes. You will give birth to a son. You will name him Jesus, meaning "The LORD Is Salvation." He will be called the Son of the Most High. He will reign over the descendants of Jacob, and his kingdom will never end."

Mary said, "How can this be, since I have no husband?"

"The Holy Spirit will come upon you," the angel told her. "GOD gives this baby to you. The child will be called the Son of GOD. Your cousin Elizabeth, who was called barren, is six months with child. She will have a son in her old age. Nothing is impossible for GOD."

"I am the servant of the LORD," Mary said. "Let it be as you have said."

Then the angel left her.

Mary felt so alone and afraid. She hurried to her cousin Elizabeth, who lived in the hill country of Judea. As soon as Elizabeth heard Mary's greeting, the older woman was filled with the Holy Spirit.

Elizabeth cried out, "Blessed are you above all women! Blessed is the child you carry! Who am I, that the mother of my Lord comes to me? When the sound of your greeting came to my ears, the baby within me leaped for joy! Blessed are you who believed that the word of the LORD would be fulfilled."

Mary's joy was great and she sang:

"My *spirit rejoices in* GOD *my Savior.*
   HE *has blessed me for all time.*"
Mary's song became a prophecy, a vision of the future.
"HE *has filled the hungry with good*
   things, and sent the rich away empty.
HE *took the mighty from their thrones,*
   and lifted up the lowly."
What GOD was doing for her was a sign of GOD's love for HIS chosen people, Mary realized. From now on, everything would be different.

Mary stayed with Elizabeth for about three months, and then she returned home.

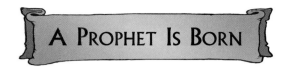
Elizabeth give birth to a son. Her neighbors heard that the LORD in HIS mercy had given her a son, and they rejoiced with her.

When the child was eight days old, the neighbors came for his naming ceremony. He was to be named Zechariah, after his father, but Elizabeth said:

"No. He must be named John."

"No one in your family has that name," the people said.

They made signs to the baby's father to ask what he wanted the child named.

Zechariah motioned for a writing tablet and wrote:

"HIS NAME IS JOHN."

Immediately Zechariah's mouth opened and he was able to speak. And he praised GOD.

All their neighbors were amazed. The story spread quickly throughout the hill country of Judea. Everyone who heard it wondered, "What will this child John become?" For clearly the hand of the LORD was on him.

And Zechariah was filled with the Holy Spirit. He spoke of Mary's son, Jesus, who was yet to be born.

"Praise the LORD, the GOD of Israel! HE has taken notice of HIS people. HE has sent us a mighty Savior, in the family of David, as HIS prophets said HE would. HE promised to remember HIS covenant with Abraham. Now HE will deliver us from our enemies so we can serve HIM without fear all the days of our lives."

Then Zechariah looked at his own baby.

"You, child, will be called the prophet of the Most High. You will go ahead of the Lord, to prepare the way. You will teach his people how to find forgiveness of their sins."

The child named John grew up and became a man strong in spirit. He lived in the desert until the day he first appeared to the people of Israel.

THE SAVIOR IS BORN

In the days after John's birth, the Roman Emperor, Caesar Augustus, ordered a census, or count, to be made of all the people in the empire. Each family had to return to the city of their ancestors to be counted.

Joseph went from the city of Nazareth in Galilee to the city of David, Bethlehem in Judea, because he was a descendant of King David. He took Mary with him.

While in Bethlehem, Mary gave birth to her firstborn son. She wrapped the baby in bands of swaddling cloth. She laid him in a manger, because there was no room for them to stay at the inn.

There were shepherds in the fields nearby, watching over their flocks through the night. An angel of the LORD appeared to them, and the glory of the LORD shone all around them, and the shepherds were filled with fear.

"Do not be afraid," said the angel. "I bring you good news to share with all the people. Today in the city of David a Savior is born. He is Christ the Lord. This is how you will know him: he is a baby wrapped in swaddling clothes and lying in a manger."

Suddenly the angel was joined by a great number of angels, praising GOD and saying:

"Glory to GOD in the highest, and on earth peace among men."

Afterward they spread the word of what the angel had told them about the Christ child. Everyone who heard their story was amazed. In her heart, Mary thought deeply about all that had happened since the angel first appeared to her.

The shepherds returned to the fields, praising GOD for all they had seen and heard.

When the angels returned to heaven, the shepherds said to each other, "Let's go now to Bethlehem and see this child for ourselves."

They hurried off and found Mary and Joseph, and saw the baby lying in a manger.

When the child was eight days old, his parents named him Jesus, as GOD's angel had commanded.

Forty days after his birth, Mary and Joseph took their baby to the Temple in Jerusalem to present him to the LORD. They offered two doves as their sacrifice. All of this was in keeping with the law of the LORD.

There was a man in Jerusalem named Simeon. He was strong in his faith, and he was waiting for the Savior to come and give the land of Israel back to the Jewish people. The Holy Spirit had shown Simeon that he would not die until he had seen the Christ. Moved by the Spirit, he went to the Temple that same day.

When the parents brought the baby Jesus into the Temple, Simeon took him in his arms and praised GOD.

"LORD, now YOU are letting me go in peace, as YOU promised," Simeon said.

"My eyes have seen YOUR salvation, which will be given to all the people."

The baby's father and mother were amazed.

Simeon blessed them and said to Mary, "This child will bring about great changes. Some will honor him. Others will hate him. The true thoughts of many hearts will be revealed. But there will be much pain in this for you."

There was a prophet there that day, a very old woman named Anna. She had been a widow for many years. She no longer left the Temple, but worshiped night and day. She came up to Mary and Joseph and praised GOD for this child who would bring redemption to Jerusalem.

Joseph and his family later returned to Galilee, back to the city of Nazareth. The child grew up there and became strong. He was filled with wisdom and the grace of GOD was on him.

THE WISE MEN

Joseph took care of Mary, and raised Jesus as his own son. But when he had first heard that Mary was with child, he had been puzzled. They were not yet married and he knew the baby was not his. While he thought about what to do, an angel of the LORD had come to him in a dream.

"Joseph, do not be afraid to take Mary as your wife," the angel had said. "She is with child by the Holy Spirit. She will give birth to a son. You will name him Jesus, because he will save his people from their sins."

After hundreds of years, the words that GOD had spoken through the prophet Isaiah were coming true. Mary's son would be Emmanuel, which means "GOD With Us."

After Joseph woke from his dream, he took Mary to be his wife. It was then that they traveled to Bethlehem, where the baby was born.

Wise men from the East came to Jerusalem soon after the birth of Jesus. "Where is the child who will be king of the Jews?" they asked people. "We have seen his star rising and have come to worship him."

King Herod was troubled by this news. Who was this new king to challenge him? The people around Herod were worried as well. They would no longer be rich and powerful if Herod lost his throne.

Herod called in his chief priests and scribes. He asked them what the prophecies said about where the Christ child would be born.

They answered, "In Bethlehem. For the prophet Micah wrote:

'You, O Bethlehem, in the land of Judah! From you will come a ruler who will be the shepherd of MY people.'"

Herod wanted to know more, so he met with the wise men in secret. They told him when the star had appeared. He counted the days and knew the age of his rival king.

"Go," he said to the wise men, "search for the child in Bethlehem. When you have found him, send me word. I too want to worship him."

The wise men went on their way, following the star they had seen in the East. It led them to a house, and inside was the child with Mary his mother.

The wise men were filled with joy. They bowed down and worshiped the child. Then they opened their treasures and gave him gifts of gold, frankincense, and myrrh.

The wise men were warned in a dream not to go back to Herod, so they left for their own country by another way.

After the wise men departed, an angel of the LORD appeared to Joseph in a dream. "Get up," the angel said, "and take the child and his mother and escape to Egypt. Stay there until I tell you.

Herod's men are searching for the child and will kill him."

So Joseph got up in the middle of the night and took Jesus and Mary and left for Egypt.

When Herod learned that the wise men had returned to their land without reporting back to him, he was furious. Since he did not know how to find the Christ child, he sent soldiers to kill all the male children in and around Bethlehem who were less than two years old. He thought that Jesus would

surely be among them. The mothers of Bethlehem wailed and cried over the loss of their children.

After Herod's death, an angel of the Lord again appeared to Joseph in a dream. "Get up," said the angel, "and take the child and his mother and return to the land of Israel. The king who wanted to kill the child is now dead."

Joseph got up and took his family from Egypt to Nazareth in Galilee. Thus the prophecy that the Savior would be from Nazareth was fulfilled.

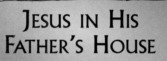

JESUS IN HIS FATHER'S HOUSE

As Jesus grew, he was filled with wisdom and GOD's favor.

When Jesus was twelve years old, his parents traveled to Jerusalem for the feast of the Passover, as they did every year.

After the feast ended, his parents began the journey back to Nazareth. They didn't realize until the next day that Jesus was not with their traveling group. Mary and Joseph looked for Jesus among their friends and relatives, but could not find him. They hurried back to Jerusalem to search for him there.

After three days they found him in the Temple, sitting with the teachers. Jesus was listening to them and asking them questions. All who saw this were astonished by the boy's understanding.

His parents were surprised to find him there.

Mary, his mother, said, "Why have you treated us like this? Your father and I have been so worried, looking everywhere for you."

"Why are you looking for me?" Jesus said. "Did you not know that I must be in my Father's house?"

His parents did not understand what he meant by this.

Jesus went with Mary and Joseph back to Nazareth. He was a good, obedient son to them. And his mother kept all these things in her heart to wonder at and think on.

The boy Jesus grew taller and wiser, and he grew in favor with GOD and the people who knew him.

JOHN THE BAPTIST PREPARES THE WAY

The Romans divided Herod's kingdom into four parts. They set a Roman governor named Pontius Pilate over Judea and Samaria. The other three parts of the kingdom were ruled by sons of Herod.

John, son of Zechariah and Elizabeth, was by this time a grown man, and he had been called by GOD. John traveled the desert wearing a garment of camel hair, with a leather belt around his waist. For food he ate locusts and wild honey. He came to the area near the Jordan River and began spreading GOD's message.

"Repent!" he shouted. "Turn from your sins and be baptized! Only by doing this will GOD forgive you. The kingdom of GOD is near!"

Crowds of people from Judea and Jerusalem came to hear him. He was fierce in telling them GOD's commands.

"You can't just say that you're sorry for your sins," he shouted at them. "If you truly want to turn to GOD, show the proof in your actions! GOD's judgment is near. It is like an axe that is ready to chop down a tree. Every tree that produces no good fruit will be cut down and thrown into the fire."

"What should we do?" asked the people.

He answered:

"If you have two coats, give one to a person who has no coat. If you have food, give some to the person who has no food."

A few tax collectors came to be baptized, and they said, "Teacher, what should we do?" For many tax collectors became rich by keeping more than a fair share of the taxes for themselves.

John said to them, "Collect no more than you should."

Soldiers asked, "What about us? What should we do?"

He said, "Don't use your power to force people to give you what you want. Be content with your pay."

People were excited and felt like something even bigger was going to happen. They began to ask whether John was the Christ come to save them.

"I baptize you with water," John answered, "but the one that comes after me is mightier. I am not even worthy to loosen the strap of his sandal. He will baptize you with the Holy Spirit and with fire.

"He is like a farmer, separating the useful part of the wheat from the stalks and chaff. He will gather the wheat into his barn, but he will burn the remains."

John spoke like this to prepare the people for the coming of Jesus.

Jesus was about thirty years old, when he traveled to the Jordan River to be baptized by John. At first John refused. "I should be baptized by you," he told Jesus. For he knew that Jesus was the Son of GOD.

But Jesus answered, "Let it be this way. It is all part of GOD's plan."

John accepted this, and Jesus was baptized.

As Jesus rose out of the water, heaven opened up. The Spirit of GOD came down to him like a dove.

A voice from heaven said:

"You are MY beloved Son. With you I am well pleased."

THE TEMPTATION IN THE WILDERNESS

Then the Spirit led Jesus into the wilderness. Jesus stayed there among the wild beasts for forty days and forty nights. He fasted the whole time, eating nothing. By the end he was terribly hungry.

Satan came to test him then, saying, "If you are the Son of GOD, command these stones to turn into bread."

Jesus answered, "It is written: 'Man does not live by bread alone. The word of GOD is more important than food.'"

Satan took him to Jerusalem and set him on the highest part of the Temple.

Satan said, "If you are the Son of GOD, throw yourself down from here. After all, it is written: 'If you trust in GOD, HIS angels will watch over you. They will hold you up, so you won't strike your foot against a stone.'"

"It is also written," Jesus said, "that you must not test the LORD your GOD."

Satan took him to the highest mountain and showed him all the kingdoms of the world and all their glory. This was the greatest temptation of all.

Satan said to Jesus, "Bow down and worship me, and all the kingdoms of the world will be yours."

Jesus said, "Get away from me, Satan! It is written, 'You must worship the LORD your GOD, and serve only HIM.'"

Satan saw that he could not tempt Jesus; so he left. And, behold, angels came and attended to Jesus.

Soon after, there was a marriage in Cana of Galilee, and Jesus' mother was there. Jesus and his followers were called to attend.

During the celebration, the guests asked for more wine. And Jesus' mother said to him, "There is no wine."

Jesus responded, "Woman, what is it you wish me to do? The hour of my mission is not yet come."

Still, his mother said to the servants, "Whatever Jesus says to you, do it."

In the corner of the room there were six stone water pots, used in the Jewish washing ritual, which could each hold twenty-five gallons. Jesus pointed these out to the servants, saying:

"Fill those six water pots with water." And the servants filled the water pots up to the brim.

"Now," said Jesus, "fill a cup from one of the water pots and offer it to the master of the wedding feast."

Again the servants did as Jesus said.

When the master of the feast tasted from the cup, he found it to be excellent wine, and he did not know where it had come from (though the servants knew its source). The master called to the bridegroom and said:

"Every man serves the very best wine at the beginning of a feast, and serves the poor wine last, when the guests have drunk well and will not notice. But you—you have served the best wine last."

Thus did Jesus begin his miracles in Cana, showing his glory; and his followers believed in him.

NICODEMUS SEEKS JESUS

Jesus went to Jerusalem for Passover. While he was there, a Pharisee named Nicodemus came to see him. Nicodemus was a leader of the Jews, but he was afraid to be seen with Jesus. He had questions he didn't want to ask when other people were listening, so he came to Jesus at night.

He said, "Rabbi, we know that you're a teacher who has come from GOD. No one can do the wonders that you do, unless GOD is with him."

Jesus answered, "I tell you the truth: No one can see the kingdom of GOD without being born again."

"How can anyone who is old be born again? Is it possible to go back to one's mother and be born a second time?" Nicodemus didn't understand that Jesus was talking about the soul being born again, not the body.

Jesus answered, "I tell you the truth: No one can enter the kingdom of GOD without being born through water and the Spirit. What is born of flesh is flesh, and what is born of the Spirit is spirit.

"Do not be surprised when I say, *You must be born again*. The wind blows where it wishes, and you hear its sound, but you don't know where it comes from or where it goes. You believe in the wind, though you can't see it. So it is with the Spirit."

"How can this be?" said Nicodemus.

"You are a teacher of Israel, and you don't know these things," Jesus replied. "If you don't believe me when I tell you about earthly things, how will you believe me when I speak of heavenly things? Only by placing their faith in me, the Son of man, can people be saved.

"For GOD loved the world so much, HE gave HIS only Son, so that everyone who trusts in him will not die but have eternal life.

"This is what I tell you: Light has come into the world, but the human race has loved darkness rather than light, because their evil deeds could be hidden in the darkness. Those who do good deeds live in truth and come into the light of GOD."

After this, Nicodemus became a secret disciple of Jesus.

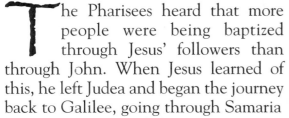

THE WOMAN AT THE WELL

The Pharisees heard that more people were being baptized through Jesus' followers than through John. When Jesus learned of this, he left Judea and began the journey back to Galilee, going through Samaria

When he reached the Samaritan city of Sychar, near the land that Jacob had given his son Joseph, Jesus stopped to rest. Tired from the journey, he sat down by Jacob's well, just outside the city. It was about noon, and the sun was high overhead. His followers went ahead into the city to buy food.

A Samaritan woman came to draw water from the well. Jesus said to her, "Will you give me a drink?"

The Samaritan woman said to him, "But you're a Jew! Jews and Samaritans have nothing to do with each other. How can you ask me for a drink?"

Jesus answered, "If you knew what a gift GOD has for you, and if you knew who I am, you would be asking me for water. I can give you living water."

"You have no bucket, sir," she answered, "and the well is deep. Where do you get this living water? Are you greater than our ancestor Jacob, who gave us this well and drank from it himself, with his sons and his cattle?"

Jesus said to her, "Whoever drinks this water will be thirsty again, but whoever drinks the water I give will never thirst. The water I give will become a spring of water within, welling up with eternal life."

"Sir," said the woman, "give me this living water, so I won't be thirsty and have to keep coming here to draw water."

"Go, call your husband, and come back here," said Jesus.

"I have no husband," she replied.

Jesus said, "That is true, for you have had five husbands, and the man you have now is not your husband."

"Sir, you must be a prophet to know all this about me," the woman said. "Can you answer this question for me?

Just then his disciples returned. They were surprised to find him talking to the woman, but none of them questioned him.

The woman left her water jar and went into the city. She said to the people, "Come! See a man who has told me everything I ever did. Can this be the Christ?"

The people who heard her story left the city to go see Jesus.

Meanwhile, the disciples offered Jesus food, but he would not eat. "I have food to eat that you don't know about. I'm refreshed in a way you don't understand."

The disciples wondered if someone else had given him food.

"What nourishes me is doing the work of God," Jesus explained. "Look around. See how fast the work is going. Look! The fields are ripe for harvest. On the same day the seed has been planted, the harvest is ripe. Look! I just spoke to the woman today and already the Samaritans are coming to me."

Many of the Samaritans believed in Jesus because of what the woman had said: "He told me everything I ever did." They begged Jesus to stay in their city, and he stayed for two days.

During his stay, his words convinced even more of the Samaritans, and they became believers. They said to the woman, "We believed at first because of what you told us, but now we have heard him ourselves, and we know that he is the Savior of the world."

Our ancestors worshiped here on this mountain, but you Jews say we must worship in the Temple in Jerusalem."

Jesus said, "Believe me, where you worship is not important. God is Spirit, and you must worship HIM in spirit and truth."

"I know that Christ is coming," the woman said to Jesus. "When he comes, he will explain everything."

"You are speaking to Christ," Jesus said. "I am he."

FISHERS OF MEN

Herod's son, Herod Antipas, ruled Galilee. John the Baptist dared to say harsh things about this powerful man. John accused Herod Antipas of breaking the law by taking his brother's wife as his own. To keep John silent, Herod ordered him to be put in jail.

After John's arrest, Jesus returned to Galilee. He told the good news of GOD to all who would listen.

"The time has come," Jesus said. "The kingdom of GOD is near! Ask GOD's forgiveness for your sins and believe the good news!"

He healed those who were sick and cast out evil spirits. He taught in the synagogues, and the people who heard him wondered at his wisdom. Stories about Jesus spread throughout Galilee.

After a time, Jesus returned to Nazareth, the town where he had grown up. Jesus went to the synagogue on the Sabbath as he always had. He stood up to read the Scriptures, and they handed him the scroll of the prophet Isaiah. He unrolled the scroll and found where it was written, "The Spirit of the LORD is on me, because HE has anointed me to preach good news to the poor. HE has sent me to proclaim liberty to the captives and to restore sight to the blind, to set at liberty those who are oppressed and to proclaim the year of the LORD's favor."

Jesus rolled up the scroll, returned it, and sat down. All eyes in the synagogue were on him.

He said, "Today this Scripture came true as you listened."

People were amazed at how well he spoke and how knowledgeable he was.

But some said, "Isn't he the son of Joseph, the carpenter? Isn't his mother named Mary? How does a man from such a humble family come to speak like this and perform great works?"

They began to doubt Jesus.

"You wonder why I have not healed people in Nazareth as you have heard I did in Capernaum and the other towns," Jesus said to them. "I tell you, no prophet is honored in his own town."

These sayings angered the crowd in the synagogue. They rose up and forced Jesus to leave the city. They led him to the edge of a cliff and wanted to throw him over the side, but Jesus simply pushed through them and went on his way.

One day, on the shore of the Sea of Galilee, a great crowd came to hear Jesus teach. Jesus saw two empty boats beside the lake, left there because the fishermen were washing their nets. Jesus got into Simon Peter's boat and asked him to row out a little way from the shore. Then Jesus sat down and taught the people from the boat.

When he was finished, he said to Simon, "Go out into the deep water and let down your nets for a catch."

"Master, we worked all night and caught nothing!" Simon answered. "But since you ask it, I will let down the nets."

They caught so many fish that the nets began to break! Simon waved to his partners in the other boat to come and help. When both boats were filled with fish, they began to sink.

Shocked by the enormous number of fish they had caught, Simon fell down at Jesus' knees and said:

"I am not worthy of such help from you, O Lord, for I am a sinful man."

Simon's partners, James and John, the sons of Zebedee, were also amazed by the great catch.

Jesus said to Simon:

"Do not be afraid. From now on you will be fishers of men."

The men pulled their boats up on the shore; and Simon, James, and John left everything behind to follow Jesus.

JESUS, THE TEACHER AND HEALER

Jesus and his disciples traveled to Capernaum. On the Sabbath he went into the synagogue there and taught the people. They were astonished at the way he spoke to them. People were used to being taught by the scribes, who repeated what they had learned from other teachers of the law. But Jesus spoke as if he knew God's law for himself and could speak about it on his own authority.

In the synagogue that day was a man who had been taken over by an evil spirit. The man screamed, "What are we to you, Jesus of Nazareth? Have you come to destroy us? I know who you are! You are the Holy One of God!"

"Be silent!" Jesus commanded the spirit. "Come out of him!"

The spirit threw the man down on the floor, but it left the man's body without harming him.

The people watching were amazed. "What is this?" they said. "Jesus commands evil spirits and they obey him!"

Jesus left the synagogue and went to Simon Peter's house. The family told Jesus that Simon's mother-in-law was lying in bed sick with a high fever. Jesus went to her, took her hand, and raised her up. The fever left her then, and she began to serve Jesus and his companions.

When the sun set, the people of the town brought all those who needed healing to Jesus. He cured many who were sick and he cast out many demons.

Early in the morning, while it was still dark, Jesus got up and found a quiet place where he could be alone to pray. Simon and others from the town came looking for him. When they found him, they tried to convince Jesus to stay.

But Jesus said, "I must go to other cities and towns so I can proclaim the good news. This is why I was sent." And he left them to spread the good news of God's kingdom throughout the region.

While Jesus was visiting one of the cities of Galilee, a man with leprosy came to him. People believed that a person became diseased with leprosy

because he had sinned against GOD. Such a person was thought to be unclean, and no one wanted to be near him. In a show of great faith, the man with leprosy fell on his knees before Jesus and pleaded, "If you are willing, you can make me clean."

Jesus said, "I am willing." He stretched out his hand and touched the man. "Be clean!"

Instantly the leprosy disappeared and the man was healed.

Jesus ordered him, "Say nothing about what happened here. Instead, go to Jerusalem and show the priest that your leprosy is gone. Give a gift to the Temple to thank GOD for this healing."

But the man was deeply grateful to Jesus. He told everyone he met how Jesus had healed him.

People came to Jesus from all directions, and great crowds gathered. He continued to spread the good news and he healed many who were sick. But Jesus often retreated to the lonely places in the wilderness to pray by himself.

Stories about Jesus soon reached the pious Pharisees and the scribes who studied and taught the law of Moses. These men wanted to know if Jesus was following the law. They worried that people would no longer listen to them but follow Jesus instead.

Pharisees from Jerusalem, and towns all over Galilee and Judea, traveled to Capernaum to see Jesus for themselves. They went to the crowded house where he was teaching and sat nearby. Soon the door was blocked with people who had come to see Jesus.

Four men came up to the house, carrying a paralyzed man on a mat. They could not get to the door, so they climbed onto the roof. They made a hole in the roof tiles and lowered the man on the mat into the house, directly in front of Jesus.

Jesus saw that these men had great faith that their companion could be healed. He said to the man on the mat, "Friend, your sins are forgiven."

The Pharisees and the scribes thought to themselves, "How dare this man speak like this! No one can forgive sins except GOD!"

Jesus knew the questions the Pharisees had in their hearts. He said to them,

When Jesus left the house, he saw a tax collector named Matthew sitting at the booth where people came to pay their taxes.

Jesus said to him, "Follow me."

And Matthew left everything, and got up and followed him.

Matthew held a great feast at his house in honor of Jesus. Tax collectors and people from other professions came and sat down with Jesus and his disciples.

The scribes and Pharisees asked Jesus' disciples, "Why does your teacher eat with tax collectors and other sinners?"

Jesus heard them and answered, "It is not the healthy people who need a doctor, but those who are sick. I have not come to save those who are already good. It is the sinners who most need to be saved."

On the Sabbath, Jesus once again taught in the synagogue. There came a man with a withered hand, and the Pharisees watched to see whether Jesus would try to heal him. Work on the Sabbath was forbidden according to Jewish law, so if Jesus healed the man, the Pharisees could accuse Jesus of breaking the law.

Jesus saw the Pharisees and knew what they were thinking. He said to the man with the withered hand, "Come and stand in front of everyone."

Then Jesus said to the scribes and Pharisees, "I ask you, what does the law ask us to do on the Sabbath? Should we do good or do harm?"

The scribes and Pharisees were silent.

Jesus turned to the man and commanded, "Stretch out your hand."

The man did this, and his hand was restored to health.

The scribes and the Pharisees were furious. They left and began to talk about how they could destroy Jesus.

"Why do you question what I have done? Which is easier: to say to the paralyzed man, 'Your sins are forgiven,' or to say, 'Rise and take up your mat and walk'? You need to know that the Son of man has the power and the right to forgive sins here on earth."

Then Jesus said to the man who could not walk, "I tell you, get up, pick up your mat, and go home."

The man immediately stood up and picked up his mat. He walked home, praising GOD.

The people watching were amazed, saying, "We never saw anything as wondrous as this!" And they praised GOD.

THE SERMON ON THE MOUNT

Jesus went alone on a mountainside and spent the night in prayer. In the morning he chose twelve of his disciples to be apostles, his special messengers. The twelve were: Simon, whom Jesus named Peter; Andrew, who was Simon's brother; James and John; Philip; Bartholomew; Matthew; Thomas; James the son of Alphaeus; Simon the Zealot; Judas the son of James; and Judas Iscariot, who would one day betray Jesus.

The apostles walked with Jesus down to a level place where a great crowd had gathered. Many of Jesus' disciples were there, as well as people from all Judea and Jerusalem and the seacoasts of Tyre and Sidon. They came to hear Jesus and to be healed of their diseases. Some tried to touch Jesus, for they believed that his power could heal them.

And Jesus taught them, saying:

Blessed are the mild in spirit, for theirs is the kingdom of heaven.

Blessed are they that mourn, for they shall be comforted.

Blessed are the meek, for they shall inherit the earth.

Blessed are they that do hunger and thirst after righteousness, for they shall be filled.

Blessed are the merciful, for they shall obtain mercy.

Blessed are the pure in heart, for they shall see GOD.

Blessed are the peacemakers, for they shall be called the children of GOD.

Blessed are they which are persecuted for righteousness' sake, for theirs is the kingdom of heaven.

Blessed are you, when men shall revile you, and persecute you, and shall say all manner of evil against you falsely, for my sake.

Rejoice, and be exceeding glad, for great is your reward in heaven, for so

persecuted they the prophets which
were before you.

You are the salt of the earth; but if
the salt has lost its flavor, where will
that salt be needed? It would be of no
use, but to be cast out and trodden
underfoot.

You are the light of the world. A city
that is set on a hill cannot be hid.
Neither do men light a candle and then
put it under a bushel, but on a candle-
stick, so that it gives light to all that are
in the house.

Let your light so shine before men,
that they may see your good works, and
glorify your Father WHO is in heaven.

I say this to all of you: Love your enemies, do good to those who hate you,
bless those who curse you, pray for those
who hurt you. If someone slaps you on
one cheek, offer the other cheek also. If
someone takes your coat, give him your
shirt as well. Give to everyone who asks
you, and if anyone takes something that
belongs to you, do not ask them to give
it back.

Do to others as you would have others do to you. If you love only those who love you, how does that help you in GOD's eyes? Even sinners love those who love them. If you do good things only for those who do good things for you, how does that help you in GOD's eyes? Even sinners do that.

But love your enemies and do good to them, and lend expecting nothing in return. Your reward will be great in heaven. You will be children of GOD, WHO is kind even to the ungrateful and the selfish. Be merciful, just as your heavenly Father is merciful.

Do not collect for yourselves treasures on earth, where moth and rust destroy all things over time, and where thieves break in to steal. But collect for yourselves treasures in heaven, where neither moth nor rust will corrupt, and where thieves do not break in and steal. For wherever your treasure is, there is your heart also.

No man can serve two masters. Either he will hate one and love the other, or he will hold to the one and despise the other. You cannot serve GOD and worldly treasures.

Therefore I say to you, do not worry about this earthly life: what you shall eat and drink, what you shall wear. Is not your life more than food and more than clothing?

Behold the birds of the air. They neither plant nor reap, yet their heavenly Father feeds them. Are you not more precious than they?

Consider the lilies of the field. They do not toil, nor spin yarn. And yet I say to you that even Solomon in all his glory was not dressed like one of these.

If GOD so clothes the grasses of the field, which live today yet will be cast into the oven tomorrow, shall HE not much more clothe you, O you of little faith?

Therefore, take no thought, saying, "What shall we drink?" or "What shall we wear?" for your heavenly Father knows that you need all these things.

First seek the kingdom of GOD, and HIS righteousness, and all these things shall be added unto you. Take therefore no thought for tomorrow, for tomorrow

will take care of itself. Today's concerns are enough for today.

Do not judge, and you will not be judged. Look not for faults in others, but look instead at your own faults. Why do you see the speck of sawdust in your brother's eye and not notice there is a log in your own eye? First take the log out of your own eye, and then you will see clearly to take the sawdust out of your brother's eye.

Do not give that which is holy to the dogs, nor cast your pearls before swine, lest they trample them, and then turn against you.

Ask, and it shall be given you. Seek, and you shall find. Knock, and the door shall be opened to you. For everyone that asks receives, and he that seeks, finds; and to him that knocks, it shall be opened.

Beware of false prophets who come in sheep's clothing, but who are truly wolves. You shall know them by their fruits. No good tree produces bad fruit, and no bad tree produces good fruit.

People with good in their hearts do good deeds and speak good words. Evil people do evil deeds because there is evil in their hearts. You will be able to tell what is in a person's heart by listening to his words."

Not everyone who says to me, "Lord, Lord," shall enter into the kingdom of heaven. But he that does the will of my Father shall enter heaven.

Everyone who hears my words and lives by them is like the wise man who built his house on a rock. The rains fell and the floods came. The winds shook the house, but it did not fall, because it had been built on a rock.

But everyone who hears my words and does not live by them is like the foolish man who built his house on the sand. The rains fell, and the floods came, and the winds blew and beat against the house; and it fell. And great was the fall of it.

And it came to pass, when Jesus had ended these sayings, the people were astonished at his teachings, for he taught them as one having authority, and not as the scribes.

A Roman commander had a favored slave who was sick and near death. When the Roman heard about Jesus, he sent Jewish elders to ask Jesus to come heal his slave.

The elders pleaded with Jesus, "The Roman deserves your help because he loves our people and built our synagogue for us." They were worried Jesus would not help a man who was not a Jew.

Jesus started toward the commander's house, but the commander sent his friends to meet Jesus on the road with this message: "Lord, I am not worthy to have you come under my roof. That is why I have not asked you to come myself. All you have to do is say the word, and my servant will be healed. I am a soldier and am used to orders. I know that when you give an order, it is always done."

When Jesus heard of this man's faith, he turned and said to his many followers, "Not even among the people of Israel have I found such faith."

The commander's friends returned to his house and found the slave was already healed.

Now, John the Baptist was in prison during this time. John's disciples visited him and told him about the great works that Jesus was doing. John sent two disciples to ask Jesus:

"Are you truly the Savior we are waiting for?"

When they found Jesus, John's disciples saw him heal many sick people.

They watched him cast out evil spirits and give sight to the blind.

And Jesus said to them, "Go tell John what you have seen and heard. The blind see, the lame walk, and the deaf hear. The dead are raised up, and the poor receive the good news of GOD's kingdom. Blessed is he whose faith stumbles but remains strong."

After the two disciples left, Jesus spoke to the crowd about John.

ahead of you to prepare the way.'

"I tell you, no one born of woman is a greater prophet than him. But the least person who has been born again into the kingdom of GOD is greater than John."

The people who had been baptized by John knew that Jesus spoke the truth. But the Pharisees and scribes did not agree. They had refused to be baptized by John.

Jesus said to the Pharisees, "You are like children, refusing to dance when you hear cheerful music and refusing to cry when you hear sad songs! When John the Baptist came, not eating food and not drinking wine, you said, 'Why does he fast? He must have a demon inside him.' The Son of man comes, eating and drinking, and you say, 'Look! Why does Jesus eat and drink? He should be fasting.' "

The Pharisees were offended that Jesus was a friend of sinners. The Pharisees and their followers tried to obey all the rules in the Law of Moses to please GOD. They taught that obeying GOD was necessary to earn GOD's forgiveness.

Jesus taught that forgiveness wasn't a reward, but a gift. He said that obeying GOD comes from experiencing GOD's love and forgiveness.

A Pharisee named Simon wanted to see for himself what sort of person Jesus was, so he asked Jesus to eat with him. Jesus went to the Pharisee's house and found more than a simple supper. Simon had invited some of his friends, and had served a formal meal. Jesus joined them, and the meal was served.

While they ate, a woman entered Simon's house uninvited. She had lived a very sinful life until she heard about Jesus. Now she wanted to honor Jesus and seek forgiveness for her sins.

"What did you go out into the wilderness to see?" he asked. "A weak man, a reed shaken by the wind? No! What did you go out to see? A man clothed in fine clothes? Those who are beautifully dressed live in a king's court, not the wilderness. So what did you go out to see? A prophet? Yes! And I tell you, he is more than a prophet. John is the one written about in the Scriptures, where it says: 'I send MY messenger

The woman carried a little stone jar of sweet-scented ointment. She went and stood near the feet of Jesus, weeping, and her tears fell onto Jesus' feet.

The woman removed her headscarf and unpinned her long hair. She bent down and wiped Jesus' feet with her hair, crying and kissing his feet tenderly the whole time. She then rubbed Jesus' feet with the ointment.

Everyone in the room was watching. Simon said to himself, "If this man were really a prophet, he would have known that this woman is a sinner. He would never have let her touch him."

"Simon," said Jesus, "I have something to say to you."

"Teacher, tell me," Simon answered.

Jesus said, "There were two men who borrowed money from a moneylender. One owed five hundred days' wages, and the other fifty. When they could not pay, he forgave them both. Now, which of them will love him more?"

Simon answered, "The one who was forgiven more, I suppose."

"You are correct," said Jesus. He pointed to the woman and said, "Do you see this woman? I entered your house, and you gave me no water to wash my feet. But she wet my feet with her tears and wiped them with her hair. You gave me no kiss of welcome, but she kissed my feet. You didn't anoint my head with oil, but she anointed my feet. She has shown great love, and so her sins—which are many—have been forgiven. But the one who is forgiven little, shows little love."

Then Jesus turned to the woman and said, "Your sins are forgiven."

The other guests began asking each other, "Who is this man that he thinks he can forgive sins?"

Jesus said to the woman, "Your faith has saved you. Go in peace."

THE PARABLE OF THE SOWER

Jesus traveled throughout the land preaching and healing. Out of one woman, Mary Magdalene, he cast seven devils.

One day near the sea, where a multitude had gathered, he stepped into a boat and spoke in parables saying:

"A sower went out to sow his seed. And as he sowed, some fell by the wayside, and the birds ate them up. Some fell among the stones where there was little soil, and when the sun rose they were scorched; and being rootless, they withered. Some fell among thorns, and the thorns sprang up and choked them. But others fell onto good soil and brought forth fruit, some a hundredfold, some sixtyfold, some thirtyfold."

And after he had taught, he cried, "He that has ears to hear, let him hear."

The disciples asked him, "What does this parable mean?"

And Jesus said, "To you is given to know the mysteries of the kingdom of GOD, but to the others I speak in parables, that seeing they still may not see, and hearing they still may not understand. Now, the meaning of the parable is this:

"The seed is the Word of GOD. Those by the wayside are they who hear. Then the wicked one comes and takes away the word from their hearts, lest they should believe and be saved.

"The seeds that fall on stones are they who, when they hear, receive the word with joy, but having no roots they believe for just a while and wither under temptation.

"Those that fall among thorns are they who, when they have heard, go forth and are choked with the cares and riches and pleasures of this life, and bring no fruit to perfection.

"But the seeds on the good soil are they who, with honest and good hearts, having heard the word, keep it and bring forth fruit with patience."

Jesus spoke another parable, saying:

"The kingdom of heaven is like a mustard seed, which a man has taken and sown in the field. It is indeed the least of all seeds; but when it is grown, it is the greatest among plants and becomes a tree, so that the birds of the air come and build nests in its branches."

Jesus Calms the Sea

One evening while teaching on the shores of the Sea of Galilee near the city of Capernaum, Jesus said to his disciples, "Let us row across to the other side."

They left the crowd and climbed into boats. As they rowed across, a terrible storm rose up without warning. The wind tossed the boat and waves rushed in over the sides.

Jesus was asleep on a cushion in the back of the boat. The disciples rushed to wake him.

"Teacher!" they cried. "Don't you see that we are going to die? Won't you save us?"

Jesus woke up. He ordered the winds to stop, and said to the sea, "Be still."

And the winds stopped and the sea was still.

He asked his disciples, "Why were you afraid? Do you have so little faith?"

They were in awe of what Jesus had done. "Who is this, that even the wind and the sea obey him?" they asked each other.

THE POSSESSED MAN

When they arrived on the other shore, in the country of the Gerasenes, the disciples saw Jesus command demons.

As Jesus stepped out of the boat, he was met by a man who had been possessed by demons for a long time. This man had been living outside of the city. He wore no clothes. He spent every night and day in the caves on the mountainside, shouting and cutting himself with stones. The man was so strong that no one could keep him tied, not even with chains.

The man bowed down before Jesus. Then he shouted, "What am I to you, Jesus, Son of the Most High GOD? I beg you, don't torture me!"

Even before the man had finished shouting, Jesus said, "Come out of the man, you evil spirit!"

Then Jesus asked the man, "What is your name?"

"Legion!" he replied, for there were thousands of demons inside him—as many as soldiers in a Roman army legion.

The demons begged Jesus not to send them away. There was a large herd of pigs feeding nearby on the hillside, and the demons asked Jesus to allow them to go into the pigs.

Jesus consented, and the demons left the man and went into the pigs. The herd of two thousand pigs then rushed down the steep bank and drowned in the sea.

Those who were tending the pigs ran off to tell the story, and many of the people they told hurried to see for themselves what Jesus had brought about.

When they came to Jesus, the man who had been possessed by the legion of demons was sitting calmly at Jesus' feet. The man was dressed and in his right mind. Those who had seen him cured of the demons told the others what had happened. People were very frightened by what they heard, and they begged Jesus to leave.

As Jesus got into the boat, the man who had been possessed asked to go with him. But Jesus sent him away, saying, "Go back to your own people and tell everyone what GOD has done for you."

The man went and proclaimed in the city how much Jesus had done for him.

THE HEALING POWER OF FAITH

When Jesus returned from the country of the Gerasenes, a great crowd welcomed him. They had been waiting beside the sea for his return.

One of the leaders of the synagogue, a man named Jairus, came and fell at Jesus' feet. Jairus begged for his help, saying, "My twelve-year-old daughter is near death. Come lay your hands on her so she will live!"

Jesus went with him and the crowd followed, pressing close upon him. There was a sick woman in the crowd who had suffered greatly for many years. She meekly came up behind Jesus and touched his robe.

Immediately she could feel that she had been healed.

"Who touched my clothes?" Jesus asked.

His disciples said, "A crowd as big as this pressing in on you, and still you can say, 'Who touched me?'"

Jesus said, "I know that someone touched me. I felt the power flowing from me."

The woman, afraid and trembling, came and fell down before him. She told him in front of everyone why she had touched him, and how she had been healed.

"Daughter, your faith has healed you," Jesus told her. "Go in peace."

While he was still speaking, some men came from Jairus' house and told Jairus that his daughter had died. "There is no need for Jesus to come now," they said.

Jesus heard them, and said to Jairus, "Don't be afraid. Trust me. She will be well."

When Jesus arrived at the house, everyone was crying and grieving. He said, "Don't weep and wail. She isn't dead, just asleep."

They laughed at him. How could he say something so untrue?

Jesus went to see the girl. He drove everyone out except Peter and James and John, and the father and mother of the child.

He took hold of the child's hand and said to her, "Little girl, get up!"

Immediately she stood up and walked around.

The parents were amazed. Jesus ordered them to tell no one about this healing, and to give the girl something to eat.

THE MISSION

Jesus called the twelve apostles together. He gave the apostles power over diseases and demons so they could heal people. He sent them out two by two to proclaim the kingdom of GOD.

"Take nothing for your journey. No walking stick, no bag, no food, no money. Do not take an extra set of clothes," Jesus told them.

"When you are invited to stay in a house, stay there until you leave that town. You will not always be greeted warmly. Wherever they don't welcome you, when you leave that town, shake the dust off your feet as a sign we will not visit there again."

The apostles left him then. They proclaimed the good news in the villages and towns. They healed many who were sick, and cast out many demons.

More and more people learned of Jesus and his good works. Not all of them realized he was the Savior they had been waiting for. Some thought he might be another prophet, come to tell them about a savior yet to come. Other people said that Jesus was the prophet Elijah, returned to earth from Heaven.

THE DEATH OF JOHN THE BAPTIST

ohn the Baptist was still in prison, having stirred the ire of Herod Antipas, the ruler of Galilee. Herod had taken his brother's wife, Herodias, as his own. Since Herod already had a wife, and Herodias already had a husband, John the Baptist had publicly spoken out against this. "The marriage is against the law," he told Herod.

By his words, John made an enemy of both Herod and Herodias, and Herod had John arrested and thrown into prison. He knew that John was a holy man and very powerful, so he kept him in chains but did not kill him.

Herodias thought that John the Baptist should die, and so she plotted against him.

It happened that Herod held a feast, inviting all the great men of the kingdom to celebrate his birthday. Salome, the daughter of Herodias, danced for the king and his guests. They were so pleased by her dancing that King Herod offered her a reward. "Ask for whatever you want," Herod told the girl, "and I will give it to you. Even if it be half my kingdom, I will give it to you."

Salome went out of the hall then and said to Herodias, her mother, "What should I ask for?"

"The head of John the Baptist," said Herodias.

The girl eagerly returned to the king and said, "I want you to give me, at once, the head of John the Baptist on a platter."

The king could not break a promise made in front of all his guests. So he ordered a guard to kill John the Baptist. The guard brought in John's head on a platter and gave it to Salome, and Salome gave it to her mother.

When John's disciples heard this terrible news, they came for John's body and placed it in a tomb.

Jesus had just heard about John's death when the apostles returned from their travels. They were anxious to tell Jesus of their travels and teachings, but Jesus stayed their talk and said:

"Let us find a lonely place and go rest there for a while."

When the crowds saw Jesus leaving, they followed him to the shore of the lake. Even though he was very tired and in mourning over John's death, he looked at the people with compassion. He saw that they were like sheep without a shepherd. He spoke to them about the kingdom of GOD, and he healed those who were sick.

LOAVES AND FISHES

The day passed and Jesus continued to minister to the crowds. The disciples came to him and said, "It is late, and this is a deserted place. Send the people to the villages and countryside to find lodging and something to eat."

"Don't send them away," said Jesus. "Give them something to eat."

"But how?" asked Philip. "How could we buy so much food? There are five thousand people here. Even if we had two hundred pieces of silver, we couldn't buy more than a small bite for each person."

"How much food do you have?" asked Jesus. "Go and find out."

They did as he said, and Andrew came back to report.

"There's a boy here who has five small loaves of barley bread and two dried fish," he said. "But what good is

that for so many?"

"Bring it to me," said Jesus. Then he said to his disciples, "Make the people sit down in groups on the green grass."

When the people sat down, they made one hundred rows of fifty each.

Jesus took the five loaves and the two fish, looked up to heaven, and blessed the food. He broke the loaves into pieces and gave the bread and fish to the disciples to set before the crowd.

Even though the bread and fish were barely enough to feed one person, after Jesus blessed them there was enough food for everyone. Thousands of people ate, and all were satisfied.

Jesus said to his disciples, "Collect the food that is left over. Don't let anything be wasted."

And the disciples filled twelve baskets with pieces of bread and bits of fish.

JESUS WALKS ON THE WATER

Jesus sent the multitudes away, and asked his disciples to get into the boat and row to the other side of the lake. He stayed behind to say good-bye to the crowd, then went up on the mountain by himself to pray.

Jesus came down to the shore alone before night ended. He saw his disciples out in the boat in the middle of the lake, working the oars and fighting the wind and waves to keep the boat upright.

Just before sunrise, Jesus went out to the boat, walking on top of the water.

When the disciples saw a figure moving over the waves, they cried out in terror:

"Behold—a ghost!"

But Jesus spoke to them, saying, "Take courage. It is I. Do not be afraid."

Peter answered him and said, "Lord, if it is you, let me come to you on the water."

"Come," Jesus said.

And Peter came down out of the boat and he walked on the water to go to Jesus. But when he saw the strong wind, he became afraid and he began to sink.

"Lord, save me!" he cried.

Jesus stretched forth his hand and caught him, and said to Peter, "O you of little faith, why did you doubt?"

When Jesus had come into the coasts of Caesarea Philippi, he asked his disciples:

"Who do the people say that I am?"

They answered, "Some say John the Baptist, but others think you are Elijah. Still others say that one of the prophets has risen from the dead."

"But you—who do you say I am?" Jesus asked.

"You are the Christ," Peter said.

And Jesus said, "You are blessed, for flesh and blood has not revealed this to you, but my Father in heaven. You are Peter—the Rock. And upon this rock I will build my church."

Jesus ordered them to tell no one that he was Christ the Savior. Then, for the first time, he spoke to them about how he would die.

"The Son of man must suffer many things," Jesus said. "He will be rejected by the elders and the chief priests and scribes. He will be killed, and on the third day he will be raised from the dead."

Afterward, Jesus spoke to the crowd that had gathered.

"If anyone wants to follow me, he must give up everything and take up his cross and follow me. For whoever wants to save his life will lose it. But whoever loses his life for my sake will save it.

"Nothing you can gather here on earth is worth anything compared to what you will receive in the kingdom of heaven. And those who are ashamed of me and my words now, will see that I am ashamed of them when they stand before GOD the Father."

And when Jesus and Peter had stepped into the boat, the wind stopped. His disciples were amazed by what they had seen, saying:

"Truly you are the Son of GOD."

They crossed over the lake and landed at Gennesaret. The people of that place recognized Jesus and sent messages all over the region telling of his powers. Wherever he went after that, people brought the sick to him for healing. So great was their faith that they begged to touch the hem of his robe, knowing that was all they needed to be healed. And so it was. Everyone who touched him was healed.

Several days later, Jesus took Peter and James and John and led them up a high mountain to find a quiet place for prayer.

As Jesus was praying, his disciples saw something wondrous happen. The robes Jesus wore shone dazzling white, and Elijah and Moses appeared in glory to speak with him.

Peter and the others were frightened and amazed. Peter said to Jesus:

"Master, it is good that we are here. Let us make three temples, one for you, one for Moses, and another for Elijah."

As he said this, a cloud came and overshadowed them. A voice came from the cloud, saying:

"This is MY Son, MY beloved. Listen to him."

The disciples looked up then and saw that Elijah and Moses had disappeared. No one was there except Jesus.

As they walked down the mountain, Jesus commanded the three men, "Tell no one about what you saw until the Son of man rises from the dead."

The disciples argued among themselves what "rises from the dead" could mean, and then they asked, "Why do the scribes say that Elijah has to come first, that he has to appear on earth before the Christ?"

Jesus answered, "Elijah does come first, to restore all things. I tell you, Elijah has already come, and they did to him what they wished. Like Elijah, the Son of man will also suffer and be treated with contempt."

The disciples understood that Jesus meant John the Baptist was like the prophet Elijah. John had prepared the way for Jesus to announce the kingdom of GOD. Like Elijah, John had suffered at the hands of unbelievers.

When they reached the bottom of the mountain, a great crowd was waiting. There were scribes and teachers of the law there, arguing with the people in the crowd.

A man came to Jesus out of the crowd and said, "Teacher, I beg you, look at my son, my only child! A spirit seizes him and he cries out. It shakes him until he foams at the mouth and grinds his teeth, and his body goes stiff. I begged your disciples to cast out the evil spirit, but they weren't strong enough."

Jesus said to him and the people of the crowd, "Why do you have so little faith? How long will I bear you?"

Then he said to the man, "Bring your son to me."

When the evil spirit saw Jesus, it tormented the boy. His body shook and he fell to the ground, rolling around and foaming at the mouth.

Jesus said to the father, "How long has this been happening?"

"From childhood," the father answered. "The spirit often threw him into fire and water to try to destroy him. If you can do anything, please help us."

Jesus said to him, "Don't you know that all things are possible for the one who believes?"

The father cried out, "I do believe! Help me when I don't believe!"

Jesus scolded the evil spirit and said, "I order you, spirit, come out of this boy and never bother him again!"

With more shouting and shaking, the spirit came out. The boy lay on the ground, and many said, "He's dead." But Jesus took hold of the boy's hand and raised him up.

Later, the disciples asked Jesus, "Why couldn't we cast out the spirit?"

"That kind of spirit can only be driven out by prayer," Jesus answered.

Then he said to his disciples for the second time, "The Son of man will be given into the hands of his enemies, and they will kill him. But after three days he will rise again."

The disciples still didn't understand what Jesus meant, and they were afraid to ask him to explain.

In the days that followed, the disciples argued over which of them was the greatest. When Jesus realized what was in their hearts, he said, "If anyone wants to be first among my disciples, he must put himself last and serve all the others."

Jesus called a little child to stand beside him, and he said to his disciples, "Whoever receives this child in my name, receives me, and whoever receives me, receives the ONE WHO sent me. Whoever is least among you will be great."

THE LORD'S PRAYER

And it came to pass that after Jesus had been praying, one of his disciples said to him: "Lord, teach us to pray."

And Jesus said to them, "When you pray, say:

Our Father WHO *is in heaven,*
holy is YOUR *name.*
YOUR *kingdom come,* YOUR *will be done*
on earth as it is in heaven.
Give us each day our daily bread,
and forgive us our sins as we forgive
those who sin against us.
Do not lead us into temptation,
but deliver us from evil."

Jesus taught them that prayer was the way to ask GOD for help. He explained that sometimes they would have to keep praying again and again for the things they needed.

"Ask, and you will receive. Do not be afraid. Ask. Stretch out your hand. GOD wants to give you a gift.

"GOD is like a parent who listens to the needs of his children. No earthly father would give a snake when the child asks for a fish, or give a scorpion when the child asks for an egg. So, if human beings who are sinful still know how to take care of what their children need, imagine what gifts the heavenly Father has in store for you."

The Pharisees and scribes still did not want to believe in the message that Jesus brought them about God's kingdom, for Jesus welcomed ordinary people and sinners to come and be saved.

So Jesus said to the Pharisees:

"What man among you, if he has a hundred sheep and lost one of them, doesn't leave the ninety-nine in the wilderness and go after the lost one until he finds it? And when he finds it, he joyfully sets it on his shoulders. When he gets home, he calls together his friends and says to them, 'Rejoice with me, for I have found my lost sheep.'

"Just so, I tell you, there will be more joy in heaven over one sinner who asks forgiveness than over ninety-nine righteous people who do not need forgiveness.

"Or what woman, if she has ten coins and loses one coin, doesn't light a lamp and sweep the house, searching carefully until she finds it? And when she finds it, she calls together her friends and says to them, 'Rejoice with me, for I have found my lost coin.'

"Just so, I tell you, there is joy among the angels of God over each sinner who asks forgiveness."

389

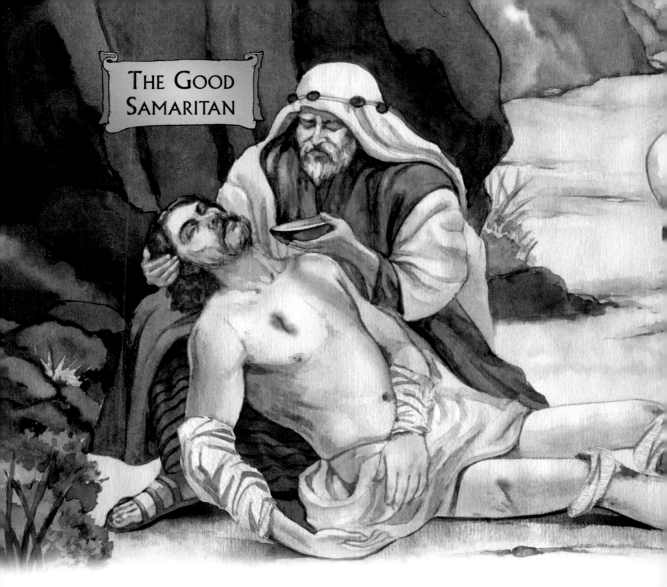

A scribe who studied and taught the Law of Moses came to challenge Jesus. He asked:

"Teacher, what do I have to do to gain eternal life and go to heaven when I die?"

"What is written in the Law of Moses?" Jesus asked him.

The scribe answered, "You must love the LORD your GOD with all your heart, and with all your soul, and with all your strength, and with all your mind. And you should love your neighbor just as you love yourself."

"That is the right answer," Jesus said. "Do that and you will go to heaven."

"Well, then, who is my neighbor?" asked the scribe.

Jesus answered with this parable:

"There was a man who was traveling from Jerusalem to Jericho. Along the way he was attacked by robbers. They stripped him of his clothes and beat him and went away, leaving him half dead.

"Now, a priest happened to be going down that road, and when he saw the man he did not stop to help him. He crossed to the other side of the road. Likewise a Levite, a Temple minister who also knew the Law of Moses, passed by the man without stopping to help him.

"Then a Samaritan came down the road. When he saw the injured man, he had compassion. He wrapped up the

Jesus told another parable, saying: "There was a man who had two sons. The younger one said, 'Father, when you die, part of what you own will be mine. Give me that part now.' So the father gave him his share.

"The younger son gathered all he had and traveled to a far country where he wasted all his money on foolish living. Then there was a great famine. He had nothing to eat, so he worked for a man of that country who sent him into his fields to feed the pigs. This son would gladly have eaten what the pigs ate, but no one offered him any.

man's wounds, pouring on oil and wine to clean them. Then the Samaritan brought him to an inn and took care of him. The next day, the Samaritan took out two silver coins and gave them to the innkeeper. He said, 'Take care of him until he is well. If it costs more than this, I will pay the rest when I come back.'

"Which of these three," Jesus asked, "was a neighbor to the man who was attacked by the robbers? The two men of his own country who passed him by, or the stranger from Samaria?"

The scribe said, "The one who showed mercy on him."

Jesus said to him:

"Go and do likewise."

"He came to realize the mistakes he had made. 'The men who work for my father have more than enough food, but here I am, starving among pigs,' he said. 'I will go home to my father and beg to be taken back, even if it means becoming one of his servants.' And so he got up and headed home.

"But while the young man was still a long way off, his father saw him and had compassion. The father ran to his son and wrapped his arms around him and kissed him.

"The son said, 'Father, I have sinned against heaven and against you. I no longer deserve to be called your son.'

"But the father said to his servants, 'Hurry, bring the best robe and put it on him. Put a ring on his finger and shoes on his feet. Prepare the fatted calf. We will feast! My son who was dead to me is alive again. He was lost and now is found.' And they began to celebrate.

"When the older son returned from his work in the fields, he heard music and dancing. He asked one of the servants what this meant.

"The servant said, 'Your brother has come home. Your father has slaughtered the fatted calf in celebration.'

"The older son was angry to hear this and refused to join the feast. His father came out and pleaded with him, but the older son said, 'All these years I served you, and I never disobeyed your orders. You never gave me even a young goat so I could feast with my friends. But then this son comes, who wasted all the money you gave him, and you slaughter the fatted calf for him!'

"The father answered, 'Son, you are always with me, and all that is mine is yours. We celebrate today because your brother was lost, but now he is found.' "

JESUS AND THE CHILDREN

And it happened one day, when Jesus was preaching, that there were many who came with their young children, that Jesus might touch them.

But the disciples discouraged and scolded them and tried to keep the children away from Jesus.

And when Jesus saw this, he was displeased, and said to his disciples:

"Let the little children come to me. Don't forbid them, for of such is the kingdom of heaven.

"Truly I say to you that whosoever will not receive the kingdom of GOD like a little child will not enter heaven."

And Jesus took the children in his arms, put his hands upon them, and blessed them.

A Servant to All

The disciples were on the way to Jerusalem, and Jesus was walking ahead of them. Then Jesus called the twelve apostles apart from the others, and told them for the third time that his death was coming.

"We are going to Jerusalem," he said, "and everything that was written by the prophets about the Son of man will happen. He will be handed over to the chief priests and the scribes to be sentenced to death, then handed over to the Romans. They will mock him and spit on him and whip him. He will die on the cross, and on the third day he will rise again."

They listened to his words with fear, but the apostles still did not understand what events would unfold when they reached Jerusalem.

James and John, the sons of Zebedee, came and asked Jesus for a special sign of his favor. They said, "Grant that we will sit, one at your right hand and the other at your left, in your kingdom."

Jesus said, "You know not what you are asking. Can you drink the cup that I drink?"

James and John answered, "We can."

But Jesus was speaking of his suffering and death, and they did not understand.

"You will drink my cup," Jesus said, "but I cannot promise you will sit at my right hand or at my left. Those places belong to those who are chosen by my Father."

The ten other apostles were angry when they heard what James and John had asked. Why should they be placed higher than the rest?

Jesus called them all together and said, "You know that in this world there are governors over the people, and even greater rulers who are set over those who govern. It must not be this way among you. Whoever wants to be the greatest among you must be the servant to you all. For the Son of man did not come to be served but to serve his people. He will give his life to gain freedom for many."

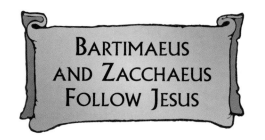

BARTIMAEUS AND ZACCHAEUS FOLLOW JESUS

Near Jericho, a blind man sat by the road as Jesus passed by with his disciples and a great crowd of followers. The blind man was a beggar and his name was Bartimaeus.

When he heard the crowd going by, Bartimaeus asked the people around him what was going on.

"Jesus of Nazareth is passing by," they said.

Bartimaeus called out to Jesus, "Son of David, have mercy on me!"

The people in the crowd scolded the beggar and told him to be silent, but he shouted again, "Son of David, have mercy on me!"

Jesus stopped and ordered that the man be brought to him.

The blind man left his robe behind and came to Jesus.

"What do you want me to do for you?" Jesus asked.

Bartimaeus said, "Lord, I want to see again."

"Your faith has saved you," said Jesus, and immediately the blind man received his sight.

Bartimaeus followed Jesus then, giving thanks to GOD.

Jesus entered Jericho, where there lived a rich man, a tax collector named Zacchaeus, who wanted to see him. Zacchaeus was too short to see over the crowd, so he ran ahead and climbed a sycamore-fig tree to get a better look.

When Jesus and his disciples passed below that tree, Jesus looked up and said, "Zacchaeus, hurry down here, for I must stay at your house today."

Zacchaeus came down right away and welcomed Jesus with joy.

When the crowd saw this, they grumbled, "Jesus has gone to stay at the house of a sinner."

But Zacchaeus said to Jesus, "Here, Lord! Right now I will give half of everything I own to the poor. If I have cheated anyone of anything, I will pay him back four times over."

Jesus said, "Today salvation has come to this house. This man too is a child of Abraham. The Son of man has come to seek and save those who are lost."

Even though Jesus had healed many people and performed miracles, not all believed that he was the Savior, the true Son of GOD. Some were angry that a man such as Jesus would make these claims. The disciples began to be afraid. Hadn't Jesus been telling them that the time of his death was growing near?

In the town of Bethany, two miles from Jerusalem, a man named Lazarus was dying. His sisters, Mary and Martha, sent a message to Jesus, saying, "Lord, your friend Lazarus is very sick."

When Jesus heard the message, he said, "This sickness will not end in death. It will bring glory to GOD, and to the Son of GOD."

Although Jesus loved Lazarus and his sisters, he did not leave right away. After two days had passed, he said to his disciples, "Our friend Lazarus has fallen asleep, but I am going now to wake him."

The disciples said, "Lord, if he has fallen asleep, he will get better."

Then Jesus told them plainly, "Lazarus is dead. I'm happy for your sake that I was not there to save him. Now you will see something that will bring you to greater faith. Let us go to him."

But Thomas expected the worst. He worried that Jesus was in danger because of the people who did not believe he was truly the Son of GOD. Thomas said to the other disciples, "Let us go with Jesus so we can die with him."

When Jesus reached Bethany, Lazarus had already been dead and in the tomb four days, and many people from Jerusalem had come out to comfort Martha and Mary.

Martha heard Jesus was coming and went out to meet him on the road. When she saw Jesus she said, "Lord, if you had been here, my brother would not have died. But even now I know that whatever you ask from GOD, GOD will give you."

"I am the resurrection and the life," Jesus told her. "Whoever believes in me, even though he dies, will live; and whoever lives and believes in me will never die. Do you believe this?"

She said to him, "Yes, Lord. I believe that you are the Christ, the Son of God."

After she said this, she went into the house to find her sister Mary. Martha spoke to her quietly so the guests wouldn't know that Jesus was nearby.

"Mary," she whispered, "the teacher is here. He's calling for you."

Mary got up and rushed out. Jesus had not yet come into the village, but was still waiting on the road where Martha had met him.

When the guests saw Mary hurry out, they followed. They thought she was going to the tomb.

Mary saw Jesus and fell at his feet, saying, "Lord, if you had been here, my brother would not have died."

When Jesus saw her crying, and all those with her crying, he was troubled.

"Where have you laid him?" he asked.

"Lord, come and see."

And then Jesus wept.

"See how he loved him," people said.

But some of them asked, "Couldn't the one who gave sight to the blind have kept this man from dying?"

Jesus loved Lazarus, and he was filled with sadness about his friend's death. But he wept for the people around him who did not have faith.

Jesus went to the tomb, a cave with a large stone covering the entrance.

"Take away the stone," he ordered.

Martha said, "Lord, by now there will be a smell. He has been dead four days."

"Did I not say that if you believe, you will see the glory of God?" Jesus asked.

So they took away the stone.

Jesus looked up and said:

"Father, I thank you for hearing me. I know that you always hear me, but I say this now so that the people standing here will believe that you sent me."

Then he called in a loud voice:

"Lazarus, come out!"

The dead man came out of the tomb. His hands and feet were wrapped in burial cloths, and cloth covered his face.

"Take off the burial cloths and let him go free," Jesus commanded.

And so they did. Lazarus had been brought back to life.

Many of the guests who had come to

comfort Mary and Martha saw this miracle and put their faith in Jesus. But others went to the Pharisees and told them what Jesus had done.

The chief priests and the Pharisees called a meeting of the ruling council of the Jews, the Sanhedrin.

"What are we going to do?" they asked each other. "This man Jesus is doing amazing works. If we let him go on like this, everyone will believe in him. If we look weak, the Romans will come and destroy our Temple and our nation."

Caiaphas, who was high priest that year, said:

"You people do not understand the situation, nor do you understand that it is better for one man to die for the people than for the whole nation to die."

The high priest Caiaphas was unknowingly prophesying that Jesus would die for the nation of the Jews, and that his dying would bring together all of God's children.

From that day on, the council members plotted how they would have Jesus put to death.

When the people heard that Jesus was near Jerusalem, they came together in a great crowd, hoping to see him enter the city. The people also wanted to see Lazarus, whom Jesus had raised from the dead. The chief priests were angry that so many people were putting their faith in Jesus.

Just outside Jerusalem, Jesus called two of his disciples and said to them, "Go into the village opposite the hill covered with olive trees. As soon as you enter, you will find a young donkey, one that has never been ridden. Untie the donkey and bring it here. If anyone asks why you are untying it, say, 'The Lord needs it.' "

The disciples did as he had ordered. As they untied the donkey, people asked them, "Why are you untying that donkey?"

"The Lord needs it," replied the disciples, and the people let them go away with the donkey.

They brought the animal to Jesus, throwing their cloaks over it as a saddle for Jesus to sit upon. Jesus rode the young donkey from the Mount of Olives to Jerusalem. Along the way, people spread their robes on the ground in front of him, and others waved palm branches.

As he rode into the city, crowds of people went before and after him, crying out in praise. "Blessed is the King who comes in the name of the LORD!" they shouted joyfully. "Peace in heaven and glory in the highest!"

Some of the Pharisees came up to him and said, "Teacher, tell your disciples to stop shouting."

Jesus answered, "I tell you, if they are silent, the stones themselves will shout."

"What can we do?" the Pharisees said to each other. "The whole world has gone over to him."

When Jesus saw the city of Jerusalem laid out before him, he wept, saying, "If you only knew today the things that would bring you peace, but they are hidden from your eyes. The time is coming when enemies will surround you and hem you in on every side. They will kill everyone inside the walls of Jerusalem. They won't leave one stone in this city standing on top of another—all because you didn't recognize this as the time when the Lord is coming to you."

THE MONEYCHANGERS IN THE TEMPLE, AND THE FIG TREE

Jesus came into Jerusalem and entered the Temple. He looked around; but since the hour was late, he did not stay. He went with the twelve apostles to the nearby village of Bethany to spend the night.

The next day as they returned to Jerusalem, Jesus was hungry. When he saw a fig tree in the distance, covered with leaves, he went to it, looking for figs to eat. But there was no fruit on the tree. It was not yet the season for figs.

"No one will ever eat fruit from you again," Jesus said to the tree.

When he arrived at the Temple that day, Jesus was angry to see people selling oxen and sheep and doves in that holy place. The moneychangers were doing business there as well.

Jesus overturned the tables of the moneychangers and the benches of those selling doves. He cast out of the Temple everyone who was buying and selling there, along with their goods and their animals.

"You have made my Father's house a marketplace!" he cried. "It is written, 'My house will be a house of prayer for all nations.' But you have made it a den of thieves."

He remained at the Temple throughout the day, and the blind and the lame came to him for healing. When the chief priests and the teachers of the law saw the wonders he did, they were not pleased. When they heard that even the children were shouting out in praise of Jesus, the priests were angry.

"Do you hear what the children are saying?" they asked Jesus.

"Yes," Jesus replied. "Have you never read in the prophecies that the children would praise my coming?"

He left the Temple then, and again spent the night in Bethany.

In the morning, on their way back to Jerusalem, the disciples came upon the fig tree that Jesus had cursed the day before.

Peter said to him, "Look, Lord! The fig tree has withered and died, all the way to the roots."

Jesus said, "A fig tree that produces no fruit will be destroyed."

When the apostles asked him how he had caused the fig tree to wither so quickly, Jesus replied, "If you have faith and do not doubt, not only could you do the same thing to the fig tree, but you could order this mountain to move, and it would do so. If you believe, you will receive whatever you ask for in prayer."

JESUS TEACHES IN THE TEMPLE

In the days that followed, people gathered in the Temple courtyard every morning to listen to the teachings of Jesus.

The chief priests and the scribes and the elders feared Jesus' influence over the people who came to listen. One day the priests and the scribes came up to Jesus while he was teaching and asked, "Who gave you the authority to come here and do these things? How can a man who has not studied the law claim to know so much about what GOD wants? Tell us."

Jesus answered, "You answer my question first, and then I will answer yours. Tell me: when John baptized people in the river, did his authority come from GOD in heaven, or from people here on earth?"

The priests argued with each other about how to answer. If they said John baptized because GOD in heaven gave him the power to do it, then Jesus would ask them why they did not believe John's word that Jesus was the Savior. If the priests said that John baptized without heaven's approval, the people would be angry with the priests, for the people believed that John was a true prophet.

So the priests refused to answer at all. "We cannot tell," they told Jesus.

"Then I will not tell you with what authority I do these things," Jesus said to them.

Jesus returned to his teaching. He told the people a parable to help them understand what GOD expected of them.

"A man planted a vineyard," Jesus said, "and he rented it to some farmers. The tenant farmers were to give him fruit from the vineyard as payment for letting them use the land. When the man sent his servant to collect the fruit, the farmers beat the servant and sent him away empty-handed. Then the man sent another servant, and again the tenants treated him shamefully and sent him away empty-handed. He sent a third servant, and this one too was beaten and thrown out of the vineyard.

"Then the man who owned the vineyard said, 'What should I do? I will send my beloved son. Perhaps they will respect him.' But when the tenants saw the man's son, they said to each other, 'This is the heir. Let us kill him, and then his inheritance, this vineyard, will be ours.' And they did just that. What will the owner of the vineyard do?"

People in the crowd answered, "He will come and destroy those tenants, and give the vineyard to others who will give him the fruit."

Jesus said to them, "As the Scriptures say, the stone that the builders reject will become the cornerstone of the LORD's building. I tell you that the kingdom of GOD will be taken from you if you do not believe, and it will be given to others who will harvest its fruit."

In this way, Jesus revealed that he was working to build GOD's kingdom. Jesus was not afraid of how these leaders on earth would judge him. The scribes and the priests wanted to arrest him then and there, but they were afraid the people would try to stop them.

The priests and scribes went away, but soon sent spies to listen to Jesus and try to trick him into saying something that would put him in trouble with the Roman officials.

"Teacher," the spies said, "we know that you speak the truth about God's way, no matter what other people want you to do. So tell us: is it right for us to pay taxes to the Romans, or not?"

Jesus knew they wanted to set him at odds with the Romans. "Why are you trying to trick me?" he asked. "Bring me a coin."

They brought one, and he said, "Whose picture is on this coin, and whose writing?"

"Caesar's," the spies answered. Caesar ruled the Roman Empire, including the land of the Jews.

Jesus said, "Give to Caesar the things that are Caesar's, and to God the things that are God's."

The spies were amazed by his answer, and they went away, but the Pharisees returned to further question Jesus.

"Teacher, which is the greatest of God's commandments?"

Jesus answered, "Love the Lord your God with all your heart, with all your soul, and with all your mind. This is the first and greatest commandment. The second is this: Love your neighbor as you love yourself. Everything else in God's Law rests on these two commandments."

While the Pharisees were gathered around him, Jesus asked, "What do you think of the Christ? Whose son is he?"

"The son of David," said the Pharisees. They expected the Savior to be a warrior king, like David, who would fight to free Jerusalem from foreigners.

Jesus said, "In one of his songs, David called the Christ his Lord. If the Christ is David's Lord, how can he also be David's son?"

After that, no one dared to ask Jesus any more questions.

Then Jesus said to the crowd and his disciples:

"The scribes and Pharisees teach the laws of Moses. You must do what they say, but not do what they do. They preach good things, but they don't practice what they preach. They weigh you down with heavy rules, but they do not try to help you carry these burdens. They make a show of following the small rules, but they pay no attention to the most important parts of the law: the teachings about justice and mercy and faith. This is like straining the fleas out of the food yet swallowing a camel instead.

"When the Pharisees do a good deed, they make sure people see it. They walk around in long, showy robes and receive attention in the marketplace and the best seats in the synagogues and the places of honor at the feasts.

"They clean the outside of the cup and the plate, but not the inside. They are greedy for money and they cheat the poor. They are like whitewashed tombs, beautiful on the outside, but inside full of dead men's bones and filth.

"I send wise men and prophets among you, but they are killed and crucified by men like these."

Jesus looked up and saw the rich men casting their gifts into the treasury. And he also saw a certain poor widow casting in two mites, coins of little worth.

And Jesus said, " Truly I say to you, that this poor widow has cast in more than all of the others. For the rich men have cast in merely the surplus of their abundance. But she, in her poverty, has given all that she had to live on."

Jesus looked around the Temple and said, "O Jerusalem, Jerusalem, killing the prophets and stoning those who are sent to you. How I want to gather your children together, as a hen gathers her chicks under her wings, but you are not willing to let them come to me. Your house will be ruined and left empty.

"I tell you, you will not see me again until you say, 'Blessed is he who comes in the name of the LORD.' "

Some people heard Jesus teach and said, "Truly, he is the prophet that Moses spoke about."

Many agreed. "This is the Christ, GOD's anointed one," they said.

"But Jesus is from Galilee," others protested. "Do the Scriptures not say that the Christ must be descended from David, and come from Bethlehem?" And so the people were divided.

The chief priests and the Pharisees sent the Temple guards to arrest Jesus, but the guards came back without him.

"Why didn't you bring him?" the priests and Pharisees asked.

"No man ever spoke like this man," the guards replied.

"Has he fooled you too?" demanded the priests. "Do you see any of us, any of the leaders, who believe in him? The common people may follow him, but they don't know the law of Moses as we do. They will be cursed, all of them!"

But Nicodemus, the Pharisee who had become one of Jesus' disciples, said, "Since when does our law judge a person without first giving him a chance to tell his story?"

WARNINGS ABOUT THE FUTURE

As Jesus walked out of the Temple, one of his disciples said to him, "Teacher, look at these enormous stones. How beautiful these buildings are!"

But Jesus said to him, "Look at these great buildings all around us. The time is coming when every one will be thrown down, and not one stone will be left on top of another."

Later that day as Jesus rested on the Mount of Olives opposite the Temple, Peter, James, John, and Andrew spoke with him privately.

"Teacher," they asked, "when will the Temple be destroyed? What sign should we watch for to know that these fearful things you speak of are about to happen?"

Jesus said:

"Beware; people may come claiming to be me. Don't believe them. And do not be alarmed when you hear reports of wars. Nation will fight against nation and kingdom against kingdom. There will be earthquakes and famines. But the world will go on.

"People will hate you because of me. They will arrest you and persecute you. You will be brought before kings and governors because of me. But worry not about what to say, for the Holy Spirit will speak through you. Those who stand firm in their belief will be saved.

"Heaven and earth will pass away, but my words will not pass away. But of that day and hour, no man knows; no, not even the angels of heaven, but my Father only. Watch, therefore, for you know not what hour your Lord will come. Be ready, for the time when you do not expect it, the Son of man will come.

"For the kingdom of heaven will be like ten bridesmaids who took their lamps and went forth to meet the bridegroom. Five of them were wise, and five were foolish. They that were foolish took their lamps and took no oil with them. But the wise took oil in their vessels with their lamps.

"While the groom tarried, the maidens grew tired and slept. And at midnight there was a cry:

" 'Behold, the bridegroom comes! Go out and meet him.'

"Then all the maidens arose and trimmed the wicks in their lamps, and the foolish said to the wise, 'Give us some of your oil, for our lamps have gone out.' But the wise answered, 'No, we cannot, for we may only have enough for our own lamps. Go, therefore, and buy oil for yourselves.'

"And while the foolish bridesmaids went to buy, the bridegroom came, and they who were ready went in with him to the wedding; and the door was shut.

"Afterward, the other bridesmaids came, saying, 'Lord, lord, open the door to us.' But he answered, 'Truly I say to you, I do not know you.'

"Watch, therefore, for you know neither the day nor the hour when the Son of man will come.

"When the end does come, there will be signs in the sun and moon and stars, and on the earth. Enemies will surround Jerusalem. People will see the Son of man coming in clouds with power and great glory to establish his kingdom.

"The Son of man will sit on his throne and all the nations will come into his presence. He will separate them the way a shepherd separates the sheep from the goats. He will place the sheep at his right hand, and the goats at his left.

"Then the King will say to those on his right, 'Come, you who are blessed by my Father. The kingdom is yours. For I was hungry and you gave me food, I was thirsty and you gave me drink, I was a stranger and you welcomed me. I was naked and you clothed me, I was sick and you cared for me, I was in prison and you came to me.'

"Then the righteous will say, 'Lord, when did we see you hungry and feed you, or thirsty and give you drink? When did we see you a stranger and welcome you, or naked and clothe you? When did we see you sick or in prison and visit you?'

"The King will answer, 'Truly, I say to you, whatever you did for the least of my brothers and sisters, you did for me.'

"Then he will say to those on his left, 'Go, for you are cursed. Go into the eternal fire prepared for the devil and his angels. For I was hungry and you gave me no food, I was thirsty and you gave me no drink, I was a stranger and you did not welcome me. I was naked and you did not clothe me, sick and in prison and you did not visit me.'

"Then these people will say, 'Lord, when did we see you hungry or thirsty, or a stranger, or naked or sick or in prison, and didn't offer you help?'

"He will answer, 'Truly, I say to you, when you helped not the least of my brothers and sisters, it was me whom you did not help.'

"The people at his left hand will go to eternal punishment, but the righteous will go to eternal life."

THE LAST SUPPER

"In two days it will be Passover," Jesus told his disciples, "and then the Son of man will be handed over to be killed upon the cross," for he knew that his enemies were plotting against him.

Even as he spoke these words, the chief priests and elders of the people were meeting in the palace of Caiaphas, the high priest, and making plans to arrest Jesus. "But we will do it secretly, and not during the Passover feast," the priests and elders agreed, "or there will be a riot among the people."

Judas Iscariot, one of the twelve apostles, was tempted by Satan. He went to the chief priests and said, "What will you give me if I hand Jesus over to you?"

The priests promised to him thirty silver coins, and from that moment, Judas looked for an opportunity to betray Jesus to the priests.

Passover was the most important of the Jewish feasts. It was celebrated every spring in remembrance of how GOD had brought their ancestors out of slavery in Egypt. On the first day of the feast, the Passover lamb was sacrificed. Families ate roasted lamb in memory of the lamb's blood that had marked the doorways and saved their people from death in Egypt.

The disciples asked Jesus, "Where do you want to eat the Passover feast? We will go and prepare the place."

He chose two of them, saying, "Go into the city, and you will meet a man carrying a jar of water. Follow him. Wherever he enters, say to the master of the house, 'The Teacher says, *Where is the room where I will eat the Passover feast with my disciples?*' He will show you a large upstairs room, which is ready for us to use. Prepare the meal for us there."

The disciples went into the city and everything happened as Jesus had said it would. They prepared the Passover meal in the room that was waiting for them.

Jesus came to the room that evening with the twelve apostles, and they shared the Passover meal.

"How greatly I have desired to eat this Passover with you before I suffer," Jesus said, "for I tell you, I will not eat another until it is fulfilled in the kingdom of GOD."

Jesus rose and laid aside his outer robe and wrapped a towel around his waist. He poured water into a basin and washed the feet of each of his disciples, drying them with a towel.

Peter could not believe the Lord would wash their feet when they were there to serve him. "Lord, you must not wash my feet," he said.

Jesus answered, "You do not understand now what I am doing, but later you will. Unless I make you clean, you will not be one of my own."

is not greater than his master, and the one who is sent is not greater than the one who sent him."

As they ate the meal, Jesus continued to speak of the one among them who was no longer clean in spirit. "I say to you, one of you who is here eating with me will soon betray me."

His apostles were greatly upset to hear this. One after another they asked, "Surely not I, Lord!"

Jesus said, "One of the twelve, one who is dipping his bread into the bowl with me, will betray me. The Son of man will go, as it was written by the prophets, but woe to the man who hands him over to his enemies. It would be better for that man if he had never been born."

Judas, the betrayer, said, "Is it I, Lord?"

"Yes, it is you," Jesus answered. "What you are about to do, do quickly."

The other apostles did not understood what Jesus meant, thinking he was telling Judas, who carried the money-box, to buy whatever was needed for the feast.

Judas left them then and went out into the night.

Jesus took bread, and when he had given thanks, he broke the bread and gave it to the apostles, saying, "Take and eat. This is my body, which is given for you. Do this in remembrance of me."

Then Jesus took a cup of wine, and when he had given thanks, he gave it to them, saying, "Drink this, all of you, for this is my blood of the covenant, the promise which I make to you. It will be poured out for the forgiveness of all. I will not drink again of the fruit of the vine until I drink it with you in my Father's kingdom."

The apostles all drank from the cup that he offered them.

"Lord," Peter replied, "then wash not just my feet, but my hands and my head."

Jesus said, "The one who has bathed need not wash but his feet, for he is clean all over. You are clean—clean in spirit—but not every one of you is clean." For he knew who would betray him.

When Jesus had put his robe back on and joined them at the table, he asked, "Do you understand what I have done? You call me Teacher and Lord, for so I am. Now if I, your Lord and teacher, have washed your feet, you should do the same for others. I tell you truly, a servant

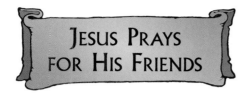

Jesus Prays for His Friends

Jesus said to the apostles, "Now God will be glorified through the Son of man. My children, I am going to leave you soon. You will look for me, but you will not find me. You cannot go where I am going.

"A new commandment I give to you: that you love one another. Just as I have loved you, so should you love one another. By this all men will know that you are my disciples: that you have love for others."

"Lord, where are you are going?" asked Peter.

Jesus answered, "Where I am going, you cannot follow me now; you will follow me later. But let not your heart be troubled, and trust in God. In my Father's house there are many rooms. I go to prepare a place for you, and I will come again and receive you to be with me. You know where I am going, and you know the way."

"But, Lord, we don't know where you're going," Thomas said. "How can we know the way?"

Jesus said, "I am the way, the truth, and the life. No one comes to the Father but by me."

"Lord, show us the Father," Philip said.

"Have I been with you this long, and you still don't know me, Philip?" Jesus asked. "If you have seen me, you have seen the Father. I am in the Father, and the Father is in me. And whatever you ask for in my name, I will do it.

"If you love me, keep my commandments. I will pray to the Father to send you another Comforter—the Holy Spirit—to be with you forever. The Spirit will teach you all things, guide you to truth, and help you remember what I taught you. I came from the Father and now I will return to the Father.

"Peace I leave with you. My own peace I give to you, a peace which the world cannot give. This is my gift to you. Let not your heart be troubled or afraid.

"This *is* my commandment: that you love one another as I have loved you. Greater love has no man than this: that a man lay down his life for his friends. You are my friends if you keep my commandment. I no longer call you servants, for everything I have heard from my Father I have shared with you. And people will know that you are my disciples by the love you have for one another."

Jesus looked up to heaven and said, "Father, the hour of my suffering is near, and my work will soon be complete. Through this suffering, glorify YOUR Son, so the Son many glorify YOU. Let this suffering reveal YOUR love to the world."

Jesus asked God to bless and watch over the disciples who had believed in his message. "I pray for the ones YOU have given to me. Protect them with the power of YOUR name, which is also my name, so they may be one, as YOU and I are one. But my prayer is not for the disciples alone. I also pray for those who will come to me through their message, that all may be one. Their unity will show the world that YOU sent me, and that YOU love them just as YOU love me."

After Jesus had spoken his prayer, they sang a hymn.

Jesus went out with his disciples to the Mount of Olives, and there Jesus said to them, "This very night, all of you will fall away, leaving me alone. It has been written: 'I will strike down the shepherd, and the sheep will be scattered.' But after I have risen, I will go ahead of you into Galilee."

"Even if they all fall away, I will never leave you," Peter replied.

Jesus said, "Truly, this very night, you will deny me three times before the rooster crows."

But Peter insisted, "Even if I must die with you, I will never deny you."

And the other disciples said the same.

THE GARDEN OF GETHSEMANE

There at the foot of the Mount of Olives, Jesus went with his disciples into the garden called Gethsemane. It was a place Judas and the other disciples knew well, a quiet place where Jesus often went to pray.

Jesus told the disciples to sit and wait while he went away from them to pray. He took only Peter and James and John with him. The three men could see how grieved Jesus was.

"My soul is full of sorrow," Jesus told them, "even to the point of death. Stay here and keep watch for me."

He went on a little farther and lay full-length on the ground, his face down. Jesus was greatly distressed by what he knew would soon happen. He prayed, "My Father, all things are possible for YOU. Let this cup pass from me—Nevertheless, not because I wish it, but because YOU wish it so."

He returned to his disciples to find that all were sleeping. Jesus said, "Peter, are you sleeping? Could not you keep watch one hour? Watch and pray that you won't be tested again. The spirit is willing, but the flesh is weak."

Then, for the second time, Jesus went off by himself. Again he prayed, saying, "O my Father, if this cup may not pass from me, I will drink it—YOUR will be done."

And again when he returned to the disciples, all were sleeping. He spoke to them, but their eyes were heavy.

416

Jesus went away to pray once more. When he returned to the disciples for the third time, he said, "Sleep on now, and take your rest. The hour has come, and the Son of man is betrayed into the hands of sinners."

Then Jesus said, "Rise; let us be going. Behold, my betrayer is near."

While Jesus was still speaking, Judas arrived, and with him was a large group of men, armed with swords and clubs, carrying lanterns and torches. The men had been sent by the chief priests and the elders of the people.

Judas had given the men a signal, saying, "The one I kiss is the man you seek. Seize him and take him away under guard."

Going immediately to Jesus, Judas said, "Master, Master," and kissed him.

"Judas, are you betraying the Son of man with a kiss?" Jesus asked.

And the armed men seized Jesus.

Peter drew his sword and struck the high priest's servant, a man named Malchus, cutting off his ear.

Jesus ordered, "Put your sword away. Those who draw the sword will die by the sword. Do you not know my Father could stop this if HE wished?"

At this, Jesus touched Malchus's ear and healed him.

Then Jesus spoke to the priests and others who had come for him, demanding, "Am I leading an army in rebellion? Why do you come with swords and clubs? Day after day I was with you in the Temple, and you did not arrest me. Instead you choose to do your work in darkness."

And the disciples scattered, leaving Jesus alone with his enemies.

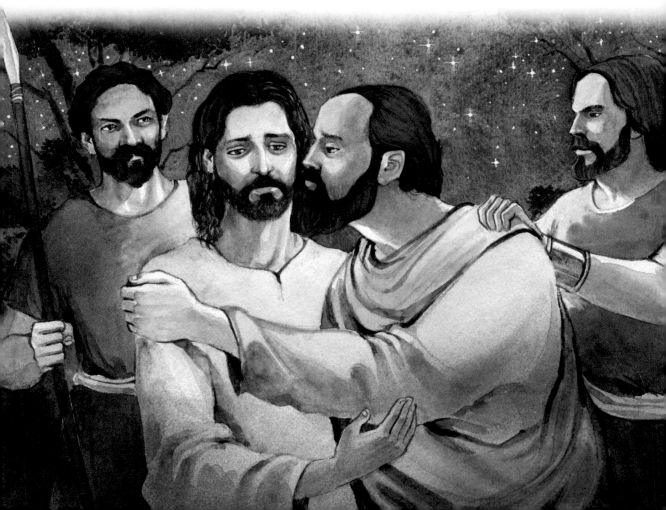

BEFORE THE HIGH PRIEST

The crowd led Jesus away to the house of Caiaphas, the high priest; and all the chief priests and the elders and the scribes met together in the middle of the night.

Peter had followed at a distance as the crowd led Jesus to this place. Peter went as far as the courtyard of the high priest's house. There Peter stood with the guards, warming himself beside a charcoal fire.

The chief priests and the elders of the council were looking for reasons to put Jesus to death, but they found none, even though many testified falsely against Jesus.

At last two men came forward and said, "We heard him say, 'I will destroy this Temple made with human hands, and in three days I will build another, not made with human hands.' "

Caiaphas, the high priest, stood up and said to Jesus, "Do you have no answer to this testimony against you?"

But Jesus held his peace.

Caiaphas questioned him: "Tell us, are you the Christ, the Son of God?"

Jesus said to him, "If I say so, you won't believe. But I say to you: In the days to come, you will see the Son of man sitting on the right hand of power, and coming on the clouds of heaven."

The other priests said, "Then, are you the Son of GOD?"

"You say that I am," replied Jesus.

The high priest tore his robes and said to the council, "Why do we need to hear more? You heard the offense against GOD. You heard this blasphemy from his own lips. What is your decision?"

"He deserves to die," they answered.

Then they spit in his face and struck him. They blindfolded him and slapped him, saying, "Prophesy to us, you Christ! Who is it that struck you?"

Peter meanwhile was outside in the courtyard. A servant girl saw him in the light of the fire and said, "You were with Jesus of Galilee."

But Peter denied it, saying, "I don't know what you're talking about."

The servants and guards standing around the fire looked at Peter. "Aren't you one of Jesus' disciples?"

"I am not!" Peter said.

Then a kinsman of Malchus, whose ear Peter had cut off, said, "Did I not see you in the garden with him?"

Peter denied again—and immediately the rooster crew.

Peter remembered the words of Jesus: "You will deny me three times before the rooster crows."

Peter went out and wept bitterly.

JESUS STANDS BEFORE PILATE

Before the sun rose, the chief priests and elders plotted together against Jesus to put him to death. They tied him up and led him away to the hall of judgment and handed him over to Pontius Pilate, the Roman governor.

When Judas, his betrayer, saw that Jesus was condemned, he repented and brought the thirty pieces of silver back to the chief priests, saying, "I have sinned by betraying an innocent man!"

"What is that to us?" the men said. "That is your problem."

Judas threw down the pieces of silver in the Temple. Then he went out and hanged himself.

The chief priests picked up the silver coins and said, "It is not lawful to put this in the treasury, for this is blood money."

And they agreed to use the money to buy the potter's field, a place where they could bury foreigners who died in Jerusalem.

The Jewish leaders would not go inside the governor's palace, for entering the home of a Gentile, a non-Jew, would

"We are not allowed to put any man to death," the priests answered; for only an official of the Roman Empire could sentence someone to death.

Pilate went back into the palace. He called Jesus to him and said, "Are you the King of the Jews?"

Jesus said to him, "Do you ask this on your own, or have others said this about me?"

"Your own nation and the chief priests have handed you over to me," Pilate replied. "What have you done?"

Jesus answered, "My kingdom is not of this world. If it were, my servants would have fought against my arrest. No, my kingdom is elsewhere."

"So, you *are* a king?" said Pilate.

Jesus answered, "You say I am a king. To this end was I born, and for this cause I came into the world, to bear witness to the truth. Everyone who is on the side of truth listens to my voice."

Pilate said to him, "What is truth?" And having voiced this, he went out to the council and said, "I find no wrong in this man."

But the priests and the elders argued, "He has been stirring up the people with his teaching all over Judea, from his home in Galilee to Jerusalem."

"If he is a Galilean, take him to Herod who is in charge over Galilee," ordered Pilate; and he sent Jesus to Herod, who was in Jerusalem at the time.

Herod was glad to meet Jesus, for he had heard about him and hoped to see him work a miracle. Herod asked many questions, but Jesus remained silent.

The chief priests and the scribes stood by, angrily accusing Jesus.

Herod and his soldiers mocked Jesus, treating him with contempt. They clothed him in a beautiful robe and sent him back to Pilate.

make them unclean before GOD, and they wanted to eat the Passover feast.

Pilate came out to meet them, and asked, "What charges are you bringing against this man?"

The chief priests had no specific charge. "This fellow is an evil-doer," they said, "or we would not be handing him over to you. We found him misleading our people and telling them not to pay taxes to Caesar, and saying that he is the King of the Jews."

Pilate said, "Why bring him to me? Judge him by your own law."

Pilate said to the council, "You brought me this man and said he was misleading the people. I have questioned him and I do not find him guilty of your charges. Neither did Herod, who sent him back to us. Jesus has done nothing to deserve death, so I will have him whipped—and then I will release him, for you have a custom: that I release to you one prisoner at the Passover. Shall I release the King of the Jews?"

But they all cried out, "Crucify this man and release Barabbas." For Barabbas was also a prisoner, arrested for murder.

Pilate sent Jesus to be whipped. And the Roman soldiers braided a crown of thorns to put on his head, and clothed him in a scarlet robe, and mocked him, saying, "Hail, King of the Jews!"

Once again Pilate went before the council. "See," said Pilate. "I am bringing him out to you, so you will know that I find no fault in him."

He had Jesus brought forth, wearing the fine robe and the crown of thorns, and presented him to the priests and the people, saying:

"Behold the man!"

When the chief priests and officers

saw him, they cried out, "Crucify him!"

And Pilate said, "I find no crime in him."

The priests answered, "According to our law, he must die, for he has made himself the Son of GOD."

"When Pilate heard this, he was afraid. He went into his palace and said to Jesus, "Where are you from?"

But Jesus gave no answer.

Then Pilate said to him, "Won't you speak to me? Don't you know that I have the power to release you, and the power to crucify you?"

Jesus answered him, "The only power you have over me is the power given to you by GOD."

Pilate brought Jesus before the crowd. Pilate sat in the judgment seat and said, "Behold your King!"

The chief priests answered, "We have no king but Caesar."

And the people cried out, "Crucify him! Crucify him! Release Barabbas!"

Fearing an uproar, Pilate took water and washed his hands before the multitude saying, "I am innocent of the blood of this man."

Then Pilate released the murderer Barabbas, and sent Jesus to be crucified.

Pilate's soldiers stripped the scarlet robe off Jesus and dressed him in his own robe. They led him through the city on the way to Golgotha, the place called the Skull, where he would die on the cross.

The soldiers forced Jesus to carry the heavy wooden crossbeam himself. As they came to the edge of the city, the soldiers saw that Jesus could carry the cross no further. They seized Simon of Cyrene, who was coming in from the country, and made him take up the cross and carry it behind Jesus.

A great crowd followed, and the women were weeping and mourning for Jesus. Jesus turned to them and said:

"Daughters of Jerusalem, weep not for me, but weep for yourselves and your children."

Two other men, both thieves, were led out of the city with Jesus to be put to death on the cross. When they had come to Golgotha, the charge against Jesus was placed above the cross in Hebrew, Latin, and Greek, so all could read it:

JESUS OF NAZARETH,
KING OF THE JEWS

And they crucified Jesus there, with the two criminals, one on the right hand, the other on the left.

Then Jesus said:

"Father, forgive them, for they know not what they do."

And the soldiers divided his garments between them, and cast lots for his robe.

Close by the cross of Jesus stood his mother, his mother's sister, Mary the wife of Cleophas, and Mary Magdalene. Jesus looked and saw the disciple standing by, whom he loved, and Jesus said to his mother:

"Woman, behold your son."

He said to the disciple, "Behold your mother." And from that hour that disciple took her into his own home.

The people stood by, watching.

The rulers scoffed, saying, "Aha! The one who destroys the Temple and builds it again in three days—come down from the cross and save yourself."

The chief priests mocked him, and the scribes said, "He saved others, but he cannot save himself. Let him come down now from the cross, so we can see and believe."

One of the criminals crucified beside Jesus joined in the insults. He ranted at Jesus, "Aren't you the Christ? Save yourself and us."

But the second criminal scolded the first, saying, "Do you not fear GOD, since you too are about to die? It is justice that we are being punished for our crimes, but this man has done nothing wrong." Then he quietly said, "Jesus, remember me when you come into your kingdom."

Jesus replied, "Truly, I say to you, today you will be with me in Paradise."

After this, Jesus said, "I am thirsty."

And a soldier lifted up to him a sponge of vinegar and bitter herbs.

It was noon, yet darkness came over the earth for three hours.

And Jesus said, "My GOD, my GOD, why have YOU forsaken me?"

After this, Jesus cried out in a loud voice, and said, "Father, into YOUR hands I commend my spirit. It is finished."

And having said this, Jesus bowed his head and breathed his last.

At that moment, the veil of the Holy of Holies in the Temple was torn in two from top to bottom. The earth quaked, rocks split, and graves were opened.

The Roman officer and his soldiers standing near the crosses were terrified. The officer said, "Truly this man was the Son of GOD."

Many women were there when Jesus died, watching from a distance. Some had followed Jesus all the way from Galilee. They had looked after Jesus while he was alive, and wanted to tend to his body now that he was dead.

The soldiers were ordered to break the bones of the three crucified men to hasten their deaths. But when they came to Jesus, they saw that he appeared dead. One soldier pierced Jesus' side with a spear, and there came out blood and water. So they broke not his bones.

That evening, a rich man named Joseph, from the town of Arimathea, boldly went to Pilate and asked for the

body of Jesus. Joseph of Arimathea was a good and righteous man, a member of the council who was a secret disciple of Jesus.

Pilate was amazed to hear that Jesus had already died. After he had confirmed Jesus' death, he gave the body of Jesus to Joseph of Arimathea.

Nicodemus was another secret disciple of Jesus. He brought nearly a hundred pounds of spices and ointments; and when Joseph took Jesus' body down from the cross, they wrapped it with spices in linen and placed a burial cloth over Jesus' face.

Near Golgotha was a garden where Joseph of Arimathea owned a tomb newly cut from the rock. The men laid the body of Jesus in there and rolled the great entrance stone in place.

Mary Magdalene and some of the other women had followed Joseph and Nicodemus to the tomb. Since it was late in the day and the Sabbath would begin at sunset, the women hurried home. They prepared the spices and ointments they would need to properly prepare the Lord's body. But the women obeyed the commandment and rested on the Sabbath.

The chief priests feared that Jesus' disciples would steal the body and claim that he had risen. Therefore they asked Pilate to place guards at the tomb and seal the stone. And it was done.

THE RESURRECTION

At the end of the Sabbath, as it began to dawn on the first day of the week, Mary Magdalene and the other women took the burial spices and ointments and carefully made their way down the path to the tomb. They asked each other, "Who can roll the huge stone away from the tomb so we can go inside?"

They were surprised to find that someone had already moved the stone away from the entrance. When they went into the tomb, the body of Jesus was gone.

"How could this be?" the women asked each other.

Suddenly an angel of the LORD appeared to them, dressed in robes that gleamed like lightning. Frightened, the women bowed down with their faces to the ground.

"Why do you look for the living among the dead?" the angel asked. "He is not here. He has risen. You will see him again in Galilee. Remember what Jesus told you: 'The Son of man will be delivered into the hands of his enemies. He will be crucified, but on the third day he will rise again.' "

Mary Magdalene, Joanna, Mary the mother of James, and the others ran to tell the apostles this news. But the apostles did not believe them, except for Peter, who got up with John and ran to the tomb.

When Peter saw the strips of linen lying on the ground, and found the burial cloth that had covered the face of Jesus, he was filled with wonder.

After the disciples had gone back to their homes, Mary Magdalene stood crying outside the tomb. She did not understand what had happened and why the body of Jesus was no longer there.

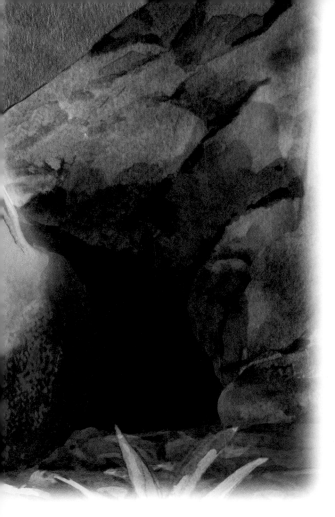

She turned around and saw a man standing before her.

"Woman, why are you crying?" she heard him say. "Whom do you seek?"

Mary thought he was the gardener, and said, "Sir, if you have carried him away, tell me where you have laid him, and I will take him away."

The man said to her, "Mary."

She looked again and he was revealed to her as Jesus.

"My Teacher!" she cried, overwhelmed with joy, wanting to embrace him.

"Do not cling to me," he said. "I have not yet gone up to the Father. But go to my brothers and sisters and tell them this: I am going to my Father and your Father, to my GOD and your GOD."

Mary Magdalene went to the disciples and said:

"I have seen the Lord!"

JESUS APPEARS TO THE DISCIPLES

That same day, two of Jesus' disciples were walking to a village named Emmaus, about seven miles from Jerusalem. Along the way they talked about all that had happened since Jesus' arrest. And it came to pass that while they discussed and reasoned together, Jesus himself came near and began to walk along with them, but their eyes were kept from recognizing him.

Jesus asked, "What is this you are talking about as you walk along? What makes you look so sad?"

One of them, Cleophas, answered, "Are you a stranger to Jerusalem? Have you not heard of the things that have happened there these past few days?"

"What things?" Jesus asked.

"About Jesus of Nazareth," they replied. "He was a prophet, mighty in deed and word in the sight of GOD and all the people. Our chief priests and rulers condemned him to death and crucified him, though we had hoped that he was the one to free our people. But there is more. Today is the third day since these things were done, and some women from our group astonished us with news. They visited his tomb early this morning but his body had disappeared. The women came back saying they had seen an angel, who told them Jesus was alive. Some of our companions went to the tomb and found it empty, just as the women had said."

Then Jesus said to them, "O foolish men. How slow your hearts are to believe all that the prophets have spoken.

Was it not necessary that the Christ should suffer these things and enter into his glory?"

Then, beginning with Moses and all the prophets, Jesus explained to them all the parts of the Scriptures that talked of the Christ.

They drew near to the village of Emmaus, and Jesus was going to walk on, but the men stopped him, saying, "Stay with us, for it's nearly evening and the day is almost over." So he went in and remained with them.

When they sat down to eat together, Jesus took the bread, and blessed and broke it. As Jesus gave the bread to the disciples, their eyes were opened and they recognized him. Then he vanished from their sight.

The men said to each other, "Did not our hearts burn within us while he talked to us on the road, when he opened the Scriptures to us?"

They rushed back to Jerusalem that very hour and found ten of the apostles gathered with other disciples who told them, "The Lord has risen indeed, and has appeared to Peter!"

Then the travelers told what had happened on the road to Emmaus, and how they recognized Jesus when the bread was broken.

Now, the disciples had kept the doors closed in the room, for they were afraid of the chief priests and the council coming after them, since they were followers of Jesus. Yet while they were talking about the vision of Jesus on the road to Emmaus, Jesus himself suddenly appeared.

"Peace be with you," he said.

The disciples were startled and frightened, for they thought they had seen a spirit.

"Why are you troubled?" Jesus asked.

"Why are there questions in your hearts? It is truly I. Behold my hands and feet. Touch me and you will see I am real. A spirit does not have flesh and bones." He held out his hands and feet so they could see for themselves.

The disciples rejoiced, but they were still amazed to see him there. Jesus asked for something to eat and they gave him some broiled fish and honeycomb. He ate it while they watched.

"Peace be with you," he told them again. "As the Father sent me, so I am sending you."

He breathed on them and said, "Receive the Holy Spirit. If you forgive anyone's sins, then their sins are forgiven." Then Jesus left them.

The disciples were filled with new life and power, and they weren't afraid.

One of the apostles, Thomas, did not arrive in time to see Jesus. When he came, the other disciples told him, "We have seen the Lord!"

But Thomas said to them, "Unless I see the mark of the nails in his hands, and touch the wound in his side, I won't believe it is really him."

Eight days later, the disciples were together in the same room, but this time Thomas was with them. Again, the doors were shut, but Jesus came and stood among them.

"Peace be with you," he said.

Jesus immediately turned to Thomas and said, "Reach out your finger and touch the nail marks in my hands. Reach out your hand and feel the wound in my side. Trust and believe."

Thomas answered and said to him, "My Lord and my GOD!"

"Thomas, you believe now that you have seen me," Jesus said. "Blessed are they who have not seen, yet have believed."

After this, Jesus told his disciples to return to Galilee, and Jesus showed himself again to his disciples by the Sea of Galilee.

Peter, Thomas, Nathanael, James and John, and two other disciples were together on the shore. Peter told them he planned to go fishing, and the others said they would go along. They were out in the boat all night and yet they caught no fish.

As the sun was rising, they saw someone standing on the beach. It was Jesus, but they did not recognize him.

"Friends, do you have any food?" the man on the shore called out.

"No," they answered.

The man said, "Cast your net on the right side of the boat, and you will find fish."

They did as he said and caught so many fish that they could not pull the

caught," Jesus said to them.

Peter went and hauled the net ashore. It was full of large fish, a hundred and fifty-three of them. Yet, though it was heavy with fish, the net was not torn.

Jesus said to them, "Come and have breakfast."

And knowing it was the Lord, none of them dared ask him, "Who are you?"

So Jesus took the bread and gave it to them, and the fish likewise.

When they finished breakfast, Jesus said, "Peter, do you love me above all else?"

"Yes, Lord. You know I love you," replied Peter.

Jesus said to him, "Feed my lambs."

Then Jesus asked a second time, "Peter, do you love me?"

"Yes, Lord. You know I love you."

"Take care of my sheep," said Jesus.

And then for the third time Jesus asked, "Peter, do you love me?"

Peter was hurt that Jesus had asked him this three times. He said to Jesus, "Lord, you know everything. You know I love you."

Jesus said to him, "Feed my sheep. You are a fisherman no longer, but the shepherd of my flock. I tell you truly, when you were younger, you dressed yourself and walked wherever you wished. But when you are old, you will stretch out your hands and someone else will bind them and take you where you do not wish to go."

With these words Jesus revealed that Peter would glorify GOD by dying in HIS service.

"Follow me," Jesus commanded Peter.

Peter turned and saw John following them. "What about him, Lord?"

Jesus said, "What is that to you? Follow me."

heavy net up into the boat.

John said to Peter, "It is the Lord!"

When Peter heard that it was the Lord, he jumped into the sea and began swimming to shore. The others stayed in the boat, dragging the net full of fish behind them.

When they reached the shore, they saw a fire of coals on the beach, with fish cooking on it, and bread.

"Bring some of the fish you have

Jesus appeared to his disciples over a period of forty days, speaking to them about the kingdom of God. "John baptized with water," he said, "but you will be baptized with the Holy Spirit not many days from now."

Jesus spoke to his eleven apostles for the last time on Mount Olivet in Galilee. They bowed down and worshiped him.

Then he said to them, "All authority in heaven and on earth has been given to me. Go, therefore, for I send you to make disciples of all nations. Baptize them in the name of the Father and of the Son and of the Holy Spirit, and teach them to follow the commands I have given you. Behold, I am with you always, even to the end of time."

Then he lifted up his hands and blessed them, and as he was blessing

them, he was lifted up, and a cloud took him out of their sight.

While they were looking steadily toward heaven, behold, two men dressed in white robes stood beside them and said to them, "Galileans, why do you stand looking up into heaven? This same Jesus who was taken up from you into heaven will come again in the same way as you have seen him go."

And they returned to Jerusalem with great joy, and went to the upper room where they were staying. The eleven apostles devoted themselves to prayer, along with the women and Mary the mother of Jesus, and his brothers.

Peter stood up and said that an apostle should be selected to take Judas' place. Two men were named. The eleven prayed, drew lots, and Matthias was chosen.

Seven weeks after Passover was the feast of Pentecost, the Jewish celebration of the first fruits of the harvest and God's gift of the Law.

That year, the hundred and twenty disciples were gathered together in one place for Pentecost. Suddenly there came a sound from heaven, like the rush of a mighty wind, and it filled the house where they were sitting.

There appeared to them tongues of flame that came to rest on each one of them. And they were all filled with the Holy Spirit and began to speak in different languages, as the Spirit led them.

Now, there were Jews staying in Jerusalem for the feast, devout people from every nation under heaven. And when they heard of this news, they gathered in a large crowd and were confounded because each man heard them speak in his own language.

They were amazed and they marveled, saying, "Are not these people Galileans? How can we hear them speaking in our own native languages? We are Parthians, Medes, and Elamites, people of Mesopotamia, Judea and Cappadocia, Pontus and Asia Minor, Phrygia and Pamphylia, Egypt and the parts of Libya near Cyrene, and visitors from Rome. We are Jews and converts to Judaism, Cretans and Arabs—but we hear them telling us in our own languages about the mighty works of God. What does this mean?"

But others mocked the Galileans, saying, "They are full of new wine."

Then Peter stood up with the eleven other apostles and said to them:

"People of Judea and Jerusalem! These people are not drunk, as you suppose, for it is only nine o'clock in the morning. This is what was spoken of by God through the prophet Joel. He said, *'When the Lord comes, I will pour out MY Spirit on all human beings. Your sons and your daughters will prophesy, your young men will see visions, and your old men will dream dreams. I will pour out MY Spirit on MY servants, men and women, and they will prophesy. I will do mighty works in the heavens above and on the*

earth below. At the end, everyone who calls on the name of the Lord will be saved.'

"Listen, Israelites! Jesus of Nazareth was sent to you by GOD. It was GOD's plan for Jesus to be handed over and crucified, but GOD raised him up! We saw him. We are witnesses. He was lifted up and now he sits at the right hand of GOD. GOD promised him that HE would pour out the Holy Spirit. Now you know for certain that GOD has made Jesus both Lord and Christ—this same Jesus that you crucified."

When the men heard this, they were cut to the heart.

"What should we do?" they asked.

Peter said, "Repent and be baptized in the name of Jesus Christ for the forgiveness of your sins. Then you will receive the gift of the Holy Spirit. The promise is to you and to your children and even foreigners—to everyone the LORD our GOD calls."

Peter spoke a long time, teaching and encouraging them, and those who received his word were baptized. About three thousand souls were added that day, the first fruits of GOD's harvest.

Since that day, awe came over everyone, and many signs and wonders were done through the apostles. And the LORD added to their number daily those who would be saved.

THE LAME BEGGAR AT THE GATE

Peter and John were going up to the Temple at the time of the afternoon prayer, when a man, lame from birth, was being carried to the Temple gate called Beautiful.

The lame man sat at that gate every day, begging for money from the people who were going to the Temple. When he saw Peter and John, he put out his hand.

Peter and John looked at him intently, and Peter said, "Look at us."

The lame man looked directly at them, expecting money. But Peter said, "I have no silver or gold, but I give you what I have. In the name of Jesus Christ of Nazareth, rise up and walk!"

Peter took the beggar by the right hand and raised him up, and immediately the man's feet and ankles were made strong. He leaped up and stood on his feet and walked with them into the Temple, leaping and praising GOD.

All the people saw him walking and heard him praising GOD, and they recognized him as the beggar at the Beautiful Gate. They were filled with amazement at what had happened to him.

Peter said to them, "Israelites, why are you amazed? Why do you stare at us, as if we had made him walk through our own power? It is faith in the name of Jesus that made this man well—the same Jesus whom you delivered to Pilate to be crucified, and whom GOD raised from the dead. We are witnesses! Friends, I know you acted in ignorance, like your rulers. Now repent and turn to the LORD, so your sins will be blotted out."

While Peter was speaking to the people, the priests and the Temple police arrived and were angry that Peter and John preached of Jesus and the resurrection. They arrested them and held them overnight.

But many of those who heard the word believed, and the number of them was five thousand.

The next day, Peter and John were brought before the elders and scribes and the ruling council, who asked them, "By what power or name did you do this?" pointing to the healed man.

Peter was filled with the Holy Spirit, and he said, "Rulers of the people and elders, let it be known to you and all Israelites: It was by the name of Jesus Christ of Nazareth, whom you crucified and GOD raised from the dead, that this man is standing before you well. Jesus is the only one, and his name is the only name, that can save us."

When they saw such boldness from uneducated men, the leaders were puzzled. But they looked at the man who had been healed standing beside them, and were silent. They ordered Peter and John to go outside while they met privately.

"What should we do with these men?" they asked each other. "Everyone in Jerusalem can see this mighty work they did. We cannot deny it. But we need to stop this witnessing from spreading any further among the people."

They called them back in and commanded, "Do not speak or teach any more to anyone in the name of Jesus."

But Peter and John answered, "You must judge whether it's right in GOD's sight for us to listen to you rather than to GOD. But we cannot stop speaking about what we have seen and heard."

The council threatened them but let them go, for the people were praising GOD for the healing of the lame man.

Upon their release, Peter and John went to their friends and reported what the chief priests and the elders had said. Then they all pleaded with GOD, saying:

"LORD, help us speak YOUR word with boldness. Stretch out YOUR hand to heal and do mighty works through the name of Jesus."

The place where they were meeting began to shake, and they were all filled with the Holy Spirit, and they spoke the word of GOD with boldness.

THE NEW COMMUNITY

The people who came to faith in Jesus devoted themselves to the apostles' teaching and fellowship. They met daily at the Temple and broke bread together in their houses. They shared food gladly, and every day the LORD added more to their number. The apostles gave witness with great power to the resurrection of the Lord Jesus, and GOD's favor was on them all

The whole community was one in heart and soul. No one among them was in need. None of them kept any of their possessions private; they had all things in common. When someone had a need, those who owned land or houses sold them and brought the proceeds and laid it at the apostles' feet, and it was distributed to the needy.

Joseph, a Levite, sold a field that belonged to him and brought the money and laid it at the apostles' feet. He was a kind man, and the apostles called him Barnabas, meaning Encourager.

But a man named Ananias and his wife Sapphira sold a piece of property and held back some of the money. Ananias brought part of the money and laid it at the apostles' feet, as if he were giving the whole amount.

Peter said, "Ananias, why did you allow Satan to fill your heart with the thought of lying to the Holy Spirit? No one forced you to sell the land, and no one made you share the proceeds. But why did you keep back part of the money and lie about it? You haven't lied to us, but to GOD."

When Ananias heard these words, he fell and died. The young men got up and wrapped his body in a sheet and carried him out and buried him.

Three hours later his wife Sapphira came in, unaware of what had happened.

Peter said to her, "Tell me, was this how much you sold the land for?"

"Yes, it was," she said.

Peter said, "Why did you plot to test the Spirit of the LORD? Listen! The feet of the men who buried your husband are at the door, and they will carry you out."

She immediately fell at Peter's feet and died, and she was buried beside her husband.

And awe came over the community and all who heard about these things.

GAMALIEL'S GOOD ADVICE

Many signs and wonders were done among the people through the hands of the apostles. Many more believers were added to the Lord, both men and women. They carried the sick out into the streets and laid them on mats so that the shadow of Peter passing might fall upon some of them. The people came into Jerusalem from the surrounding towns, bringing the sick and those afflicted with unclean spirits, and they were all healed.

The high priest and the Sadducees were filled with jealousy, and they arrested the apostles and put them in the public jail. But in the middle of the night an angel of the LORD opened the jail doors and brought them out, saying:

"Go to the Temple and speak to the people the message of life."

441

Hearing this, the apostles went to the Temple at daybreak and taught the people.

That morning the council met and sent to the jail to have the apostles brought out. But when the officers arrived at the jail, the apostles were gone. Returning to the council, they reported, "We found the jail locked up tight, and the guards standing at the door, but when we opened it, no one was inside."

Then someone came and told them, "Behold, the men you put in jail are at the Temple, teaching the people."

So the captain of the Temple went with some officers and arrested the apostles, quietly and without violence, for fear that the people would be so angry they would stone the police.

When the apostles were brought to the council, the high priest questioned them, saying, "We commanded you not to teach in this name, but you have filled Jerusalem with your teaching and you accuse us of shedding his blood."

Peter answered, "We must obey GOD rather than men. The GOD of our ancestors raised Jesus, whom you killed by hanging him on a tree. We are witnesses to these things, and so is the Holy Spirit, whom GOD has given to those who obey HIM."

The council members were furious and were of a mind to kill the apostles. But there was a Pharisee on the council named Gamaliel, a teacher of the law who was greatly respected by all the people. He stood up and told them to put the apostles outside while he spoke.

Then he said to them, "Israelites, be very careful what you do with these men.

STEPHEN, FULL OF GRACE

In these days, some of the Jews spoke Greek and followed Greek customs. Others spoke Aramaic yet followed Hebrew customs. As the number of disciples increased, the Greek disciples grumbled against the Hebrews. They complained that when food was given out every day, the Greek widows were neglected.

The apostles called them together and said, "It's not right for us to abandon the Word of God to serve tables. Therefore, friends, you choose from among yourselves seven men of good reputation, full of the Spirit and wisdom. We'll assign this duty to them, and we'll devote ourselves to prayer and the service of the Word."

They were pleased with what the apostles said, and they chose Stephen, a man full of faith and the Holy Spirit, and six others, including Philip, to be deacons. The apostles prayed for them and laid their hands on them.

Stephen, full of grace and power, did mighty signs and wonders among the people. When some people from a synagogue debated with him, they were not able to resist the wisdom and spirit of his words. They were angry, and they plotted secretly to have some men say, "We heard Stephen speak blasphemy against Moses and God."

They spread this rumor and stirred up the people against him. Stephen was seized and brought to the council, and false witnesses spoke against him, saying, "This man never stops speaking

Others have appeared and claimed to be the Christ. They gathered followers and were killed. Their followers were scattered, and that was the end of it. I tell you, keep away from these men and leave them alone. If this movement is of human origin, it will fail. But if it comes from God, you won't be able to overthrow it. You might even find yourselves fighting against God."

The council took Gamaliel's advice and did not kill the apostles. They had them beaten and ordered them not to speak in the name of Jesus.

Therefore the apostles went out rejoicing that they were considered worthy to suffer for the name of Jesus. Every day in the Temple and in the houses where they met, they never stopped teaching and preaching that Jesus was the Christ.

against the Temple and the law of Moses. We heard him say Jesus of Nazareth will destroy the Temple and change the customs Moses gave us."

The whole council looked intently at Stephen and saw that his face was like the face of an angel.

Then the high priest said to him, "Is this true?"

Stephen said, "Men, brothers, and fathers, listen. The prophets have told us that the Most High does not dwell in temples made with hands. And which of the prophets did your ancestors not persecute? They killed those who announced the coming of the Righteous One, whom you have now betrayed and murdered. You received the law like a gift from angels, and you didn't keep it."

When the members of the council heard these things, they ground their teeth in rage against him. But Stephen, full of the Holy Spirit, looked intently toward heaven and saw the glory of God and Jesus standing at the right hand of God.

"Behold!" he said. "I see the heavens opened, and the Son of man standing at the right hand of God."

But the council cried out with a loud voice and put their hands over their ears and rushed upon him. They threw him out of the city and stoned him.

And the witnesses laid down their cloaks at the feet of a young Jewish man named Saul, a Roman agent.

As he was being stoned, Stephen prayed, "Lord Jesus, receive my spirit." He kneeled down and cried out in a loud voice, "Lord, do not hold this sin against them." And then he fell asleep in death.

Saul saw and heard this, and he approved of the killing.

The day that Stephen was killed, a great persecution rose up against the church in Jerusalem, and the whole community, except the apostles, scattered throughout Judea and Samaria.

Saul was ruining the church in Jerusalem. He went into house after house and dragged off men and women and sent them to jail. But those who were scattered went all over Judea and Samaria, preaching the word.

Philip went to a city in Samaria. When he proclaimed Christ, an enormous crowd gathered. Unclean spirits came out of many, and many who were paralyzed or lame were healed. There was much joy in that city.

But there was a man in the city named Simon who amazed the Samaritans with his practice of magic. He told them he was a great man, and everyone believed him, from the richest to the poorest. "This man is the great power of GOD!" they said.

This had been going on for some time before Philip arrived with the good news about the kingdom of GOD and the name of Jesus Christ.

Many of the Samaritans were baptized, men and women, and even Simon. After he was baptized, he went around the city with Philip, for he was amazed by the mighty works Philip was doing.

When the apostles in Jerusalem heard that the Samaritans had received the word of GOD, Peter and John came and prayed for the Samaritans to receive the Holy Spirit. They had been baptized in the name of the Lord Jesus, but the Spirit had not yet fallen on any of them.

Peter and John laid their hands on them and they received the Holy Spirit.

When Simon saw that the Spirit was given through the laying on of hands, he offered money, saying, "Give me this power, so I also may lay my hands on someone to receive the Holy Spirit."

Peter said to him, "May your silver perish with you, for thinking you could obtain the gift of God with money! You have no share in this work, for your heart is not right. Repent, and pray to the Lord to forgive you."

Simon answered, "Pray to the Lord for me, so that nothing you said will happen."

THE ETHIOPIAN ON THE ROAD TO GAZA

The apostles testified in Samaria and then returned to Jerusalem, proclaiming the Gospel to many villages of Samaritans on their way back.

But an angel of the Lord said to Philip, "Get up and go toward the south, to the road that goes down from Jerusalem to Gaza."

This was a deserted land with few travelers on the road.

Philip got up and went, and he saw a chariot with a royal crest, rolling down the road behind a team of horses. The man being driven was the treasurer of Candace, queen of the Ethiopians. He had come to Jerusalem to worship and was on his way home, and he was reading the Scriptures as he rode along.

The Spirit said to Philip, "Go up and join this chariot."

When he came close, Philip could hear the man reading out loud from Isaiah the prophet. Philip recognized the Scripture, which described the suffering of the servant of God, and he

asked, "Do you understand what you are reading?"

The man said, "How can I, unless someone guides me?" And he invited Philip to ride with him in the chariot.

The passage of the Scripture that he was reading was this:

Like a sheep he was led to the slaughter. Like a lamb silent before its shearer, he did not open his mouth. In his humiliation, justice was denied him. Who can describe his generation? For he was cut off out of the land of the living.

The Ethiopian said to Philip, "Please tell me, who is the prophet speaking about: himself or someone else?"

Beginning with this Scripture, Philip told him the good news. "Jesus fulfilled GOD's plan for HIS Creation," Philip explained. "When you look at Jesus, you see what GOD is like. You can know that GOD is love, because HE gave up power and came to us as a servant and suffered on the cross for our sins."

As they went along the road, they came to some water, and the Ethiopian said, "Look! Here is some water. Is there any reason I cannot be baptized?"

He ordered the driver to stop the chariot, and he and Philip went down into the water, and Philip baptized him.

As soon as they came up out of the water, the Spirit of the Lord caught Philip up and took him away. The Ethiopian returned to the chariot and went on his way, rejoicing.

Philip found himself beside the seacoast. He proclaimed the Gospel to all the towns until he came to Caesarea.

SAUL MEETS JESUS ON THE ROAD TO DAMASCUS

Saul was still breathing out threats and murder against the Lord's disciples when he went to the high priest and asked him for letters to the synagogues at Damascus. He planned to go there to look for followers of Jesus, men or women, and bring them back in chains to Jerusalem.

The priests gave him what he asked for, and he set out. As he was on the road to Damascus, a light from heaven flashed all around him. He fell to the ground and heard a voice saying:

"Saul, Saul, why are you persecuting me?"

He said, "Who are you, Lord?"

The voice answered, "I am Jesus, whom you are persecuting. Get up and go into the city, and you will be told what to do."

The men who were traveling with Saul were speechless, for they heard the voice but saw no one.

Saul got up, but when he opened his eyes, he could not see, and he had to be led by the hand into Damascus. For three days he was blind, and did not eat or drink.

There was a disciple in Damascus named Ananias. The Lord said to him in a vision, "Get up and go to the street called Straight. At the house of Judas ask for a man from Tarsus named Saul. At this very moment he is praying and

seeing a vision of you coming in and laying your hands on him so he can regain his sight."

Ananias answered, "Lord, I've heard from many people how much evil this man has done to your saints in Jerusalem. Now he has come with letters from the chief priests to arrest everyone who calls on your name."

"Go!" said the Lord. "He will carry my name to foreign nations and kings and the children of Israel. I will show him how much he must suffer for the sake of my name."

Ananias went to the house and found Saul and laid his hands on him.

"Brother Saul," he said, "the Lord Jesus has sent me so you can regain your sight and be filled with the Holy Spirit."

Immediately it was as if scales fell from Saul's eyes, and he regained his sight. Then he arose and was baptized.

After eating and regaining his strength, Saul stayed with the disciples in Damascus for several days. He went to the synagogues and immediately proclaimed Jesus, saying:

"He is the Son of GOD!"

Everyone who heard him was amazed and said, "Isn't this the man who tried to wipe out the followers of Jesus in Jerusalem? He has come here to bring them back in chains to the chief priests."

But Saul increased in strength and confused the Jews of Damascus with many proofs that Jesus was the Christ. This went on for a long while, and the Jews began to plot against him to kill him.

Saul found out they were watching for him at the city gates day and night. In the middle of the night, Saul's friends helped him escape by lowering him down the side of the city wall in a basket.

When Saul arrived in Jerusalem and tried to join the disciples, they were afraid of him until Barnabas took him to the apostles. He told them how Saul had seen the Lord on the road and preached boldly in Damascus, and then they welcomed him.

Afterward, Saul preached openly in Jerusalem. He debated with some of the Jews, and they went looking for him to kill him. When the disciples found out that Saul was in danger, they took him to the port at Caesarea and sent him by ship to Tarsus.

Then the church in Judea and Galilee and Samaria had peace and grew in faith and numbers.

MIGHTY WORKS OF PETER

As Peter traveled among the believers, he did works as amazing as the works of Jesus. He came to the town of Lydda, where he found a man named Aeneas, who had been in bed for eight years, paralyzed. Peter said to him:

"Aeneas, Jesus Christ heals you! Get up and make your bed."

Immediately Aeneas arose. All who lived in and near Lydda saw him, and they turned to the Lord.

There was a disciple living in Joppa named Tabitha. She was full of good works and loving deeds for the poor. She fell sick and died, and her family prepared her body for burial and laid her in an upstairs room.

When the disciples heard that Peter was nearby, they sent two men to plead with him to come right away. Peter got up and went with them to Joppa where they took him to the upstairs room.

All the widows were there, crying and showing the many shirts and coats Tabitha had made for the poor while she was with them. Peter sent them all out of the room and kneeled down and prayed. Then he turned to the body and spoke to her as Jesus had spoken to the daughter of Jairus, saying:

"Tabitha, get up!"

The woman opened her eyes, saw Peter, and sat up. He took her by the hand and lifted her up from her bed. Then he called the disciples and widows and presented her alive to them.

The report of this went out all over Joppa, and many believed in the Lord. And it came to pass that Peter stayed in the city for many days with Simon, a leather worker.

PETER AND CORNELIUS

At Caesarea there was a man named Cornelius, a Roman centurion, who believed in God and gave generously to the needy and prayed without ceasing. He saw in a vision one afternoon an angel of God come in and say to him, "Cornelius."

He stared at the angel in terror and said, "What is it, Lord?"

The angel said, "Your prayers and gifts have gone up to God. Now send men to Joppa to ask for a man named Peter. He is staying with Simon, a leather worker, whose house is beside the seas. Peter will tell you what you are to do."

When the angel left, Cornelius called two of his servants and a devout soldier from among his servants. He told them everything he had seen and heard, and sent them to Joppa.

The next day, while Cornelius' men drew near to Joppa, Peter went up to the flat roof of Simon's house to pray, awaiting the noonday meal.

While the meal was being prepared, Peter fell into a trance. He saw heaven open, and something like a great sheet came down, lowered by its four corners to the ground. On it were all kinds of animals and reptiles and birds of the air. Each one was impure according to Jewish law.

A voice came to Peter, saying:

"Get up, Peter; kill and eat."

Peter said, "No, Lord. For I have never eaten any of these forbidden unclean animals."

Again the voice came to him, and it said, "What God has made clean, you must not call unclean."

This happened three times. Then the sheet was suddenly taken up to heaven.

While Peter was puzzling over the meaning of the vision, the three men sent by Cornelius had arrived and now stood before the gate. They called out, asking whether Peter was staying there.

The Spirit said to Peter, "Three men are looking for you. Arise and go downstairs. Do not hesitate, but go with them, for I have sent them."

Peter went down to the men and said,"I am the one you seek. Why have you come?"

They said, "Cornelius the centurion, an upright and God-fearing man,

respected by the whole Jewish nation, was directed by a holy angel to send for you and hear what you have to say."

Peter invited them into the house; and the next day he went with them, he and six disciples from Joppa.

When they arrived in Caesarea the next day, they found Cornelius waiting for them, along with his family and close friends. As Peter came in, Cornelius met him and fell down at his feet and worshiped him. But Peter lifted him up, saying:

"Stand up. I am a man like yourself."

Then they went into the house, talking together.

When Peter found the many people gathered there, he said to them, "You know it is forbidden by Jewish law for a Jew to associate with or visit anyone of another nation. But GOD has shown me that I must not call anyone unclean. Therefore, I came without hesitation as soon as I was sent for. Now tell me why you sent for me."

Cornelius recounted his vision to Peter, adding, "I sent my servants to you at once, and you have been kind enough to come. Now we are all here in the sight of God, to hear everything you have been commanded by the Lord."

Peter said, "Truly I now know that God has no favorites, but HE accepts those in every nation who fear HIM and do what is right. The Word of the Lord was sent to the children of Israel, proclaiming the Gospel of peace through Jesus Christ, Lord of all. This word was proclaimed throughout Judea, beginning from Galilee after the baptism of John. God anointed Jesus of Nazareth

with the Holy Spirit and with power. He went about doing good and healing all who were oppressed by the devil, for GOD was with him.

"We are witnesses to everything he did in Judea and Jerusalem. They put him to death by hanging him on a tree, but GOD raised him on the third day.

HE revealed him, not to all the people, but to us who were chosen as witnesses. We ate and drank with him after he rose from the dead.

"He commanded us to preach to the people and to testify that he is the one ordained by GOD to judge the living and the dead. He is the one spoken of by all the prophets. Everyone who believes in him receives forgiveness of sins through his name."

While Peter was speaking, the Holy Spirit fell on all who heard the word. The Jewish believers who came with Peter were amazed, for the gift of the Holy Spirit had been poured out upon Gentiles.

Peter declared, "Is there any reason to refuse water baptism to these people who have received the Holy Spirit just as we have?"

He commanded them to be baptized in the name of Jesus Christ. Then they asked him to stay with them for a few days.

When the apostles and the believers in Judea heard that Gentiles had received the word of GOD, they were critical of Peter. But Peter told them how GOD had directed him to declare the message of salvation to Cornelius and his whole household.

"As I began to speak, the Holy Spirit fell on them, just as it did on us at the beginning. Then I remembered the word of the Lord, how he said, 'John baptized with water, but you will be baptized with the Holy Spirit.' If GOD gave the same gift to them that HE gave to us when we believed in the Lord Jesus Christ, who was I to resist GOD?"

When they heard this, they argued no more, but glorified GOD, saying, "GOD has given the Gentiles the opportunity to turn to HIM and live."

LIFE FOR THE CHURCH AND DEATH FOR HEROD

About that time, King Herod Agrippa laid violent hands on some who belonged to the church. His grandfather, Herod the Great, had tried to kill the baby Jesus, and his uncle, Herod Antipas, had beheaded John the Baptist. Now Herod Agrippa arrested and beheaded James the brother of John. When he saw that this pleased the Pharisees, he also arrested Peter.

Herod put Peter in prison and handed him over to four squads of soldiers to guard him until after the feast of the Passover.

But the church was praying for Peter.

The night Herod was planning to turn Peter over to the Pharisees, Peter was bound by two chains, sleeping between two soldiers, and sentries stood guard before the prison door. Suddenly an angel of the LORD appeared, and a light shone in the prison cell. The angel struck Peter on the side and woke him, saying, "Get up quickly." And the chains fell off his wrists.

Then the angel said, "Get dressed and put on your sandals." He did so, and the angel said, "Wrap your cloak around you and follow me."

Peter followed the angel, but he thought it was merely a vision.

They passed the first and second guards and came to the iron gate leading into the city. The gate opened by itself, and Peter and the angel went out and passed on through one street, and then the angel departed from him.

Peter came to himself and said, "Now I'm sure the LORD has sent HIS angel. HE rescued me from the hand of Herod and from all that the Pharisees intended."

He went to the house of Mary, the mother of John Mark, where many disciples had gathered to pray. As Peter knocked at the gate, a maiden named Rhoda came to answer. She recognized Peter's voice, but in her joy she forgot to open the gate. Instead, she ran in and told everyone that Peter was standing at the gate.

They said to her, "You must be mad."

When she insisted, they said, "It is not really Peter. It is his angel."

Peter continued knocking; and when they finally opened the gate, they were amazed to see him. He motioned with his hand for them to be silent, and he told them how the LORD had brought him out of the prison.

Then he said, "Tell Jesus' brother James and the others about this," and he left and went to another place, to hide from Herod.

At daybreak, there was great confusion among the soldiers over what had become of Peter. When Herod searched for him and could not find him, he ordered that the guards be put to death.

Herod left Judea and went to his palace in Caesarea to meet a delegation of Phoenicians. On the day of the meeting, he put on his royal robes, took his seat on the throne, and made a public speech.

The people shouted, "This is the voice of a god, not of man!"

Herod accepted their praise and worship, and immediately an angel of the LORD struck him, and he died in agony.

And the word of GOD grew and multiplied.

457

A Good Governor and an Evil Magician

The disciples who scattered because of the persecution traveled as far as Phoenicia, Cyprus, and Antioch, speaking the word only to Jews. But some went to Antioch in Syria and preached of Jesus to the Gentiles. The hand of the LORD was with them, and many turned to the LORD.

When the church in Jerusalem heard about this, they sent Barnabas to Antioch to investigate. He rejoiced when he saw the grace of GOD among the new believers. Barnabas was a good man, full of the Holy Spirit and faith, and with his encouragement, many more were brought to the Lord. He went to Tarsus to look for Saul, and when he found him, he brought him to Antioch to help teach the people of the church.

Saul no longer went by his Hebrew name. He used his Greek name, and became known throughout the land as Paul.

And it was in Antioch that disciples were called Christians for the first time.

In these days, prophets came to Antioch from Jerusalem. One of them, a man named Agabus, stood up and foretold of a great famine coming over all the world. The disciples in Antioch decided that each should give as they could to relieve the brothers and sisters in Judea. They sent money with Barnabas and Paul, and they delivered the collection to the elders of the church in Jerusalem. When they returned to Antioch, Barnabas and Paul brought the young disciple named John Mark back with them.

It came to pass that one day while the prophets and teachers in the church at Antioch were praying and fasting, the Holy Spirit said to them, "Set Barnabas and Paul apart to do my work."

They prayed and fasted some more, and they laid their hands on Barnabas and Paul and sent them out, along with John Mark. The Holy Spirit led them to the port of Seleucia, and from there they sailed to the island of Cyprus.

When they arrived in the city of Salamis, the two disciples proclaimed the word of GOD in the synagogues,

with John Mark assisting.

They next traveled across the island to the city of Paphos, where they met a magician, a false prophet by the name of Elymas, who served as counselor to the Roman governor of Cyprus, Sergius Paulus.

Now, the governor was a man of intelligence, and he sent for Barnabas and Paul, for he wanted to hear the word of GOD. But Elymas the magician opposed them, seeking to turn the governor away from the faith.

Paul was filled with the Holy Spirit and he looked intently at Elymas and proclaimed:

"You son of the devil! You enemy of righteousness, full of deceit and evil tricks! It is time to stop twisting the straight paths of the LORD. Now, behold! The hand of the LORD is upon you, and you will be blind and will not see the sun for a season!"

Immediately mist and darkness fell on Elymas, and he went around seeking someone to lead him by the hand. The governor was amazed to see this, and he became a believer.

PAUL AND BARNABAS
IN ASIA MINOR

PHRYGIA

GALATIA

5 Antioch

LYCAONIA

PISIDIA

6 Iconium

PAMPHYLIA

7 Lystra

8 Derbe

CILICIA

4 Perga

Tarsus

Attalia

1 Antioch

Seleucia

SYRIA

CYPRUS

2 Salamis

3 Paphos

MEDITERRANEAN
SEA

Nazareth

Paul and his friends set sail from Paphos to Perga, a port city in Pamphylia, a Roman province in Asia Minor. John Mark left them and returned to Jerusalem, and Paul and Barnabas went on by themselves through the mountain passes and up into the hills of Galatia to the city of Antioch-Pisidia.

They were in Antioch on the Sabbath day, and they went into the synagogue and sat down. After the reading of the law and the prophets, the rulers of the synagogue said to Paul and Barnabas, "Brothers, if you have any word for the people, say it."

Paul stood up and said, "Israelites and Gentiles who have come here to worship GOD, listen to me! The GOD of Israel kept HIS promise to our ancestors and sent a Savior, Jesus. But the people of Jerusalem and their rulers did not recognize him. They did not understand the message of the prophets that they hear every Sabbath. So, as the prophets said they would, they killed him. But GOD raised him from the dead, and he appeared to his disciples. Now we are his witnesses, and we bring you the good news: through Jesus Christ, everyone who believes is freed from sin and death."

And on the following Sabbath, almost everyone in the city came to hear the word of GOD. But when certain of the Jews saw the crowd, they were filled with jealousy, and they disputed what Paul said and insulted him.

Paul and Barnabas spoke boldly, saying, "It was necessary for the word of GOD to be spoken to you first. But since you push it away and judge yourselves unworthy of eternal life, we turn to the Gentiles, as the LORD spoke through the prophet. HE was speaking about Jesus when HE said, 'I have set you as a light for the Gentiles, to bring salvation to the ends of the earth.'"

The Gentiles were glad, and they glorified the word of GOD. Many believed and the Word of the LORD spread all over the region. But the Jews stirred up other people to persecute Paul and Barnabas. These people were rich and powerful, and they drove them out of their district. Paul and Barnabas fled for Iconium, but the disciples they left behind were filled with joy and with the Holy Spirit.

When they arrived in Iconium, Paul and Barnabas went into the synagogue and spoke, and many believed, both Jews and Greeks. But the unbelieving Jews stirred up the Gentiles and poisoned their minds against the believers. Paul and Barnabas spoke boldly for the LORD, and the LORD gave them power to do signs and wonders, but still the people were divided.

When Paul and Barnabas heard of a plot to have them stoned to death, they fled to Lystra and Derbe, in the province of Lycaonia. They preached the good news there and in the surrounding region.

Now, in Lystra was a man who couldn't use his feet. He was lame from birth and had never walked. As he was listening to Paul speak, Paul looked intently at him and saw that he had faith, and he said in a loud voice:

"Stand up straight on your feet!"

The man leaped up and started to walk.

When the crowds saw what Paul had done, they shouted in their own language, "The gods have come down to us in human form!"

The people called Barnabas Zeus, the Greek king of the gods. Because Paul was the chief speaker, they called him Hermes, the messenger of the gods. Then the priest of Zeus, whose temple stood in front of the city, brought oxen and garlands of flowers to the gates, so the people could offer sacrifices to Paul and Barnabas.

When Barnabas and Paul were told of this, they tore their clothes and rushed out into the crowd, shouting, "Friends! Why are you doing this? We are only human, like you! We came to bring you the good news so you would turn away from these worthless things to the living GOD WHO made the heaven and the earth and the sea and all that is in them."

But even with these words, the apostles barely managed to stop the people from offering sacrifices to them.

But there came to Lystra certain Jews from Antioch-Pisidia and Iconium who turned the people against them. They stoned Paul and dragged him out of the city, thinking he was dead. But when the disciples gathered about him, he rose up and went into the city.

The next day, Paul went with Barnabas to Derbe. After they preached the Gospel to that city and made many disciples, they returned to Lystra and Iconium and Antioch-Pisidia. They strengthened the disciples and encouraged them to keep the faith. They selected elders for every church, and with prayer and fasting they committed them to the LORD.

Then they passed through the province of Pisidia and returned to the port of Pamphylia. After they spoke the word in Perga, they went down to Attalia. From there they sailed to Antioch in Syria and returned to the church that had sent them.

When they arrived, they told them how GOD had accomplished the work that the Holy Spirit had sent them to do, and how HE had opened a door of faith to the Gentiles.

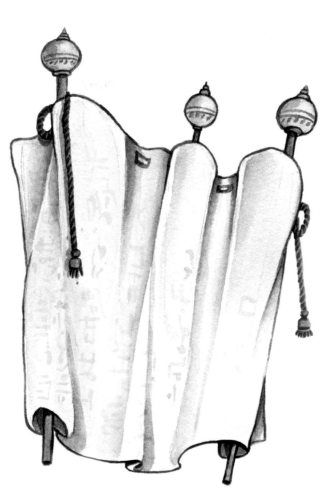

It happened that men from Judea came to the church in Antioch and said to the Gentiles, "Unless you first become a Jew, you cannot be saved."

Paul and Barnabas argued fiercely against them, and the church sent them and some others to take the matter to the apostles and elders in Jerusalem.

There, the Pharisees in the church stood up and said, "It is necessary for Gentiles to follow the whole law of Moses, and Gentiles must become Jews before they are baptized."

The apostles and elders considered the matter, and after much debate, Peter stood up and spoke.

"Friends," he said, "you know that in the early days GOD sent me to speak the word in the household of Cornelius. GOD gave those Gentiles the Holy Spirit, just as HE did to us. They did not need the law to be clean in the sight of GOD. GOD cleansed their hearts by faith. So why do you annoy GOD by burdening these Gentiles? You know that we and our ancestors found the law a burden. We believe that Jews and Gentiles will be saved through the grace of the Lord Jesus, not by keeping the law."

The whole assembly was silent.

Then Barnabas and Paul told about the mighty works GOD had done through them among the Gentiles. After they finished speaking, James, the brother of Jesus, said:

"Friends, listen to me. GOD called our ancestors out from the nations to be a separate people. The prophets say the Gentiles must come to the Jews to find the LORD. But when they come, we must not trouble them. Let us just ask them to follow a few rules, so they can eat with brothers like these Pharisees, who follow the law of Moses."

The apostles and elders and whole church agreed with what James said. They chose Judas Barsabbas and Silas to go with Paul and Barnabas to report their decision in a letter to the Gentiles in Antioch and Syria and Cilicia.

Upon reading of this decision, the Gentiles rejoiced. Judas and Silas taught them and encouraged them. Then they were sent back in peace to those who had sent them.

MACEDONIA

Philippi *4* Neapolis

THRACE

BITHYNIA

Thessolonica *5*

Samothrace

Berea *6*

MYSIA

GREECE

3 Troas

AEGEAN
SEA

ASIA
MINOR

PHRYGIA

ACHAIA

9

Ephesus

Athens *7*

Corinth

8

PAUL AND SILAS
IN PRISON

CRETE

After some days, Paul said to Barnabas, "Let us visit the disciples in every city where we proclaimed the Word of the LORD, and see how they are."

Barnabas wanted to take John Mark, but Paul refused because he had left them before the end of their first journey. They argued over this matter and then separated from each other. Barnabas took John Mark and sailed away to Cyprus.

Paul invited Silas to go with him, and together they went through the provinces of Syria and Cilicia, strengthening the churches. They also visited Derbe and Lystra, where they met a young disciple named Timothy.

Timothy was the son of a Jewish woman who was a believer, but his father was a Greek. Timothy was respected by the churches at Lystra and Iconium, and Paul invited him to join them on their missionary journey.

Paul and Silas and Timothy were joined by a Greek doctor named Luke. Luke kept a diary of their travels, and many years later he wrote about Jesus and Paul in books known as *The Gospel According to Saint Luke* and *The Acts of the Apostles*.

The four of them journeyed together through the provinces of Phrygia and Galatia, preaching to the Gentiles

GALATIA

CILICIA

Lystra
2
Derbe

Tarsus

Antioch • 1

SYRIA

CYPRUS

wherever the Holy Spirit led them.

When they came to Troas, a port in Asia Minor, a vision came to Paul in the night. He saw a man from Macedonia standing beside him, pleading, "Come over to Macedonia and help us."

Immediately they set sail from Troas and went to Samothrace, where they spent the night. The next day they went on to Neapolis, and from there to Philippi, the leading city of Macedonia, and a Roman colony.

On the Sabbath day they went outside the city gate to the riverside where they thought they would find a place of prayer. They sat down and spoke to the women who were meeting there. One of the listeners was a woman named Lydia. She was a merchant who bought and sold purple cloth. She already worshiped GOD, and now the LORD opened her heart to Paul's message.

After Lydia and her family and servants were baptized, she said, "If you think I am a true believer, come down to my house and stay with us."

They accepted her invitation and stayed in the city.

One day while Paul and his friends were going to the place of prayer, they met a slave girl who was possessed by an evil spirit that gave her the power to know the future. Her owners earned money by having her tell fortunes.

The slave girl followed Paul and his friends around the city, shouting, "These men are servants of the Most High GOD! They proclaim the way of salvation!"

She did this many days. But Paul's heart was grieved that the spirit possessed her. He turned around and said to the spirit, "In the name of Jesus Christ, I command you to come out of her!"

It came out immediately.

When the girl's owners realized they could no longer make money from her fortune-telling, they were furious. They seized Paul and Silas and took them to the Roman officials in the marketplace.

"These men are Jews," they said. "They are causing a lot of trouble in our city. They are teaching things that are unlawful for us Roman citizens."

The crowd in the marketplace joined in the attack on Paul and Silas. The officials had the two of them stripped of their clothes and beaten with wooden rods. Then they were thrown in prison.

The officials told the jailer to watch them carefully, and he locked them in the dungeon and fastened their feet between heavy blocks of wood.

465

About midnight, Paul and Silas were praying and singing songs of praise to GOD, and the other prisoners listened to them. Suddenly there was a great earthquake, so strong that the foundations of the prison were shaken. Immediately all the doors flew open and the chains fell off all the prisoners.

The jailer woke up, and when he saw the doors open, he pulled out his sword in order to kill himself; for he thought the prisoners had escaped and feared he would be blamed.

Paul called out to him in a loud voice, "Do not harm yourself! We are all here!"

The jailer ordered torches for light, and he rushed in, trembling. He fell at the feet of Paul and Silas, and then he led them out of the dungeon.

"Sirs," he said, "what must I do to be saved?"

"Believe in the Lord Jesus," they answered. "Then you will be saved—you and all your household."

They spoke the Word of the LORD to the jailer and all his family and servants. Right then and there, in the prison in the middle of the night, the jailer took them and washed their wounds, and then he and all his family were baptized. Then he brought them into his own house and gave them food. He and his whole household were overjoyed at finding faith in GOD.

When morning came, the Roman officials sent police to the prison with orders to release Paul and Silas.

The jailer said to Paul, "The officials have sent a message that you may be set free. Now you can leave this place and go on your way in peace."

But Paul refused. Instead he said to the police, "They beat us publicly without giving us any kind of a trial. They threw us into prison even though we are Roman citizens. Now they want us to leave quietly. Indeed not. They must come themselves and carry us out."

When the police told the officials that they had imprisoned Roman citizens without a trial, the officials came in person to the prison and apologized and let them out. Then they politely asked them to leave the city.

Paul and Silas left Philippi, but first they went to the house of Lydia, where they met with the believers and gave them encouragement.

467

PAUL PREACHES TO THE GREEKS

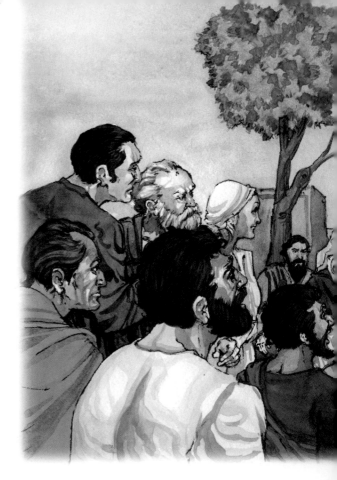

Paul and his friends traveled across Macedonia from Philippi to the city of Thessalonica, where they found a Jewish synagogue. As was his custom, Paul went in to the Jewish people and had discussions with them for three Sabbaths. He explained to them why it was necessary for the Christ to die and rise from the dead, and then he said, "This Jesus whom I am telling you about is the Christ."

Some of the Jews became believers, and so did many Greek Gentile men and noblewomen. But the unpersuaded Jews became jealous and employed some wicked men to stir up a crowd and set the city in an uproar. Then they went out and found some believers and dragged them to the officials.

"These are the men who have turned the world upside down!" they shouted. "They go against the orders of Caesar, saying there is another king named Jesus!"

The people and the rulers were upset when they heard these things. They made the believers pay a fine, and then they let them go.

But it was too dangerous for Paul and Silas to stay in Thessalonica. That night, as soon as it was dark, the believers sent them to the city of Berea.

When they reached Berea they went to the synagogue. They found the Jews of Berea open-minded and ready to listen. Every day they studied the Scriptures to see if what Paul was saying was true. Many of the Jews became believers, along with a large number of upper-class Greek women and Greek men.

But when the Jews of Thessalonica found out that Paul was preaching in Berea, they came after him. Timothy, who had stayed behind in Thessalonica, came and warned Paul to leave the city.

Silas and Timothy stayed in Berea, and the believers went with Paul by ship to Athens. They left him there and returned to Berea with a message from Paul for Silas and Timothy to join him as soon as possible.

While Paul waited in Athens for Silas and Timothy, he walked around the city and looked at the temples and statues of gods and goddesses. His spirit was troubled when he saw that the city was full of idols. He went to the synagogue on the Sabbath and argued with the people there, and he went to the marketplace every day to argue with passersby.

Some of the Greek philosophers came and made fun of him. "What is this man

babbling about?" they asked. Another answered, "He seems to be a preacher of foreign gods," for he preached to them of Jesus and the resurrection. They were curious, so they took Paul to a nearby hill, where the city council met, and introduced him to the leaders of the city.

"Tell us about this new teaching of yours," they said. "It sounds strange to us, and we want to know what it means."

Now, the Athenians loved anything that was new and different, and spent their time in gossip to tell or hear some new thing.

"Men of Athens!" said Paul as he stood in the middle of their council. "I have seen with my own eyes that in every way you are very religious. As I walked around your city and looked at the objects you worship, I noticed that you have an altar on which it is written, TO THE UNKNOWN GOD.

"This unknown god you worship is the GOD I am here to speak about! This GOD made the world and everything in it. HE is ruler of heaven and earth. HE does not live in temples made by human hands. HE does not need anything made by humans. HE does not need anything at all, for HE is the ONE WHO provides everything, including life and breath.

"In the past, GOD has overlooked your idol-making, but now HE is calling all people everywhere to turn from their idols and worship HIM. HE has set a day when the whole world will be judged by a man HE has chosen. HE has proved this by raising that man from the dead!"

When the Athenians heard Paul speak of one being raised from the dead, they mocked him. But some of them said, "We want to hear more about this."

Paul left the council, and some of the faithful Athenians went with him.

TROUBLE IN CORINTH

Paul went from Athens to the city of Corinth. There he met a Jewish couple named Aquila and Priscilla who had just arrived from Italy, for Emperor Claudius had ordered all Jews to leave Rome. Paul learned that they were tentmakers, as was he, so he stayed with them, and together they earned their living by sewing tent cloth.

Every Sabbath Paul spoke in the synagogue, teaching of Jesus. By the time Silas and Timothy arrived from Macedonia, Paul was spending all his time preaching to the Jews of Corinth.

When certain Jews opposed him, Paul took his cloak and shook it out in front of them, saying, "Your blood is on your own heads. I am clean. From now on, I will go to the Gentiles!"

One night the LORD said to Paul in a vision, "Do not be afraid. Continue to speak and teach, for I am with you. No one will harm you. I have many people in this city."

After this there were some who did try to silence Paul. They had him arrested and taken to the Roman governor. But they weren't able to harm him. The governor refused to listen to the charges against him.

Paul stayed in Corinth for a year and a half, and then he went to Syria, taking Priscilla and Aquila with him. When their ship stopped at Ephesus, Paul went to the synagogue and discussed the Scriptures with the Jews. They asked him to stay longer, but he said, "If it is GOD's will, I will be back another time."

He left Priscilla and Aquila in Ephesus and went on to Jerusalem and Antioch. And a few months later, Paul did return to Ephesus.

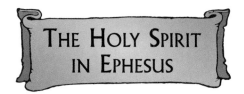

THE HOLY SPIRIT IN EPHESUS

A Jewish believer named Apollos came to Ephesus and spoke powerfully to the people about Jesus Christ. Apollos was an educated man who knew the Scriptures well, but he knew only the baptism of John.

Paul's friends Priscilla and Aquila heard Apollos speaking boldly about Jesus in the synagogue, and they took him aside and taught him more about the faith.

Then Apollos went to Corinth and strengthened the believers. With his strong arguments and knowledge of the Scriptures, he showed the Jews that the Christ was Jesus.

Meanwhile, Paul had returned and found twelve new disciples who had been taught by Apollos.

He asked them, "Did you receive the Holy Spirit when you became believers?"

"No," they answered. "We have not heard of the Holy Spirit."

Paul asked, "Into what were you baptized?"

"Into John's baptism," they answered.

"John's baptism was for repentance," said Paul. "It was a sign that you turned away from your sins. But John said we must believe in the one who came after him, who is Jesus."

When the believers heard this, they were baptized in the name of the Lord Jesus. Paul laid his hands upon them, and the Holy Spirit came upon them, whereupon they began to speak in tongues and to prophesy.

Paul stayed in Ephesus, speaking boldly in the synagogue. For three months he debated with the people, and many of them were convinced. But some of them hardened their hearts and refused to believe, and publicly insulted the way of the Lord.

Paul took his followers out of the synagogue to another building where he taught, and GOD worked miracles through Paul. The Ephesians took handkerchiefs and clothing that he had touched and gave them to those who were sick or had evil spirits, and they were healed. Many Greeks and Jews heard the Word of the LORD and believed.

When seven traveling Jewish magicians came to Ephesus, they tried to drive out evil spirits by calling on the name of the Lord Jesus. They said to the evil spirits, "We command you in the name of Jesus, whom Paul preaches."

One evil spirit answered, "I know Jesus, and I've heard of Paul; but who are you?"

The man who had the evil spirit attacked the magicians, overpowering all seven of them, tearing the robes off their backs. They fled the house naked and wounded.

When the people of Ephesus heard about this, fear and awe came over them, and they praised the Name of the LORD.

Many of the believers admitted that they had been practicing magic. They collected their books and publicly burned them, the value of these books being more than fifty thousand pieces of silver.

And the Word of the LORD grew mightily and prevailed.

A Riot in Ephesus

A silversmith in Ephesus named Demetrius had a successful business making models of the temple of Diana, the great mother goddess of Asia Minor. This business earned large profits for Demetrius and his workers. When the people of Ephesus began to believe in Jesus, they stopped worshiping Diana, and they stopped buying Demetrius' silver shrines.

Demetrius called together his workers and others in the same business, and said to them, "Friends, you know how our business depends on this work, and you've noticed that this man Paul has been convincing people all over this region that gods made by human hands aren't real gods. This is hurting our business. It's also hurting the temple of the great goddess Diana. And something even worse could happen! The magnificence of the great goddess Diana could be destroyed—the goddess whom all the world worships!"

When the workers heard this, they were furious, and they began to shout, "Great is Diana of the Ephesians!"

Soon the whole city was rioting. A mob gathered and rushed to the great outdoor theater in the middle of the city. They seized two of Paul's friends and dragged them into the theater. Paul wanted to go into the crowd, but the disciples wouldn't let him. A few important officials who were friends of Paul begged him not to go to the theater.

At the theater, all was in confusion for two hours and many cried out, "Great is Diana of the Ephesians!"

Finally the town clerk calmed the crowd. "People of Ephesus!" he said. "Everyone knows that our city is the center of worship for the great Diana, and the guardian of her temple. No one can deny it. Do not do anything you'll regret later. These people bring no harm to the temple. They haven't insulted our goddess. So why have you brought them here? If Demetrius and the silversmiths want to bring charges, let them do it in court. Right now we're all in danger of being charged with rioting! There's no excuse for this!"

When the town clerk was finished with his speech, he sent the people home.

A Long Sermon and a Sad Farewell

After the riot, Paul left to visit the churches in Macedonia and Athens and then go on to Jerusalem.

"After I've been there, I must see Rome," he said. He also hoped to go to Spain. In those days Spain was considered the end of the earth.

When he came to Troas, he met with believers in the evening on the first day of the week, when they gathered to break bread. Paul began to speak to them, and since he was to leave the next morning, he talked into the evening.

As midnight drew on, he was still talking. Many lamps were burning in the upstairs room where they were meeting, and a young man named Eutychus was sitting in the window. As Paul talked, Eutychus became sleepier and sleepier. He fell into a deep sleep and slipped, falling out of the window to the ground three stories below. When they picked him up, he was dead.

Paul went down and bent over him and held him gently in his arms. "Do not worry," he said. "He lives still."

The youth was taken home alive, and everyone was relieved. Paul returned to the upstairs room. He broke bread and ate, and talked a long while until the break of day, and then departed.

Paul was in a hurry to reach Jerusalem in time for Pentecost, so he and his friends did not stop at Ephesus. But when they reached the port of Miletus, he sent a message to the leaders of the Ephesian church. He asked that they come meet with him so he could talk to them one more time and tell them good-bye.

When the Ephesians arrived, Paul told them, "The Holy Spirit is leading me to Jerusalem. I don't know what will happen, but the Holy Spirit tells me to expect prison and suffering. I value not my own life. I only want to finish my work and the ministry I received from the Lord Jesus, to witness to the Gospel of the grace of GOD.

"I know that you will never see my face again. Take care of yourselves. Watch over the flock the Holy Spirit has put in your care. Now I turn you over to the LORD's care."

Then he kneeled down and prayed with them, and they cried as they hugged and kissed Paul.

Paul and his friends set sail. When they stopped in Cyprus, the disciples warned Paul not to go to Jerusalem. But he went back to the ship, and some of the disciples went with him to say good-bye. They knelt down on the shore and prayed together one last time.

On the way to Jerusalem they stopped at Caesarea, where they stayed at the house of Philip the evangelist, one of the seven deacons. While they were there, a prophet named Agabus came from Judea with a message for Paul.

Agabus took Paul's belt and tied his own hands and feet with it and said, "The Holy Spirit says that the owner of this belt will be tied up by the Jews in Jerusalem, and they will hand him over to the Gentiles."

When Paul's friends heard this, they begged him not to go to Jerusalem.

Paul said, "Why are you crying and breaking my heart? I am ready to go to prison and even to die, for the name of the Lord Jesus."

Since they could not change his mind, his friends said, "May the LORD's will be done."

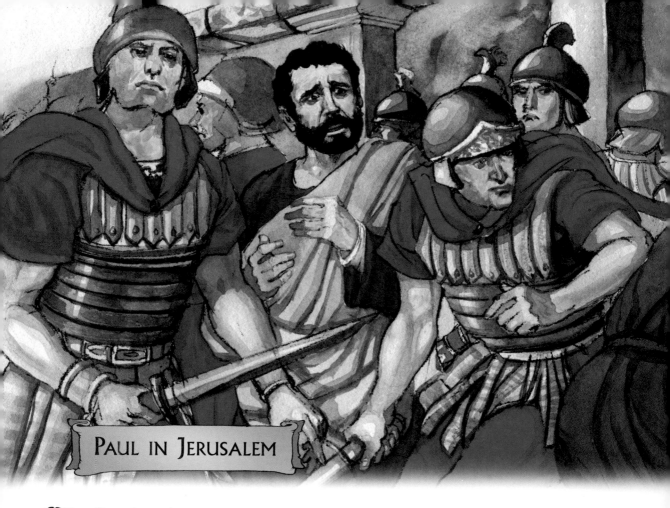

PAUL IN JERUSALEM

The disciples in Jerusalem welcomed Paul and his friends and invited them to stay with them. Paul visited James and the other leaders and told them what GOD was doing among the Gentiles. When they heard Paul's report, they glorified GOD.

Then they warned him, "Brother, many Jews have become believers, and all of them are loyal to the law of Moses. They've been told that you teach Jews who live in Gentile lands to ignore Jewish law and customs. When they find out you're in Jerusalem, who knows what might happen? You need to do something to show them that you're really a good Jew. Go to the Temple with these four men who have taken a vow. If you pay the cost of their vow completion ceremony, it will stop the rumors that you do not obey Jewish law."

The next day Paul went to the Temple and paid for the ceremony, and he arranged to return in seven days, when the sacrifices would be offered.

There were Jews from Asia Minor who saw Paul in the Temple, and they stirred the crowd up against him. They accused him of taking a Gentile into the areas of the Temple reserved for Jews. The penalty for this crime was death. A week later, Paul returned to the Temple, and they were waiting for him. They seized him and said:

"Israelites! This is the man who is going everywhere preaching against our people, our law, and our Temple. Now he has brought Gentiles into the Temple and made our holy place unclean!"

The whole city was in an uproar. A mob came running and seized Paul and dragged him out of the Temple.

While they were trying to kill him, the commander of the nearby Roman fortress heard the riot. He called out his soldiers and sent them running down the steps from the fortress to the Temple. When the mob saw the Roman soldiers, they stopped beating Paul.

The Roman commander, Claudius Lysias, went up to Paul and arrested him and ordered his men to bind Paul with two chains.

"Who is this man, and what has he done?" Lysias asked the mob.

Some shouted one thing, and some shouted another. There was so much noise, Lysias couldn't tell what was going on. He ordered the soldiers to lead Paul to the fortress, but by the time they reached the top of the steps, the mob was so violent they had to carry him away.

"Kill him!" the people shouted, rushing after Paul.

As the soldiers were taking him into the fortress, Paul asked Lysias, "May I say something?"

Lysias answered, "So you speak Greek! I thought you were the Egyptian rebel I've been hearing about."

"I am a Jew," answered Paul, "a citizen of Tarsus, an important city in Cilicia. Please let me speak to the people."

Lysias gave permission, and Paul stood at the top of the steps and motioned for the crowd to be quiet. Then he spoke to them in the Hebrew language.

"My brothers and fathers," he said, "listen to my defense."

As soon as they heard him speaking to them in Hebrew, the people were quiet.

"I am a Jew," said Paul. "I was born in Tarsus in Cilicia, but I grew up here in this city."

He told them he was a strict Pharisee, and he had persecuted the church before he met Jesus. They listened until he said, "The Lord sent me to the Gentiles."

Then they shouted, "Kill him! Rid the earth of such a man! He isn't fit to live!" They ripped their clothes and threw dust into the air to show their outrage.

Lysias ordered his men to take Paul into the fortress and whip him until he confessed as to why the people were against him. When they tied him up to be whipped, Paul said to the officer in charge:

"Is it legal for you to whip a man who is a Roman citizen and has not been sentenced?"

When the officer heard this, he went to Lysias and said, "Do you know what you were about to do? That man is a Roman citizen." For in the Roman Empire, citizens received lesser punishments for crimes and had a right to trial.

Lysias went to Paul, "Are you a Roman citizen?" he asked.

"I am," answered Paul.

"It cost me a lot of money to buy my citizenship," said Lysias.

"I was born a Roman citizen," said Paul.

At this, the men who were going to torture Paul left quickly, and Lysias became fearful when he found out that he had put a Roman citizen in chains.

PAUL BEFORE THE HIGH PRIEST

The next day, Lysias ordered the Jewish council to meet and hear Paul, so he could find out why the Jews were accusing him.

Paul looked intently at the council and said, "Brothers, I have lived my life up to this day with a clear conscience before GOD."

Ananias the high priest ordered the men standing near Paul to strike him on the mouth.

Paul said to him, "GOD will strike you, you whitewashed wall! How dare you sit there judging me by the law, while you break the law by ordering them to strike me!"

The bystanders said, "How dare you insult GOD's high priest!"

"Brothers," said Paul, "I didn't know he was the high priest. Of course, Scripture tells us not to speak against our rulers." Then Paul noticed that some members of the council were Sadducees and some were Pharisees. "Brothers," he said, "I am a Pharisee and the son of Pharisees. I am on trial here because I believe what the Pharisees teach. I believe in the resurrection of the dead."

As soon as he said this, the Sadducees and the Pharisees began to argue, and the council split into two groups. The Sadducees did not believe in spirits, angels, or the resurrection of the dead. The Pharisees believed in all these, and a noisy argument broke out.

Some of the Pharisees stood up and said, "We find no wrong in this man. So what if an angel or a spirit spoke to him?"

The argument became so violent that Lysias was afraid the council members would tear Paul to pieces. He ordered his soldiers to bring him back to the fortress.

The next night, the Lord said to Paul, "Be brave and of good cheer, Paul. As you have witnessed in Jerusalem, so you must also witness in Rome."

Early the next morning, the Jews who were working against Paul met secretly and vowed not to eat or drink until they had killed him. There were more than forty men involved. They went to the chief priests and elders and said:

"We've made a vow to taste no food until we've killed Paul. You and the council must make Lysias bring Paul to you. Pretend you want to question him more. We are ready to kill him even before he gets here."

Paul's nephew heard about the plot, and he went to the fortress and told Paul.

Paul called one of the officers and said, "Take this young man to Commander Lysias. He has something to tell him."

The officer took Paul's nephew to Lysias, and Lysias took the young man by the hand and led him to a place where they wouldn't be overheard.

"What do you have to tell me?" he asked.

"The leaders of the Jews are going to ask you to bring Paul to the council tomorrow to ask him some questions," said Paul's nephew. "But don't give in to them. More than forty men are lying in ambush for him. They've vowed not to eat or drink until they've killed him."

Lysias listened, then sent the young man away, saying, "Don't tell anyone that you've told me about this."

PAUL BEFORE GOVERNORS AND A KING

Lysias called two of his officers and said, "By nine o'clock tonight have two hundred soldiers, seventy horsemen, and two hundred spearmen ready to go to Caesarea. Also have a horse for Paul to ride, and bring him safely to Felix, the governor of Judea"; for Lysias had decided to order Paul's accusers to make their charges in front of Felix.

That night, the soldiers took Paul out of Jerusalem. In the morning they delivered Paul to the Roman governor, along with a letter written to Felix from Lysias. Felix read the letter and ordered his men to keep Paul under guard until his accusers arrived.

Five days later, Ananias the high priest and the elders arrived in Caesarea with a spokesman named Tertullus. They made their case against Paul in front of Felix, as Lysias had ordered.

Tertullus said to Felix, "We enjoy the peace you Romans have provided, Your Excellency. In every way and everywhere, we accept your administration with gratitude. Now kindly hear why we consider this man dangerous. He is an agitator among Jews all over the world and the ringleader of a new religious movement. He even tried to profane the Temple, so we seized him. Examine him yourself and you will see what we mean."

The high priest and elders joined in the charge, agreeing that this was true.

When the governor motioned him to speak, Paul said, "I cheerfully make my defense, confident in Roman justice. They cannot prove what they have charged. I worship the GOD of our ancestors, and I believe everything that is written in the law and the prophets. I have the same hope in GOD that they do—that there will be a resurrection of both the just and the unjust. My conscience is clear. The only thing they have against me is what I said to them. I am on trial for believing in the resurrection."

Felix said, "I'll give you my decision when Lysias arrives."

Paul's enemies went back to Jerusalem, and Paul was put under guard.

A few days later, Felix sent for Paul to come and speak to him and his wife, Drusilla, who was Jewish. Felix listened while Paul spoke about faith in Jesus Christ.

But when Paul began to talk about justice and GOD's judgment, Felix became nervous. "You can go now," he said. "I'll send for you again later."

Felix kept sending for Paul, but he never gave a decision. Secretly, Felix was hoping that Paul would offer him

Festus asked Paul if he would be willing to return to Jerusalem for a new trial. "I'll be in charge," Festus promised, knowing Paul did not trust the council.

But Paul knew that Festus simply wanted to please the Jewish council. "I'm in a Roman court now," he said. "That's where I belong. I've done nothing wrong. I will not let you use me to win their favor. I appeal to Caesar!"

Festus conferred with his advisers and then said to Paul, "You have appealed to Caesar, so to Caesar you will go."

A few days later, King Agrippa II, son of King Herod Agrippa I, came to Caesarea with his sister Bernice to welcome the new governor. They were there for many days, and Festus told them about Paul's case.

"When I heard the charges," said Festus, "I saw they didn't have a case. They were arguing about their own superstition, and about a man named Jesus who died and Paul says is still alive. I don't know much about such matters, so I asked Paul to return to Jerusalem. But he refused. Instead, he appealed to the emperor. He is here under guard until I send him to Rome."

Agrippa was curious. "I would like to hear this man myself," he said.

"Tomorrow," said Festus, "you will hear him."

The next day, Agrippa and Bernice came with great fanfare into the audience hall with the military and civilian officials and the important people of the city. At the command of Festus, Paul was brought in, bound with chains to the wrist of a Roman soldier.

Festus introduced Paul, saying:

"King Agrippa and honored guests, you see this man the Jews brought to me, saying he should die. I have found

money for his release. He also wanted to appear favorable to the Jews, so he left Paul in prison. This went on for two years, until Felix was replaced as governor by Porcius Festus.

When Festus visited Jerusalem, the chief priests and leaders of the Jews urged him to send Paul back to Jerusalem, so that they could ambush and kill him on the way. Festus told them to come to Caesarea to accuse Paul, and they came and brought charges they could not prove.

Paul said, "I've done nothing against Jewish law or the Temple or Caesar. The charges aren't true."

that he has done nothing to deserve death. He has appealed to the emperor, and I have decided to send him to Rome. But I have nothing definite to write to Caesar about him, so I've brought him to you, King Agrippa. After we've examined him, I may have something to write in my report. It seems unreasonable to me to send a prisoner without indicating the charges against him."

King Agrippa said to Paul, "You have permission to tell us your story."

Paul said, "I consider myself fortunate to be making my defense before you, King Agrippa, because you are familiar with the customs and controversies of the Jews. I beg you to listen to me patiently.

"I spent my early life as a Pharisee, the strictest sect of our religion, and now I am on trial for believing what my reli-

gion teaches, that GOD raises the dead. I opposed the name of Jesus in Jerusalem and persecuted the saints, but on the road to Damascus I saw a light from heaven, brighter than the sun, and I heard the voice of Jesus. He sent me to bear witness, and he said, 'I send you to the Jews and the Gentiles, to open their eyes, so they will turn from darkness to light, from the power of Satan to GOD, so they can receive forgiveness of sins

and a place among the saints.'

"King Agrippa, I wasn't disobedient to the heavenly vision. I witnessed to Jesus, first in Damascus, and then in Jerusalem and Judea, and also to the Gentiles. I urged them to repent and turn to GOD and do deeds worthy of repentance.

"For this the Jews seized me in the Temple and tried to kill me. But I have had help from GOD, and so I stand here giving my testimony. I say nothing but what the prophets and Moses said. They said the Christ must suffer—he would be the first to suffer, die, and rise from the dead. And he would proclaim light to the Jews and the Gentiles."

As Paul finished speaking, Festus shouted, "Paul, too much learning has driven you out of your mind!"

Paul said, "I am in my right mind, most noble Festus. I speak the plain truth. The king understands these things. I'm sure he knows what I'm talking about. These things were done in public." Then he turned to the king and said, "King Agrippa, do you believe the prophets? But of course you do."

Agrippa answered, "In a short time, you'll be making me a Christian!"

Paul said, "Whether short or long, I pray to GOD that you and everyone here could become as I am—except for these chains."

The king stood up, and so did Festus and Bernice and all those sitting with them. They left the audience hall and went outside, where they spoke about the case among themselves.

"This man has done nothing to deserve death," they agreed. "He should not be in prison."

Agrippa said to Festus, "The man could have been set free—if only he hadn't appealed to Caesar."

THE SHIPWRECK

It was decided that Paul should sail to Rome, Italy. He and some other prisoners were turned over to one named Julius, a Roman officer. They boarded a ship that sailed along the coast of Asia Minor, and on the way they stopped at Sidon, where Julius kindly allowed Paul to visit some friends there.

They sailed along Cyprus, and upon reaching Myra of Lycia, Julius found a large ship full of wheat from Alexandria, one of the last ships of the season to be sailing to Italy. It was late autumn, and all sea travel ceased in the winter, for the sea was too stormy for safe travel. Julius put his prisoners onto this ship.

As they sailed from Myra on the large ship, they met a strong northwest wind, which they struggled against for two weeks until they reached the port of Cnidus. Here they turned south and sailed down the coast of Crete, with all on board aware of the dangerous conditions. The ship struggled into the harbor of Fair Havens and they waited there for the wind to change.

Julius and the captain debated over staying at Fair Havens or sailing to Phoenix, a better port fifty miles away.

Paul, an experienced sea traveler, warned them, "Friends, I can see that the voyage to Phoenix will be dangerous. We might lose everything, not just the ship and the cargo, but even our lives."

Nevertheless, Julius followed the captain's advice to sail to Phoenix to harbor there for the winter. As soon as the weather was mild, they set sail. Then the danger Paul had warned about swept over them. A terrible storm came up and a great wind hit the ship, turning it away from Crete into the open sea.

The wind was so fierce, they feared being blown onto the sandbanks of North Africa. They lowered the sails, letting the ship drift at the mercy of the storm. The ship was tossed about in the tempest, and the crew threw cargo overboard to lighten their load. On the third day of the storm they threw out some of the ship's equipment.

The storm raged on, day after day, with no sign of the sun or the stars. All on board grew weak from hunger and lack of sleep. Finally, they gave up hope of being saved and waited for death.

But Paul never gave up hope. He went among the crew and passengers, comforting them.

"Friends," he said, "you shouldn't have sailed from Crete. If we had stayed at Fair Havens, we wouldn't be suffering now. But I beg you—don't give up! Not one of you will die. Only the ship will be lost. I know this for certain, for last night an angel of my GOD stood by me and said, 'Do not be afraid, Paul. You must appear before Caesar. For this reason, GOD has spared the lives of everyone who is sailing with you.'

"Be brave, friends! I have faith in GOD that it will be exactly as the angel told me. But we will have to run the ship aground on some island."

On the fourteenth night of the storm, they were being driven back and forth in the sea between Italy and Sicily when suddenly, about midnight, the sailors felt there was land nearby. They measured the depth of the water by dropping a line. It was a hundred and twenty feet deep. After sailing a little farther, they dropped another line. The water was only ninety feet deep—a sure sign that they were coming close to land.

The sailors feared they would crash on some rocks, so they threw out four anchors and prayed for daylight. They could hear the sound of the waves hitting against a shore that they could not see, and their fears grew. Intending to flee the ship, they lowered the longboat into the water.

But Paul said to Julius, "Unless these men stay with the ship, you cannot be saved."

Julius ordered his soldiers to cut the ropes and let the longboat drop into the sea and drift away.

While everyone waited for morning, Paul comforted them and encouraged them to eat. "You've had nothing to eat for fourteen days," he said. "You haven't taken a bite the whole time you've been fighting the storm. I beg you, eat something. You must if you are to survive. Believe what I say, that not a hair of your heads will be lost."

Paul took some bread and gave thanks to GOD. Then he broke it and began to eat. This cheered the crew, and they ate. When they had eaten their fill, they threw the wheat overboard to lighten the ship.

Daylight came, and they saw that they were anchored near a rocky island, with waves pounding against the shore. No one recognized the place, but they could see a bay and a sandy shore. Deciding to run the ship onto the soft ground, they cut away the anchors and let them sink into the sea, and they cut the ropes that held the steering oars. Then they raised the front sail, so it would catch the wind, and headed for the sandy beach.

The ship struck a sandy shoal and the forepart became stuck. The violent waves pounded at the back of the ship, breaking it apart.

The soldiers were afraid the prisoners would escape, so they took out their swords to kill them. But Julius wanted to save Paul, so he stopped them. He gave orders for everyone who could swim to jump overboard and head for land while the rest followed, hanging onto pieces of the wrecked ship.

Paul and all those sailing with him reached the shore safely, just as GOD had promised.

After they escaped the sea and came ashore, they learned that the island was called Malta. The natives showed them kindness and lit a fire and welcomed

them to it, for it was cold and rainy.

Paul gathered a bundle of sticks to lay upon the fire. But as he did so, a snake struck out from the heated kindling and fastened itself to his hand.

"This man must be a murderer!" the natives said to each other. "He has escaped from the sea, but justice won't let him live."

Paul shook the snake off into the fire without being hurt. The natives waited for him to swell up or drop dead, but after waiting a long time and seeing nothing happen to him, they changed their minds and said that he was a god.

Much of the land in that part of the island belonged to Publius, the Roman governor. He welcomed the crew and passengers from the shipwreck, and for three days they were his guests.

Publius' father happened to be in bed, sick with fever and dysentery. Paul visited him and prayed, laying his hands on him, and healed him. After this, all those on the island who were sick came to Paul to be healed. They bestowed honors upon him and presented him with gifts. When the time came for Paul to leave, they gave him everything he needed for the voyage.

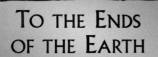

TO THE ENDS OF THE EARTH

Three months later, Paul and the others sailed away on a ship that had spent the winter at Malta. They reached the city of Syracuse on the island of Sicily and stayed there for three days. Then they sailed up the coast of Italy to Rhegium and Puteoli.

At Puteoli, Paul and his friends found some disciples and stayed with them for a week. While they were there, the brethren of the church in Rome heard that Paul had arrived and came to meet him. They traveled together to Rome on the great road, the Appian Way.

When they arrived in Rome, Paul was permitted to live in a house instead of a prison, but a soldier was put on duty to guard him.

On his third day in Rome, Paul invited the local Jewish leaders to meet with him, and he told them about his arrest and his appeal to the emperor. He said:

"Brothers, although I did nothing against the Jews or our customs, I was arrested and handed over to the Romans. They examined me and wanted to set me free, finding no reason for the death penalty. When the Jewish leaders objected, I had to appeal to Caesar. That is why I have asked to see you, for it is because of the hope of Israel that I am bound with this chain."

"We've heard nothing about you," they answered. "Not from Judea or our people in Rome. We'd like to hear what you have to say, for everyone's speaking against this new religious movement."

They made an appointment to come back, and returned with a large number of their people.

From morning until evening, Paul spoke to them about Jesus and God's kingdom. He told of his own faith and tried to convince them from the law of

Luke and John Mark and the disciples from the churches in Asia Minor and Macedonia brought news and letters, and Paul sent letters back to them. He wrote of the faith and his love for his own people. His heart ached, for most of them did not believe in Jesus.

While Paul was in Rome, a great fire broke out, and the Emperor Nero blamed the Christians. Nero persecuted the church, and many disciples were killed. Paul knew that he, too, was to die. Before he was killed, he wrote to Timothy:

"I have fought the good fight. I have finished the race. I have kept the faith."

Several years later, the Romans sent an army to Jerusalem to crush a rebellion, and they completely destroyed the city. Just as Jesus had said, the Temple was burned down and the people were scattered.

Moses and the prophets. Some were convinced, but others not. Since they disagreed among themselves, they left.

As they were going, Paul made one last statement:

"The Holy Spirit was right when HE said to your ancestors through the prophet Isaiah, *You will hear but not understand. You will see but not perceive. For your minds are dull and your ears are hard of hearing. You have closed your eyes, so you won't see, or hear, or understand. If you would open your eyes and your ears and your minds, you would turn to ME, and I would heal you.* Now you know why this salvation has been sent to the Gentiles. They will listen."

Paul stayed under house arrest for two years and welcomed everyone who came to him. Although he was a prisoner, he preached the kingdom of GOD and taught about the Lord Jesus openly.

JOHN'S VISION

THE REVELATION

In the days when the Romans were persecuting the church, a leader named John was sent to the little island of Patmos in the Aegean Sea near Ephesus. John was a prisoner because he had witnessed for Jesus.

One day on the first day of the week, the Holy Spirit fell on John, and he saw a strange and wonderful vision, like the visions of Ezekiel and Daniel. He shared the visions with the churches to encourage them to keep the faith. Jesus, the Lamb of GOD, had defeated evil already by dying on the cross. At the end of time, Jesus would come again.

John told the churches:

I heard a voice as loud as a trumpet calling to me, and I turned around to see who was speaking. I saw seven golden lampstands, and among the lampstands I saw someone who looked like a mortal man.

He was dressed in a long robe with a golden sash about him. His hair was as white as snow, and his eyes blazed like fire. His feet were shining like polished bronze. His voice sounded like a roaring waterfall. In his right hand he held seven stars. A sharp two-edged sword came out of his mouth, and his face was as bright as the noonday sun.

When I saw this person, this Son of man, I fell down at his feet like a dead man. I was filled with holy fear, for the person in my vision was the risen Lord Jesus Christ.

"Do not be afraid!" said Jesus, and he touched me with his right hand. "I am the first and the last, the living One. I

was dead, but now I am alive forever and ever. I hold in my hand the keys of death and the grave.

"Write down everything you see. Some of the things in this vision are happening now, and some will happen in the future. See the seven stars in my right hand and the seven lampstands. Here is their secret meaning: the seven stars are the angels of the seven churches, and the seven lampstands are the churches of Asia Minor."

was a circle of light like an emerald rainbow. Around the throne were twenty-four other thrones. Sitting on these thrones were twenty-four elders. They were dressed in white robes and wore golden crowns.

From the throne in the middle came flashes of lightning and loud noises and the rumbling of thunder. Seven lamps burned in front of the throne—they were the seven angels of GOD. In front of the throne was a sea of glass, as clear as crystal.

Around the throne were four living creatures, covered in front and back with eyes. The first creature looked like a lion, the second like a bull, the third had a human face, and the fourth looked like a flying eagle. Each of the creatures had six wings, and they were completely covered with eyes inside and out.

Day and night the four creatures sang without stopping: "Holy, holy, holy is the LORD GOD Almighty, WHO was, and is, and is to come."

The living creatures kept giving glory and honor and thanksgiving to the One WHO sat on the throne, the One WHO lives forever and ever.

The twenty-four elders bowed down before the One on the throne and worshiped HIM, the One WHO lives forever and ever. They threw their crowns in front of the throne and sang, "YOU are worthy, O LORD our GOD, to receive glory and honor and power, for YOU created all things. By YOUR will everything was created."

I saw a book in the right hand of the One sitting on the throne. It was a scroll filled with writing on front and back, and it was sealed with seven seals.

I saw a mighty angel who called out in a loud voice, "Who is worthy to open the book and break the seven seals?"

In the vision Jesus told me to send a message to each of the seven churches. The letters praised the churches for some things and rebuked them for others.

Then I saw a door standing open in heaven, and I heard the same voice, the voice that sounded like a trumpet.

"Come up here," said the voice. "I will show you happenings in the future."

I saw a throne set up in heaven. The One sitting on the throne was shining like diamonds. All around the throne

No one in heaven or on earth or under the earth was able to open the book, or even to look at it. I began to cry because there was no one worthy to open the book or even look at it.

Then one of the twenty-four elders said to me, "Do not cry. Behold! The lion from the tribe of Judah has won the victory. He is able to open the book and break the seven seals."

I looked at the throne and saw a being standing in the very center. It was a Lamb who looked as if he had been killed. He had seven horns and seven eyes, to see everything that happens on the earth. The Lamb came and took the scroll from the right hand of the ONE WHO was sitting on the throne.

The four living creatures and the twenty-four elders bowed down before the Lamb. Each of them had a harp and a golden bowl full of incense, which were the prayers of the saints. Together the creatures and the elders sang a song of praise to the Lamb.

I heard the voices of thousands of angels circling around the throne and the creatures and the elders. There were tens of thousands of them, a thousand times a thousand. They all sang, "Worthy is the Lamb who was slaughtered! He is worthy to receive power and riches and wisdom and strength and honor and glory and praise!"

I heard the voice of every living creature in heaven and on the earth and under the earth and on the sea. They were all singing, "Let us give praise and honor, glory and power to the One WHO sits on the throne and to the Lamb forever and ever!"

"Amen!" said the four living creatures, and the elders fell down and worshiped.

Then I saw around the throne of God and before the Lamb of God a great crowd of people, so many they couldn't be counted. They were from every nation, all tribes and peoples and languages. They were dressed in white robes, and had palm branches in their hands, and they cried out with loud voices, saying, "Salvation belongs to our God who sits upon the throne, and to the Lamb!"

All the angels were standing around the throne and around the leaders and the four living creatures. They fell on their faces before the throne and worshiped God, saying, "Amen! Blessing and glory and wisdom and thanksgiving and honor and power and might be to our God forever and ever! Amen."

Then one of the elders said to me, "Who are these people, dressed in white robes, and where have they come from?"

I said to him, "Sir, you know."

He said to me:

"These are the ones who have come out of the great persecution. They have washed their robes and made them white in the blood of the Lamb. That is why they are before the throne of God, and they serve him night and day in his Temple. The One who sits on the throne will shelter them within his presence. Never again will they hunger or thirst. Never again will the sun strike them, nor burning heat. The Lamb who is in the middle of the throne will be their shepherd, and he will guide them to springs of living water. God will wipe away every tear from their eyes."

THE CITY OF GOD

John saw visions of GOD's punishment of the wicked, and the victory of the heavenly armies over the spiritual powers of evil. He saw the One WHO was sitting on the throne judging the dead.

In his last vision he saw a new heaven and a new earth. And he wrote to the churches:

I saw the holy city, the new Jerusalem, coming down from GOD out of heaven, like a bride, beautifully dressed for her husband.

"Behold!" said a great voice from the heavenly throne. "Now GOD's home is with HIS people, and HE will stay with them. They will be HIS people, and HE will be their GOD. HE will wipe away every tear. Death will be no more. Never again will there be sadness or crying or pain. All those things are gone forever."

Then the One WHO was sitting on the throne said, "I am making all things new. Write this down, for MY words are true."

Then HE said, "It is finished! I am the

had twelve gates, three on each side. At each gate stood an angel, and above the gates were written the names of the twelve tribes of Israel.

The city was a perfect square built on twelve great foundation stones. On each stone was written the name of one of the twelve apostles of the Lamb.

The angel measured the city with a golden measuring rod. It was twelve thousand measures long, twelve thousand measures wide, and twelve thousand measures high.

The wall of the city was made of crystal-clear gems. The city itself was built of pure gold, as shiny as glass. The foundation stones were made from twelve different jewels. Each of the twelve gates was made from a single pearl. The streets were paved with pure gold.

There was no Temple in the city, for the LORD GOD Almighty and the Lamb were the Temple. The city did not need the light of the sun or the moon, for the glory of GOD filled the city with light, and its glow was the Lamb.

In the future the nations will walk by the light of the city, and the rulers of the earth will bring their glory to it. The gates of the city will stand open day after day. There will be no night. The wealth of the nations will be brought to the city. Nothing unclean or wicked will be allowed to enter—only the people whose names are written in the Lamb's book of life.

Then the angel showed me the river of the water of life. It sparkled like crystal as it flowed from the throne of GOD and the Lamb. It ran down the middle of the street, and on each side of it grew the trees of life. On the trees grew a different kind of fruit each month, and the leaves of the trees gave healing medicine for all people.

Alpha and the Omega, the beginning and the end. I will give water to the thirsty from the fountain of the water of life."

An angel came to me, saying, "Come, I will show you the bride of the Lamb."

The angel showed me a vision of the new Jerusalem. He carried me in the Spirit to the top of a great mountain and I saw the holy city coming down out of heaven from GOD. The city was shining with the glory of GOD.

A high wall surrounded the city. It